Danger in the Darkness

~Leida~

~Diabloss~

~Mettalika~

~Zephirak~

To Josh
hope you enjoy it!
best wishes

Lisa
Ryan

Danger In
The Darkness

A novel by Lara Ryan

First Printing: 2014

ISBN 978-1-312-59706-8

Explore more at www.gryphiesaga.co.uk

This book is dedicated to my wonderful parents for supporting me throughout my years, in everything I do and also to my friends for being there for me. And to those of my friends who are also writers looking to be published. If I can do it, so can you!
Keep on persevering and following your dreams and one day you will soar like a Gryphie!

<u>Prologue</u>

In a world not unlike our own, on a planet alive with many different creatures, there lived two dominant species.

The Gryphies, masters of the air, with huge bat-like wings that soared through the sky. They were the gentler of the two species, living in peace with nature and making their homes in the trees in Shernaron, their territory and the Gryphie forest. They resembled furred dragons of a type and were pyrokinetic, having the ability to breathe fire so hot that it was blue.

The other species were the Lizariaouses, land bound and lizard-like, these creatures resided in Dyarkroeen, the Lizariaous territory, their homes being caves in the barren landscape. They were vicious and warlike, armed with a row of sharp, poison tipped needles running along the length of their spines and heavy set, muscular bodies capable of fast relentless hunting.

The Gryphies and Lizariaouses lived in two huge territories, each spanning hundreds of miles. Each territory was divided into smaller ones, areas where different groups lived. For example Shernaron had the Gryphie Forest and the Steel Mountains among the areas where gatherings lived, while Dyarkroeen had mostly caves and areas like the wastelands and near the reservoir where packs lived.

Days were called "Sun Cycles", nights "Moon Cycles", a "Lunar" was a month and "Seasons" measured years – four seasons to a year. Nightmares were "Moonmares".

These two species had never really gotten along, merely tolerated each other. The Lizariaouses would not hesitate to kill an injured Gryphie they found wandering through their territory. Thus the Gryphies seemed cautious and would avoid them. The flying advantage was one thing the Lizariaouses were jealous of as well; however their skin could withstand the Gryphies' fire up to a point.

Things would have carried on this way had it not been for the Gryphies who made a mistake in saving a member of their gathering after she was attacked by Lizariaouses and whose vengeance was beginning to get out of hand.

A war was imminent.

Chapter 1
The Gryphies

A cool breeze blew through the air across the cliff tops. A lone figure sat on the cliff edge, looking out to sea. The calm wind blew through her glossy dark blue fur. The sea was calm and there were only a few clouds in the sky. Down below, sea vultures screeched and circled at the water's edge as the waves lapped against the cliff face. She watched them, thinking deeply and lifted her head up again to stare out across the sea.

Am I hungry? She wondered to herself. *No, I am just bored.*

She stood, stretching out a deep purple wing and yawned. It had been a while since the last Lizariaous attack, the last Lizariaous attack that, as usual, Leida had run away from. *I'm such a wimp* she told herself as she watched her mate, Diabloss and the others fighting for their lives. Then she turned her back and flew into the sky. Still it was better to run and keep your life than to risk it in battle like Mettalika had done.

As she sat on the cliff top now, she shivered as she thought of the dreadful thing that happened to Mettalika. When Mettalika was very young, a pack of Lizariaouses had attacked her, badly injuring her and she was dying. Under the suggestion and guidance of Mystik, the Forest elder, some Gryphies from the High Mountains where they mined and produced steel armour found her and mechanised her to save her life. She had a mechanised tail, her left back foot and right front hand were both artificial, made out of reinforced steel and she wore a helmet to cover the hideous scars on her face. Now she was always thirsty for Lizariaous blood and always on the lookout to attack them as payback for what they did to her.

Leida was a quiet Gryphie. Her fur was deep blue and she had a brown neck and chest. She had a tan mane and deep purple wings with, like all Gryphies, red talons on the third joint of the main wing bone. The underside of her wings was cream. She had five black spikes running down the length of her spine and a gray and yellow tail spade.

She spread her wings and prepared to launch herself into the air. She leapt off the cliff top and soared into the sky, her wings catching an air current and lifting her higher. The sun shone in rays and made her fur sparkle as she flew through it. She did a few backwards tailspins and corkscrews in the air and soared along the cliff edge, scattering the sea vultures. Laughing, she returned to her perch on the cliff. She looked down at the sea vultures that were regrouping and smirked. Lucky for them she wasn't hungry this time. Sea vultures were one of the main parts of the Gryphie diet and resembled seagulls.

Suddenly a shadow passed overhead as another creature circled to land. Leida stiffened, ears back and her muzzle drawn into a small snarl as she spun round, wings outstretched ready to take flight and faced the source of the shadow.

Another Gryphie, an emerald green one stood before her. He looked at her with his yellow eyes, smiling.

"That was quite a feat back there", he said admiringly.

Leida relaxed. "Oh, it's only you. I thought Zephirak had come to attack me or something."

Diabloss chuckled. "You do have excellent and unusual flying abilities you know" he remarked.

Leida blushed. "Uh, well, not really I was just having fun" She had no self confidence and found compliments hard to take. She sighed and looked out to sea. "Fun" was such a rare thing these sun cycles.

"You looked so beautiful and graceful out there" smiled Diabloss nuzzling her.

"Thanks" said Leida blushing more.

Diabloss was a huge Gryphie compared to Leida. Being a male was one reason for that, but he was also one, if not *the* best fighter of the Gryphies in that area. He was well muscled with a glossy black mane and huge black, red and gray wings. As well as having the normal red talons on the third joint of the main wing bone, he also had one on each of the four fingers of his wings. Leida had five fingers on her wings, but only the normal talons. This was because Diabloss was part Deamon and Deamon Gryphies had talons on all the wing fingers. Deamon Gryphies were one of the many sub-Gryphie species, but they were reputed to be evil and bloodthirsty. This was one of the reasons why Diabloss was such a good fighter. He had dark blue spikes running down the spinal ridge of his tail and a sharp green tail spade. He also had a small earring in his left ear.

Many of the other female Gryphies often wondered why he had chosen quiet, swift Leida as his mate, but there was something in her that only he seemed to see.

"Have there been any attacks?" asked Leida.

"There was one. Mettalika was involved in it, as usual. Ever since she was mechanised, she's gone around forcefully attacking any Lizariaous she sees. This one didn't want to fight, that was clear. It had been injured in a fight already and was retreating back to its home. Mettalika leapt out at it and challenged it. When it wouldn't fight her, she flew into a rage and attacked it full on. Not wanting to get injured any more, the Lizariaous refused to fight. It was in no shape to. At that point I flew in and separated them. The Lizariaous ran off. As for Mettalika, she broke free of my hold and also ran off. To circle the area and encounter that Lizariaous again, I've no doubt."

"She'll get herself killed", said Leida, shaking her head.

"No she won't. She's unstoppable. All she wants to do is kill every last Lizariaous there is. Offence, not defence like the rest of us" snarled Diabloss.

"Did she ever destroy those who nearly killed her?" asked Leida.

"They were the first. She found them and killed them slowly and painfully from what I heard. She's getting out of control" sighed Diabloss.

"Well, I'm off on a hunt now," he said.

They nuzzled each other goodbye and he spread his wings and flexed them, before leaping off the cliff edge into the sky. Leida watched as he disappeared into the distance. She sighed and lay down, looking out at the sea.

Chapter 2
The Lizariaouses

Far away, a large, dark creature stirred. It lifted its brown, scaly muzzle and sniffed the air. A small snarl spread across its lips. Turning its head towards a sound behind it, the creature snorted. Before it stood another, similar creature, only this one was a dull red colour. It was panting and collapsed before the first creature.

"Got into a fight again, didn't you, Xalos?" snapped Zephirak.

Xalos didn't reply, but lay panting and beaten on the cold stone ground. "Well?" demanded Zephirak, rattling the needles on his back threateningly.

"I...I didn't want to fight her. She...she came at me and attacked me full on. I tried to escape, but it was no...no...no use..." his voice faded as he drifted into unconsciousness.

Zephirak looked at the unconscious Lizariaous with distaste.

Zephirak was large and well muscled, the fearsome leader of the Lizariaous pack. He was brown all over, with a few purple scales here and there. Twelve or so long, sharp needles grew out of his spine, deadly poisoned tipped weapons that he was able to shoot at enemies. He also had two curved spines on each of his shoulder blades. A short muzzle filled with razor sharp teeth and blood red eyes set in a narrow skull with three spikes coming out of the back and a long curved tail with a sharp tail-spade completed him. Both his fore feet and hind feet had opposable thumbs and sharp black claws.

Xalos was a dull weathered orange colour and much smaller than Zephirak. He didn't have as many needles or as powerful a musculature as Zephirak either. That's why Zephirak was the leader of the Lizariaouses in

Dyarkroeen. He was bigger and more powerful than all of them. If he wasn't, some other Lizariaous could battle him and overthrow him.

"KARNOS!!" he yelled. Another Lizariaous, a dark blue-black one appeared at the mouth of Zephirak's vast cavern.

"Take this retard and fix him up, he's badly injured" spat Zephirak. Karnos nodded and called in two more Lizariaouses who promptly carried Xalos out. Karnos followed them.

Zephirak sat back down and sighed. He knew Mettalika had been Xalos's attacker. His eyes flashed angrily and he threw back his head and roared. That Gryphie had been made virtually indestructible. However, she wasn't Zephirak's main cause for anger. Diabloss was Zephirak's worst rival. He was still the best fighter in the whole of the Gryphie gathering and being part Deamon, he was immune to the poisoned needles the Lizariaouses used for weapons. And if Zephirak was to accomplish his goal - becoming the undisputed ruler of Gryphies and Lizariaouses alike, he had to defeat the best fighter of the Gryphies in order to bring the rest down.

He began to think. Think of a weakness that Diabloss might have so Zephirak could get to him.

Hmm, if only Gryphies couldn't fly, is there a way to make them land bound? It would be easier to fight them if they didn't have the advantage of flying away. Is there another Gryphie that Diabloss is attached to? One he really cares about?

Zephirak sat up.

That's it! Diabloss has a mate I seem to remember. If I send out some packs to kidnap her and bring her back, I could get Diabloss to surrender, or I'd kill his

22

mate. He immediately brightened at this cruel thought and stood up.

"MORDRED!" he roared.

There was a scraping of claws approaching the mouth of the cavern and Mordred; Zephirak's favourite pack commander appeared.

"Yes sir" barked Mordred. He was considerably smaller than Zephirak and his skin was a dull grey colour with red scales here and there. He had fewer needles along his back and spiked elbows. His tail spade faced the opposite direction to other Lizariaouses.

"Mordred, take a strong pack over to Shernaron and find Diabloss's mate. Bring her back here alive," said Zephirak.

"But we don't know what she looks like," replied Mordred.

"Then spy on them and find out!" snapped Zephirak. "Go! Now!"

Zephirak watched as Mordred galloped off and laughed to himself. "Soon I will have the whole Gryphie gathering at my mercy."

He sat at the mouth of his cavern and looked out as Mordred went to the other Lizariaous soldiers' caves and rounded up three others to go and find Diabloss's mate with him.

The Lizariaous territory of Dyarkroeen was rocky, there were many bushes around the place and a lot of caves. Lizariaouses made their homes from the caves and some had been constructed by worker Lizariaouses. These were simply creatures that were stronger. Any Lizariaous that could dig through rock qualified to help with working. Their strong front claws were used mainly for killing prey, but the strongest of them could also shovel and dig through rock as well, making it easy to dig out concave niches in rock and finish the construction using their tail spades.

Zephirak's cavern was the biggest, of course and had a natural sky light in the top to let in sunlight and air because it was so big and needed ventilation.

Other than that, Dyarkroeen was fairly plain. Few trees, no rivers. A few small mountains. If they needed water, they had to travel half a mile to a large reservoir and drink. Every morning mothers would take their youngsters there so they could quench their thirst after the moon cycle and take some turtle shells to bring some back in for that sun cycle.

Zephirak decided he'd take a walk around and see what was going on around the place while Mordred was out with the soldiers.

***

Back in the Gryphie territory, Leida was getting bored with sitting around. Evening was fast drawing in and she wanted to go home. She stood up, stretched herself, turned away from the cliff edge and began the short walk back to the forest.

As she walked, she heard a soft rustling behind her. She tensed herself, but carried on walking. The rustling followed her. She narrowed her eyes and looked around, her ears turning to focus on the sounds around her. A bush moved a little way back to the side of the path. Leida stretched her wings out, ready to fly away if something came at her. However, she didn't sense any danger and curiosity finally got the better of her. She crept up to the moving bush and stood in front of it, about a metre or so away.

A small violet nose poked out through the leaves. It sniffed, twitching now and then. Leida relaxed. She knew that nose. It belonged to Lunara, a young Gryphie who was always spying on everyone, or following someone, waiting for them to play with her.

Her head popped out and looked up at Leida. She giggled and fell out of the bush.

"What are you doing out at this time? Shouldn't you be at home eating your supper?" asked Leida.

Lunara smiled. "I've had my tea."

"Oh, well I'm off home. Coming?"

Leida held a hand out to Lunara.

"K!" she laughed, tapping Leida's hand with hers.

After a while, Lunara got bored of walking and hopped up on to Leida's back for a ride.

"So, how are the flight lessons going?" asked Leida.

"Oh, they're ok. I'm getting better all the time!" replied Lunara proudly. Lunara, being only young, was just learning. She wasn't a beginning flier but all young Gryphies went to flight school and when they were older, to hunting school. Lunara wasn't old enough to hunt yet.

"I'll be taking my exam in seven sunrises from now." she said happily.

"Then I wish you luck with it" replied Leida, smiling.

Lunara suddenly leaped off Leida's back and landed on the path.

"I don't want to go home just yet, can we play a game?" she asked.

"Well I guess so. But you can't stay out too long; your mother will wonder where you are" said Leida glancing towards the sky and the setting sun shining down through the leaves.

"I know, I know. But I wanted to show you something I found this morning!" Lunara skipped off the path and into the forest, Leida following and being pretty glad they weren't anywhere near the Lizariaous territory.

Unknown to her, the pair of them were being watched. Mordred and the three soldiers he'd taken with him were hidden in the undergrowth. They had encountered Leida and Lunara as they headed into the forest, planning to infiltrate the base of the Gryphies. So now they watched them.

Mordred was wondering how long it would take to actually find Diabloss's mate since they had no idea what she looked like, let alone her name. This blue Gryphie could be his mate and the lilac one their kitten. So they watched as Leida and Lunara headed to a small waterfall by the spring.

"Follow me!" said Lunara and she jumped into the spring and disappeared behind the waterfall. Leida followed and saw what Lunara was trying to show her. It was a small cave.

"I found it this sun cycle" Lunara explained. "It makes a great hideout."

"Yes it does" Leida smiled.

Outside, Mordred held one of his underlings back.

"No! We don't know it's her! If we take back the wrong female, Zephirak will skin us alive. Wait." The other Lizariaous snarled at him, annoyed and clacked his needles.

Leida and Lunara returned and as they passed them Mordred sniffed, taking note of their scents.

They made their way along the path through the dense forest, waving occasionally to the guards that sat here and there in the trees.

The Gryphie territory of Shernaron was a vast place with trees and forests, quite the opposite of Dyarkroeen. It was about two hundred miles bigger than Dyarkroeen as well, which was another reason Zephirak wanted it as well as his own territory.

The Gryphie gathering (a large number of Gryphies living together are called a gathering, much like a large number of Lizariaouses are called a pack) Leida belonged to was living in the middle of a large forest in Shernaron. They lived in the trees, out of the way of Lizariaouses because that way, Lizariaouses couldn't sneak up on them and kill their young or them for food. Sure, Lizariaouses were fully capable of climbing, but often made a lot of noise doing so. The Gryphies' home was well guarded by lookout Gryphies so Lizariaouses rarely got to the main living area of it. Each Gryphie had their own tree, but families had the larger trees and shared. The only trees that had solitary Gryphies in were the ones belonging to Gryphies that were on their own, without a mate. Leida shared her tree with Diabloss.

There was no leader of the gathering; they all worked as equals in things. There was a wise one, a best fighter, good guards, but no leader. They were not governed by a ruler as the Lizariaouses were.

Lunara ran off to find her mother, while Leida climbed up her tree.

She sat on her food perch, looking down at the other Gryphies playing, talking and engaging in various Gryphie activities down below. Diabloss hadn't come back yet. Leida sighed and lay down on the wide branch.

"Hey!" called a voice. Leida looked down to see a minty green Gryphie with feathered wings standing at the base of the tree.

"You're Diabloss's mate, right?" she asked.

"Yes, why?" called Leida.

"He asked me to tell you that he's gone scouting and won't be back for a while, just so you don't get worried" called the other Gryphie.

27

"Oh. Who are you?" asked Leida.

"Iseera. I'm Diabloss's cousin. I live elsewhere, which is why you haven't seen me around here. I saw him out to the northwest, at the edge of the mountains. Isn't that where the Lizariaouses live?"

"Yes, that's where he normally scouts about, to see what they're up to" replied Leida.

"But why don't you just stay away from them?" asked Iseera, who's gathering was too far away to be involved in the friction between the species.

"In case they plan a surprise attack. We have guards everywhere, but they've still ambushed some of our gathering before" said Leida, climbing down from the tree.

"Oh, I…" began Iseera, but stopped as Mystik, the old wise elder of the forest, walked over to see them.

"Iseera, how are you?" said Mystik, warmly, putting a hand on Iseera's shoulder.

"Hello, Mystik. I'm fine, how have you been keeping?"

Leida watched Mystik and Iseera talking. Mystik had known Iseera from way back when Iseera was a baby and they were old friends. Leida was immediately forgotten as they caught up on what had been going on in their gatherings. Leida, feeling like the third wheel, sighed and walked away.

Feeling thirsty, she decided to head out of the forest and off to the spring to have a drink.

Unknown to her four dark shadows moved through the forest undergrowth, undetected by the guards. They watched her head out of the forest into the open and snarled.

Leida stepped up to the spring and began to drink. The water was cool and refreshing. She paused after her first mouthful. Everything was strangely quiet. She had another drink, and then listened. Not a sound was to be heard. A few moments later, she heard a twig snap. Spinning round, she felt something fall on her. She collapsed, desperately trying to get up; her eyes darting frantically around, trying to work out what it was that had fallen on her. Then she blacked out.

Chapter 3
In the Cavern

Drowsily, Leida opened her eyes. Everything around her was blurry. She shook her head, trying to make it all come into focus. She felt dizzy and weak. She couldn't move her wings either.

"So, you're awake" a voice spoke, seemingly from somewhere inside her head. Leida looked around and tried to get up. Finally things became a little more focused and she saw a dark figure standing before her. Its red eyes bored into her and she looked away.

"W…where am I?" she asked, more to herself than anyone else.

Zephirak narrowed his eyes and slinked towards her.

"Never mind where you are. You'll be staying here until I say you can go."

Everything seemed to fall into place and Leida realised where she was.

Dyarkroeen.

Leida stood up, afraid now. She laid her ears back and snarled; the fear showing in her eyes. Zephirak laughed. He could tell she was an inexperienced fighter by the way she'd handled the attack by Mordred and the small pack of Lizariaouses he had with him. Leida looked around for the way out, but there was none visible as she was right at the back of Zephirak's cavern. Moonlight shone in from a large crack in the roof and Leida made for that. She tried to spread her wings, but couldn't. She couldn't move them at all. Looking over her shoulder, she discovered her wings were tightly bound.

"There's no escape!" snarled Zephirak advancing towards her. Leida began to panic. She threw back her head and screamed a distress call.

"No one can hear you," said Zephirak calmly. Leida tried again and again but no one came to help her.

Suddenly, a long needle flew through the air, just barely missing Leida's head. She stopped, stunned.

"Another sound from you and next time it won't miss" snarled Zephirak, "now lie down and shut up, or do I have to shackle you to the floor??!"

Leida obeyed silently. Zephirak left that part of the cavern with a rattle of the dangerous needles on his back as a warning.

Leida rested her head on her hands miserably and began to cry. She'd never been caught before, she'd always run away and she'd never spent time training to fight because she'd never thought such a time would come when she was caught. She sobbed and watched her tears roll down her hands and splash onto the hard ground upon which she lay.

Diabloss arrived back in Shernaron early the following sun cycle as the sun was beginning to rise in the sky. He hated being out all moon cycle away from Leida and the rest of the gathering but he'd had a run in with a rogue Lizariaous on the way home.

Diabloss looked up at the tree he shared with Leida and smiled. He began to climb up.

"Hey, Leida, I'm back! Did you get Iseera's message? Sorry I'm so late." There was no reply. Diabloss searched the tree, but found no one, apart from one young Gryphie using it as a hiding place for a game he was playing with his friends.

Diabloss climbed back down and looked around. He saw Iseera coming down from the tree she was staying in, since she had been waiting for Diabloss's return to make sure everything was ok.

"Iseera, have you seen Leida?" he asked her.

Iseera paused, "I don't know where she is, sorry cous. I thought she was in the tree asleep like the rest of us were"

Diabloss asked one of the guards. "Have you seen Leida?"

"Your mate? Yeah, she went out to the spring last sun cycle evening. I haven't seen her come back, though" replied the guard.

Diabloss galloped off to the spring, annoyed that the rest of the gathering always seemed to overlook Leida's existence and never noticed when she could be in trouble. When he reached the spring, he sniffed around. Yes, she'd definitely been here. There were scuff-marks in the soft earth around the spring. It looked as though there'd been a struggle. Diabloss gasped as he lifted his foot. There was a small puddle of nearly dry blood where his foot had been. A few drops lead away from the puddle. He looked at his foot. It was not he who had been bleeding, however and he recognised the smell to be Leida's.

"LEIDA! NO!" he roared. Blue flames erupted from his mouth in his anger.

Diabloss spread his huge wings and soared into the sky. He had a pretty good idea of who had attacked Leida, but would he be too late? Would she still be alive? He flew as fast as he could to Dyarkroeen.

Chapter 4
Friend or Foe?

Outside Zephirak's cavern, Zephirak was just returning with some food for his "hostage" when one of the guards at the entrance called to him.

"Sir, she has been crying and breathing fire all moon cycle and we can't stop her in case she burns us. I wouldn't go in yet, unless you want to get fried"

"Shut up, Croter!" snapped Zephirak and walked past him into the cavern.

There were a few muffled sobs coming from Leida's direction. Zephirak walked over to her and dropped a lump of fresh meat in front of her.

"Eat!" he snarled. Then he walked out. Mordred came up to him. "Zephirak, sir, how do you know this plan will work?" he asked.

"Because once Diabloss sees the scene of the struggle and the blood that Leida lost, he'll guess it's us and come running to save his precious mate. And when he does, we'll be ready" growled Zephirak, leaving Mordred standing at the mouth of the cavern.

He watched Zephirak walking away and turned towards the cavern. He heard a faint sobbing that pained his heart. Mordred was completely loyal to Zephirak, but he couldn't bear the way Zephirak treated the hostage. He advanced into the dark cavern, ignoring the guards' warnings that Leida might fry him if she was scared.

As he entered the chamber that Leida was in, the sobs got louder and he saw her crouched miserably on a wide, flat plinth of rock, staring down at the meat Zephirak had left her. Her ears twitched as she heard him approach and she tensed herself, trying to move her wings. She cried out in pain as they were bound so

33

tightly, the bindings cut into her skin. She looked at him, fearfully, her cheeks stained with tears.

"It's alright," said Mordred gently, "I won't hurt you".

Leida backed away slowly, the fur on her neck standing on end. She was worn out from using her fire in panic nearly all moon cycle but she still attempted to protect herself if need be. Mordred sniffed the meat and wrinkled his nose in disgust.

"Zeph's trying to make you a cannibal now is he?" said Mordred, more to himself than to Leida. Leida's eyes grew wide in horror as she realised the meat Zephirak had given her was Gryphie meat and she began to cry again.

Mordred quietly walked over to her and loosened the bindings on her wings, cringing as he saw the bloody marks on them where they'd cut into her.

Leida curled herself into a protective ball in fear.

"It's alright, I won't hurt you" repeated Mordred as kindly as possible. He gently put a paw on her head and ruffled her fur. Leida looked up at him and sniffled, her ears laid back against her head. Mordred sat down in front of her and smiled.

"Y…you're not like the others?" asked Leida slowly, speaking for the first time.

"I am like the others, but I don't like what the master is doing to you" said Mordred slowly, "he didn't need to bind your wings so tightly, nor make you unknowingly eat your own kind. I would never go against his word, or disobey him, but he is twisted and sick when he's in a vengeful mood". Mordred looked up at the crack of light in the roof of the vast cavern and sighed sadly.

"Why did he do this, why does he want to kill us and enslave us?" asked Leida, shakily sitting up a little.

34

"Because Zephirak wants to rule over everything and anything standing in his way must be disposed of" said Mordred, gravely.

"He will never destroy us, we will fight him to the end" snapped Leida, bitterly.

"Fight *who* to the end??!!" boomed a voice from the mouth of the chamber.

Leida and Mordred spun round and faced the newcomer.

Zephirak bounded in angrily. "What were you doing talking to the hostage, Mordred?" he snarled; the needles on his back rattling threateningly. It was clear Mordred wanted to escape. His eyes flashed around franticly, wide with fear.

Leida backed up against the cavern wall, shivering. Zephirak ignored her, aiming for Mordred.

Zephirak's blood red eyes gleamed with rage. Mordred was trapped in a corner now.

"Telling her all our plans were you? Or were you just having a friendly "chat"?" his sharp teeth glinted in the dim light.

"No...I...I...was telling her that she wouldn't escape. She...she loosened her bindings and I was trying to threaten her and scare her into submission so I could tighten them again" whimpered Mordred. It was clear Zephirak didn't believe him and he pointed his needles towards him, getting ready to fire.

"Do you think I was born last sun cycle??!! You think I didn't hear you two talking about fighting me to the end?" in his rage, Zephirak didn't realise that all he'd really heard was Leida saying the Gryphies would fight him. Unfortunately, Zephirak was the sort of Lizariaous who jumped to conclusions and was distrustful of virtually everyone. The only person he really trusted was himself. He never stopped to think that Mordred might

35

not have been trying to befriend the unfortunate Gryphie.

Zephirak, stood on his hind legs and with a terrifying roar, he slashed a front paw downwards across Mordred's left eye.

Mordred cried out in pain and fled past Zephirak, yelping. Zephirak turned towards Leida. She stared up at him, terrified. He bought his paw down across the side of her face, knocking her out.

***

Meanwhile, Diabloss was speeding towards Dyarkroeen. He had only one thing on his mind - rescuing Leida.

When he reached the enormous cavern that served as a home for Zephirak, he hovered above in the shelter of two large trees that grew just behind it, watching for any sign of his mate. A few young Lizariaouses played in the dirt and some others were coming back from a hunting trip with a fresh kill. Then he noticed the guards outside Zephirak's cavern. Puzzled, Diabloss flew in closer. The guards were talking and he could just make out what they were saying.

"I don't know why the master doesn't attack them straight out. There are so many of us and only a few of them, at least in that forest of theirs" said Croter.

"Yes, but they have an advantage we don't. They have wings. We have to attack them where they are weak like taking loved ones or something they cherish, either that or be able to shoot them down from the sky" the older guard, Zarkiz replied.

"I still think it would be better to take them by force", retorted Croter.

"You think it's better to take anything by force, no wonder you never got a mate", chuckled Zarkiz.

Diabloss frowned. This still wasn't telling him where Leida was and he didn't want to go in, in case he was seen and captured himself. *I should have bought some backup with me*, he thought as he hovered a small distance away from the cavern. Then he saw Mordred. He had his tail down and looked ashamed and miserable.

"How is she? Do you know if he harmed her" he asked the guards.

"You've already displeased the master once this sun cycle, if he catches you round here again, he'll kill you. You are very brave for coming back here though; I'll give you that. I don't know what he did to her, but she isn't making any noise or flaming any more, he must have really scared her" said Zarkiz.

Mordred took a step forward. "I'll see how she is" he said.

Croter and Zarkiz aimed their needles at him.

"We can't let you in, not after you consorted with her. We don't know if you're on their side and we're not willing to help you I'm afraid, by letting you see her. Zephirak banned you from here. Now go before we tell him you showed your face here again." The guards growled threateningly but Mordred didn't back down. He stepped forward, also aiming his needles at them.

"You're either very brave or very stupid" hissed Croter.

"I'd go for the former" snarled Mordred.

"You can't take us both on and if you do, the master will get to hear about it" snapped Zarkiz. Mordred knew he was outnumbered, but he didn't want to admit it and back down. He would look foolish in front of the guards.

Zarkiz sat back. "Oh, and I suppose you want the master to do in your other eye too, for your troubles." That did it. Mordred retreated with his head down in shame. It was no good, he was outnumbered and not at any advantage and now this. He'd been extremely ashamed of the slash across his eye. It was what Zephirak did to those who'd misbehaved. Now it was recognised all around the territory that Mordred was one of those unfortunates and he'd noticed other Lizariaouses whispering about it as he'd passed them.

I used to be Zephirak's favourite and one of the best fighters, but now look at me. Reduced to nothing more than a laughing stock and ashamed to show my face. Mordred sighed and slowly walked away.

Diabloss, who had been watching all this, was stunned that a Lizariaous would worry about a Gryphie's safety. He didn't believe it was true and he wanted to go after Mordred to talk with him, but it was too risky. He stayed where he was. Now was the task of getting past the guards and getting Leida out before they followed him in and trapped him.

Mordred meanwhile had gone back to his cave to see his mate and have a nap. The other Lizariaouses also had caves, but they were not as big as Zephirak's cavern. Mordred's cave was fairly large and he shared it with his mate, Schaarl.

Schaarl was a pretty (if you could call a Lizariaous pretty) pale orange Lizariaous. She was also the envy of Zephirak, who didn't have a mate after his last one died to Mettalika. This was what really sparked off most of his vengeance.

Mordred loped in and slumped down on the pile of dry leaves that served as bedding for him and his mate. The cave had two chambers, one was for living and one was for sleeping. The sleeping quarters were at the back and Schaarl, seeing how miserable Mordred was, followed him into the sleeping quarters and sat down beside him as he slumped on the leaves.

"What is it dear?" she asked, looking down at the gash across his eye. She knew how that had happened as Mordred had made for his cave straight after Zephirak had attacked him.

Mordred sighed. "They might be our enemies, but they don't deserve to be hurt like that. Zephirak's got her; he's holding her hostage, she's already afraid and stressed, there is no need for him to be mistreating her like he is."

"It makes me sick too, but there is nothing we can do. If we attempt to rescue her, we will be treated in the same way, maybe even killed" said Schaarl, shaking her head.

"You're right, it is none of our business" sighed Mordred. He knew he couldn't argue with Zephirak, he valued Zephirak's trust too much. If he ever went against that trust, not only would he lose it, but he would also lose the respect of the whole pack and maybe even be banished from it forever.

Chapter 5
The Rescue

Diabloss watched the guards carefully. Now he had to work out how to distract them long enough to get into the cavern and rescue Leida. Suddenly he saw the large crack in the roof of the cavern. He alighted on the rocks that surrounded it and looked in. It was very dark inside, but Diabloss could just make out a form on the floor below. It was Leida. He called down to her.

"Leida, look up."

Leida slowly raised her head to look at the crack in the roof. Her face was stained with tears, but it brightened up when she saw her mate. Diabloss tried to hold in the shock and pain of seeing her like that.

"Can you get up?" he called down quietly. She nodded and slowly stood, whimpering as she moved her wings.

"Is there anyone around down there?" asked Diabloss.

"No, only me" replied Leida, her voice cracking.

Diabloss squeezed himself through the hole in the roof and jumped silently down next to Leida.

Tears of joy streaming down her cheeks, she nuzzled him lovingly and he put an arm round her.

She leaped back, yelping in pain as his arm touched her bound wings.

"What have they done to you?" said Diabloss and with a quick swipe of his claws, the bindings fell to the ground.

"It was horrible," cried Leida, "Zephirak knocked me out, he tried to shoot me with those needles on his back and he tried to feed me Gryphie meat.

Diabloss's eyes shone in anger.

"When I've dealt with him, Zephirak won't be able to walk, let alone treat Gryphies like that. We've got to get you back to the safety of the Forest." He said. "Can you spread your wings?"

Leida spread her wings slightly, cringing in pain. She collapsed in a heap, sobbing.

"I'll never be able to fly again", she cried.

"Of course you will" comforted Diabloss, "the wounds made by the bindings will heal very quickly if I can get you back to Mystik so she can put some herbs on them. Meanwhile, we've got to think of how to get you out of here. If you can't fly then we can't get out of the hole up there, plus in here it's hard to stretch our wings out to gain lift. We'll have to go past the guards. I'll create a diversion while you slip away. Do you think you can do that?"

Leida nodded, choking back a sob.

Outside, the guards, Croter and Zarkiz were chatting about the availability of fresh prey in the area.

Suddenly, Diabloss charged out of the cavern breathing fire and roaring angrily.

"What the...?" yelled Zarkiz, jumping out of the way.

"Huh?" Croter, also taken by surprise spun round and came face to face with a very angry Diabloss.

Diabloss snarled and flamed at him.

"What the hell are you doing here, Gryphie?" yelled Croter, staring at Diabloss in disbelief.

"Oh, just a flying visit" growled Diabloss and flew into the air.

Just as he'd hoped, the guards chased him, firing needles at him. Diabloss expertly dodged them and yelled, "Is that the best you can do?" while flying on his back.

This made the guards really angry, and roaring; they fired faster at Diabloss in a fit of rage.

Leida looked out of the cave warily. She sniggered when she saw the hapless guards chasing Diabloss with no hope of capturing him. She looked around and focused on a small Lizariaous who was watching her. She put her ears back, but then realised it was only a juvenile. He put his head on one side and said, "Whatja doin'?"

Leida thought quickly. She was good with kids and used to all the stuff that the young Gryphies got up to, so she replied "I'm hiding, don't say anything, I mustn't let my friends find me."

She put a finger to her mouth and whispered, "Shh" then she slunk away.

The little Lizariaous watched her for a moment then skipped off to find his friends.

Phew, thought Leida as she headed out of Dyarkroeen.

Diabloss meanwhile was still being chased by the two Lizariaous guards and he was having great fun annoying them.

"See these? These are wings, they're useful aren't they?" shouted Diabloss to the two guards. The guards roared angrily down below.

Diabloss needed to keep them occupied for just a minute longer, just enough time to wear them out a bit more.

The guards ran past Mordred's cavern and Mordred and Schaarl stuck their heads out to see what was going on. Mordred chuckled when he saw Diabloss teasing the guards and guessed that he'd come to rescue Leida. He only hoped Zephirak wouldn't see Diabloss and also guess.

He didn't need to worry, though because Zephirak was on the trail of a Mettalika sighting. Some Lizariaouses to the north had spotted Mettalika and Zephirak hoped to catch her unawares and ambush her. She normally hung around in the north and Zephirak's packs had set a lot of traps around there. Zephirak knew he couldn't fight her single-handedly, so he relied on traps to capture and disable her. If he could find her, then he could set a trap to capture her. However, she usually outsmarted most of the traps or escaped from the ones that caught her. If Zephirak found her and saw her getting caught, he could fire a needle at her and weaken her. He just had to find her first and this was the difficult part. Mettalika was smart and silent. She could move around easily without being seen or heard so Zephirak was putting himself in some danger going after her.

However, the feelings of vengeance he had towards her were bigger than his sense of personal safety. For taking the life of his mate and countless other Lizariaouses, he wanted to destroy her.

Chapter 6
Rage

Leida had finally made it out of Dyarkroeen and was well on her way back to the forest. Her wings still hurt her and she was very tired, but she kept on. She'd never walked all the way from Dyarkroeen to the Gryphie forest before, she'd always flown. She realised that on foot, the distance seemed much longer and more tiring. Finally, she had the forest in view and she wanted to run, but didn't have the strength, so she carried on walking slowly.

She was just wondering how Diabloss was getting on deterring the guards, when something flew past her. It was Diabloss.

"How did you get on?" asked Leida.

"Heh, those guards didn't even know what to do except run around, roaring and shooting needles at me. What a pair of idiots!" laughed Diabloss. "How are your wings? Are they still sore?"

"Yes, they still hurt", replied Leida, "but we're nearly home. Mystik can heal them with some herbs."

"Yes, then what you need is a good moon cycle's rest and in the morning, you'll feel much better" said Diabloss gently.

"Thanks for rescuing me, I was so scared back there, I thought Zephirak was going to kill me, or worse."

"I wouldn't have let him hurt you, you know that. I would have got you back no matter what it took. You mean everything to me and if I ever lost you, I don't know what I'd do."

Leida smiled warmly at him. "I love you, Diabloss." She said quietly.

"I love you too, dear" he replied landing next to her. He walked alongside her the rest of the way back to the forest.

Zephirak stormed back to his cavern after an unsuccessful search for Mettalika. He was not happy. He hadn't seen hide or hair of the Gryphie and now he was tired after so much searching.

Croter and Zarkiz were sitting either side of the mouth of the cavern, standing guard.

After Diabloss had flown away, they'd gone back to check on Leida, but had found she'd gone and realised what Diabloss's plan had been. They knew Zephirak would kill them if he found out they'd let her escape, so in the end, they'd decided it was best to be still standing guard when Zephirak got back and pretend nothing had happened.

Zephirak stepped up to the mouth of the cavern and looked at them.

"How is she?" he asked.

Croter was the one who replied. "We haven't heard anything from her all evening, Sir." Well, if Zephirak killed him, at least it wouldn't be for lying.

Zephirak snorted, "The stupid creature's probably still knocked out." He smirked and went inside.

It was dusk now outside and the interior of the cavern was even darker than usual. Zephirak blinked to adjust his eyes to the dark.

He went into the chamber Leida was being held in and looked around. There was no sound of her breathing and he couldn't make out the shape of her body, either.

"Hmm" he murmured, slightly puzzled. *I wonder where she could be.* He walked over to the plinth of rock she had fallen onto when he'd knocked her out. The meat was still there, and a few flies buzzed round it.

Zephirak sniffed at it. It was untouched. He snarled, rage building inside him.

"GRYPHIE!" he roared into the darkness. No one answered him. His voice echoed around in the vastness of the cavern.

He rattled the needles on his back angrily and bounded outside.

Croter and Zarkiz had heard him roar and they cowered a little when he stormed out.

"WHERE IS SHE?" he snapped at them.

"L…last time we ch…checked, Sir, she was in there" whimpered Zarkiz.

"Well she isn't now. You've let her get away. She's escaped!" yelled Zephirak.

"She couldn't have Sir, we never saw her come out" said Croter, truthfully.

"Well she has" growled Zephirak in a low, threatening tone, his eyes narrowing. "And since *you* let her escape, *you* can take a pack out and get her back. In her condition, she can't have gone too far. Go. Now!"

Croter and Zarkiz ran off to gather together a pack. They knew Diabloss had distracted them while Leida escaped and she was probably home by now, but they didn't dare tell Zephirak. So they got together a pack of Lizariaouses to scout around.

Mordred was one of these.

***

Meanwhile, back at the forest, Leida and Diabloss had made it home. They went straight to see Mystik in her ancient tree home.

"Mystik?" called Diabloss, walking in.

46

"Yes?" came the reply and Mystik stepped into view. Her tree was hollowed out and she lived inside it. It was truly enormous and very, very old. Some Gryphies said that Mystik was as old as the tree itself. She was also very wise and knew cures and remedies for nearly anything. It was her idea to mechanise Mettalika to save her life, but Mystik soon regretted it once she knew what Mettalika had set her life on doing after that.

"Leida was captured by the Lizariaouses and they bound her wings tightly, injuring them very badly. Do you have any healing herbs that we can put on them?" asked Diabloss.

"Why yes, I should have. Come on in and we'll see what we can do, dear." Mystik gestured for Leida to go inside and she followed. Leida looked back at Diabloss.

"I'll be in the tree if you need me, just call. You can't sleep in the tree in your condition" he said.

"Don't worry, she can sleep in my home for this moon cycle." said Mystik.

"Thank you Mystik" said Diabloss. He gave Leida one last loving look before going back to the tree and climbing up.

Leida didn't have the strength to climb up with her body and wings that weak.

Mystik looked around her home for the herbs. Shelves had been roughly carved out of the walls and many leaves and dried things lined them. Many of the things Leida had never seen. Mystik looked at her wings. Then she selected some herbs.

"Hmm, it seems I'm out of wing wort. We'll have to send someone to go and get some" said Mystik and went to the mouth of the hollow tree and called out for some help.

Sinxo, a young orange and black Gryphie with a white and black mane and black stripes on her body arrived.

"Want a scout?" she asked. She was younger than Leida, but only by a few seasons. She was fast and one of the best scouters and finders in the gathering.

"Yes, will you go and find some wing wort for Leida please?" asked Mystik.

Sinxo nodded and galloped off. She knew where everything grew in the forest.

She walked along the edge of a small stream. The wing wort grew around here somewhere. All she needed to do was find it. That was the hard part. Wing wort plants are very small. They have tiny green leaves and the only way you can easily spot them is by their big purple-blue flowers. Unfortunately, they only flower at certain times of the seasons. Right now it was late spring and they didn't produce flowers until late summer.

Sinxo sniffed the ground with her soft nose. Her nose was very keen, another reason why she was a good scouter. She sniffled and snuffled around, her eyes to the ground. Suddenly she came across something odd. She took a good look at it and leaped back. It was the claw of a Lizariaous. Just lying there in the grass.

Sinxo reached down and picked it up. She examined it carefully. It was black and shiny. It also looked to be quite old. It must have been lost a few lunars ago...but how? Sinxo turned it around it her fingers, thinking.

Suddenly, there was a rustle and something leaped out, right in front of her, taking up an attack position. The creature straightened up when it realised it was only another Gryphie. Sinxo jumped, but even after she saw who it was, she was still tense. It was Mettalika.

Her red fur was dirty and un-cared for and her steel plates shone dully. She was big and muscular from all the training and fighting she'd been doing against the Lizariaouses. She had no mane along her neck, it had moulted long ago and she had only three fingers on her wings, one talon of each was steel, the others were blue.

She raised her artificial claw in a gesture. "Thought you were a Lizariaous for a moment" she said gruffly.

I'm glad I'm not thought Sinxo, then said "I'm looking for some wing wort for Mystik, have you seen any?"

"What's wrong with ol' Mystik?" asked Mettalika.

"It's for Leida's wing. It's damaged and Mystik had run out of wing wort to heal it with."

"How'd it get damaged?"

"I don't know. But it looked bad, so I have to find the herb quickly, or it will get infected."

Mettalika grunted and shrugged. "I don't know." Then, quite suddenly, she ran off.

Sinxo wondered why Mettalika had left so suddenly, but remembered that she was a solitary now and not really used to the company of others after she alienated herself from the gathering. Thus, she was not really used to helping others. She only cared for herself now because she felt she only had to look out for herself. There were Lizariaouses to destroy and she was determined to get them all, even though unknown to her, it was impossible to do alone. Besides, the Gryphies didn't want to fight and avoided it at all times. They only ever defended themselves, not went on the offensive, like Mettalika did as Diabloss had stated earlier.

Sinxo watched her go for a while and then her thoughts suddenly drifted back to the wing wort.

She looked around again and saw some against a rock by the stream. She carefully picked it up and then ran back to Mystik's tree with it.

"I've got it, Mystik!" she yelled and ran up to Mystik and Leida who was laid out asleep on her medical plinth.

"Shh!" whispered Mystik and put a finger to her mouth. "Leida's asleep. She needs her rest, don't wake her. Put it on the rock over there and leave. Thank you for retrieving it for me."

Sinxo nodded and put the wing wort on the rock that served as a table for Mystik. She'd ask her about the Lizariaous claw later. She still had it with her and she took it back to her tree.

Mystik meanwhile took the wing wort and mashed it up in a hollowed out turtle shell. She added a drop of water to it and it turned to a liquid. It was nearly ready. She sprinkled some flower dew on it for freshness and then applied it to the injured parts of Leida's wings. Leida didn't stir; she was in a deep sleep. After the wing wort cream had been applied, Mystik wrapped Leida's wings in some large leaves so the medication didn't come off and could work while Leida slept. Leida flinched when the leaves were wrapped round her wings.

Then Mystik retired to her bedding of fresh leaves and lay down. Soon she too was asleep.

Diabloss couldn't sleep. He missed Leida's company. In the time they had been mates, he'd never been without her even a single moon cycle. He tossed and turned and shivered. Even though the summer was close, the moon cycles were still cool and without Leida to snuggle up to, he was cold. At last, with a sigh he was drifting off to sleep. However, he didn't get to sleep long, as a screech broke through the silence of the moon cycle.

Chapter 7
The Dream

There was movement from every tree in the forest as Gryphies everywhere woke up with jumps and starts, interrupting their dreams of wild flights and fantasies of what life might be like or how they'd wish it to be like without Lizariaouses constantly hindering and thwarting them.

Many voices filled the chill moon cycle air and some baby Gryphies cried for their parents. Diabloss sat up. He was the only one who recognised the scream of terror. It was Leida and she was in trouble. He leaped down from the tree and ran to Mystik's old tree.

Inside, Leida was crying while Mystik tried to comfort her.

"Leida? What's wrong?" asked Diabloss rushing in so fast the contents of the shelves nearly fell from their places.

"A...a dream, it was a dream..." sniffed Leida.

"Yes, she had a dream she was back in Dyarkroeen, back in Zephirak's cave" explained Mystik.

Diabloss nuzzled her to reassure her and she smiled a little, then her face crumpled with pain as she moved her wings to shift her weight on the plinth.

Diabloss went to the entrance of the tree and called out that it was a false alarm. Then he returned to Leida's side. Leida settled down a little and tried to explain her dream, finding it may go away quicker if she told someone about it.

"I...I was back in his cavern. No one knew I was there. I c...couldn't leave and no one came to me...I had no food...I became weaker and weaker...sun cycles went by...no one came...I couldn't move, I was paralysed. I got...th...thinner and thinner and then *they* came. They came at me from all sides, eyes glowing red in the darkness. Hidden things that lurked in the shadows...danger...danger in the darkness...I...I couldn't escape. They were closing in so fast now. I could hear them breathing, they knew I couldn't escape...couldn't fight back. My muzzle was bound. I couldn't open it...everywhere...they..." she trailed off and closed her eyes, relating to the dream in pain as it came flooding back to her in her mind.

"There there, it's all gone now. It was a dream, nothing more than a dream" comforted Diabloss.

Leida sobbed. "It...it was so real" she sniffed.

"Dreams often are" said Mystik, "but it is really all in your mind. Once you wake up everything returns to normal and you know it was only a dream."

"I'll stay with her for the rest of the moon cycle" Diabloss told Mystik.

Mystik nodded and retired once again with a weary sigh.

Leida slept nearly all through the moon cycle after that, waking up just once. This time, it was because her wings were hurting her. It was hard to sleep without lying on them, as she'd nearly always lain on her back at moon cycle as well as her front, despite, her mother telling her when she was younger that lying on her back was bad in case something attacked her in the middle of the moon cycle and her soft tummy was exposed.

The next morning, Diabloss was the first to awaken in Mystik's old tree. He stood up and stretched, then went outside and stretched his wings, since the width of the tree was too short for his mighty wingspan. He looked back in and saw Leida asleep, a peaceful expression on her face. It seemed her moonmares had stopped.

As the sun shone in on her eyes, Leida stirred and slowly opened them, squinting against the early morning sunlight. Diabloss walked back in and stood in front of her, shielding her eyes from the light so she could adjust them.

Leida sat up slowly, groaning with the effort. The walk from Dyarkroeen back to the gathering the previous sun cycle had been tiring and her legs ached. She stretched her wings out a little, wincing with the pain that still lingered there in her muscles and in the deep wounds she'd suffered. She felt a little as though she was still bound when she had her wings folded. It felt as if the bindings were still there.

"How are you this morning?" asked Diabloss.

Leida yawned, then replied; "I feel a little better."

Mystik came from her bedding at the back of the tree and smiled. "It is good to see you up and about, Leida. You were brave last sun cycle."

"No I wasn't. I got caught by the Lizariaouses and nearly killed too" sighed Leida.

"Well, at any rate, you were lucky to escape" remarked Diabloss.

"No, Leida, you were brave enough to go out and leave Dyarkroeen when Diabloss distracted the guards. You could have run into Zephirak" Mystik told her.

"How do you know what happened?" asked Leida.

"Well last sun cycle when Diabloss told me you'd been captured by the Lizariaouses, I guessed he must have distracted them while you got away. We have guards around the forest, so I assumed they too must have guards outside Zephirak's cave to make sure you didn't get away. I know many things because I have been around many more seasons than you." She chuckled and went to find some breakfast, leaving them in the old tree.

Diabloss walked out. "Come on Leida. Let's see if we can find some breakfast too" he suggested. Leida nodded and followed him.

***

As they walked down the earthy path to the spring for a morning drink before their hunt, Leida looked around nervously. She feared an ambush and didn't really want to go back to the spring again. Anything could be out there waiting for her.

Diabloss noticed her behaviour and started a conversation up.

"What was it like in Zephirak's cave?" he asked her as they walked.

Leida shuddered as she related to it. "It was very dark and cool, dry too, but I could smell death all around me. It was a nasty place, full of evil…like a mist clouding the air, contaminating all good that entered. However, there was one Lizariaous who seemed different. He was a grey colour with red areas on his body and lean. He was younger than Zephirak. He loosened my bindings, but Zephirak found him and attacked him. I never saw him again. He told me he thought what Zephirak was doing was bad and he shouldn't treat me in the way he was doing. He said he liked him, but he still thought it was cruel."

"I saw him too. He was confronting the guards outside the cavern; he seemed to be worried for your safety. He had a slash across his eye" said Diabloss, remembering

"That was where Zephirak attacked him."

"I wonder why a Lizariaous would care so much about a Gryphie."

"He told me he didn't. He just thought it was bad for Zephirak to treat me like dirt" said Leida quietly.

"It makes me wonder if there are members of the pack that don't like what Zephirak's doing. After all, he's the only one who thinks he has a reason to attack us."

"Maybe there are, but Mettalika has killed many of the pack. However, they still outnumber us and they are strong. The vengeful ones won't give up easily. I know I never want to go back there though." Leida shuddered at the thought.

Meanwhile, Croter, Xarkiz, Mordred and the other three Lizariaouses that were with them hadn't found Leida. They had searched all moon cycle, thinking they'd find her asleep somewhere and that she would never have made it far without having to sleep and rest. Well, the three other Lizariaouses had that in mind. Croter, Xarkiz and Mordred knew very well that Diabloss had helped her escape. Maybe there was a slight chance they hadn't made it back and had stopped for a rest, but Diabloss would be with her and they wouldn't be able to get near her.

"Why don't we just go back? There's no point in carrying on this search; its plain we'll never find her, not with Diabloss there too. For all we know, she could have flown home on his back or something" said Xarkiz.

Croter snapped at him. "Have you any idea what Zephirak will say if we return empty clawed? He'd kill us 8 times over before we fell to the ground, that's what! Do you really want that to happen?"

Xarkiz shook his head looking down.

Mordred stepped up. "Why don't we just go home and tell him we found some creature eating her or something?" he suggested.

Croter thought. "Hmm...that might work. We'll say we came across a QuadraFelieon devouring what was left of her. Yes. I think he'll buy it. At least you're good at doing something, Mordred." Croter looked him straight in the eye. "If Diabloss hadn't saved her and we'd have let you in to see her a second time...I wonder if she'd still be our captive or if she would have "mysteriously" escaped anyway."

Mordred snarled at him. "How dare you think that I would have helped her escape! I am no friend to Gryphies. I live and serve Zephirak. No one else."

Croter smirked and turned away, commanding the others. "You three! Here, now! We saw a QuadraFelieon eating her, let's return and tell the master. We can't bring her back now."

The soldiers regrouped and returned to where Croter, Xarkiz and Mordred were and they all made their way back to Dyarkroeen.

Far away in the forest, Sinxo had been waiting for Mystik to return from her hunt. Even though she was old, she was still a very good hunter, using the power of surprise instead of speed to catch her prey.

Sinxo yawned, the early morning sun shining down on her deep orange fur. She had the Lizariaous claw with her.

Soon, Mystik returned with her kill - a small forest deer.

"Oh, Sinxo! What are you doing here? I hope you haven't come for some of my breakfast. It took a lot to get it this morning. I left too late to ambush them when they were asleep due to last moon cycle and I overslept a bit" she said.

"No, I've come to show you what I found last sun cycle" explained Sinxo. "It's a Lizariaous claw. I found it in the grass while looking for the wing wort. How do you think it got there?" She gave the claw to Mystik, who took it and examined it carefully.

"Hmm, it's not new. See how it has been weathered? Also, it is green in places where moss has been growing on it. I'd say its owner died of old age. Nothing hunts Lizariaouses."

"So Mettalika didn't kill it then?"

"No, she goes mainly for the younger ones that have a lot of life left. Ones that can live for a good few more seasons and bring suffering for us...or so Mettalika thinks. Ah, that is one thing I regret. It was fate that she died. It was her time to go and I helped to stop it. Saving her life was a bad decision of mine and only worsened our situation." Mystik sighed sadly. "In helping her, I ruined her life and also destroyed the lives of many others. And many more to come."

Sinxo put a hand on her shoulder. "Don't blame yourself; you were trying to help, to do what was best and save the life of your fellow Gryphie. You didn't know it would turn out like this."

"Ah, but you see I should have done. I panicked and made the wrong decision. I should have known better than to mess with the natural way of life. Now Mettalika is alone and a murderer and she will not stop until she has every last one of them. We are peaceful; we don't take lives in earnest as she is doing. It is wrong. In a way, that makes her worse than Zephirak himself."

Sinxo's eyes widened. "That can't be. No Gryphie would sink to his level, not even Mettalika, surely."

Mystik just gave a weary sigh.

"Do you want the claw? You could use it in a medicine or something" asked Sinxo.

"No, you keep it, I have a lot I collected from Mettalika's victims" replied Mystik. "Now, if you don't mind, I am going to eat my breakfast" and she took her kill to the back of her tree to eat it.

Sinxo stood up and walked out of Mystik's tree on her hind legs so she could carry the claw in her hand. Outside, she met Lunara playing with her friends. They ran up and asked to have a look at the claw. Sinxo showed it to them.

"Wow! That's cool!" yelled Lunara.

"Here, you can have it if you want," said Sinxo, "I don't really need it." She gave the claw to Lunara. Lunara beamed.

"Really? Wow, thanks! Hey guys! I'm the evil Lizariaous and you all have to run from me and my sharp claw!" The young Gryphies all ran around screaming, laughing and shouting as they fled from Lunara who roared and chased after them.

Sinxo watched them for a while, then turned and went back to her tree.

Leida and Diabloss meanwhile had caught two forest deer. Leida had had problems catching hers because her wings didn't work very well. Every time she went to catch one, she automatically went into flight as she usually did, as flying was faster than running. And every time she did this, it caused her pain and she tripped up and landed on her face. She finally managed to catch one by leaping out of a tree. By this time, Diabloss had nearly eaten all of his. Leida did a sort of body slam on hers and knocked it unconscious. Then she started to eat it, sitting next to Diabloss.

"Well done" said Diabloss, looking at her admiringly. "You used your head and found a new way to catch one." He hadn't helped her on purpose, as he wanted to know if she could solve the problem on her own.

"Umm…Leida, I was thinking something over last moon cycle and I wondered if you'd agree if I suggested it" he said quietly.

"What is it?" asked Leida.

"Well, they caught you easily last sun cycle. If you had been training, then they wouldn't have and you would have been able to protect yourself better instead of panicking. I was thinking maybe I could train you a bit; teach you some things about attack and defence. What do you say?"

Leida looked doubtful. "Next time, I'll be more careful. I wasn't keeping my ears and senses open. It was quiet when I went to the spring; I should have suspected something."

"Yes, but if you slip up again, they might not take you hostage. They might kill you."

Leida thought this through. "Very well" she said, "I will train."

Chapter 8
In Training

To the east of Shernaron, there was a large open field where a lot of Gryphies trained for battles and in case they were attacked by Lizariaouses. A Gryphie was the coach, a well-trained Gryphie, who knew every single art of battle there was. He knew how to breathe not only the famous Gryphie blue fire, but also ice as well. That required expert skills and not even Diabloss could do it. A Gryphie had to be born with a fault in its fire chamber in order to breathe ice. Few Gryphies were capable of doing it. The coach was old, but not as old as Mystik. Every single guard had learnt their skills from him; even Mettalika had been in his class once.

His name was Strassor. He had jet-black fur with streaks of blue around his eyes and on his legs. His wings were normal peach colour and he had a massive tail blade with six sharp razor edged points.

Strassor could be seen yelling orders to a few training guards and soldiers. They ran around obstacle courses and used their fire to help them in ways Leida had never seen before.

For example, if they were loosing altitude in flight too fast, breathing fire at the ground helped them to land more slowly. Some plants were too dense to crawl or climb through, so breathing fire at them made them brittle so they could easily be barged through.

Diabloss and Leida trotted up to Strassor.

"Strassor, this is Leida, my mate. Would it be ok if you trained her in your class? She knows few skills and has already been captured once by Lizariaouses. She needs your help to train her properly" said Diabloss.

"Aye, that be true. She looks in poor shape to be trainin' this sun cycle," said Strassor in his unusual regional accent. "'Er wings don't look too good to me. Come back tomorrow young 'un an' I'll tell yea how ter fight prop'ly." Then he turned back to the other Gryphies and started barking orders out again.

Diabloss and Leida walked away. "We'll have to come back tomorrow," said Diabloss.

"How did he know about my wings?" asked Leida.

"Strassor's got very keen eyesight. He must have seen the wounds on them. By tomorrow, they should have healed over. We'll come back tomorrow and you can start training."

Croter, Xarkiz and the others walked up to Zephirak's cavern. Zephirak was sitting outside, enjoying the morning sun. He saw them coming and stood up.

"Well, where is she then?" he asked.

Mordred stepped forward. "Long gone now, Sir. A QuadraFelieon was just finishing her off when we found her" he explained.

"There was nothing we could do, she was just too weak," Croter added.

Zephirak snarled. "Damn! That was the route to Diabloss's undoing. Now we have nothing that he will risk his life for so we can capture him. You morons! You should have protected her better." The needles on his back rattled in anger and he retreated, seething, into his cavern.

Croter looked at Mordred.

"Do you think we escaped?" he murmured.

"I should think so, but Zephirak will be in a mood for a good few sun cycles, we'd better avoid him until he gets over it" he replied.

They all went back to their own home caves to lay low for a bit.

Mordred went home to Schaarl, who looked worried when she saw him.

"What happened?" she asked.

Mordred sighed and explained. Finally he said, "I'm glad she escaped, but Zephirak will still not stop. He's in his cavern scheming away now, plotting to find a way to destroy the Gryphies' best fighter and make it easier for us to enslave them and for what? Just so he can be master of another race of creatures. What is a master if the subjects all hate him and don't come willingly to his aid? There will be turmoil. Any Gryphies that escape will set up some kind of a freedom fighting team surely and there will be an all out war between our species. Well if it comes to that, I for one will have nothing to do with any of it. I'd rather move away than die fighting in a pointless war brought on by our corrupt ruler."

"Yes, but Mettalika did kill his mate all those seasons ago" said Schaarl quietly.

"Yes, *all those seasons ago*, sixteen seasons ago. Zephirak should have let it pass. He knows that it was Lizariaouses that nearly finished her off when she was young and defenceless. Just because there was a food shortage. Gryphies and Lizariaouses have never really been allies, but at least they tolerated each other. So in a way, *we* were the ones who started this thing. After the death of his mate, Zephirak sent hunters out to kill Gryphies for our food. I would never touch one, but some of us have developed a taste for them." Mordred shook his head in sadness and confusion. "I...I just want it all to stop." He lay down.

"Because if it doesn't soon, we will *all* be in danger. In danger of wiping each other out completely."

The next sun cycle, Diabloss and Leida were up bright and early. They caught breakfast and headed over to the training fields to see Strassor.

"Mornin'!" he yelled heartily as they trotted up to him.

"Ah, I see yer wing's better young 'un!" he smiled.

Leida nodded. Her wing felt much better thanks to Mystik's herbal remedies.

"Let's be 'avin' a look at yer then!" said Strassor and Leida walked up to him.

"Hmm…hmm…ah! Aye, you be fit ter train this sun cycle" he said after checking her over and making sure her wings worked properly.

"Now, we start with general agility courses. The most important thing ter remember is that if yer wings be broken, yer must escape usin' speed." He pointed to the course ahead. "This be where yer startin'. Lessee how fast you can get roun' that there obstacle course."

Diabloss found that this would probably not be all that interesting and went to patrol the south border of Shernaron for Lizariaouses.

Leida waved to him as he left and walked to the start of the course. Strassor took her into the air so she could see the layout of the course and figure out a way to get across. Then she landed again.

Ahead of her lay an obstacle course not unlike one seen in army training camps.

First, there was a wooden platform a few feet off the ground, followed by a ramp with a rope bridge across water to a ledge the other slide. Beyond the ledge there was a dirt slide with sharp rocks at the bottom to be jumped over. After that there were thick bushes. Some had prickles and some were infested with snakes. Leida shivered. After those came a deep pool about 30 feet long and beyond that a pit full of sand. Then there was another wooden platform that finished the course off.

"Off yer go then. I want to see first how yeh handle that there obstacle course. Good luck." Strassor told her.

Leida took a deep breath and started off. She jumped onto the platform and ran up the ramp. Then very carefully and using her wings for balance, she crossed the bridge. Once on the other side she slid down the dirt slide rather uncomfortably on her bottom, narrowly missing the rocks, then faced the bushes. She gulped.

First was the dense one. She forced her way through it. Next came the prickly one. She couldn't walk round it, as there were low walls either side of the bushes so that very thing couldn't be done. So instead she jumped up on the wall and walked along it, past the prickly bush and past the one with the snakes. Then she jumped back down and carried on. Next was the deep pool. She had to jump in and was shocked and scared that she couldn't touch the bottom of it. She floundered around panic stricken.

Strassor flew above her.

"Calm yerself! Don't be so tense! Just swim across. The body is naturally buoyant and if yer don't struggle, yer won't sink" he yelled to the struggling blue form below that was Leida desperately trying to keep her head above the surface of the deep greenish grey-blue water that seemed determined to draw her under.

She stopped struggling and took deep breaths to calm herself, then began to doggy-paddle across the pool. She swam faster and faster, desperate to get out and finally made it to the other side.

She stood panting for a minute and looked to see what still lay ahead of her. It was the sandpit. She sighed in relief and exhaustion and walked forward and across the sand.

Suddenly she felt her feet being pulled downwards by an invisible force. It was quicksand! Leida struggled and, as with the water, the more she struggled the deeper she went. Now she was up to her ankles in it.

"What did I tell yer 'bout strugglin'?" came Strassor's voice from above.

Leida stopped and stood stock still now. She looked down and very slowly and carefully tried to pull a front foot out of the sand. It worked. She eased the other three feet out and leaped to the side before she could sink in again. Finally she collapsed on the wooden platform that finished the course, panting.

Chapter 9
Lessons

Strassor alighted beside her. She looked at him hopefully.

"Did I do ok?" she asked.

"Well, yeh cheated a bit and yer knowledge of defence is poor" he replied looking at her. She looked ashamed and down hearted.

"But we can soon fix that!" he added. "Time fer some lessons I think Leida."

Strassor jumped onto the wooden platform and pointed to the ramp and bridge. "Yeh did these well an' remembered to use yer wings fer balance on the bridge, which is good." He walked up and along the bridge, coming to the slide at the other end. Leida followed on the ground, sometimes flying up to get a better look at what he was talking about.

"Fer the dirt slide, yeh have ta remember that seein' as yeh can't use yer wings on this, ter get down, yeh gotta improvise. Use yer back feet to slide down on an' jump when you get near the rocks so yeh don't crash into 'em." He demonstrated this and after the jump, landed about a foot away from the rocks and just in front of the first bush.

"Dense bushes like this one can be easily overcome by using fire and burnin' 'em ter ashes. It be a lot easier to break through a bunch of dry brittle sticks than ter try an' get through a thick bush an' strain yerself."

Strassor didn't demonstrate this, as Leida would need the bush when she tried all this out afterwards.

"The same goes fer the prickly bush. Now that there snake one can be overcome by using yer wings ter shield yerself from the snakebites. Gryphie wings be one o' the best forms of armour an' can shield most

things even to some extent the fire of another Gryphie."
He told her. Leida watched with interest as he walked
through the snake bush, gathering his wings about him
and using them as a shield around his body.

"If they get too close, flick them away with yer wing.
Yeh dun' want 'em getting' too close 'cos if they happen
ter get underneath ya, they can do considerable
damage to yer belly, so dun' let 'em bite yer there, it'll
hurt!" he explained as he walked.

Leida nodded and acknowledged his words every so
often, paying deep attention to him.

He carried on to the pool. "Now, yeh never know
how much deepness a pool has until yer in it. If yeh find
yer can't touch the bottom, yeh must swim an' keep
yerself afloat. As I said before, the body is naturally
buoyant an' won't sink so easily if yer don' struggle.
Swim as slow as yeh like, especially if yeh can't see the
other side. Yeh dun' wanna drain yer energy too quickly,
yeh want enough to take you across." He swam slowly
and easily across the pool and came out the other side
ready for the sand.

"Are yeh followin' me so far?" he asked. Leida
nodded. "Yes, I understand so far" she said.

Strassor nodded and looked across the quick sand.
"Fer something like this, it be best ter take a giant leap
across an' clear it without havin' ter touch it. That way
yeh won't be risking yer life tryin' ter get out."

He leaped across easily as he was larger than Leida
and his legs were longer. Then he stepped up on the
platform.

"There. Course completed. Now that weren't so
hard, were it? Now you try!" he said, motioning to the
course.

Leida swallowed, hoping she'd remember all he'd
told her and flew to the beginning of the course.

The first part of the course she did much the same until she reached the dirt slide. Then she sat back on her haunches and glided down surprisingly easily on her back feet. She suddenly saw the rocks coming and nearly forgot to jump however.

"That were close!" yelled Strassor from the air, watching her.

No kidding thought Leida. The bushes now lay ahead of her. She breathed fire over the first and second ones, roasting them well and barging through each of them as Strassor had shown her. Next was the snake bush. Leida had dreaded doing this one. She crept through, making sure her wings were practically wrapped around her whole body and nearly tripping over them a couple of times. The bush was alive with snakes and they all attacked her, but not able to get a good grip on the smooth skin of her wings.

However she wasn't paying enough attention and one got underneath her. Fortunately she trod on its head and squashed it by accident so never really realised what a close call she'd just had.

After she'd completed that, she stretched her wings out thankfully the other side of it and looked on to her next obstacle, the pool.

Carefully she got in and shivered as the cold water touched her once again. Still, swimming helped to keep her warm and she was soon across a lot easier than the last time.

Now for the sand. She backed up to the edge of the pool, took a running jump and cleared most of the sand. However she fell just slightly short and landed right in it.

"Aaah!" she screamed, trying to get herself free of the sand that tried to suck her into its depths.

"Dun' panic!" yelled Strassor, "remember what I said!"

Leida did remember, but instinct kicked in and she opened her wings, using them to help pull her out of the quick sand. Then she landed on the platform beyond, panting. Strassor landed beside her.

"Well, yeh did better than last time" he said. "Congratulations anyway. You must return tomorrow so we can work on yer weaknesses."

Leida nodded. "Did…I do…well?" she asked, wanting to be sure she wasn't a complete failure.

"Well enough" replied Strassor and walked off to see some more Gryphies who had just arrived for training.

Leida's first lesson was over. She went to find Diabloss.

***

Zephirak paced up and down, getting ever more distraught over the fact that Leida was dead, or so he thought. He had made quite a mark on the floor of his cavern from where he'd been pacing. He sat down on the plinth of rock where Leida had been held hostage and raked a claw down the hard surface of it, leaving a deep scratch mark. His red eyes narrowed in anger as he racked his brain for any ideas of how to bring Diabloss down.

Finally, he decided to focus his vengeance on Mettalika. None of the traps the scouters had set had caught her or even come near to catching her. The most any of them had caught were a few deer and one had caught a Furmine that had escaped after a scout released it thinking it was dead.

They had tried everything on Mettalika. Snares, pit traps, caves that they lured her into and closed a rock across the opening, but every time she'd escaped with little or no trouble. Most of the time she had used her wings for escape, also with her heightened strength from killing and hunting so much, she could escape the snares because invariably they would close on one of her steel body parts as well.

They had attacked her with their needles, but her armour was too strong. They had tried to ambush her and get her down on the ground by jumping on her at the same time, but she would simply spread her wings and fly up until they had all fallen off her. She was insidious and unstoppable it seemed. The hurt deep inside her and her hunger for revenge burned strong and it had never waned, in all her seasons of killing and destroying the thing that plagued her...Lizariaouses.

But how to dispose of her, she has no weaknesses and no one she cares about. The only way we could bring her down is to somehow rid her of that armour. She is killing more and more of us, even to the point of attacking mothers who take their children out on hunting trips and destroying the new life. Wait...she scavenges too. Yes, poison! We shall poison her! Zephirak was very proud of that idea. He stood up with an evil grin.

It was true. Although Mettalika mainly relied on Lizariaouses for food, she also ate forest deer and finding or stealing a fresh one from another creature was a great opportunity.

Now all Zephirak needed was a poison that was scentless and tasteless and the only place he knew where to find something like that was near the marsh. There grew a plant, a poisonous plant, a plant known as Umbrabane. It had large flat leaves and black flowers. The leaves were very thick and by squeezing them, it could be milked for its poison. The poison was deadly for nearly all creatures. When consumed, the victim would experience hallucinations followed by sickness and then death.

All I have to do is kill a forest deer and fill it with poison, then leave it for her in a place she will find it. He thought.

He went to find Hytarious and Karnos, his two best soldiers.

Chapter 10
Death by Poison

Karnos was relaxing in the sun with his youngsters. He had two little boys and an older girl. His mate had been a victim to Mettalika when she was pregnant with the fourth baby. Karnos's dark blue/black scales shone in the sunlight. He was well conditioned, as he had not fought for a while. He had red stained claws from fighting and nine very long needles along his spine and a few brown scales here and there where he had been injured and the correct pigment had not grown back again with the new scale. He had a long thin green tail spade with small spines all along it.

The youngsters played, laughed and rolled around in the dust, even the older sister joining in.

Suddenly a shadow cast over them and they stopped playing. It was Zephirak. The youngsters ran back to their father again, as they weren't used to him.

"Karnos, you are required to aid me now" announced Zephirak, "this way." He gestured with his paw and turned.

"Ok, you three go and play now. Look after your brothers, Silpharius!" Karnos told the young ones and they ran off to continue their game elsewhere. Karnos followed Zephirak.

Soon they came across Hytarious. He was sitting on the ground staring into the sky and looking at the clouds, trying to figure out if it would rain or not anytime soon. He had a mate but no youngsters, since she refused to bear them.

He was a very dark brown with only seven needles on his back. He had grey feet and a grey tail, the tip of which was missing and thus, the tail spade as well. No one knew how he had lost it, only that it wasn't there for some reason best known to Hytarious.

"Hytarious, report for duty now!" barked Zephirak and immediately the Lizariaous stood to attention.

"Now I have both of you here, I have a job for you. You are to go down to the marsh to the east of Dyarkroeen and retrieve the poison of an Umbrabane. Then you are to kill a forest deer, poison the meat and leave it as bait for Mettalika, somewhere where you are positive she will find it. I suggest you find her and then leave it in her path. Hide well to make sure she takes it and then bring her back to me. Is this understood?"

"Yes sir!" Karnos and Hytarious yelled in unison.

"Good. Now go!" Zephirak told them and they galloped off.

"I can't think why Zephirak doesn't just give up on it," said Hytarious.

"Because Gryphies are a nuisance, especially this one" replied Karnos.

"Yes, but we're the ones risking our lives here. I've seen that thing kill. She's brutal and deadly. We are no match for her."

"Now listen here! We will be well hidden when she finds that meat and soon enough she will be eating it, then she will die. After the first mouthful she won't even be able to see us long enough to attack us, let alone anything else. Now just calm down will you? Let's get that poison."

"And what do you propose we put it in?"

"Hmm, you have a good point. Well, we'll kill the deer first then."

"And have the smell with us? She'll smell a dead animal's blood and come running...or something worse will" pointed out Hytarious.

Karnos thought about this and finally replied, "well you pick a leaf and I'll kill the deer. Then we'll put the poison straight in."

Hytarious nodded in agreement and they set off.

The marsh was humid and quiet save for the occasional croaking frog. They looked around and it was Karnos who found the plant. He called Hytarious over and he picked a leaf carefully.

"Don't get it on you, you might swallow it" said Karnos.

Hytarious nodded. "I am fully aware of that. Now let's find a deer so we can finish this."

They crept out of the marsh carefully and quietly, Hytarious holding the leaf as gently as possible so as not to poke it and waste some of the poison. Finding a forest deer was the hardest part. They had to be very careful, as most of the forest was on the Gryphies side of Dyarkroeen and if any guards saw them, they would alert the gathering, Mettalika would get wind of it and their plan would be blown.

Hytarious sat down on a moss covered rock and waited while Karnos hunted for a deer. About half an hour later, he heard scuffling and struggling then a cry and Karnos emerged with a dead deer in his jaws. He'd caught himself a fairly large one too and Hytarious, who hadn't had a decent meal for a while looked longingly at it. Karnos dropped it at his feet.

"We'll find Mettalika first, then lay the bait and poison it quickly before she passes it," said Karnos. "Then we'll hide in these bushes at the side of the path and watch her. I will find her. Then give you the signal. You lay the meat in her path and put the poison on it, on the top here." He pointed out a place on the deer's flank where Mettalika was most likely to sink her teeth first.

"Understand?"

Hytarious nodded.

"Good, I will find her now." Karnos ran off, leaving Hytarious with the meat. In a few minutes he returned.

"This way, follow me," he said and they set off the way they'd come.

Mettalika was on the trail of a scent. It was in fact their scent, Karnos and Hytarious.

Hmm, Lizariaouses and their scent is fresh. They rarely travel down to the marsh for food or water. I wonder why these went there. She thought to herself. The reason for the Lizariaouses apparent journey puzzled her.

In the bushes, Karnos pointed out to Hytarious where to place the meat and he obediently placed it there. Then he poisoned it. Not a moment too soon, either. Since Mettalika was following their trail, she had followed them and headed directly for the path that the meat lay in. Hytarious had just enough time to jump for cover before she rounded the corner and saw it.

Meat? She went and sniffed at it. *Fresh and abandoned or maybe its dispatcher will return for it.* She grinned. Well they wouldn't find it if they did come back.

She was just about to take a bite right from the flank where the poison was, when out of the corner of her eye, she saw a slight movement in the undergrowth. A small snarl spread across her lips and she very slightly turned her head towards the cause of the movement, tensing her body in case it was another Gryphie who would challenge her for her meal or a Lizariaous who shouldn't be foolish enough to be around her.

Her ears pricked up, listening for the slightest sound of an intruder breathing or shifting around. All was quiet now. However, she decided to take a look around before continuing with her meal. She could lose it to another creature, but if there were Lizariaouses around, it meant she'd get a meal anyway.

She straightened up and walked slowly up and down the path, looking around. It was then she saw it. The tip of a needle sticking up from the leaves of a bush to the side of the path near where the meat lay.

With a roar, Mettalika coiled her body and then leaped forward into the bush, pushing out Hytarious who was hiding there. Being tensed up, the needles on his back were not relaxed and so instead of being laid down along his spine, they stuck straight up in the air as normal, giving him away and costing him dearly.

He tumbled out and ran for it. It was the only way to go. Mettalika made for the air to give herself a gain on him then dived down on his tail, grabbing it by the tip in her paws as that was a weak spot. This was her normal method of tackling a Lizariaous. Usually they had tail spades however to get a good grip on. This one hadn't. This one she had tackled before. Hytarious had encountered her before and escaped. Karnos from his hiding spot realised this now. He realised why Hytarious had never spoken of how he had lost his tail spade.

Hytarious's tail slipped out from Mettalika's claws and he carried on running. Mettalika flew round him, landing in front of him and blocking his path.

"So we meet again" she snarled. Hytarious tried to turn and run the other way but Mettalika swung her tail round with force, the steel tail blade hitting him in his side and knocking him down.

Within seconds she was upon him, his needles useless now he was on his side as they could only shoot outwards. She sank her teeth into his neck and with a twist of her head snapped it as though it were a twig.

You may have escaped once, Lizariaous, but you do not get a second chance.

Karnos, shivering now in his hiding place waited around no more and escaped while she was preoccupied with her new kill.

Their plan had failed and cost another life. Zephirak would not be happy.

Chapter 11
Further Training

Nearby, Leida stood stock-still listening. She and Diabloss had heard Hytarious's scream.

"What was that?" she asked Diabloss.

Diabloss shook his head. "I'm not sure. Probably something being killed by something else or something."

Leida laughed. "So how many somethings is that?" she giggled. Diabloss grinned and shrugged.

"Think we should go and check it out?" asked Leida.

"I'll go," said Diabloss, "you stay here in case it's dangerous." He flew off, preferring the safety of the air in case whatever caused the creature to scream was still hungry. Not many things killed Gryphies, but there were a few such as QuadraFelieons. They would take young or weak Gryphies.

Leida pouted. *Can't protect myself? Of course I can! I fly away from danger. It's easy to escape it. Danger. Humph! I can do fine on my own; just because Diabloss is the strongest fighter doesn't mean he has to always be looking out for me.*

She sat thinking all this as he returned.

"Mettalika has made a kill. I saw her eating it. It was a Lizariaous, a brown one" he told her.

Leida sighed. "I should have known," she said.

Diabloss nuzzled her. "Don't worry, everything changes. One sun cycle Mettalika will be gone and we will all live in peace."

"Zephirak would still remain though." Leida pointed out.

"I was thinking a while back about going and trying to reason with him. Maybe Mettalika is the problem. I believe she may be the reason Zephirak hates us so much. After all, it was her who killed his mate." Diabloss told her.

"It's too dangerous. I don't want you risking your life in Dyarkroeen just to reason with a Lizariaous who simply won't agree."

Diabloss sat up. "That gives me an idea. That other Lizariaous, the grey one. He seemed worried about you didn't he? Maybe I can get him to agree and find as many Lizariaouses who are on our side too, or at least don't like the way Zephirak treats them. With his own kind as well agreeing that Mettalika is the problem, maybe Zephirak will be more likely to come to his senses."

"I dunno. It's still a big risk…"

"But if it works it will mean peace between us and that's worth a risk." Diabloss seemed set on his idea now.

Leida sighed. It was a good idea, but she was worried for her mate. He was the only one who understood her. Without him, she'd be alone, she knew she would. She had few friends and was too quiet to make more.

***

However, hers was nothing compared to the worry that Karnos was going through right now.

He had stopped on the outskirts of the reservoir and was miserably worrying about what he was going to do. For one thing, Zephirak didn't expect another failure. Karnos knew about Croter and Xarkiz and how mad Zephirak had been when they came back without Leida. He thought Hytarious's mate should know however and went to tell her. She was devastated and ran into her cave in tears.

80

Karnos wondered if he'd done the right thing. Now word would get out of Hytarious's death even if he didn't tell Zephirak.

Slowly he took the short walk to Zephirak's cavern. Zephirak was no where to be seen. He must be inside. Karnos went in.

There was a large main entrance chamber and at the back of it, a smaller passage leading to the rest of the labyrinth. Zephirak's cavern was part of a vast cliff face and the cavern went far into the cliff. It was a natural thing, but had been modified by Lizariaouses for living in. Things like holes for air and skylights had been added. The chamber that had held Leida was part of an extra piece of rock on the side of the cliff. The crack in the top was large enough obviously for a Gryphie to carefully squeeze through since Diabloss had done so in rescuing Leida. Diabloss was large too. Zephirak sometimes used the cave when he did not want to go out. Sun shone in through the crack and he could soak it up while still staying inside.

Karnos used his nose to sniff in the darkness and his eyes where light shone in. As he went deeper in, it became rather damp and clammy. There was a certain smell of dead things about it, since Zephirak normally took food indoors to feed on and saved it if it was too big to devour at one sitting. Karnos didn't like it much. A few stalactites hung down here and there from the ceiling.

At last he found Zephirak sitting chewing lazily on a large bone.

"Zephirak, sir... I...I have news for you." He said timidly.

Zephirak looked up. "Karnos? Did I say you could enter?"

"N...no sir, but I have important new for you. It's bad I'm afraid."

"Bad?" Zephirak didn't like this, Karnos could tell from the tone of his voice.

"Yes sir." Karnos was now in two minds whether or not to run.

"Come on, get it out then!" said Zephirak sitting up.

"We got the Umbrabane, Sir and killed the deer. Everything was going fine and Mettalika was about to take a bite from it when Hytarious moved and she saw him. She killed him sir." Karnos tensed himself ready to run. If Zephirak was going to react in the way he expected, he'd need to.

Zephirak was silent for a while. His rage was so great now, of vengeance and hatred that he couldn't even speak.

"S...sir?" asked Karnos after a while. All he could see were two red eyes glowing in the darkness. He could hear Zephirak's breathing get heavier and suddenly erupt into a mighty roar of sheer unadulterated rage.

Karnos yelped and ran for it.

As he ran he could hear Zephirak screaming in the distance.

"I will get you Gryphie! You and your kind! You will not know pain until you have seen what I can do! Now it is time for you to pay Mettalika! PAY!"

The last word echoed in the darkness and echoed in Karnos's mind for many sun cycles after that.

***

Back in Shernaron, Diabloss and Leida had gone back to the forest for some rest and relaxation in the sun. The young Gryphies played around and Mystik sat outside her old tree, gazing at the sky.

"Training was hard," said Leida as they climbed to the top of their tree to rest on the large thick branches on top in the sun. "I kept trying to find the easy way out all the time."

"Yes, that's just like you. You have to learn tactics and think ahead though." Diabloss told her.

"I know" replied Leida.

All afternoon they spent in the warm sun. Gryphies love sun. Other than that their favourite weather is the kind you get on mild to cool sun cycles with a light rain and a mist. Gryphies love that more than anything. They hate the cold however, especially frost. Snow they do not mind as much and young Gryphies delight in playing in the snow and making tunnels and such in the deepest snow. Older Gryphies enjoy it too, but not as much.

Gryphies don't get sunburn or heat stroke either, mainly because they are pyrokinetic.

As the sun began to set, Leida woke Diabloss up. She was hungry and wanted to go and hunt for some food. Diabloss agreed and they went to hunt for their dinner.

Upon returning, they discovered their tree had been taken over by young Gryphies playing hide and seek in its dense leafy branches. Diabloss had one of the biggest trees in the forest and Leida had moved in with him when they fell in love. Her tree had been on the outskirts of the forest, rather small and cold in the winter. Needless to say Gryphies prefer evergreen trees that keep their leaves in the winter so they have some shelter against the cold. Diabloss's tree was evergreen, but Leida's old one wasn't.

"Come on you lot! Shouldn't you be having your tea now?" asked Leida to the young Gryphies.

Hiryasis, Lunara's best friend said; "our mums said we could play a bit longer though!"

"Come on Hiry! We can go play somewhere else anyway," said Lunara.

Hiryasis looked glum. Len laughed. Hiry was a pale blue colour. Most young Gryphies are pastel shades and their fur deepens as they get older. Lunara was pale lilac and Len was pale yellow. A few more of their friends poked their heads out from the leaves, some looked sad and others laughed. Some were shy and you could only see their eyes peeking out.

"We'll eat on the ground, but you'd better have finished your game by the time we've finished our food!" said Diabloss.

The young Gryphies nodded and carried on playing. Not for long however, as their mums soon called them home. They flew and those who couldn't, climbed down from the tree.

"Thanks for letting us stay a bit," said Lunara before running off to her tree. Leida waved to them. She liked the young Gryphies that lived in the forest and they liked her because she didn't order them around or tell them off like some of the other adults.

"I have to go back for training with Strassor tomorrow." Leida said to Diabloss.

"I'll come and watch if you like and see how you're getting on" he replied.

"Thanks" smiled Leida.

The next morning, after breakfast, Leida and Diabloss returned to the training grounds once again. They came early like they had the previous morning, as none of the other trainees would have arrived and Strassor could give his full attention to Leida.

Strassor was relaxing on a large rock. He got up very early indeed, much earlier than anyone in Shernaron most likely and had already had his breakfast long ago. He was prepared for his pupils to come at any time they liked.

Diabloss and Leida walked over to him and they greeted each other.

"So yer back fer more trainin' are yeh? A wise choice, Leida." He smiled. Strassor liked pupils who were determined to train and had willpower.

"Yes, I would like to improve on what I was bad at last sun cycle" said Leida.

Strassor nodded. "Very well" he said, "let's see what yer can do this sun cycle then."

Once again, Leida found herself at the beginning of the obstacle course.

As before, she got through easily. The sand soon came at the end though and once again she fell short. When she finally pulled herself out the other side, she sighed.

"I'll never get the hang of it."

"Sure yeh will. Yeh just need ter practise yer jumpin'." Strassor told her.

"But I can't jump very far without my wings" sighed Leida miserably. Gryphies are quite heavy creatures and getting off the ground without the use of their great wings is pretty hard. They're nimble enough and can climb trees, but jumping isn't one of their strong points really.

"I'll help you practise with your jumping" said Diabloss. Leida nodded and they practised all morning until Leida was worn out. She still couldn't jump very far even at the end of this however.

"Well, if it gets bad, you'll hafta rely on yer wings fer long jumps across things" said Strassor.

Leida tried the course again and this time only just made it to the other side of the sandpit, but at least she made it.

Diabloss ran to her and put his arms round her in a warm embrace.

"Well done Leida!" he said. Leida smiled, proud of herself now.

"Tomorrow, we'll start on physical fighting training and how ter defend yerself," said Strassor.

"Fighting?" asked Leida with more than a hint of fear in her voice.

"Aye, like them there." Strassor pointed to a pair of male Gryphies fighting against each other in a mock battle. They looked really violent, flaming and biting each other.

Leida looked worried.

"You have to learn things like that if you want to defend yourself properly." Diabloss told her.

"I know," said Leida, "but I'm so used to running away. Even when I was young I ran away from the other youngsters when they teased me."

"Well, you'll soon learn how ter defend yerself in battle. It's much easier to chase the enemy away than be chased by the enemy and wear yerself out running, then end up gettin' caught or somethin'. They won't challenge yeh again if yeh fight back an' show' 'em who's boss."

Leida looked at Diabloss and Strassor. They were both large and looked a good match for anyone. She didn't think she'd have a chance.

"See yer tomorrow then." Strassor's words broke into her thoughts.

"Uh, yes, see you tomorrow." She and Diabloss walked away from the training grounds.

"I think you did really well this sun cycle, Leida. You deserve a treat," said Diabloss. He suddenly flew off and returned with a fresh young Ground Bird, a Gryphie delicacy. Ground Birds are very shy and are rarely seen.

She wondered how Diabloss had got one so fast, but didn't think much about that. It was gone in one bite.

"Thank you." She smiled and nuzzled him. Diabloss growled gently followed by a murr, a contented sound that resembled a cat's purr.

Diabloss was proud of Leida and the way she'd tackled the problems she'd faced on the course in the training grounds.

Chapter 12
The Furmine's News

Zephirak hadn't had such a peaceful moon cycle.
Half his cavern was crushed and battered from where
he'd thrown a tantrum through the moon cycle. Since
Karnos had run out, Zephirak had remained in his
cavern plotting, scheming and not getting anywhere.
Most of his angst was because of that. He had no idea
how to get to the Gryphies now, short of calling an all
out war and attacking them by force to drive them into
submission. But they still had both Mettalika and
Diabloss and with both of them the Lizariaouses were
still at a disadvantage.

The rest of Dyarkroeen had been kept awake most
of the moon cycle with Zephirak's roars and the crashes
of the cavern being bashed around.

Schaarl and Mordred huddled together in the back of
their cave trying to block out the noises that echoed
around from their hearing. Xarkiz, Croter, Karnos and
the other guards and soldiers shuddered, just glad that
Zephirak hadn't taken it out on them.

Most thought that he was losing his mind and to a
certain extent that was true. His rage had driven him to
a nearly mindless existence.

The next morning however, he had worn himself out
and he was sleeping peacefully in his cavern where he'd
finally collapsed from exhaustion the moon cycle before.

Everyone else in Dyarkroeen was up and going
about their daily business when the light shining in from
the roof of his cavern slowly awakened the sleeping
Zephirak. He yawned and sat up, his rage now calmed
as he came to his senses and his memory returned as it
does after a moon cycle of sleep.

When he came to the mouth of his cavern, some of the younger Lizariaouses ran off back to their caves in fear.

A small blue creature ran past him. It was a Furmine. Furmine are very intelligent creatures and resemble weasels except that they are odd colours like blue and red. Zephirak took aim and pounced on it. The Furmine cried out and tried to wriggle away.

Zephirak held it up by its tail and sneered. "Oh yes little Furmine. So intelligent, but not intelligent enough to plan revenge. I'm sure the QuadraFelieon who ate Diabloss's mate has no idea how much it ruined my plans."

"Diabloss's mate Leida?" squeaked the Furmine.

"Yes. About my only really good plan subject." Zephirak snarled and prepared to deliver a killing blow on the Furmine when it spoke up again.

"Leida lives! I saw her with Diabloss the other sun cycle training. She is not dead. A silly tale that is if you heard she was eaten by a QuadraFelieon. That is unless you made a mistake and saw..." it trailed off as Zephirak interrupted it.

"She's *alive*? You mean my soldiers lied to me? They LIED?" Once again his rage was mounting although this time is was mainly surprise. He dropped the Furmine, who ran off quickly, glad it could live another sun cycle.

Zephirak threw back his head and roared, calling Croter and Xarkiz to him along with Mordred too.

They all came running a little worriedly as they wondered whether their leader was still in a rage.

"What did you say happened to Diabloss's mate?" asked Zephirak quietly.

"She was killed Sir, a QuadraFelieon was the culprit," answered Croter.

"Yes, we saw it with our own…"

"SILENCE!" roared Zephirak breaking into Xarkiz's sentence.

The guards quivered with fear. Mordred however was quick thinking and wondered if Zephirak had found out she wasn't really dead.

"Well, we *think* we saw her, Sir. It certainly was a similar Gryphie, blue and everything" he said.

"Well it wasn't her" said Zephirak, "a little Furmine told me it saw her alive with her mate in the training grounds of Shernaron."

Croter and Xarkiz looked ready to flee.

"Then we made a mistake. We apologise with the utmost humbleness, Sir" said Mordred bowing his head.

"Yes, we were very silly in making such a mistake, Sir" said the other two in unison.

Zephirak snarled at them. "As a punishment you will set to work on the fixing of the reservoir. It has sprung a leak and lower Dyarkroeen is getting flooded from it. Go and join the workers."

"But Sir, we are not strong enough to…"

"Silence! Go NOW!" roared Zephirak and they ran off like they had had their tails bitten.

"As for you, Mordred, you will clean my cavern while I go out for the sun cycle."

Mordred looked ashamed of himself. "Yes Sir" he replied.

Zephirak nodded and walked off, rattling his needles in annoyance.

Now Zephirak's plans for vengeance were renewed with the news that Leida was still alive. He figured he'd go and get her himself. It would be easier than getting soldiers to do it and he could be sure of achievement.

***

Diabloss and Leida had gone out for a flight together in the balmy early summer air. The gentle wind ruffled their manes as they flew lazily through the sky. Leida for now was content that she'd got this far with the training. She was trying to forget about the events of the next sun cycle, as she was still worried about the physical training in case she got hurt.

Diabloss was doing his best to comfort her and it was working. All she needed was a confidence boost to help her because that was what she lacked; confidence.

They flew, circling and swooping in the air, laughing and having fun. A Gryphie feels most free when in the air flying around. It gives them a view over the land and the trees. They can see all around themselves. That is how they like it best.

Down below, Diabloss spotted Zephirak heading towards Shernaron. He frowned and pointed it out to Leida. She shuddered, glad that she was in the air and he couldn't get her.

"What do you think he's up to?" she asked Diabloss.

"I don't know. But I don't like it. He's heading towards Shernaron Forest and that's bad. I must fly and warn the others. The mothers must make sure they have all their kittens in and safe. You keep an eye on him here and track what he does, ok?" said Diabloss.

Leida nodded and he flew off.

However, not all the kittens were safe. Little Lunara had wandered away exploring on her own. She hadn't realised how far she'd wandered and she was now out of the boundaries of Shernaron. Soon she'd wandered into Dyarkroeen and not realising the danger she was in, started her favourite game of spying.

Hiding behind a rock, she spied on some little Lizariaouses playing a game and then she saw a larger one walk right past her. She'd never seen a Lizariaous close up and although she knew they were dangerous, curiosity burned and she stayed where she was. One of the young Lizariaouses ran behind the rock and banged into her. He screamed and leaped back.

"Ah! What are you?" he yelled.

"I'm a Gryph...uh...Lizariaous hunter!" replied Lunara suddenly remembering she still had the claw Sinxo had given her and deciding to play a trick.

"Lizariaous hunter? Pah! You're too small!" said the other.

Lunara waved the claw around. "This guy thought so too!" she growled.

The Lizariaous youngster looked terrified. "You won't...hunt me will you?" he asked.

"No, you're too small" she replied. He looked relieved. "Good, 'cos I get hurt easily!" he said. "I'm Jadariol, what's your name?"

"Lunara" replied Lunara.

"Ok, Lunara, wanna play hide and seek with us?" he asked her.

Lunara nodded. Hide and seek was her favourite game. The both ran off together to join the rest of Jadariol's friends.

With Zephirak away, the clan was more relaxed and didn't really think about much, just lazed around in the sun. No one seemed to notice there was a Gryphie playing around with the Lizariaouses. Most of the time Lunara was hidden. However, she was soon found out when she hid in Mordred's cave. Schaarl had just returned from a hunting trip and Lunara was hidden behind a piece of rock in the cave entrance. Schaarl tripped over her tail as she came in. It made her drop the meat she was carrying and she spun round to see what had tripped her. What she saw was a little Gryphie youngster cowering behind a rock and hoping she wouldn't be seen.

"Who are you?" asked Schaarl.

Lunara looked up at her but didn't sense any hostility from the Lizariaous, only surprise.

"I'm L…lunara" she replied, stuttering. "Please don't hurt me, I'll go now." She stood up.

Schaarl picked her up. "You're a Gryphie, you shouldn't be here, what are you doing…" but she was broken off as a sharp yell interrupted her speech.

"SCHAARL! She's a Lizariaous hunter! Put her down or she'll kill you!" It was Jadariol.

Schaarl looked surprised and then started laughing. "Oh will she? And how will she kill me?"

"She has a claw from a Lizariaous she killed! Show her, Lunara!" said Jadariol excitedly.

Schaarl put Lunara down and she feebly produced the claw and showed it to her. Schaarl looked at it.

"This is an old claw; it looks as though it's just the shedding of a claw anyway. I think our friend here probably just found it lying around. Am I right?" she asked Lunara.

Lunara looked down. "My friend gave it to me" she said quietly. Lizariaouses shed their claws like cats, but the sheddings are so thick, they are often mistaken for actual claws, not just the outer layer of one.

Jadariol looked a little disgusted. "So you're not a hunter? That's just lame."

Lunara sniffed.

"Come now, let's not get upset. You should be going back home now little one. I'll walk you to the edge of Dyarkroeen and see that you cross into the Outlands safely. Jadariol, run along and play" said Schaarl.

Jadariol ran off.

Schaarl and Lunara walked to the edge of Dyarkroeen and stood on a large cliff looking over at the Gryphie territory of Shernaron.

"There, now off you go."

Lunara thanked Schaarl and made to go down the hill. Then suddenly she saw blue fire rising out of the forest and into the sky. She recognised it as a call for her to return by her mother. If a youngster is too far away to hear the mother's cries for it to return, the mother shoots fire into the air as a signal that the youngster can't miss. By the irregularity of the flaming, it looked as though Lunara's mother was desperate and worried about her.

Lunara took to the sky after a quick wave to Schaarl. Lunara's flying was getting better, however she didn't have the strength to fly for extreme distances and couldn't make it all the way back to the forest in one go. She'd have to land.

Schaarl watched her go and then turned. It suddenly occurred to her that Zephirak might be around but the young Gryphie was in the Outlands now and out of her hands. If it got into trouble, Schaarl could do nothing. Lizariaouses, with the exception of soldiers and hunters, never left Dyarkroeen.

Lunara landed a few miles away from the edge of the Forest and started walking until she got the strength back in her wings again. Her wings felt to her what a person's legs feel to them after they've run a long distance so she had to rest them. She walked instead of sitting for a rest, so she would get there faster. She had no time to waste. Her mother wanted her for some reason and it seemed desperate.

Chapter 13
Reasoning

Meanwhile, Leida had been keeping an eye on Zephirak as he neared the forest. Diabloss returned and told her that Lunara wasn't with her mother.

"We'll have to hope she's safe somewhere in Shernaron" he said, watching Zephirak closely. Luckily they were flying pretty high up and he hadn't noticed them.

"No, I'll go and make sure she isn't in trouble" said Leida. She was fond of Lunara and didn't like to think of her getting hurt. "What if Zephirak comes into our territory? Have you called backup?"

"Yes, but before they come, I think now is the time to try and reason with him. You look for Lunara and I'll fly on down and see if I can talk with him about the whole Mettalika situation" replied Diabloss. Leida gave him a worried look and opened her mouth to say something but Diabloss bustled her away and flew down to Zephirak.

Zephirak saw his approach and snarled; stiffening and readying his needles. Diabloss landed close by, watching him closely and raising one hand in a non-threatening gesture.

Zephirak snarled again "What do you want?" Diabloss edged closer. "To reason with you. Both Gryphies and Lizariaouses have one problem in common. Mettalika. If we teamed up and fought her together, we could be rid of her forever and could live in peace again. She killed your mate; I know that's where most of your fury comes from. Would you consider that?"

Zephirak paused for a moment and then burst out laughing. "You really think she's the only problem I have with Gryphies? Ha! You have to be kidding yourself. I don't just want to get revenge on Mettalika for what she did; I want to rule over all of you. So here's my reasoning. Surrender to the Lizariaouses and then we can live in...peace. That is the only way I will submit to your idea, if you, all of you submit to us."

Diabloss stepped back shocked and appalled. So this was what he was heading for by kidnapping Leida and trying to get to Diabloss that way. Zephirak obviously knew that Diabloss was the gathering's best fighter and he wanted to take that from them too. Well, that as may be but there were other soldiers in the gathering who could fight just as well, although they were not as strong. He should have known it was stupid to try and reason with Zephirak. He tried again, he figured he may as well, since backup wasn't here yet and he had Zephirak where he wanted him as opposed to risking himself going to Dyarkroeen.

"But why? We won't come willingly and it would be more of a hassle surely for you to do that? You're sinking to Mettalika's level by trying to rule over us too and you will end up dying in the process. Is ultimate domination really worth that?" Diabloss urged him to reconsider.

"Yes. I'd say it is. If I die, there are plenty of others who would take my place and fight on." Zephirak sneered at him. "Stop trying to be the hero Diabloss."

"But if you die then what would be the point?"

"I will have lived out my purpose and died honouring what I lived for. Besides, look at you, you're part Deamon. Deamon Gryphies are another subspecies that never got on well with purebloods. Why would you even care? You should give it up and go back to the Dark Plains. There is no war there and once I have assumed my place as ruler, we won't bother you. How does that sound for a compromise?" Zephirak looked Diabloss straight in the eyes.

"No, I am an example of Deamon and pureblood coming together in unity and giving birth to a new generation that's another step closer to the ultimate goal of us all, living in harmony despite our differences. My mother was Deamon but she would have died defending my pureblood father as he would her. But then, you're too narrow-minded to see that!" snarled Diabloss.

Zephirak's annoyance started to rise a little at that remark. "Actually, you're an example of going backwards in evolution. Instead of keeping the Deamon strain strong, you introduce weak genes of the pureblood in and weaken yourselves through your stupidity and "affection" towards each other. You are not as strong as your mother was, despite being a male. But you can't help that, your mother was a foolish excuse for a Deamon Gryphie" he spat.

Now Diabloss's temper started to rise. "How DARE you speak of my mother that way. You never even knew her!" A ball of blue started to form and glow in his jaws.

"No, but my father did and he told me how pathetic she was joining the gathering from the forest. It's weak Diabloss, WEAK! Your whole species is weak. And that is why you need a decent leader such as myself to strengthen you and control you." Zephirak had now started walking in a half circle before Diabloss, rattling his needles with enthusiastic joy at making Diabloss so angry.

Diabloss spread his wings out and opened his mouth wide, blue fire erupting from his jaws straight at Zephirak's smug face. Zephirak closed his eyes and countered, firing needles right back at Diabloss. The needles shot through the fire, the poisoned tips igniting and flying straight at Diabloss. He retaliated, stepping

97

back and folding his wings in front of him as a shield against the fiery needles.

Zephirak thrashed his tail angrily and Diabloss growled in response, the pair of them staring each other down.

***

Leida had been pretty much unaware of the fight that was taking place. She had far too much on her mind looking for Lunara and worrying as usual. She dare not cry out for the youngster while being so close to Zephirak. She was scared at being so close to him in case she was seen and attacked again but the fear for her young friend's safety was far greater.

It was then that she spotted Lunara, heading right towards Zephirak and Diabloss in a wide arc and trying not to get spotted. She was creeping on her belly close to the ground, her wings folded close about her as protection and resembling a small purple rock with a head. Leida watched her, not daring to fly down and get her out of there in case Zephirak saw. Then Lunara just stopped. This was when the flaming and needle throwing started. She'd stopped out of fear. Leida looked at Zephirak and Diabloss sizing each other up, circling now, all thoughts of conversation gone and only wild instincts still remaining.

Leida thought she'd take the chance and flew down in a torpedo shape for speed, ready to tackle Lunara and pick her up, getting her out of there.

Unfortunately, Zephirak saw her swoop down out of the corner of his eye. His brain working on overdrive, he knew if he could get Leida in some way and threaten her life, Diabloss would submit. He spun round with lightning reflexes, firing out a needle and getting Leida's leg, fortunately for her just skimming it. A small spray of blood flew out and she panicked and plunged to the ground. A normal Gryphie would have carried on since the wings were undamaged and carried out the plan but this was Leida and now she was terrified she'd been poisoned. She landed badly on one of her wings and screeched out in distress. Zephirak bounded up to her, closely followed by Diabloss. Zephirak reached her first and stood in front of her.

"Take another step and I'll kill her, Diabloss." Zephirak grinned, showing off his sickle like teeth in a nasty malicious snarling smile.

Diabloss stopped on the spot. His eyes were wide with horror and worry. Sweat clung to his fur as his adrenaline surged to a peak.

"No...." he trailed off.

Zephirak now had a paw wrapped around her throat, his long black claws digging into her painfully and unpleasantly. She choked a little, fearfully. This was it. She was going to die. Lunara snuggled underneath her, terrified and trying to hide. Leida felt the little Gryphie's body shivering violently and her soft fearful whimpers.

"Or, maybe I should kill her anyway. What would you do then with your spirit broken along with your mate's neck?" Zephirak was enjoying this.

Diabloss pulled his ears back. "Then you would be as bad as Mettalika. She killed your mate, how will killing mine make things any better?"

"Because, you will know the pain I've suffered..." Zephirak spoke through gritted teeth, tightening his grip around Leida's throat. She thrashed about panicked but couldn't escape. Zephirak had most of his weight rested on her body, forcing her down with sheer anger and spite.

Suddenly everything turned blue. There were roars of anger and the sound of wings all around them, taking Zephirak by surprise and making him loosen his vice grip on Leida. She kicked out from under him with her back legs, desperate to get away, fear and instinct leading her. She knocked him off balance and grabbed Lunara in her mouth, pulling herself up and stumbling away as fast as she could.

Behind her, Zephirak roared and fired needles at his assailants. She could hear Diabloss's angry roars too but she never looked back.

The backup had arrived and the soldiers, 6 of them, had flown in to break up the fight. They forced Zephirak back and got him on the run. He fled back towards Dyarkroeen, most of his needles used up and his own fear kicking in.

The soldiers landed beside Diabloss.

"Are you alright Sir?" asked one.

"No, I am not! What the hell took you so long?? Zephirak could have killed Leida while you were ambling about." Diabloss shot out a ball of flame angrily at the soldier.

"Sorry Sir, it took me a while to group the other soldiers, the ones you asked for were busy with other tasks so I waited for them to arrive."

"BUSY WITH OTHER TASKS?? Then you should have brought different soldiers you moron! What the grik were you thinking? This was Zephirak I wanted backup against, not just one of his cronies." Diabloss snarled, enraged.

"Look, I don't have time to sort you idiots out. You are some of my best soldiers and yet your brains still fail you. I'll call you later, all of you and we can talk about this. Right now I must get to Leida; I think she may have been poisoned." Diabloss took to the sky and flew off, his great wings sweeping through the air.

The soldier called after him. "You wanted the best and that was the only reason I waited, Sir!"

Diabloss ignored him and headed back to the Gryphie Forest.

By the time Leida reached the clearing in the forest, she was dragging her left back leg where she'd been hit and her jaws were aching from carrying Lunara. Lunara was still shaking and tears were streaming down her cheeks. Being only young, she still wasn't sure what was going on and the events had scared her. Especially Leida screeching and her chokes when Zephirak had hold of her.

Leida, panting violently, staggered into the clearing, dropped Lunara and collapsed. Some guards had followed her in, wondering what was wrong and also for protection since they could see she'd been attacked and her attacker might still be around.

Lunara's mother, Shen, ran over to her frightened kitten and Lunara whimpered, running to meet her.

"What happened?" asked Shen.

Lunara was too choked up with confusion and tears to speak at first. Her mother allowed her to calm down and explain.

"I'm sorry, Mum. I shouldn't have wandered so far away from home. It's my fault Leida was attacked by...by...Zephirak" and she burst into tears again.

"Attacked by Zephirak?" Shen looked puzzled and worried.

Leida spoke for the first time. It hurt to speak but she'd caught a little of her breath back. "Don't be angry at Lunara. I was terrified Zephirak would see her and flew down to get her while Zephirak was distracted by

Diabloss." She coughed and tried to sit up. She managed to half sit, keeping the weight off her hurt leg.

"But what was Lunara doing there in the first place?" asked Shen, concern clouding her pretty face. All young Gryphies were completely banned from wandering into what was known as the Outlands, the stretch of desert-like plain between Shernaron and Dyarkroeen.

Lunara spoke again. "I went...ex...exploring and wandered too far. I was trying to get back when I saw Zephirak and Leida saved me." She was careful not to mention where exactly she did go exploring and the fact she wandered into Dyarkroeen without realising it. Shen would ground her and it was most likely her father would give her a good rebuff for her troubles.

"Lunara! You should always keep an eye on where you are! I know you love to explore but it's too dangerous. We aren't at peace like we were when I was growing up, you must stay in Shernaron. Next time Leida won't be there to save you, I don't want to lose you." Shen nuzzled Lunara. "Now, go back to the tree and stay there until your father gets home. We'll see what he has to say about this."

Shen went up to Leida.

"Thank you for saving my kitten" she said gratefully. "I am so sorry for her behaviour. If there is anything I can do to help you or if you need anything in return in the future I will be there. I can't tell you how grateful I am, risking your life to save my kitten..." she trailed off, trying desperately not to think about what may have happened if Leida hadn't saved Lunara.

"Make sure Lunara stays in Shernaron in the future, Shen. Next time she probably won't be so lucky." It was Diabloss who had spoken this time.

Leida looked up at him and whimpered with relief and pain. Diabloss nuzzled her and folded a wing around her, pulling her close to him.

Shen nodded at Diabloss's advice and returned to her tree and her tearaway daughter.

The guards had dispersed when Diabloss appeared. Diabloss just held Leida for a long while. He had no idea what to say to her. He'd feared for her life so much. Zephirak had nearly gotten to him and made him submit. If those soldiers had arrived any later...

Finally Leida spoke. "I...I think I've been poisoned."

Diabloss almost leaped back, staring at her. "No. No, he can't have poisoned you too... Where did he hit you?"

Leida showed him and Diabloss sniffed her leg where the gash was.

"No, I can't smell any poison; I think it just skimmed the surface. But it's better to be on the safe side." He leaped up their tree in huge bounds and returned with some anti-venom. It had been made by Mystik and was only really effective on poisoning if it was either caught quickly or there was only slight poisoning.

Diabloss dripped a single drop on Leida's leg. She winced but looked relieved.

"Can you climb up the tree?"asked Diabloss. Leida nodded and they climbed up to their wide sleeping perch just over half way up.

Leida lay down and Diabloss sat next to her. Her wing wasn't badly damaged luckily; she'd just strained it a bit.

For a while, neither of them spoke. Both were just calming down.

Finally, Leida spoke quietly. "I didn't know what else to do; Zephirak would have killed Lunara if he'd seen her."

"Zephirak is a sick freak" replied Diabloss solemnly. "It's not just Mettalika he wants gone. He wants to rule over Gryphies and Lizariaouses alike. He wants to be leader of all of us. If we back down, that is the only way he said peace will be restored." He looked down, thinking over what had happened and mulling over the awful things Zephirak had said, taunting his heritage and his parents, threatening the life of his mate and being smug the whole time, knowing he was getting to Diabloss.

"But...why? Why does he want to control all of us?" asked Leida, puzzled.

"He said it was because Gryphies are weak. For example, the way Deamons and purebloods sometimes interbreed. The stronger Deamon breeding with the weaker pureblood, he doesn't understand things like that. If you ask me, Zephirak is worried that with our flying ability, we will be able to defeat him first. In truth, although we can fly, they can shoot those needles high into the sky and with enough precision, hit us fairly easily." He stopped, looking at Leida, unable to get the awful image of her plunging down after she was hit out of his head.

"We only ever defend, we've never been a threat to him or the others" continued Diabloss.

"Then maybe" Leida began, a strange look in her eyes, "it's time for us to go on the offence."

Chapter 14
Plans and Training

Over in Dyarkroeen, Zephirak had reached his cavern and was attempting to hide his obvious breathlessness and shock. He had composed himself on the way back, slowing down his pace having realised that the enemy Gryphies weren't following him. He cursed and swore to himself, angry with his own smugness and for rubbing it in Diabloss's face instead of going straight ahead and killing Leida when he first got hold of her. Next time he wouldn't pause to mock even though he enjoyed it so.

He approached the cavern, hearing sounds inside. He bounded in. He was in no mood to deal with youngsters who may be playing in his cavern, they should know better than to trespass. Then he saw the tail spade pointing the wrong way and realised it was only Mordred. He remembered now, he'd told Mordred to clean his cavern while he was out. It was early evening now and the cleaning was nearly finished.

Mordred stood to attention as Zephirak approached.

"Did you have a nice walk Sir?" he asked.

Zephirak snarled. "No, I didn't. Now get out."

Mordred hurried out; a little disappointed he'd received no praise for his hard work all afternoon. Zephirak was always in a temper he thought.

Zephirak went into his sleeping chamber and lay down on the dry grass that served as a bed. He was angry with himself but even angrier with the Gryphies. The event had only made him hate them more.

He started muttering to himself angrily.

"Why didn't I just kill her? Hmm, because if she was dead it would serve no purpose. I need her." He was still thinking of the original plan he'd had to lure Diabloss back to Dyarkroeen and capture him or threaten to kill Leida and get him that way. Nothing else had worked and the female was such a little wimp, it wouldn't be hard to keep her hostage until Diabloss got there. Zephirak snarled and mulled it over in his mind, getting ever more angry about his own foolishness. It had felt good to mock Diabloss and insult his upbringing but ultimately the mockery had been in vain. There would be time enough for mocking once he had Leida and Diabloss was at his mercy.

Mordred had headed back to his cave after Zephirak yelled at him. Schaarl was lying outside in the warm sun and she smiled as he approached. Mordred sat next to her and sighed.

"What is it honey?" she asked him, noticing his slumped posture.

Mordred sighed again. "It's Zephirak. He came back in a rage and hadn't even noticed what I'd done in his cave. I thought I did a good job. Ah well, he's never grateful for anything these sun cycles. He's so lost in the whole Gryphie thing."

"Oh, speaking of Gryphies, a young one found her way into our territory earlier" Schaarl said quietly so no one else would overhear.

"Really? Is she ok? Did she get out, because Zephirak will kill her if he finds her." Mordred looked concerned.

"Yes, she left. I took her to the edge of Dyarkroeen and watched her fly off. I'm sure she's fine."

Mordred sighed again. "Good, I'm glad she's ok" he replied.

"She was a cute little thing. I still don't know why Zephirak just doesn't drop it. I guess because we're outside looking in and don't understand what's going through his head." Schaarl looked thoughtful.

"We don't need to understand. No one can understand. Our leader has gone crazy with hatred, misery, regret, longing and mourning for his mate. I can see how he's upset but honestly, bringing a war to our territories is not the answer."

"I know, but there's no way you can change his mind or even talk to him and suggest anything else...is there?"

Mordred sat up. "Yes! I can at least try that. He's always trusted my advice and if I suggest other ways around it, maybe he'll listen! I'm one of his best fighters and his favourite commander. It's worth a shot right?"

Schaarl looked unsure. "That scar on your face says differently I'm afraid."

Mordred raised a paw to his face and touched the scar, looking troubled. "I think I'll wait for his temper to calm a little before I try this."

***

Over in Shernaron, Diabloss was having words with his squad.

"What happened to your common sense back there??" he demanded.

A younger female Gryphie spoke up "I'm sorry Sir, we just assumed you wanted the best fighters since it was Zephirak"

"Yes but if they were unavailable then you need the next best thing. Use your grikking heads! If Zephirak had killed my mate, I would have had the lot of you fired and put to work in the metal mountains and you would never fight again, do you understand me?" Diabloss snarled and his eyes flashed angrily.

The female backed down and lowered her head submissively. "Yes Sir."

Diabloss looked around. "And the rest of you?"

They all nodded and mumbled apologies.

Diabloss blasted one with his fire, a warning shot. "I SAID, AND THE REST OF YOU?" he roared angrily, his voice echoing all around the forest.

They all stood bolt upright to attention and did the high wing salute. "Yes Sir!" they barked in unison.

"That's better" Diabloss spread his huge wings wide, blocking out the sun in black and red, showing his dominance and power. "Don't let such foolishness happen again."

They all saluted again and stood in a row. He had ten of them, the best fighters around. They were his personal arsenal of soldiers that took on the biggest and most dangerous fights. The squad was made up of six males and four females. The males all had power in brute strength and the females were swift and skilled in martial arts style fighting, able to dodge any Lizariaous needles that came at them and give just as much as they took. The males had large and powerful wings; they were excellent at hand to hand combat with Lizariaouses and strong jaws, strong enough to crack through Lizariaous bones.

These were the select few, ones that had been raised to be soldiers, ones that showed potential as kittens and had spent all their lives honing their strength and skill. They battled, they lived for the fight and they were totally loyal to Diabloss. Only he had the power to command them and they had chosen to be fighters. Some with such skills never wanted to use them and although they were encouraged to make use of them, no Gryphies were ever forced into it. They had to choose to fight, to protect the gathering, to never let their fire go out and above all to have the loyalty and courage to go into battle blazing for victory. Those who only went in half hearted and were not one hundred per-cent positive they wanted to be a soldier of this kind would never get anywhere and would most likely be killed in battle. They only went in for the toughest battles that regular soldiers would lose in.

Diabloss took off into the sky with one huge flap of his wings and hovered a little over them. "Now, go back and have an hour's training. Then you may go to your trees."

They all saluted once more and flew into the sky as one complete and synchronised unit, flying off in perfect formation.

Diabloss watched after them. He was proud of them but they were all younger than him and not as experienced. In their line of work, injuries were common and sadly if they were injured too badly, it affected their skills and they had to retire. Nothing less than absolute fighting perfection could be on that squadron. There were many other squads that were used for everything else but Diabloss wanted his personal one to be the absolute best, especially if there would soon be an all out war. He flew back to his tree and found Leida looking a little better. He landed at the top and climbed down instead of walking through the forest. Leida was sat outside the hollow in the trunk of the tree that served as their indoor sleeping quarters. Diabloss climbed down beside her and nuzzled her softly.

"Feeling better?" he asked.

She nodded. "Yes, I am. I was a little shaken up back there but I'm fine now. However I have been thinking and tomorrow when I have my first fighting lesson, I will try extra hard. I refuse to be a wimp any more. I will not run. I will stay and fight. I won't cower in fear; I will be the one dealing out the fear. And above all, I will show any Lizariaous who dares to try, why they shouldn't mess with us. They attack, I will defend but if they continue I won't hesitate to hurt them."

Diabloss watched her, taken aback a little. Leida had always been shy and quiet, she'd never wanted to fight or hurt. Even now she only wanted to hurt them if they hurt her first but the recent events had really changed her. She had a wild look in her eyes, she wanted to learn to defend herself and deal out a beating. Diabloss smiled; if Zephirak tried to take her again, he knew this time she'd be ready. And Zephirak would be in for a big surprise if and when that sun cycle came. However, she had a lot to learn about fighting. She'd always been his little sweetheart, ever since they'd met and she had relied on him heavily, not being that independent or willing to be more adventurous. Still, from the moment he'd laid eyes on her he could sense there was something special about her. He only hoped she would be brave enough to endure what was in involved in learning to fight. Luckily it would start off easily.

Diabloss held her to him. "I'll be with you every step of the way so you have nothing to worry about" he said quietly.

Leida smiled and cuddled against him. "I'm so glad I have you with me, you help give me confidence."

"That's what I'm here for!" grinned Diabloss.

Evening was drawing in and Mordred had finally gotten up the courage to go talk to Zephirak. Schaarl had wished him luck and warned him to get out of Zephirak's cave if he was feeling hostile. Mordred was feeling less than brave about the whole thing but he wanted to suggest other ways than trying to control the Gryphies. Zephirak and a handful of other Lizariaouses wanted this but the majority of them weren't bothered. All the soldiers were for it but that was probably mostly because they had to obey orders and any who suggested otherwise would be killed. Unlike the Gryphies who were given a chance to opt out of being a fighter, young Lizariaouses with soldier parents were raised as soldiers, whether they wanted to be them or not. If they didn't, they were threatened. If they still didn't, then they were killed. Youngsters born to soldier parents had no other choice in the matter. Thankfully for them though, raised in a fighting environment, not many wanted to do anything other than follow in their parents' footsteps. It was the same for the young of workers and diggers. Raised to only know such career choices and they just went along with it.

Mordred had had loving parents. His father was a commander and his father before him. Mordred came from a long line of the best and that was why Zephirak had him as his right hand Lizariaous. However of course, lately, things had been frictional between them. Mordred had mentally kicked himself many times for daring to get so close or speak so kindly to a hostage, especially one in Zephirak's cave. That had shattered most of the trust Zephirak had in him. He was sorely worried that Karnos would take his place. Karnos never offered advice, he only followed orders and as his name suggested, carnage and death were his specialities. He was the commander just below Mordred. Zephirak seemed to favour those who only followed orders and didn't suggest things lately. Still, Mordred had to at least try.

Chapter 15
Unwanted Advice

Zephirak had calmed down. He was currently eating a fresh kill of a cave cat he'd found lurking around nearby. Cave cats were small stripy catlike creatures that lived around the Lizariaouses caves. Any empty caves would likely have families of these little felids in and some caves were kept empty for just that reason; a ready food source.

Mordred had reached Zephirak's cavern and was lingering outside. He saw Jadariol and his friends run past. Jadariol stopped as his friends ran on.

"Hey, are you visiting the Master?" he asked.

Mordred mentally shuddered at that name for Zephirak as he had stopped using it now. Hearing others call Zephirak "Master" made him realise even more that he was wise to just call Zephirak Sir. "Err yes, I'm visiting Zephirak."

"Then why are you standing outside?" Jadariol put his head on one side in puzzlement. He was a reddish colour and had shorter needles since he was only young. He was the son of Karnos. He had a double bladed tail spade and largish paws since he was still growing. Black scales were here and there on his body and Mordred knew he would grow into a ferocious fighter and soldier. He had that look about him. Now however, he was just a kid, a naive innocent youngster who spent most of his time playing. What really unnerved Mordred was that Jadariol looked up to and completely respected Zephirak. He was his hero. And, like with a few others, he referred to Zephirak as his master.

Mordred brushed these thoughts aside and entered Zephirak's cavern, giving a dismissive swish of his tail to the youngster, who returned to his friends to carry on their game.

Mordred suppressed a shudder, it was best to get these feelings out of the way before he encountered their angry leader. He took a deep breath of the cool musty air and stepped solidly forward into the darkness.

However as with most advances into Zephirak's cavern, Zephirak had spotted him long before he spotted Zephirak.

"And what do you want, Mordred?" he heard the low grumbling voice of Zephirak in the darkness.

Mordred tried not to look too taken by surprise but he honestly had no idea which direction Zephirak's voice was coming from and thus had no idea which way to turn in answering him. Not knowing where he was was the most frightening part.

"I came to talk, Sir. I need to talk about this whole situation with the Gryphies and I had a few ideas I thought you might like to hear." He stood tall, facing forwards, head raised high so as not to show how nervous he was. He'd always respected Zephirak but also feared him. Back when Zephirak's mate had still been alive, Zephirak had been more tolerant and pleasant to be around. But now he was more unpredictable than ever and Mordred feared him. Still, it was not his job to show this fear and he tried to imagine nothing had changed when he spoke to their leader.

He saw Zephirak's red eyes shining dimly to his right.

"Very well, what is it you have to say to me." The voice was calm and level. Mordred was surprised by this.

"I..." but he was interrupted as Zephirak told him to sit down and shoved some meat towards him. Mordred obeyed and ate some of it before he continued.

"My idea was this, Sir. Instead of fighting the Gryphies, why don't we find Mettalika and kill her? We can get an army out to find her if need be and track her down. Go all out with scouters and searchers. Once she's gone, peace will reign again, or at least tolerance like we used to have with them. We can easily overpower her, she is just one Gryphie."

Zephirak seemed thoughtful. Mordred could just make him out in the dim light.

"We've done similar to that before though and it didn't work." He countered.

"Yes, but we can get an army out, like I said. Our best fighters and trackers. Before, we only used a few individuals, a couple of packs here and there..."

"Which she wiped out" interrupted Zephirak.

"I know, Sir...I..."

"And she could end up killing our best fighters."

"Yes, but if we outnumber her enough, corner her or something, she won't have a chance. Please consider this. It would benefit all of us." Mordred looked hopeful and tried to hide it with his serious face.

Zephirak chuckled. "You don't really have any real plan do you? I mean, this is only an *idea*. It could all fall through and then what would you do? If you wish to take out an army and kill her, then you must plan it carefully. Track her in advance; try to corner her when she goes to drink or something. She's escaped every trap we've ever used. We even failed in poisoning her. Why do you think going all out like that would actually succeed?"

"Because it will! We'll plan it out carefully and catch her. This is only an idea so far, Sir. I need to get some packs together and the best fighters we have, half the army and anyone else who wants to join in. Surely once she's dead, we can end this senseless fighting?"

"I've started to get a taste for their flesh. Besides, why do you care? You seem to give too much of a grik about them. Why?" Zephirak's eye flashed a little dangerously and his words were spoken with a snarl.

"I don't particularly, Sir. It's just that one sun cycle soon, Schaarl and I are going to start a family and I don't want to bring up our youngsters in the middle of a war. I want to ensure their future and the safety of their own young's future. Surely you can see that? Don't you want to take another mate and put this trouble behind you? You want to live the rest of your life taking revenge on a whole species when it was only an individual who hurt you?"

"Hmm, you have a point." Zephirak moved closer to him, close enough so that his muzzle was nearly touching Mordred's ear. "But you see, there's one flaw in your little "idea for a perfect life" and do you know what that is?"

Mordred's body was completely tense. "N...no Sir..." he tried not to stutter but couldn't help himself.

"The flaw is..." Zephirak paused, the silence extremely uncomfortable for Mordred. "If we don't control all the Gryphies, it will happen again. We can destroy Mettalika but there may be those who support her and want to follow in her footsteps, do you understand me?"

Mordred had expected Zephirak to yell, the levelness of his voice made him even more nervous because Zephirak was being unpredictable.

"But surely those who followed her, if any, wouldn't be as powerful?" he gingerly spoke.

"Not if they get themselves "upgraded" with mechanical parts by those steel worker Gryphies from the mountains. Then what would you do with your great idea?"

Mordred sighed, it was hopeless. It seemed nothing would change Zephirak's mind on the subject. "So what do we do then? Find and kill Mettalika and then make the other Gryphies surrender?"

"Yes, in whatever order. I have a few plans of my own. I had an idea this sun cycle, but we'll go with your idea about capturing and destroying Mettalika if you like." Zephirak had moved away from Mordred now and was completely calm on the matter.

Mordred was the exact opposite. He still couldn't understand what Zephirak was up to. "What is your plan, if I may ask Sir?"

Zephirak laughed. "Oh, don't worry about that, it will soon come to fruition. It doesn't involve you but I know it will definitely work. Do you wonder why it doesn't involve you?"

Mordred shook his head. "I'm sure whatever you have planned will go smoothly, Sir."

"You don't even have the slightest concern that you have nothing to do with it?"

"Well, I suppose I do wonder a little. I mean, I've always been let in on your plans and you ask me for advice quite often." Mordred was in fact, wondering very much but he didn't want to let on.

"It's because I don't trust you as much as I did, Mordred. Ever since the whole scenario with that Gryphie I had in my cavern and then her mysteriously escaping. I thought she had gotten out herself but then when I found out Diabloss had rescued her; that made it worse. And you; going in to talk to her. You will have to work hard for me to trust you as much as I used to, Mordred."

"But Sir, I went to check that she hadn't escaped. I was nowhere near your cave when I saw Diabloss creating a riot there." Mordred tried to defend himself.

"No, but you could have gone and recaptured her while Diabloss was dealing with Croter and Zarkiz. It amazes me the stupidity of the Lizariaouses in this pack. They all panic and none of them think half the time. I think all of you could do with some serious training. Situation training is what all the soldiers, trackers, scouters, anyone who can fight needs. Before you go out to get Mettalika, you must get all the soldiers under your command to do some training exercises. We could all do with some training and effort put in to this pack. Then when the time comes for our sun cycle of victory, we will all be ready. If you put an effort in, Mordred, you will get on my good side again. Until then, go and get in shape. I am going to prepare some plans for situation training this evening and at sunrise we will start seriously." Zephirak turned his back to Mordred as a sign for him to leave.

"Yes, Sir." Said Mordred and trotted out of the cavern, trying to look as cheerful and determined as possible. He needed to stay on Zephirak's good side so Zephirak wouldn't realise his true intentions. Mordred wanted nothing to do with the war and if Zephirak tried to wrongly imprison the Gryphies, Mordred would have no choice but to go against Zephirak. However he suspected that once Mettalika was dead, Zephirak would calm down about the whole thing. He worried most about how happy Zephirak was. An angry Zephirak was a force to be reckoned with but a happy Zephirak was something to be truly worried about. What was this plan of his? Well, at least he hadn't been too harsh about the whole not trusting thing.

When Mordred got back home to Schaarl, he told her all about it.

"So he wants to get rid of Mettalika but still rule over the Gryphies?" she asked.

117

"Yes, but I'm sure after she's gone; Zeph will come round and not bother with the others. I think it's probably only revenge that Zephirak wants. Once she's died at his claws, he'll feel much better."

"Do you want Mettalika dead for what she's doing, Mordred?" asked Schaarl.

"Hmm, I think it would benefit both sides if she was destroyed. I wonder why it hasn't occurred to the Gryphies to kill her. Still, they've only ever been defensive and wouldn't take the life of one of their own. So it's up to us to take her out for the good of everyone. She's asking for it after all by needlessly killing Lizariaouses. If she didn't do that then we'd have no reason to kill her. You'd think she'd be happy to have been given another chance at life but apparently not. We had to kill something when there was that food shortage. Come to think of it, it's no one's fault really, what happened. I thought about taking a few Lizariaouses who were against the war and moving away." Mordred was pondering the situation.

"That wouldn't work. Do you remember Shevronn? Well he took some away who didn't agree with what Zephirak was doing and they were all found by Zephirak and some others and killed for betrayal. I wouldn't want that to happen to anyone even if some of us managed to escape."

Mordred listened to this and looked surprised and sad. He hadn't heard about that.

"Well" he continued, "We'll kill Mettalika. I am happy to kill, I just think it's pointless to try and rule over everything. I have no idea what Zephirak would gain from that. Once he governs over everything, what will he do then? I suppose just sit there and gloat over his little empire." Mordred spat the last sentence with distaste.

"Don't worry honey; we'll all live in peace one sun cycle. It will be like it used to be. If we can just see this through, bad things can't last forever" Schaarl put her paw on his and smiled. Mordred half smiled back.

"Yes, you're right. We'll put this plan in motion, train up, get Mettalika and then it will be over, I'm sure of it."

They sat together outside their cave and watched the sun set. For once it was peaceful in Dyarkroeen and they hoped for more evenings like this. Mordred was worried about going and looking for Mettalika. He'd never let on of course but he hoped his idea wouldn't be in vain.

Chapter 16
First Fight

The sun had started to rise over the Gryphie Forest.
Leida and Diabloss had decided to sleep outside that
moon cycle since it was mild and quiet. So they slept on
the wide branch that grew out of their tree just under
their indoor sleeping quarters in the hollow of it.

Leida was the first to awaken. She yawned and
gazed at Diabloss sleepily. He was still fast asleep. Her
state of half consciousness slowly bought her memories
back to her. This sun cycle was the one she'd do her
first fight training. She looked forward to it and dreaded
it at the same time.

Looking forward to it because it meant that she could
improve but dreading it in case she got hurt. Still, you
can't fight without getting hurt and she understood this.
Being a naturally worrying type, she still had her doubts
but when she thought about Zephirak, it made her want
to fight for the rights of the whole gathering.

Diabloss slowly stirred and smiled at her.

"I see you're awake already" he said quietly.

"Yes, I was thinking about the training I'll be doing
this sun cycle."

"Are you ready for it?" asked Diabloss, sitting up and
yawning.

"I'm ready. I will do my best as I always try to do. I
think I did ok with the previous training although there
are still weaknesses I need to work on but I think I can
escape easily enough. I've been running away all my life
after all." she sighed and looked down.

"Well not any more, I'm sure with the right training
you'll soon be a match even for my soldiers" grinned
Diabloss.

Leida blushed a bit and smiled. "I doubt that"

"You need to have more faith in yourself and gain some confidence." Diabloss put an arm round her and pulled her close. Leida snuggled up to him.

"I know, I just sometimes feel that I can't seem to do anything right. I get injured every time I encounter trouble, I've been kidnapped, nearly killed by Zephirak..." she trailed off as he interrupted her.

"Yes and yet you survived it all and want to improve and fight more! Listen Leida, I am proud to have you for a mate. I saw something special in you when we first met and now it's really showing!"

Leida just looked down at the branch and smiled. Once again compliments were hard for her to take. Finally she looked up and nodded.

"Yes and I'll make you even prouder. I will fight, we will win, we will beat the Lizariaouses and bring back peace to both our territories."

"That's the spirit!" Diabloss grinned. "Now, let's go get some breakfast and head over to the training grounds." He stood and climbed to the top of the tree to take off. Leida followed him and they flew off together to the cliffs to catch their morning meal of sea vultures.

Over in Dyarkroeen, Mordred was arranging his soldiers. Croter and Zarkiz were among these. Technically they were only guards but Mordred wanted all the Lizariaouses, or at least as many fighters as possible to train. He needed to teach a large enough group and impress Zephirak. Zephirak was currently putting the situation plans into action. The training would take place in a large open area of Dyarkroeen; this was where training was usually done. There were a few caves around but the rocks and other things that had been in the way to hinder the soldiers had been moved by workers to create the training grounds. The Lizariaouses who lived in nearby caves had to stay out of the way or they would get hurt. So they mostly either left their caves and visited other friends or went hunting or simply sat at the mouth of their caves and watched the training. Some even let their youngsters watch and learn from the soldiers.

Zephirak had set up several situations for the soldiers to work their way out of. They had to be prepared for anything Mettalika could throw at them. This included flying, breathing fire, hand to hand combat and also they needed to cover various other skills such as stalking her and ambushing her. Ideally they would need to surround her and force her to surrender. Not that she would of course, they would surround her and basically attack her at the same time, making it fast so she didn't know what was going on. There would be no slow death because chances were, mocking her and annoying her, saying they had the upper hand would give her enough time to attack back, take most of them out and escape.

Zephirak was warming to the idea now; he was getting in the spirit of it and was pretty cheerful about it. Once again, while Mordred was happy about this, he also feared it in case anything went wrong, Zephirak's nice mood was spoiled and he took his temper out on those around him.

For the flying test, targets were placed on long poles high up and the soldiers had to fire their needles at them, aiming of course for the bull's eye. That represented Mettalika's wings. Although a needle through the skull would soon bring her down since Gryphies didn't have thick skulls like Lizariaouses, Mettalika had a steel helmet on. Their needles couldn't penetrate that. Also her belly was protected by a steel plate. She had a long mechanical whip-like tail and the helmet on her head had a long spike on it. She sometimes charged her enemies and used it to great effect. She had steel claws on her right front hand and left back leg which could cause a lot more damage than her real claws could. The soldiers had to aim to bring her down and then leap on her at the same time. It had to be carefully co-ordinated however, or they would end up attacking each other at such a close and confusing range and not Mettalika. Her neck was unprotected. The neck was what they were aiming for, several soldiers holding her down and one biting down on her neck to kill her. In fact two biting her neck at the same time would be just as useful Zephirak was thinking. As he set out the equipment, it made him realise all the more that this was the first real time that they had even thought properly about how to correctly bring her down. Mostly they'd just gone out with no proper plans, intending to kill her with relative ease. Even with ambushes there hadn't been as many soldiers as were really needed and that was most likely why they had failed so often.

Aside from the high targets, he'd set up the fire breathing test. Basically the fire had been replaced with water and there was a young Lizariaous with a pump device that sprayed water over the soldiers. He sat on top of a large rock at one end of the training field. The soldiers would have to dodge this. Although Lizariaouses could take some flaming, due to their thick skin, too much would burn them and so dodging was still in order or they would get seriously scolded.

Finally a cave cat had been tied to a long length of rope for the final attack. Cave cats weren't as big as Gryphies but it would have to do. Basically the soldiers had to leap on it and dispose of it with a bite to the neck. Well, they would pretend to bite its neck. Zephirak wanted it kept alive so they could try over and over and perfect the moves.

Mordred had lined his soldiers up, planning to have them take the tests one at a time to see for a start how each of them did. The test with the cave cat was left until last. They would have a go at that one after they had perfected the others. The cave cat itself was rather disgruntled at being tied up and tried to escape in various ways until it wore itself out and lay down to watch the training.

Zephirak stepped up next to Mordred and examined his troops.

"Hmm....good so far" he looked at each one and nodded. Mordred had gathered about 54 soldiers. This wasn't all of the soldiers in the entire territory of course, to have them all sent out would be foolishness but it was a start and they had never used this many against Mettalika before.

The soldiers stood completely tall and to attention in the presence of Zephirak. Each one wanted to impress him. Some of them knew that they would mess up the various training activities simply because they were so self conscious in Zephirak's presence.

Zephirak walked the line of them and returned to Mordred, sitting beside him.

"Very well" he said, "BEGIN!" The first soldier ran out to the fire test. The target test would be next. After these tests had been perfected, then the killing test would be taken. Mordred intended to split the soldiers into two groups. The first group would perfect the tests and then attack the cave cat as a pack. Since there were so many soldiers to get through, they may not get to the other group until the following sun cycle but at least the second group would get to watch the first in action, learn from them and hopefully do a bit better when it came to their turn.

Croter and Zarkiz were in the second group, near the end since that was where the guards had been placed. Guards were generally good at fighting but specialised in protection and defence, not attacks. By placing them at the end of the second group, Mordred hoped they would pick up more training tips by watching the others.

The first soldier returned, soaked through at not being able to dodge the "fire" fast enough. It would be a long sun cycle.

***

Back in Shernaron, Leida and Diabloss had finished their breakfast. Leida had eaten two sea vultures and Diabloss had had five of them. He insisted that she not eat so much that it would fill her up and make her movements slow when fighting. So she had eaten two to take the edge off her appetite. Diabloss told her he always fought better when a little hungry anyway. Leida loved her food and was a little put out by this.

They headed to the training grounds and as usual, there was Strassor, overseeing the other Gryphies in training.

"Ah, Leida, it be good ter see yeh!" he said brightly trotting up to them.

Leida greeted him and smiled. "Yes, I'm here to start my training for fighting" she replied. She suddenly felt very self conscious and also felt what she'd just said, in trying to sound eager and impressive, she just sounded a bit silly. Her wings dropped a little.

"Ye'll be fine, I can assure yeh" Strassor reassured her. "Now, come with me and we'll go over some basic moves."

Leida followed him, looking back at Diabloss every so often. Diabloss lay down where he was to watch them. They walked a little way away and Strassor turned to Leida.

"Ok, first thing yeh gotta learn is blocking attacks. The less yeh be gettin' hurt, the better really. Now, we be blockin' attacks by using our wings as shields, the same as yeh did on that there obstacle course with the sharp thorns. This 'ere shield will block fire attacks and fer the most part, block physical attacks too. However yeh gotta be careful with physical attacks because if yer wings're torn or damaged, yeh may as well give up. A grounded Gryphie be pretty much useless. Yeh still have yer fire but without the ability to fly, yeh lose a big advantage over the enemy, Lizariaous or otherwise. Yeh got that?"

Leida nodded. "Yes Sir."

"Good." Strassor leaned his head back and let out a call. Another Gryphie swooped down. This one was a deep purple with a black mane and wings. He had the strangest claws, they were kind of transparent.

"Yes Sir." He said with a small bow.

"This here's my son, Odax. Yeh'll be training with him fer basic defence.

Odax turned to Leida and smiled kindly. "You'll be fine, I do defence training all the time and you won't get hurt...well, much anyway..." he sniggered. Leida looked considerably more worried.

"Odax! Don't be teasin' the poor girl. Just get on with the training and take it easy on her, it be her first time." Strassor glared at him.

Odax looked guilty. "Sorry Sir! Come on...er..."

"Leida" said Leida quietly.

"Leida then, we'll go over here to train" Odax told her and started to head to where he had pointed. Leida followed, finding it very odd that he called his father "Sir" as opposed to "Dad" or "Father" she brushed it off though, now was not the time to think of such trivial things.

Odax stopped and turned to her. "Right, my father probably told you about using your wings as shields. I want you to dodge my fire and when you can't dodge, to block it with your wings, got that?"

Leida nodded. "Yes Sir!"

"Er, don't call me Sir, ok? Just call me Odax....I'm not really a high enough rank to be referred to as "Sir" by anyone just yet" Odax laughed and readied himself.

Leida smiled. She liked him and didn't feel at all afraid or threatened that he may harm her intentionally. She seemed to have a special sense where she could sense how others felt towards her and she felt relaxed around Odax.

She readied herself also and prepared for his first blast. She watched him carefully, figuring that if she could be aware of little signs an enemy made before they flamed, that it would make it easier to dodge in time. The same would apply to the needles of the Lizariaouses.

Odax let out the first blast, short and sharp. Leida dodged with little effort. It seemed he was starting out slowly to begin with.

"Good so far" he said. "Now, dodge this!" He let out a large blast of blue flames, but Leida still dodged them.

"Excellent. Now see if you can dodge this!" He let out a blast of flames large enough to engulf her and too big to dodge. Leida was flamed full on with it and leapt back with a small yelp.

"Ok that's where you made a mistake. If it's too big or too many needles to dodge then you gotta shield yourself, yeah? Now, try again."

Leida had been paying too much attention to what he was telling her. When he'd said to dodge it, that's what she tried to do instead of using her own logic to work out that it was too big to dodge and use her wings instead. She decided to use her brain this time.

Odax let out another blast, this one was as big as the last had been and she shielded herself swiftly, not letting any of the blue flames get around her wings.

"That's great! Ok, now for the big one" Odax inhaled deeply, he intended this blast to be long and violent.

Leida had been observing when he was about to release and even though he'd inhaled deeply this time, previously she'd been quick enough to dodge because she noticed his chest expand very slightly just before he released his flames. Her powers of observation would be useful to her in battle.

She readied herself, wings folded in front of her, ready for his attack.

"No! Fold your wings normally. Don't forget your reflexes. In battle you won't have your wings constantly shielding you from their needles or it will hinder your movement. So get them out when I blast you." Odax explained. Leida nodded and folded her wings normally.

Odax inhaled again and blasted her full on. Leida swiftly blocked him with her wings. She kept them there but he kept on flaming her. Soon it was starting to hurt her and singe her wings. She closed her eyes, gritted her teeth and stood firm. However, eventually she fled backwards to escape the pain. Odax stopped his blast.

"Well that was stupid. Anyone with a brain would have flown up into the air and away once they realised the flow of fire or needles wasn't going to stop. Lizariaouses can't fly so if you need to get past some and they're firing needles at you that much you wait for a good chance, ready yourself and fly up and over them as fast as you can. Use your head and use your reflexes, you got that?"

Leida nodded, her wings stung her badly and were smoking a little.

"Sorry, it was foolish of me to try and withstand it. I thought you would stop."

"Stop? What is your head made of? Rock? Because that's how it sounds to me. I wouldn't stop and you're gunna be facing a whole army of Lizariaouses. Try to stand there and withstand their needles. Go on, just try it. You'd be dead and poisoned within seconds. The longer you stand there, the more likely that a needle will pierce your wing and poison you. Our wings are tough but even they can't withstand that many needles. So in order not to be poisoned, the wings are an aid, a shield but not armour. Do you understand this?" said Odax, all the while looking right at her.

Leida nodded again. "Yes Odax, I'll remember that."

"Good. Now, how are your wings? Can you continue?"

"Yes, they'll be ok."

"Good because in battle it will hurt a lot more than this but you must keep fighting until your body can't take any more. To give up as soon as you get a slight graze would be admitting defeat and we will never win that way, should a full on war start. I will blast you again. This time remember what I've told you." He readied himself, not even waiting for a reply and blasted her as he had before, not stopping or faltering.

Leida stood her ground, shielding herself with her wings, waiting for a chance where she could take off quickly and flying into the sky. The fire caught one of her back feet but she ignored the unpleasant stinging sensation and carried on, flying over Odax. She landed behind him as he stopped flaming and was about to say something when suddenly she was jumped upon by another Gryphie. He pinned her and she couldn't get away.

Panicked, she flamed everywhere, tiring quickly. In her panic she never aimed, missed the Gryphie completely and wore herself out.

The Gryphie was now laughing at her. Odax she could see stood a little way away watching them.

"ODAX!! Help!" she screamed but her oppressor removed himself and allowed her to stand. She stood, fell backwards and fled back to Odax, trying to escape.

"Well that was pathetic" said the newcomer pointedly.

"This is her first lesson as you know, Otuss." Replied Odax calmly.

"Yeah but...you really think *that* will make a soldier?" Otuss pointed at Leida and sniggered. Leida growled threateningly at him but stayed behind Odax.

"Aww look at the little wussy kitten! What a pathetic excuse for a Gryphie. And Diabloss's mate too...what does he see in you, baby? Maybe he needs his eyes checked or somethin'?" Otuss burst out laughing again, openly mocking Leida and making her anger worse.

Leida stepped forward a little, growling louder. Otuss was bigger than her but smaller than Odax. He was a green-blue colour with a short white mane. He was blinded in one eye as well and had a huge scar across his chest. He had an extremely sharp looking tail spade and his teeth hung out when his muzzle was shut since they were somewhat oversized. This gave a nasty threatening look about him. In fact he reminded Leida of a Lizariaous in disguise as a Gryphie or a Gryphie who was trying to look like a Lizariaous.

"Ooh you think yer tough? Come get me then, baby!" he opened his wings wide in a mocking gesture and waved his tail.

Leida was very angry by now. Sure she was bad at this but she was only just beginning and this newcomer apparently didn't know that. She had been proud of how she'd overcome most of these tasks even with the problems she'd had and she wasn't about to let any stuck up bully boy ruin it for her.

"Aww the little kitten too scared?" Otuss mocked.

"That's IT! You don't come here out of the blue and interrupt my training lesson!" growled Leida.

"Hey you tell him, sport! Go show him what for!" yelled Odax. Spurred on by his encouragement, Leida charged forward, wings out as balance and leaped on Otuss, pushing him backwards. Swiftly, Otuss reversed her attack, overpowering her and flipping her on her back.

"You're dead." He murmured, close to her ear and bit down on her neck.

Leida closed her eyes, gritted her teeth, panicked completely and kicked her back legs up into his stomach, raking her claws along it. Otuss pushed his body right down on her, preventing her legs from moving any further along his belly and wrapped his tail around hers, pulling it out painfully.

Leida screamed and just lay there shivering and waiting to be killed.

"That's enough, Otuss." It was Odax.

Otuss mumbled in annoyance but got off Leida. Leida didn't move, just lay whimpering.

Odax came over and helped her up. "This is Otuss, my younger brother. He teaches physical training. Fighting in hand to hand combat. And that was a test.

Otuss laughed. "And you did awful! Man, you panicked so badly it was painful to watch!"

Leida sat there and just felt void of all energy. "I'll never be a good fighter will I? I mean, Otuss said that too. He was right. All I ever do is panic and mess things up."

"Na, you'll be a fighter. You had the right idea, the claws to slice my belly open and all that. I'm just more experienced than you and stronger. When fighting Lizariaouses, you gotta aim for their bellies anyway, get 'em on their backs and defenceless. They can't shoot needles while lying on their backs after all." Otuss explained. "In any case, you'll be training with me next."

"Oh great." Leida murmured.

"Haha it's not that bad! You'll do fine, baby." Otuss turned and walked away.

"Where's he going? Aren't we training for the fighting now?" asked Leida.

"Nope, that's enough for this sun cycle. Your sessions will get longer with each but the fighting is the hardest and right now you're suffering from shock and fatigue, it's no way to fight. Now we go and tell my father how you did." Replied Odax.

"Oh great." Leida said again.

They found Strassor overseeing some young Gryphies who were learning to fly. Lunara was among these and she wanted to say hi to Leida but the female Gryphie who was with them told her no, since she was in a lesson. Lunara pouted about this.

"Well how did yeh do?" asked Strassor.

"Awful" replied Leida.

"She wasn't that bad. She got the hang of dodging and shielding fast enough. But the surprise trick training from Otuss went not so well. She has some of the right ideas but she panics and lets her anger take over too much" said Odax.

"Ah yes, anger can give yeh strength but not speed. You need both in battle. Speed be important if yer pinned and yeh need to get away quickly and take the enemy by surprise, knock him off balance and escape." Strassor told Leida. Leida nodded, listening carefully.

"All in all she did ok. I've seen worse anyway." Odax finished just as Diabloss came up. He'd watched the whole thing.

"Not bad, Leida!" he said, smiling.

He's seen worse thought Leida. I bet worse was actually some kitten or an old guy. Not someone her age with her level of energy and supposed skill. She sighed.

"Don't worry, yeh'll get better" said Strassor. "Come back tomorrow fer physical training!"

Leida nodded, forced a smile and walked off with Diabloss. Strassor watched them go.

"She shows promise, Sir. If she gets over her confidence and anger issues she will be a good fighter. I saw how she observed me when I was fire training her." Odax said quietly.

"Yeah, she'll be fine. A few more lessons will sort her out. I were noticing her observational skills before. I'll have ter tell Otuss ter be going easy on her to begin with though, when she panics, like with anyone else, she don't think straight." Strassor pondered as Diabloss and Leida left.

Leida was quiet for a while, then she said "Odax said he's seen worse" and sighed.

Diabloss spoke quietly. "He has seen worse. He trained Mettalika."

"Mettalika?" Leida was puzzled now. It never occurred to her that someone might have trained her too.

"Yes. Strassor and Odax both trained her but she was never any good at it. That was why she was attacked so easily by those Lizariaouses."

"But now she goes around killing loads of them with ease, how did she get so much better?" asked Leida.

"After she was saved and mechanised, she trained herself. Harsh, intensive training. Also her armour makes her stronger, especially in those parts of her body which have been entirely replaced like her hand and foot. She's hard to kill too, they can't pierce her skull or get her belly, those are the main parts that Lizariaouses aim for. Due to her training, her flight muscles are also stronger, not only can she stay in the air for extended periods of time without tiring, she can also pack a real punch with those wings of hers in hand to hand combat. But to begin with, she couldn't fight at all, she was worse than you."

"Oh, thanks" replied Leida sarcastically.

"Hey, I have faith in you, you show promise and I know you'll make a great fighter! You will fight alongside me" Diabloss said proudly.

"Alongside you? You think I can get that good?"

"Yes and even if you don't, you'll be by my side because you're my mate and I love you." Diabloss smiled at her as they walked.

Leida smiled back. It was always comforting to have Diabloss by her side; he brought out her confidence and made her think more positive.

She only hoped the fierce looking Otuss would go easy on her and he wouldn't hurt her too badly. She didn't trust him. He seemed unpredictable. It also annoyed her greatly how he kept referring to her as "baby" she wasn't a baby; she was an adult and expected to be treated as such. She hated those who treated her like a kitten and not an adult. She was young but often others thought she was younger than she actually was. She had that look about her and a certain kind of naivety.

However, she was learning. Diabloss also had some training plans for her too.

The Lizariaouses were still hard at work training. Most of the soldiers were completing the tasks quickly and efficiently. Mordred was proud of them. The first few had been rather slow and gotten drenched by the water. They all had good aim for the targets though. Although aiming for Mettalika's wings was never any easy feat. The targets didn't move much, her wings were always on the move so it meant that they would be more of a challenge to hit. Zephirak thought to himself to install some moving targets that moved like her wings. Then it occurred to him to use sea vultures and tie them to rope. They weren't as big targets as Mettalika but he figured that if he made the soldiers aim for smaller things, then aiming for Mettalika's wings would be easy. So he got Croter and Zarkiz to catch ten sea vultures. The soldiers who were good at the target practise would get a chance on them. The sea vultures would die with one hit so only a few soldiers were trained in hitting moving targets since sea vultures weren't that easy to catch unless you could fly yourself and they didn't have time to catch a whole load of them.

Zephirak stood beside Mordred. It was well into the afternoon now and the soldiers hadn't stopped for rests unless it was someone else's turn. They were still on the first group and were nearly down to the cave cat task.

"How are they doing?" asked Mordred.

Zephirak looked positive. "I think this time we'll really get her. She doesn't stand a chance. We'll train them and keep training until there is no way they can lose. I will not have another failure and I will not lose another pack."

Mordred smiled, feeling proud of his choices of soldiers and how well they were doing. He felt positive also, for the first time in a long time.

"Yes, good work Mordred" Zephirak smiled.

Mordred lowered his head in respect. "Thank you, Sir" he said.

Zephirak nodded. Yes, this plan could not, would not fail.

Chapter 17
The Solitary

Somewhere between both Shernaron and Dyarkroeen, something stirred. It was Mettalika. Her heightened senses scanned the area for Lizariaouses or anything else she could kill for a meal. Her fur was dirty and neglected and her steel armour had a dull glow. Her red fur helped to disguise the blood that was constantly on her arms and legs. The steel was reddish from all the things she'd killed. She never stayed in one area. If she did that then others would know to avoid it. There were certain areas she preferred. She rarely met other Gryphies. Apart from Sinxo, there hadn't been many others around and she only bumped into Sinxo because Sinxo was a scouter. Mettalika rarely flew, it gave away her position. But she did love to fly up and target unsuspecting Lizariaouses, swoop down on them and kill them from the air. Her steel claw could grip the needles without fear of harm and snap them all off. She'd use both her artificial claws when doing this and her tail which was the most useful of her false limbs.

She hadn't eaten since the morning and was feeling hungry. She usually liked to catch a Lizariaous for lunch. A decent sized one would last her the rest of the sun cycle and she only needed something small in the evening. She didn't just catch them for food though; mostly she did it for fun in her own twisted way. She liked to torture them. She was a wretched creature, no better than Zephirak since she was still stuck in the past, unable to let go and vindictive because of this. She had no friends but she rarely felt lonely since she could never go back to the gathering even if she wanted to. To apologise and admit she was wrong, to see the error of her ways was something she would never do. As far as she was concerned, *they* were wrong, not her. After she'd been mechanised and healed, she returned to the gathering and tried to get others to join her in her fight. They'd all been against it though, not interested. So there had been a food shortage, it hadn't lasted long anyway, just a season. Mettalika had explained her anger at the Lizariaouses trying to kill Gryphies for food but the others had ignored her, Gryphies being naturally peaceful, they didn't want to start battles and make it worse.

In her anger at never being a good fighter, Mettalika had gone out and trained herself. She didn't want anyone laughing at her for not being able to defend herself from attack. She was young admittedly, but there hadn't been anyone in the gathering, ever, who was so bad at fighting as she had been. She had been clumsy and just couldn't get the hang of anything. Over lunars of hard training she slowly began to improve by pushing herself and then pushing herself more. The armour helped a lot and soon she was strong and efficient in battle. She returned to Strassor's training grounds and challenged him, wanting to show him how good she'd become.

Strassor accepted the challenge and they fought. But she had become too good. In fact Odax had to rush in and separate them because Mettalika was getting too cocky and threatening.

Strassor warned her not to ever fight another Gryphie or he would remove her armour and let the Gryphies from the high mountains melt it down for scrap. This scared Mettalika but she was still determined to recruit some other Gryphies to help her. She had decided over her lunars of training, to go and kill Zephirak's mate. Destroy something the leader of the Lizariaouses held dear and ruin his life like he'd commanded his pack to ruin hers. They would have killed her had it not been for Diabloss and his soldiers chasing them off when they heard the commotion. So Mettalika went to find Diabloss. Back then her fur wasn't dirty and her steel was shining. When she moved, her muscles rippled from the intense training and she looked powerful and intimidating. As she entered the forest, younger Gryphies either stared at her in awe or ran to hide.

She found Diabloss and his mate sat under their tree talking. Mettalika had always had something for Diabloss but she was ashamed of her bad fighting and training skills and felt this was why Diabloss had chosen Leida instead of her. A small snarl crossed her lips as she saw them together, her heart tinged with jealousy. She'd show Diabloss how much better she'd gotten and he would join her. Surely he wanted a mate who was a good fighter and swift in the air. So she went and asked him to go with her since she had something to show him. Diabloss showed interest and left Leida under the tree as he followed Mettalika out of the forest and into a clearing near the edge of Shernaron.

Here, Mettalika showed off her skills and asked him what he thought. Diabloss was impressed and suggested she joined his soldiers. But Mettalika had other ideas. She asked him to go with her to Dyarkroeen and help her kill Zephirak's mate. Taken aback, Diabloss refused. Mettalika grew angry. She told him that they were both the best fighters in the Forest and that it would be easy. Diabloss still refused.

"We don't need a war, Mettalika. They aren't taking Gryphies any more. Just drop it. You have become a good fighter and for that I respect you because you trained hard but forgive the Lizariaouses and leave it."

Mettalika snarled. "Then if you won't help, I will go myself."

Diabloss tried to stop her but she tore one of his wings with her tail. She could have killed him or at least tried but her feelings for him wouldn't allow that. After putting him out of commission for following her, she flew to Dyarkroeen and was lucky enough to spy Zephirak's mate, Salvariss outside their cave in the sun asleep. Mettalika flew in, creeping round the cave and sliced Salvariss's throat with her tail before she could awaken. Zephirak, returning home with a kill, saw Mettalika's killing blow happen before he could do anything about it. He charged forward but Mettalika flew into the air and mocked him.

"You tried to kill me but failed. You and your kind will regret attacking Gryphies. We are not food and you have no right to hunt us. For what you have done, I will hunt you, I will hunt your kind and I will kill your soldiers and young and make you see the wrong in your selfish acts. I am Mettalika. I am unstoppable and I am your worst moonmare. Your kind will fall because of your foolishness." Mettalika struck a threatening pose in the air, making sure Zephirak could see every last inch of pointed, shining steel and flew off, leaving him to mourn the death of his beloved mate.

And so it began. Mettalika's reign of terror for Lizariaouses.

Zephirak, in his anger, told his hunters that Gryphie meat would be on the menu from now on and sent out his first pack to capture or kill Mettalika.

Mettalika was walking through the swamp, the memories of all this on her mind. To an extent she felt lonely sometimes. Being a solitary; a Gryphie on its own with no gathering or friends was hard. But then she remembered her hatred for the Lizariaouses and the loneliness disappeared.

She was also angry and hurt that Diabloss never wanted her. Even after she'd trained and shown off her skills. The sun cycle he told her he wanted nothing to do with her plans and tried to stop her was constantly on her mind. She'd thought about killing Leida but it would never make Diabloss love her, only hate her. So she'd tried to let him go. She was a solitary, she needed no one. Her mind was so far away with her own thoughts that she didn't notice her path was being crossed by a young Lizariaous. It was Jadariol.

She may not have noticed him if he hadn't stopped her to talk to her.

"Hey, I'm lost, can you help me?" he asked boldly, seemingly unaware that he was facing the greatest Lizariaous killer of all time.

Mettalika couldn't believe he hadn't heard of her. But this made it even better, she would enjoy this kill. And he was young and fresh too; she rarely got the chance to devour a youngster even though they were one of her favourite things to kill.

"I can help you" she said with a nasty grin. "I can help you to die."

"Die? Err...no...I'd much rather live. If you could point me in the right direction of..." but he was cut off as Mettalika hit him, sending him bowling over into the mud. Jadariol realised her true intentions now and started to run away but his legs were short compared to hers and he didn't get far before she was in front of him. He tried to fire needles at her but his aim was bad in his fright and he missed her completely.

Mettalika's tail swung round and the end of it sliced off his remaining needles. Jadariol fell backwards, whimpering in fear now.

141

Mettalika just laughed. "I'll enjoy devouring you, young one" she sneered and pounced on him, biting down on one of his front legs and breaking it easily. Jadariol screamed in pain and fear, struggling desperately to escape. Mettalika lay down, holding him like a cat with its prey. Jadariol was crying in distress, tears rolling down his cheeks.

"Aww don't cry, you deserve to die. You're nothing but Lizariaous scum. I bet you wish you'd been born a powerful Gryphie like me. Then I wouldn't be killing you, your leader, Zephirak would do that instead. When I was your age, a pack of your soldiers tried to kill me and look at me now. I'm their worst moonmare."

Mettalika held the struggling Lizariaous down although his constant kicking with his back legs was starting to annoy her. He placed her artificial claw on one of his back legs and pressed down. Jadariol felt his bones crack slowly and painfully and he screamed again.

All the commotion had attracted someone else. Sinxo. She was out hunting and she slunk over to see what was happening. What she saw horrified and sickened her to the pit of her stomach. Mettalika torturing a poor little youngster. She hated that Mettalika killed the Lizariaouses but it made it even worse when she tormented them, especially the youngsters.

She had to stop it.

Sinxo bounded out suddenly, flaming and taking Mettalika by surprise and she let go of Jadariol. Jadariol crawled under a nearby bush to hide.

"What do you want?" demanded Mettalika.

"I want you to stop. Killing Lizariaouses is cruel enough without torturing and tormenting their children." Sinxo snarled, sizing Mettalika up. She was bigger than

Sinxo by quite a bit and Sinxo knew she would lose in a fight against Mettalika, she wouldn't stand a chance.

Mettalika laughed. "They *all* deserve to die. Even this little wimp. Why do you care?"

"Because he's a kid. Don't you have any morals at all?"

"Not really, no. He was an easy snack, besides he was stupid enough to walk right into my path. He deserves to be killed for not being careful enough." Mettalika held her wings out in a threatening manner, letting Sinxo see through body language; that she could and would attack at any time.

"Let me have him" ventured Sinxo.

"Why should I?" demanded Mettalika.

"Look, he's gunna die anyway from shock so if I take him back to Dyarkroeen, he can be used as a threat; so they can see the damage you do to them. I don't like Lizariaouses either but don't you think this is going too far?"

"I've eaten their young before. I'm used to it" replied Mettalika.

Sinxo was starting to think she was in a losing argument. She had to somehow save the poor kid. Mettalika was getting impatient and she turned her back to Sinxo.

"Leave me alone to finish my kill in peace" she said quietly.

"But..." Sinxo began but Mettalika cut her off. "I said LEAVE. Or I'll kill you instead."

Sinxo backed away and turned to go. She looked over her shoulder but noticed that Mettalika was having trouble finding the young Lizariaous.

Sinxo thought to have a look for him herself, he can't have gotten far in his condition.

She circled around where she saw he'd hidden; he must have gone in that direction. Mettalika was by now, getting very annoyed at not being able to find him. Then Sinxo saw a tail spade stuck out from under a nearby bush. He seemed to have gone to hide in a bush he deemed to be far enough away that Mettalika wouldn't find him. Well it had worked so far but it wouldn't for very long. She'd smell his blood sooner or later over the stench of the swamp.

Sinxo snuck up to him and parted some of the leaves of the bush. He stared at her, shivering in sheer unadulterated fear.

"Keep quiet, I'm going to save you but we don't have much time, I must get you out of here before Mettalika sees I'm trying to rescue you. Can you walk?" Sinxo spoke quietly, keeping an eye out for Mettalika. She could see her but thankfully Mettalika was far enough away that so far, she couldn't hear them talking.

"I c...can't...w...walk...she....she b....broke my...le...legs..." whimpered the little Lizariaous.

"All of them?"

"N...no...just..two..."

"Ok, I'm gunna pick you up. Don't scream, no matter if it hurts. If you scream, she'll kill us both. Ready?" Sinxo decided to pick him up by his scruff and she lowered her muzzle to him.

Jadariol nodded shakily.

Sinxo picked him up quickly, trying to be as gentle as possible and slowly backed away, out of the bush. Mettalika was now facing the opposite direction and thrashing about in some nearby bushes, thankfully unaware.

Sinxo quickly turned and bounded off with her precious cargo, wanting to get as far away from the marsh and Mettalika as possible. So she headed to the safety of Shernaron.

Jadariol was in tears, he had no idea where she was taking him but every little jolt as she bounded along hurt him.

Soon they reached the Gryphie Forest and Sinxo approached the guards, passing them. Suddenly, one leaped in front of her.

"What is that?" he demanded. "It looks like a Lizariaous. Why are you bringing it to the forest?"

"I rescued him from Mettalika, he's badly injured, I need to get him healed and his legs set in wood because they are broken. Please let me pass" she pleaded, putting Jadariol down so she could speak.

"No, leave the Lizariaous here and we will put it out of its misery." The guard was adamant and his comrade had stepped up beside him once he realised that persuading Sinxo not to take the Lizariaous into the forest was going to be hard.

Sinxo stood her ground. "I risked my life fending off Mettalika to save this little guy and you are not gunna stop me taking him to Mystik" she growled.

"If you take him in, others will come looking for him. We don't need that right now. Leave him here, he can go home by himself if he wishes or you can take him home. Either way, he's not passing."

Sinxo was really starting to get angry now. "He has two broken legs, he can't make it back to Dyarkroeen by himself and the journey is too long for me to take him back carrying him in my mouth. I am taking him in to see Mystik and that is final."

"No, we won't let you. If you take another step, we will use force to stop you" replied the guard. His comrade readied himself to flame Sinxo and Jadariol if necessary. Jadariol was getting upset again and started to whimper.

Sinxo growled in annoyance. "Then I will go in by air. You will not stop me" It was then she realised what a stupid thing that was to say, since the guards knew her plan now.

"Well we will stop you now cos we know about it" chuckled the guard.

"What's going on?" The voice came from behind Sinxo. It was Diabloss. He and Leida had returned from their relaxing afternoon together.

"Sinxo wants to bring a Lizariaous into the forest. We won't let her pass" explained the guard.

"A Lizariaous? What's all this?" Diabloss looked at Sinxo with a demanding expression on his face, wanting an explanation.

"I rescued him from Mettalika. She was going to kill him. He's only a youngster and she was torturing him. I brought him back here so Mystik could heal his broken legs" Sinxo said quietly. "Was I wrong to rescue him?"

Leida looked at Jadariol. "No, you weren't wrong to rescue him. Look at him, he's terrified and in pain. He needs to be healed. We'll take him to Mystik and see what she has to say about the situation." She looked at Diabloss for confirmation and Diabloss nodded.

"Yes. Stand aside" he motioned to the guards and they stood obediently aside, letting Diabloss, Leida and Sinxo carrying Jadariol again to pass them.

The four of them headed into the forest and came to the clearing. Sinxo took Jadariol to Mystik.

Mystik was outside her tree and saw Sinxo approach. So did Lunara. And she recognised Jadariol. Shen held her back though.

"It's a Lizariaous, what are you doing? Leave it be, it's none of our concern, Lunara." Shen warned her.

146

"But when I went to Dyarkroeen, he was the one I saw, there was a bunch of them, kids my age and I played with him. What's wrong with him? Why doesn't he see me?" Lunara wanted so badly to go and say hi.

"He looks in pain. What is Sinxo doing bringing a Lizariaous into the forest, harmed or otherwise? We'll have the whole pack on our backs if we bring Lizariaouses into the forest. Did she kidnap him?" Shen was puzzled over the whole situation.

Sinxo put Jadariol down and explained to Mystik what had happened.

"Hmm, well, we can't leave him to die. We can put wood on his legs to help them heal better and use my herbs on him" said Mystik carefully examining Jadariol.

"Then do I take him back to Dyarkroeen?" asked Sinxo.

"I was thinking about that. They aren't good at healing their wounded, especially not when the wounds are this bad. He will need his dressings changed every sun cycle and he will take about a lunar to heal. If we send him back, we may as well kill him because Lizariaouses are known to kill those who are wounded this badly rather than work to get them better, especially if the survival or healing chances are low. This one may not walk properly ever again..."

At those words, Jadariol started crying harder and the eyes of the whole forest were upon him, wondering what the noise was about.

"However, I have the right herbs that will heal his legs like new. If he is left with me, he will heal fine. If we take him back after he is healed, we can use him as a peace offering, show that there are no hard feelings and we aren't all like Mettalika. Mettalika hurt him but we heal him. Maybe we can agree to a truce that way."

147

Sinxo nodded, thinking this was a good idea. Mystik was the wisest Gryphie she knew and had been her mentor for many seasons. Half the scouting jobs that Sinxo did were looking for herbs for Mystik.

"Now, Sinxo, pick him up and bring him over to the healing bed. I will need the wood splints, the healing herbs of Shinnohron and the antiseptic balm. Since he was injured in the marsh, dirt could have gotten into his wounds and poisoned them. We need to clean them. His front leg is broken cleanly and the back leg is only fractured, seems like you saved that one in time. I applaud your bravery, Sinxo."

Sinxo felt flattered at this and did as she was told, putting Jadariol on the bed where he lay down, exhausted and Mystik moved around preparing his wounds, cleaning them and setting the wood splints.

All the time Mystik talked to Jadariol comfortingly and worked on him gently and carefully.

Jadariol behaved himself, didn't make too much noise and tried to be brave.

Mystik asked him things to help take his mind off the discomfort.

"Why were you out in the swamp?" she asked.

"I was wandering around and I guess I didn't realise how far I'd wandered away from Dyarkroeen" replied Jadariol, wincing as Mystik applied the herbs to his wounds before splinting his legs.

"Ah yes, we can all forget where we are sometimes. But you must be more observant, you are lucky Sinxo found you when she did or you would not be alive now. You would be inside Mettalika's belly."

"I didn't know she'd kill me. She said something about helping me to die but I thought she was joking." Jadariol tried not to pull away in pain as Mystik splinted his back leg.

"Didn't you know who she was?" asked Sinxo.

"I'd heard of Mettalika but I didn't know what she looked like, no one ever told me that" explained Jadariol.

Mystik thought about this and found it rather odd. After all, Mettalika was the number one enemy of all Lizariaouses and she assumed teaching youngsters to fear her was one of the first things they would be told by their parents. Surely they didn't try to keep the horrible truth from their children? Telling them what she looked like was also important, so they knew what to look out for and keep away from.

"What had you been told about her?" Mystik asked him.

"She's bad and she'll kill you" replied Jadariol.

"But you were never told what she looked like?"

"I don't think so. At least, I don't remember my Dad telling me. My Dad is a commander in the army. He was the one who told me about her. My mother was killed by her when I was very young."

Mystik figured maybe he planned on telling him when he was a little older but all the same she was shocked that Mettalika had taken the kid's parent and yet the other parent wouldn't describe her to him. Especially not one born into a family whose father was in the army. Any Lizariaous parent with any sense would make sure their child was well educated about Mettalika as soon as possible. Mystik wondered whether Lizariaouses cared about their youngsters as much as Gryphies cared about theirs. But then again maybe since Mettalika had taken the mother, the father was simply trying not to get too deeply into the subject or did not wish to speak of it.

She finished splinting Jadariol's legs.

"There, you mustn't walk on them; you must lie and rest ok? They will heal soon enough with rest. They will heal crooked if you move them too much though and it will hinder your walking." Mystik told him.

Jadariol nodded and moved carefully into a more comfortable position lying down.

Mystik expected him to say that his father would be worried but he said nothing. She thought even more that the parents of Lizariaous youngsters didn't care as much as Gryphie parents.

Sinxo was putting things away and Mystik went and sat outside again to leave Jadariol to rest.

Lunara was outside, trying to see in. She knew it was Jadariol and she had snuck away from Shen to see if she could talk to him.

Mystik saw her and smiled.

"Hello Lunara, what brings you here this sun cycle?" she asked.

"Err...well...I know the Lizariaous kid in there." Lunara explained how she'd wandered too far and met Jadariol in Dyarkroeen. "Can I go see him please?" She looked sweetly at Mystik, hoping to win her over.

Mystik smiled. "Of course dear, but don't be too long because he needs his rest. However it will do him good to have a friend his age around."

Lunara jumped with glee and skipped into the tree to see Jadariol.

Jadariol was lying down with his head rested in the dry grass that served as bedding.

"Hi Jadariol!" squeaked Lunara with joy.

Jadariol looked up. "Hey I remember you, the Lizariaous hunter" he laughed. "Caught any recently oh great hunter?"

Lunara blushed. "Well...not recently...they seem to be getting away from me hehe"

Jadariol just rolled his eyes.

"What happened to you? I heard you were hurt and now I can see you've been hurt." Lunara looked concerned.

"I bumped into Mettalika. Heard of her?"

Lunara's eyes widened in fear. "She did that to you?" she motioned to Jadariol's broken legs.

"Yeah...I was lost and she just wanted to kill me. It was horrible. She tormented me and threatened me" Tears came to Jadariol's eyes as he remembered. "It hurt a lot and I didn't know why she was doing it. I hadn't done anything to her and yet she still wanted to kill me. Why? I know she goes round killing my kind. Why does she do it?"

"Because she's mean. She was attacked by Lizariaouses when there was a food shortage and ever since, she's killed them. She had her revenge in killing Zephirak's mate but she just kept on going afterwards. We all hate her anyway; she's not welcome in the forest any more and never will be." Lunara explained. "I can't think how a Gryphie could ever be so cruel. We like peace; she goes against all of it."

Jadariol listened carefully. "Well I hope I never see her again" he said. "My Dad is a commander in the army and he says Mettalika will die. What do you think of that?"

"I know Mettalika won't hurt me or my kind so it doesn't affect me whether she lives or dies. I met her once; she never said anything to me. I think she ignores kittens. She seemed cold and distant though." Lunara looked down. "I really wish we could just all be friends though, like you and I are. Maybe we should make the grown-ups see that? If we can be friends, why can't they?"

"Because grown-ups like to fight. Well most of the ones in my pack do. They get satisfaction from it; they live to fight." Jadariol shrugged. "I like fighting."

"But you wouldn't kill someone without reason would you? Like Mettalika does?"

"No, not unless they annoyed me or threatened my pack. I wish I was older, I would kill Mettalika. She's horrible, she deserves to die. She killed my mother." Jadariol growled and then winced from his injuries.

Lunara didn't reply. She was shocked that Mettalika had taken the life of his parent. Mettalika had hurt someone Lunara considered to be a friend as well and she didn't like her at all now. Previously she felt Mettalika could change or be forgiven but she was beginning to see the cruel harsh reality of the situation.

They sat and chatted a while longer until Lunara was called home to go to bed. Jadariol closed his eyes and rested for the moon cycle. His dreams were haunted with Mettalika's voice, threatening and cruel in his ears.

Over on Diabloss and Leida's tree, they were talking about the fight training. Leida was still a little under confident.

"Just think of me and how much I love you, how proud I'll be once you pass your training." Diabloss told her.

Leida smiled. "I will. I train for you but I train for the good of all of us, for the good of the gathering. I don't want to be useless and I won't be. I will have my use!" Leida had decided not to doubt herself any more. She had gone too long doubting and having no faith in herself and she'd never be a good fighter if she didn't believe she could do it. Her heart and soul had to be in it completely for her to succeed.

"I wonder how the Lizariaous kid is doing" she wondered, gazing towards Mystik's tree.

"I should think he'd ok. They're resilient to most things. He was in a pretty bad state though." Diabloss looked a little concerned.

"I think she's going too far picking on youngsters" Leida murmured.

"She doesn't usually, only if they cross her path. She doesn't go looking for them at least. That little one, Sinxo said he was lost. It's unusual for a young Lizariaous to wander away from Dyarkroeen like that. We wander and so do our kittens but that's only because we can fly. I noticed he was friendly with Lunara too." Diabloss looked thoughtful.

"Yes, if only we could bridge the gap like them. Children often don't care about differences, they don't see it. All they see is a potential friend their age, someone to play with and who likes the same things as them. Sometimes innocence is a good thing." Leida smiled.

Diabloss's face clouded. "Yes but somehow if Zephirak knew about them I don't think he would accept it like we do. He would keep them from each other. I'll have to find out more about that kid. Like who his parents are."

"For all we know he could be the son of Zephirak" Leida pointed out.

"No, Zephirak has no kids. In fact I heard that his mate was pregnant when she was killed. That of course made his feelings of vengeance for Mettalika far worse."

"That's awful" said Leida looking shocked. She wasn't that bothered about having kittens but it didn't mean no one else wanted to and to take not only the life of a mother but her unborn babies too was just unthinkable. Especially if it was done in malice.

"Heheh, Mettalika liked me. She had feelings for me many seasons ago but was never happy that I wouldn't accept her." Diabloss sat up.

"What? You never told me that" Leida looked with interest now.

"Well it didn't need telling. She trained and showed off her skills to me but I wasn't interested. Even before I met you I wasn't interested. There was always something not right with her. She hated losing and that was the main problem with her training. Whenever she got it wrong she would get so angry with herself that she'd never get it right. It would cloud her aim, judgement and techniques. Only when she really put her heart into it, made herself train by herself and forget her own stupidity did she become as good a fighter as I always knew she was. I invited her to join my ranks but she only wanted to have me help her kill. I refused; I even tried to stop her but to no avail. I always hope that one sun cycle she will learn her lesson. Sadly that sun cycle looks very far away and highly unlikely. It's a shame, a waste. She had potential once." Diabloss looked genuinely sorrowful for Mettalika's plight.

Leida looked down. "Well so long as no one else joins her."

"They won't. She has no respect from us now and while at one time we were willing to forgive and take her back, she is forever banished. We can never accept a murderer who kills in cold blood and for no reason except hate. It is not our way." Diabloss yawned. "Well, we have a long sun cycle tomorrow. We'd better get some sleep sweetheart."

Leida agreed and they slept in the hollow of their tree this moon cycle, curled up together.

Chapter 18
Physical Skills Tested

The training had gone well in Dyarkroeen. The first group of soldiers would move onto physical hand to hand sparring the following sun cycle while the second group would do the fire and target practise. All the sea vultures had been used and there were a few soldiers who needed to work on moving target practise so the following sun cycle they would be sent out into the "field" to practise that.

Evening drew in and the remaining soldiers all returned to their caves for some well earned rest.

"How did we do Sir?" asked Mordred.

Zephirak looked satisfied. "I am happy with the progress of this sun cycle. There are still some things that need to be worked on but it's a brilliant start, Mordred. You are earning back my respect. I see you are working very efficiently and once again I remember why I chose you to be my number one commander."

Mordred looked thrilled. "Thank you Sir, as always, it is an honour working in your presence. My ranks will make you proud. This time we will get Mettalika, there is no doubt of it."

"There is a lot more training needs to be done before we can move to Mettalika. I want those guys to be ready, more ready than they've ever been. There is no room for failure this time. If your plan doesn't work, Mordred, then I will have you working as a digger the rest of your life and train the soldiers for full on war. This is your last chance at Mettalika. If it doesn't work then I will go for the bigger plan and take down the Forest. Do you understand me, Mordred? This is your last chance to impress me. Right now you're doing a good job of it but if you fail, you know what will happen."

155

Mordred saluted. "Yes Sir, I understand. We will not fail you. In fact we will bring back Mettalika's corpse for you to do as you wish with. Take her steel and have it as a trophy."

"You won't need to. I will be coming with you. I have decided I will deal the killing blow to the neck." Zephirak replied.

"But, then why have you been having me train them for that as well?" asked Mordred, puzzled.

"Because you never know when it might be useful. Mettalika is not the only Gryphie you know. On the tiny chance that others come to her rescue we will need all the skills available from everyone to make it work and take her out efficiently with minimal damage to the ranks."

"Yes Sir." Mordred replied, saluting again.

"Now, to your cave. We need to rest up for tomorrow. It will become more intense for those already basically trained." Zephirak turned and walked off, not waiting for any kind of reply.

Mordred took some meat to the cave cat that was still tied up and returned to his own cave. Schaarl was outside waiting for him.

"Did it go well?" she asked as he passed her and headed into the cave. She followed. She'd got him some fresh meat and he sat and ate it hungrily since he hadn't had a bite to eat all sun cycle.

"It went well enough" he replied in between mouthfuls. "Except we can't fail with this. If we do, Zephirak is going to declare all out war. He's determined to take someone's life, whether it's Mettalika or all the other Gryphies."

"How do you know he won't just do that anyway, even if you do destroy Mettalika?" Schaarl said darkly.

Mordred looked troubled and growled in frustration. "I don't. But I do seriously think that once Zephirak has taken her life, he won't be so worried about the others. He will be accompanying us and deliver the killing blow. He wants to see her die himself and ensure we don't mess up again."

Schaarl sighed and lay down. All this talk of death worried her. "Well I for one look forward to the sun cycle when we can all live in peace and not have to worry about being killed by Mettalika, ruled over by a tyrant like Zephirak or being forced into a battle that is pointless."

Mordred had finished his food and he lay beside her and nuzzled her reassuringly. "It will be ok, it will take some time but I promise it will be ok honey. Then we can raise a family in peace and safety."

Schaarl rested her head on him and sighed. She hoped so.

Zephirak walked back to his cave feeling achievement of the sun cycle's events. Things were going well. The soldiers were being trained and if they failed to kill Mettalika again, well that training would come in very handy for declaring war and taking the Forest by force. He chuckled to himself as he went to sleep that moon cycle.

***

A new sun cycle dawned over the Forest. Leida and Diabloss were already awake. In fact they had caught their morning meal and had brought it back to the forest to eat it. Diabloss wanted a few words with Jadariol before they left for Leida's training that sun cycle.

Mystik was awake too and was sorting out Jadariol's dressings, checking them over. He hadn't slept well.

157

Finding it hard to move and then it hurting him when he tried to lie properly or comfortably had been a huge hassle and he was very tired still. That, coupled with the moonmares he'd had didn't make for a very good moon cycle's sleep.

"Hold still please, yes I know it hurts. The pain will go in time. Let me see, ah yes, the bleeding has stopped. I'll just give you a clean dressing there..." Mystik talked to him while she checked him over until he was organised again.

"Now, I have brought some food for you." She placed a dead sea vulture before him.

"Do you um...have any forest deer?" asked Jadariol.

"No, they are hard to catch although they do provide food for a good few sun cycles. This will do you for now anyway." Mystik smiled at him. "Now, eat up, it will make you stronger. Don't stop eating or you will fade away to nothing."

Jadariol ate the food gratefully. He was hungry but he would miss eating cave cats, they were his favourites.

Outside, Diabloss had finished his breakfast and he trotted over to Mystik's tree. Mystik was outside eating her own meal, another sea vulture.

"Mystik, may I see the kid?" asked Diabloss.

"You may, when he has finished eating. Why do you wish to see him anyway?"

"I want to find out more about him. If he is the son of a high ranking general or commander, they may come looking for him. If he is the son of a digger or general worker then I doubt they would bother. How long do we keep him?" asked Diabloss.

"Until he is healed. You can then take him back to Dyarkroeen as a peace offering to show that we are not

158

vengeful and forgive what they did to Mettalika; that we aren't all like her." Mystik explained.

"Well I hope it will work. Still, it sounds like a good enough idea." Diabloss replied.

"I want to make up for the mistake I made seasons ago with my idea of saving Mettalika. It was the worst decision I have ever made and now we are all suffering for it." Mystik recalled her decision with regret.

"You weren't to know that would happen. You are still the oldest and wisest in the gathering. Many of the younger ones look up to you as a teacher and learn from you." Diabloss smiled.

"Maybe so but I will have the regret of choosing to save her for the rest of my life unless I can fix what I did wrong those seasons ago. I think Jadariol has finished his meal now." Mystik didn't look round to see if he had, she could just sense he was resting again.

Diabloss nodded and headed into the tree. He swallowed as he saw the form of poor little Jadariol on the makeshift bed near the back. The kid's breathing was a little laboured and he kept gritting his teeth and wincing. The remains of the sea vulture lay nearby in a pile of feathers. Usually Lizariaouses ate the whole of their kill, even the bones. Diabloss worried that the kid might stop eating because of his weakened condition. Plus he would have to have careful exercise. Not being able to stand on his legs for a few weeks would weaken his walking. Both Gryphies and Lizariaouses were relatively fast healers so in about a lunar Jadariol would at least have healed enough to walk again. His back leg would heal first and it was easier to limp around while keeping a front leg off the ground.

"Hey there" said Diabloss, trying to sound friendly and calm. He'd never been much good with youngsters.

Jadariol looked up. "Hi" was the one word reply.

159

Diabloss smiled and sat next to him. "Can you tell me about what happened?" he asked.

"Sure, I was attacked by Mettalika. I was lost and trying to get back to Dyarkroeen. She attacked me, broke my leg and then tried to break my other leg" Jadariol's ears drooped. "I don't want to talk about it any more. Ask Lunara or the old one if you need to know." He sighed and winced again.

"Ok, what kind of a family do you come from? They need to know you're safe" Diabloss made the last part up to persuade Jadariol to tell him.

"My Dad is in the army. He also heals the wounded. My mother was killed by Mettalika when I was very small. I don't remember her." Jadariol sighed again.

Diabloss frowned. So, Mettalika had gotten the kid's mother and now the kid himself. He wondered if she had a grudge against that family. If the father had attacked her and she was getting revenge once again. She seemed to hold grudges on everything. And the father was a healer? Even more interesting. But the kid wasn't worried about his father being worried.

"And I have two siblings" Jadariol went on; "Silpharius is my older sister. My younger brother is Gandrix."

"And are they quite safe? They weren't out there getting lost with you were they?" Diabloss was worried they may have fallen victim to Mettalika as well and not made it.

"No, they're back in Dyarkroeen."

"How did you wander so far out and get lost? You weren't playing with them?" Diabloss asked.

"No, I was by myself. I was hunting. I wanted to make my first kill and impress my Dad. I wandered out away from Dyarkroeen to be as far away as possible so no one would find me and send me home. I asked

Mettalika for directions but she just wanted to kill me."
Jadariol sniffed, he was getting worked up and upset
now so Diabloss figured it would be best to leave it. He
had all the information he needed. He didn't bother to
find out the name of Jadariol's father since he wasn't
going to tell him they had his kid safe, it would be a
surprise for when the kid was better.

"Ok, well you rest and get better soon!" Diabloss
smiled and trotted out.

Jadariol watched as he left and rested his head on
his paws. Why was everyone always asking him things?
He was getting tired of it; he just wanted to be left alone
to rest.

"Well? What did he say?" asked Leida when
Diabloss returned to her.

"His father is in the army and a healer as well. That
was interesting. What was more interesting was that he
said his mother had been a victim of Mettalika when he
was very young. It made me think that Mettalika is now
targeting families. Tearing them apart by picking them
off one by one. I don't know how much more of this I can
handle." Diabloss shook his head.

"How did he get out there by himself?" asked Leida.
That had been puzzling her.

"He told me he was out hunting. He wanted to make
his first kill and impress his father."

"Poor little guy. Mettalika has no morals, no heart."
Leida snarled.

Diabloss shook his head. "I don't suppose talking to
her would help either."

"Well it certainly didn't help Zephirak."

"No, I think she'll carry on doing this until she dies."
Diabloss looked at his claws. "Whenever that will be."

"You aren't thinking of killing her yourself are you?
We never kill our own kind." Leida looked shocked.

"No, I just don't know when this madness will end" Diabloss looked at the sky, noted the position of the sun and turned to Leida. "But we need to think of that some other time. Right now it's time for your training! Come on." He got up and started up their tree to take off for the training grounds.

Great, thought Leida. *Otuss is going to thrash me.*

They took off and soon arrived at the training grounds.

Strassor was expecting them.

"Ah I see yeh be here then, Leida!" he walked up, smiling.

Otuss was beside him smirking, his teeth sticking out at unnerving angles. Leida figured he was trying to be friendly but his appearance made him look rather creepy.

"You ready for this sun cycle's lesson, baby?" he asked. He looked as though he was going to burst out laughing at any given moment, almost insinuating Leida was some kind of joke.

Leida looked him straight in his good eye. "Yes. Bring it on. I can handle whatever you throw at me." She snarled.

"Heheh I doubt that very much. You're just a beginner. You have no idea what the grik to do in battle. All you know is dodging and running like a kitten baby. The wuss's way out. Haha pathetic! But I'll make a soldier and fighter of you yet. Come on."

Leida looked at Diabloss who stepped up beside her and nuzzled her. "You'll be fine. He's a good trainer." He told her.

"Good?" mumbled Leida so only Diabloss could hear. "He's already making fun of me and he hasn't even seen what I can do yet. I don't like him. Isn't there anyone else who could train me instead?"

"No, Strassor is using his sons to train you because he feels that you should be trained by the best. You're my mate, I expect greatness of you, Leida and you must do your best. Impress Otuss; show him what you're truly made of. Gain his respect and he'll take back the mocking words. Make him surprised and impressed at the talents I know you have. You are graceful in the air and have the fire in you. You even risked your life to save Lunara. Now go out there and show him." Diabloss nudged her towards Otuss who was now halfway across the training grounds.

Leida sighed and followed Otuss. She hoped Diabloss was right.

"Come on, baby! We aint got all sun cycle!" yelled Otuss as he'd reached the place they would train.

"I'm coming!" Leida ran to catch him up and arrived by his side.

"Ok, first of all you need to know how to defend yourself. Like when I pinned you last sun cycle. Defence is the first priority because someone like you would easily be pinned and killed with little or no effort from a Lizariaous."

Leida opened her mouth to counter him but shut it again. He was her trainer and he didn't want Diabloss to be ashamed of her for arguing.

Just you wait, she thought, I'll show you what I'm really made of and make you eat those words.

"Now, a Lizariaous's weakest place is the belly. Slice that open and you're home free. When I pinned you last sun cycle and you kicked out with your back legs you had the right idea. Throw your attacker off or slice him. But don't let him press his weight on you because you won't have the strength to push up. They're heavier and stronger than us. Yes, even stronger than me or Diabloss. They always use weight to an advantage with a grounded Gryphie. So, this is our first training. I'm gunna pounce you and you must try to push me off. Don't worry about hurting me, I'm used to it. Hence all these scars."

Leida didn't care about hurting him, she didn't like him anyway which was probably a good thing because she could pretend he really was a Lizariaous and not regret anything. He looked enough like one with those teeth anyway. Maybe that was why he was a fight trainer.

"Are you ready?" Otuss asked.

"Yes, come at me" replied Leida, readying herself.

Otuss laughed, then his face contorted into a twisted snarl and he went for her. Leida was taken by surprise and shock at his hideous grimace and stepped back, momentarily put off by it. She quickly gained her composure and stiffened, her tail thrashing and she growled in response. First, she decided she wouldn't let him get near her to pounce on her. She shielded herself with her wings and backed up but he leaped over her, got her from behind and flipped her over on her back, holding her down with his claws. Leida's heart was racing, adrenaline pumping and she thrashed out with her back legs, she didn't merely kick, the movement was a huge fast reaction powered by adrenaline and fear. She winded Otuss completely, knocking him back and this gave her a chance to grip her back feet on his sides and dig her claws in painfully. Otuss screeched and snarled in anger at being taken by surprise like this. He backed down but he seemed to be fighting an inward battle before he got off her. She could see he wanted to repay the damage.

Panting, he stumbled a little way away and sat, regaining his composure and checking himself over for damage.

Leida got up and crouched, watching him. She didn't mean to be that rough with him. She was surprised at her own reaction. She had panicked again of course. She knew he wouldn't hurt her but the face he pulled before he went for her was one of pure hatred and malice, something evil and cruel. This had made her doubt his true intentions and somewhere inside she feared he would have killed her had she not defended herself properly.

Otuss's head was bowed. He glanced at her, his eyes narrowed.

"Well that was...unexpected. What the grik were you thinking? I wanted you to push me off...but wow. You should have stopped when you heard me yelling."

Screaming more like, thought Leida. Still, she looked ashamed. "Sorry, it was kind of a reaction. My body wanted you off me and so that's what my legs were doing."

"Yeah but you should have stopped when you winded me. In a fight, winding your opponent will knock them back, you can escape and you could've done back there too, just pull yourself out and get away. But you couldn't even do that. You're such a grikking baby. What? You thought you'd give me a taste of my own medicine? It was *training* and we don't go that far in fight training. If we did, I would simply kill you. There are limits."

Leida avoided eye contact and laid her ears back. Man, he was taking this too far. He should be proud of her that she had been resourceful. It then dawned on her that he was mad she'd gotten the better of him and it had turned out in the opposite way to how he thought it would. She smirked inwardly. So she did have the fire within her, Diabloss had been right. She had noticed

Otuss making the decision whether or not to fight back or get off her though and she didn't like that.

Otuss stood up. "Ok, well I want to see how you escape if I pin you the other way. If a Lizariaous jumps on top of a Gryphie, it prevents them flying away. Only the strongest Gryphies can get airborne with a Lizariaous on their back and throw them off so I know you wouldn't be able to do that but at least try to throw me off and get in the air. Ok, baby?"

Leida nodded, she decided to play submissive. She also suspected that he had chosen to do this next since it meant she wouldn't be able to get her claws on him and he would be at an advantage.

"To make it more natural, I'll chase you. Don't just stand there and allow me to jump on you. You wouldn't do that in battle and you won't do that now. I'll get you when you least expect it because they will always take you by surprise. Are you ready?" Otuss stood tall; Leida could see marks on his sides from where she'd dug her claws into him. She hadn't drawn blood but the fur was ruffled there.

She nodded. "Ready" she said and trotted off. Behind her, Otuss's face contorted into that twisted smile again and he chuckled. Yes, she showed potential but that only meant he could really test her mettle by making it extra hard for her. There was no reason to go easy. She wanted to learn to fight, he'd teach her. The hard way.

Leida wandered further away from him, trotted and ran a few steps and then walked, keeping on the lookout for him simply because she couldn't help it. She was expecting him to jump on her at any moment. She looked across the grassy plain, watching other Gryphies training. She saw Odax flying in the air and watched as he did somersaults and loop the loops, flaming some other student.

Her mind was distracted and Otuss knew it. He ran up behind her, jumping into the air and leaping on her, pushing her to the ground in one motion, digging all his claws in roughly. Leida, taken by surprise completely, screamed and was forced down. She struggled and flapped her wings, well she tried to. They had been folded and Otuss had intended to keep them that way. He was holding them closed with his claws. She got one out and flapped it around, trying to get him off her, of course her wing didn't reach that far and in the way she wanted it to. His claws dug in deeper as he maintained his grip, laughing maliciously.

Oh yeah, you enjoy your grikking job, don't you? Leida thought with spite. She wondered if he'd killed any Lizariaouses, she suspected he had and that he had killed them with satisfaction too.

He was a lot heavier than her. Male Gryphies were heavier set than females anyway, the female being slimmer and more delicate unless she was trained in advanced combat in which case she gained a few muscles as she became stronger. Leida wasn't though, she wasn't very strong. But the pain he was inflicting upon her was starting to make her lose her temper. She really, really disliked him a lot. She tried turning her head to flame him but she couldn't turn it far enough.

"Give up yet, baby?" she heard him sniggering in her ear. Leida merely growled, not giving him the satisfaction of a worded reply.

She bucked her back legs upwards but only succeeded in falling over as they left the ground. Now she was flat on her belly.

"Well that was a stupid thing to do. You're dead for sure once your feet are taken from beneath you. There is no way you can stand up again. Only strong Gryphies buck their bodies like that, ones who could actually knock the opponent off them. You'll never be strong enough to do that. You need to think of other ways. One little snap of my teeth and your neck is broken, you're dead." Otuss laughed and got off her. Leida lay there pathetically, panting and trying to get her breath back.

Otuss stood beside her. "Get up then. Don't lie there like a lazy slob."

Leida slowly pulled herself into a sitting position. She looked at him grudgingly.

"We're gunna have to work on this one, baby. Ok, here's a tip. If a Lizariaous leaps on you, chances are you'll have your wings folded. The enemy is at a big advantage if they hold them closed. It means less limbs that can struggle and throw them off. So when you walk on the battlefield, hold your wings out like this, don't fold them completely, just hold them at the ready." He demonstrated this. "You got that?"

"Yes." Replied Leida and stood up, holding her wings as he did. She nearly said "Yes, Sir" but she quickly bit her tongue. She would never refer to him as "Sir" since she had no respect for him.

Otuss pulled one of her wings out a bit, roughly. "No; like that. Then when they jump on you, they will grab a hold on your back and not your wings. This leaves the wings free to move and they can't do anything about it. If they get a grip on them, they will rip them and you won't be able to fly. Ripped wings are the hardest things to heal. If holes in them don't heal, it's hard if not impossible to fly properly ever again. They are your most important part. If you were as strong as me, you could fly into the air with the enemy on your back and drop them from a height, hopefully smashing them on the ground below. Some jump off once they realise you are taking off but it's the ones who hold on for dear life who are the fun ones." He stopped talking as he had erupted into laughter at this. "They make such wonderful breaky noises."

Leida felt sick. Maybe this guy was a Lizariaous disguised as a Gryphie. She had thought that many times. He was too vile to be a member of her species. She also doubted he had a mate.

"So, we will try again. But this time for grik's sake, be ready." Otuss waited for her to walk off.

Leida hated how he swore so much. "Grik" was usually only used when the speaker was very angry or annoyed. It was a nasty word in the Gryphie language. Lizariaouses also used it. It was about the only universal swear word the two species shared and it meant something vile and disgusting. Well, then it suited Otuss thought Leida.

Once again she was lost in her own thoughts and he caught her unawares. Except this time at least her wings were ready. She had made sure to hold them folded but not flush to her body. She felt him land on her but he did it silently, only growling once he had made contact with her soft fur.

Leida roared, her wings flapping about and she ran a few steps with him on her back. He laughed and dug his claws in deeper, however he was struggling to stay on her, she mentally noticed this and smirked. She flapped her wings and started running.

On her back, Otuss was thinking she was stupid to try to take off. He knew she was trying to prove herself but decided to let her do as she wished, he was curious as to whether or not she would manage to get off the ground with him on her back. He highly doubted it.

Leida was flapping furiously, she reared up on her hind legs but he clung on. She had hoped he would fall off because even she knew that he was too heavy to allow her to get off the ground. But nevertheless, she carried on, kicking off the ground with her feet. Otuss tried to get a grip on her neck and force her into submission but she was moving too much and he couldn't manage it, most of his attention was spent on trying to keep his grip on her. If he could just stay on long enough to wear her out, she was flailing around like a trapped sea vulture.

But Leida kept on going, kept persisting and finally managed to get off the ground. It was hard and her wings felt like they would explode from the effort but very slowly she was managing to rise a little into the air. Her back feet were still touching the ground as she kicked out one at a time. The motion of her wings kept smacking Otuss about and he couldn't hold on much longer. A Lizariaous would dig its claws in deeper to maintain a hold but of course this was training and Otuss wouldn't allow himself to do that. Much as he found her to be annoying, he knew that if he hurt her badly, Diabloss would be on him and he would not take it lightly. Otuss had seen Diabloss punish one of his soldiers once. It had not been pretty.

Leida gave a huge roar and with one final, massive effort, her wings swooped up and she took off, knocking Otuss right off her and onto his back on the ground. With his weight gone, she found it much easier to move and flew into the air, then back down, landing a little way away. Her wings ached badly and she couldn't have stayed airborne for long, she needed to rest them.

Otuss rolled over and stood up. Well, it was a foolish thing for her to do, try to take off with him on her back, given her lack of strength but he couldn't deny that she was determined. He had expected her to use her wings as weapons and whack him right off her back like she should have done. She was trying to prove herself, he knew that. She would have a lot of proving to do before her training was finished.

Leida slumped, wings on the ground either side of her, hanging limp.

Otuss went up to her. "Well, you got me off but that was pretty stupid."

"Why?" asked Leida. "I got you off didn't I? That was what I was supposed to do, wasn't it?" She was annoyed that once again he had a problem with how she handled things.

"Yeah, you did. But you also wore yourself out. The thing is to be fast, use your wings to whack 'em around a little, smack them in the face, use your wing claws. Lift your wings and get them in a headlock. If you lift them right, you can actually grab the enemy and throw them off. Like this." He demonstrated, lifting his wings where the thumb-like part was and pretending to grab and throw an invisible Lizariaous off him.

"That's why we keep our wings ready. They're our greatest asset against these guys. Now look, you've worn yourself out. We'll have to stop for this sun cycle. You're getting better but you're still pathetic, baby."

Leida looked disgruntled. She wished he'd give her more credit. He was right of course; she shouldn't have tried to show off like that. She felt as though she had embarrassed herself.

"Come back at sunrise and we'll carry on. And next time, no grikking showing off. You have nothing to prove, I already know you're pathetic without you demonstrating that. You only make an idiot of yourself." He turned to leave.

Leida opened her mouth to tell him that he had to admit that she had impressed him earlier with the whole winding and throwing off thing. But she closed her mouth again, sighed, got up, turned around and walked off the other way. She glanced over her shoulder as she walked, seeing Otuss talking to another student. She knew training would be hard but she at least expected some encouragement. She walked back to where Diabloss was waiting. He was laid out on a large rock, his usual watching place and he sat up as she approached.

"Hey, what's up? You look disheartened." Diabloss looked at her with concern.

"Oh it's just Otuss. He won't give me any credit. We did a training procedure where he rolled me over and pinned me. I kicked up and winded him, then I dug my claws into him hard and he got off. I got it right and all he did was complain." Leida snarled.

"Well he's a tough coach. He's just like that. I saw what you did. I sensed he was impressed but it's only the beginning. It's easy to impress with a few lucky shots. If he's impressed in the long run and you can really get the better of him in battle, then he will compliment you."

"Yes, I know. But I was foolish and wore myself out. I shouldn't have shown off."

"Well you'll know next time. I think you're doing well. Let's go get some food and afterwards you can train with me, a little homework. You can show me what you've been learning and how well you are doing. I'm sure you will impress me because I can see you've improved nicely." Diabloss smiled and Leida cheered up a little. She would be more relaxed and happy training with Diabloss and also doing this "homework" meant that she would hopefully improve in leaps and bounds and show off her fast learning ability. Otuss might not compliment her but at least he would see she was putting her heart and soul into it.

"Yes, I'd like that. I'll have a rest and we can train a bit on the edge of the forest. Could you catch my food for me? I'm very tired."

Diabloss nodded. "It's not a problem" he replied and they left the training grounds.

The soldiers in Dyarkroeen were also busy training still. They had gotten onto the second group and the soldiers were doing well. Croter and Zarkiz had messed up a little, only being involved in guarding most of their lives. Direct combat was taking some getting used to. No one much bothered guards and so, although they were trained to fight like any other soldier, they never had the chance to really, so they got out of practise.

The cave cat exercise had also been successful. They had gone through about three cave cats. Even without killing them the trauma and fright was too much for them and they had to be killed when they were reduced to shivering bundles.

Most of the soldiers had been sent out to hone their skills now they knew what kind of training to do and would do this for a few weeks. Mordred had given them all a talk about how important this was. They couldn't fail. He even went so far as to lie and say that if they didn't bring down Mettalika, they would all be either killed or reduced to work as rock diggers. He knew the soldiers would be punished if they failed but also knew that Zephirak wouldn't fire that many soldiers. No, it would be he, Mordred, who would bear the bitter brunt of shame and humiliation by being a digger. Not only that but it was likely that Zephirak would also parade him around as someone who had failed and use him as an example to other commanders of what they would be reduced to should they fail. He couldn't mess up. His life and reputation depended on this. With these words to the soldiers, they trained themselves hard at all hours, having only one break for food and only stopping for a rest when they literally could not keep going.

Mordred hadn't seen Zephirak at all that sun cycle. He had woken up early in the morning and got the soldiers organised with the training exercises and Zephirak hadn't even bothered to come and see how they were doing. Mordred found this odd but it also gave him a chance to try and get the soldiers all passing their tasks and going off to train by themselves so that if enough passed, maybe Zephirak would be more impressed. The first group was gone and the second group was half way through the basic exercises.

"What the grik are you doing?" Mordred yelled at Croter who had decided to fire needles at the Lizariaous with the water spraying device.

"Getting the problem at its source, Sir!" yelled back Croter.

"You're supposed to dodge it you fool, not attack. Do you really think you could aim right with a Gryphie flaming you like that? Look, you're soaked. If that was real fire you would be a ball of flames by now. Go and sit out, watch the others train for a while and learn from them you moron."

Croter grudgingly wandered over to the side and sat down moping and grumbling. Well he had thought it was a good idea even if his commander didn't.

Zarkiz laughed. "Croter you idiot! I knew you'd mess up."

"Shut up Zarkiz!" snapped Croter.

"Oooh, can't take a little criticism? You'll never be as good as me, watch me when I'm out there, pick up some tips."

"Look you stuffed up egomaniac; I can take criticism, from my *commander*, not you. I happened to have been being smart by getting the problem at its source and not just running away."

"Hey, I was only giving you tips, just trying to help. You heard what Mordred said about it anyway, don't stand there trying to take out a Gryphie who's flaming you for all they're worth. Unless you want to be a pile of ash of course!" Zarkiz could stand it no longer and burst out laughing.

Croter could stand it no longer and cuffed him across the face with a paw.

"Hey, take a joke! Cos you sure looked like one out there!! Hahaha!" Zarkiz snorted.

Croter growled. "One more word out of you about it and I'll be using *you* as target practise."

"Fine, fine whatever. Honestly you need to learn to laugh at yourself...cos, well, everyone else was!" Zarkiz had gotten into the swing of it and couldn't help himself now.

Croter was getting really angry by this time. "I gave you a chance, now shut the grik up!!" He pushed Zarkiz over and leaped on him, his claws at Zarkiz's throat and his needles aimed at Zarkiz's head. He pushed down. Zarkiz struggled beneath him, his tail thrashing and trying to get a grip round Croter's leg so he could throw him off. Zarkiz tried to protest but only succeeded in making choking noises.

"This is what you get for not dropping things" growled Croter and pushed down harder on Zarkiz, digging his claws into his skin and growling deeply, his eyes looking directly into the eyes of his comrade.

Mordred heard the scuffles and growls, he looked round to see them both fighting and watched for a while to see if they would break it up by themselves. Fights never usually got serious enough for deaths to occur, only injury which was sometimes pretty major. In which case, the commanding officer would separate the fighting soldiers. When Mordred saw they didn't split up, he stepped in, running up and yelling.

"Hey, you two, cut it out! Save the fighting for practise."

Croter appeared not to hear, his mind and anger solely directed at Zarkiz.

"Croter, I said, cut it out!" growled Mordred and shot a needle at Croter. It hit him in the side and Croter yelped in surprise, getting off Zarkiz when he realised it was Mordred who shot the needle.

"Sorry Sir. He was mocking my training attempts on the field." Croter explained and pulled out the needle. Lizariaous poison doesn't affect Lizariaouses.

"Then tell him to shut up about it but don't lose yourself over it." Mordred scolded.

"I did Sir. He wouldn't shut up so I thought I'd shut him up."

"You should have ignored him then. Were you born last sun cycle? Getting pulled in and annoyed by stupid remarks. And Zarkiz keep your dumb opinions to yourself in the future. Now both of you sit and wait to be called up again. And no more fighting!" Mordred turned and stalked off. The training was hard enough and the sun cycle was long enough without soldiers getting into scraps. He honestly didn't need that as well.

Croter sighed and sat down. Zarkiz sniggered. "And that's what you get for being pulled in by my remarks. I was only having some fun."

"Shut up" was Croter's only reply and he turned his back to Zarkiz to watch the other soldiers training.

Chapter 19
Homework

Over in Shernaron Leida and Diabloss had finished their meal and were now at the edge of the forest ready for Leida to show Diabloss what Otuss had taught her.

Diabloss did his best Lizariaous impression and pounced on her, pinning her down on her back. Leida tried to kick out but she was afraid of hurting him so she used the soles of her feet instead of digging her claws in. This made no effect on Diabloss.

"Come on Leida, throw me off! Dig your claws in and get rid of me."

"I...can't. I don't want to hurt you."

"You won't hurt me. Well, you may a little but I don't mind, I'm supposed to be a Lizariaous and you wouldn't be afraid of hurting one of those, would you?"

Leida shook her head.

"Well then, show me what you've learned from Otuss."

Leida readied herself and suddenly kicked against Diabloss's belly, digging in all her claws and raking them along it in an unpleasant and painful manner, pushing him at the same time and he toppled backwards, giving her time to slide out from under him and escape.

"Excellent! That's it. Now, I'm gunna keep coming at you. Chances are that they will try to bring you down one at a time or in a pack so as soon as you escape from one of them; you will have to escape from another and another, all over again. Now, let's begin the proper practise!"

Leida nodded, determination showing in her face and she readied herself again.

Diabloss pounced on her again and again, pushing her onto her back with ease and trying to keep her pinned long enough to bite down on her neck. Each and every time, Leida kicked him off. After about the 8th time, she was struggling to get him off her as her back legs were tiring.

Diabloss sat back and had a rest, as did she.

"That's great! You're doing very well. I am impressed at your stamina. We will do this training once a sun cycle, working up the amount of times I try to pin you each time. Soon your legs will be strong enough to keep going for a long while and defend yourself very efficiently. How are you feeling?"

Leida was panting a little. "Well, I'm tired" she smiled. "But I think I'm doing better now. You're bigger and heavier than Otuss so it's harder to flip you off me. Have I scratched you much?" She looked worried.

"No, I'm fine. I trained some of my soldiers, or at least helped them practise in between training with Strassor. So I'm used to it." He smiled warmly and Leida felt reassured.

"Next we will have a little go at dodging my fire. Pretending again that I am a Lizariaous of course!" He grinned.

Leida laughed. "What about you jumping on my back? Should I train for that too?"

"No not this sun cycle. It takes more energy than dodge practise and I think you've lost enough energy for one sun cycle. You need to be feeling rested enough to carry on tomorrow. The more we train and practise, the stronger you will become, the more energy you will have and the longer you will be able to keep training. Sessions can last a good few hours then and you will improve very fast. So, let's begin." He got up and so did Leida.

Diabloss shot a few blasts at her and she dodged each one. Then he slowly worked it up with longer and longer blasts of fire. She flew and he tried to shoot her down from the sky too. Leida dodged them all and only got skimmed by one once, it caught her leg.

After this, Diabloss sat back down. "Ok, very good, I am impressed. Once again your legs got hit though. You need to hold them closer to your body when you fly and try to keep them under you more when you run. And don't forget to use your wings as a shield when you're on the ground."

Leida nodded, listening to his advice carefully.

"I think you're doing great my love. You show great potential where speed and acceleration are concerned and your stamina isn't bad." He put a hand on her shoulder and smiled. "Well done."

Leida blushed. "I'm glad it impressed you at least."

"Of course it did! But I may be biased since I love you." He nuzzled her softly.

Suddenly they heard flapping wings. It was Kayto, one of Diabloss's squadron of elite fighters and he landed nearby.

"Diabloss, Sir, Mettalika has been causing trouble again. There's a massive fight broken out to the east of the swamp. She's attacking a couple of young Lizariaouses but a Gryphie has been caught up in it too. She's paranoid! She attacked the Gryphie because he was nearby and she thought he was with the Lizariaouses. She seems to think everyone is turning on her for some reason." Kayto blurted out, panting and frantic.

"She must have seen Sinxo rescuing Jadariol" Diabloss murmured.

"You have to come and help. Five more of us are there but she has all three of the victims cornered and we can't pass her to get to them."

"I'm coming. I'll see you later, Leida" Diabloss gave Leida a quick lick on the cheek and took off with Kayto to go to the rescue.

Leida watched them fly off thinking how brave and respected her mate was, pride growing in her heart.

She decided to take a walk to the cliffs and sit to think for a while. So she headed away from the forest and towards the coast of Shernaron. Her mind was filled with thoughts of training and getting better. She was thinking about any small things she did that she needed to improve upon.

Suddenly something flew past her head. She thought it was a sea vulture and ignored it. Another flew past and she turned to the direction it came from. They weren't sea vultures, they were needles and they were coming from a pack of three Lizariaouses, a hunting pack.

Leida tried not to panic. She was very lucky that the needles had missed but now they knew she was aware of their presence and they attacked full on.

Leida's ears went back and she ran, using her wings as a shield. Some needles bounced off them. She needed to take off but stretching her wings to do that would leave her body exposed. So she decided to run to the cliff edge and take off there. She could hear them growling and mocking her, hungry for her blood. Not much further now though, she was confident that she would make it. The fastest Lizariaous had run up beside her now. Generally, because they were heavier, Lizariaouses couldn't run as fast as Gryphies. However, they had much more stamina. Gryphies, more at home flying, had more strength in their wings than their legs and could fly for far longer periods without tiring. So a pack of hunter Lizariaouses would try to prevent a

Gryphie taking off and running it down until they could run level with it and take it out that way.

Leida snarled at the Lizariaous who snapped and shot a needle at her. She flapped her wing and hit it away. He fired another and she hit that away too. Otuss had never told her she could bat needles away with her wings. Another had come up beside her now, a female hunter. She shot needles at Leida too but Leida batted those away. Leida focused most of her concentration on running; she didn't want to slow down for even a moment because it meant the other Lizariaous could catch up. The one who would leap on her back. The third hunter would always leap on the back of the victim while the other two ran either side to make sure the victim slowed or stumbled. Since Leida had been training most of the sun cycle, she did not have as much energy as she would normally.

Come on, I can do it, just a little further. She willed herself to keep on, dying to take off and give her legs a rest. Finally she saw the edge of the cliff. It was there in her sights, she felt hope rising. She would escape! She was putting her training into action and she would escape!

But the third hunter had launched himself at her. She was now slow enough that he could leap on her. She stumbled and yelped as she felt his claws make contact with her back and dig in. She couldn't stop, if she did, she would be dead. With one final surge of energy, Leida approached the cliff edge and launched herself off with her passenger on board. She spread her wings as she leaped. He hadn't been able to pin her wings since she had had them gathered about her as a shield and had kept using them to bat away needles. As her feet left the cliff and she went over the edge, the weight of the Lizariaous on her made her fall a few feet before she

181

could gain lift again, her wings sweeping forwards in huge powerful motions. The other two stood on the cliff edge still firing needles at her, not seeming to care that if she fell and died on the rocks below, so would their comrade.

Leida now tried to throw off the Lizariaous. But he wouldn't move. He clung like a limpet to a rock and his claws were dug in so deep that they were starting to draw blood. Leida knew there was only one thing for it.

She flew upwards in a long, slow curving motion. Then she looped upside down and he fell off. She finished the loop and hovered, watching him fall. He fell in the sea because by that time, she had flown a little way out. She saw him swimming to shore, disgruntled and heard his angry grumbles. Leida laughed at her achievement. Over on the cliff edge the other two watched her angrily.

"Damn you, Gryphie!" they yelled. Leida flew closer. Maybe target practise for real would be good training.

"I'll give you another chance" she called to them, flying ever closer. "See if you can hit me. If you can then you get a meal, but if you can't then I have made a fool of all of you!"

They pointed their needles right at her, waiting for her to move a little closer.

Leida pulled a face. "You couldn't hit the backside of a forest deer! You have awful aim. You're pathetic examples of hunters!"

This really made them mad and they started firing needles at her. She dodged them all and hovered, mocking them still. The female Lizariaous fired another needle at Leida and it narrowly missed her leg. This reminded her to keep her legs close to her. She flew in right above them.

"Come on, I'm so close and yet you still can't hit me!"

She swished her tail disrespectfully and pulled another face.

They shot the needles right up at her but she swerved off to one side and they all missed.

Leida laughed at them. The hunters got evermore angry and their aim got even worse because they weren't concentrating. Leida had found a new tactic. She was good at dodging so she could afford to play with them until they got so angry that they could no longer aim properly.

She flew inland more and they followed her. She could easily fly faster than they could run though and, becoming a bit bored and satisfied that her dodging skills were really good, he left them way behind.

Leida flew over the forest, cart wheeling and swooping about, feeling more achievement than she had ever felt before. She had done it. For the first time in her life she had taken on a pack of Lizariaouses with skill and courage. She had been confident that she had the upper hand and she had even managed to use her aerial skills to knock off an attacker.

The training was working! She couldn't wait to tell Diabloss. She even felt like boasting about it to Otuss although she doubted that he would even bother to say it was good. She suspected he would tell her off for playing with the enemy. But she didn't care. She saw Sinxo flying in the distance and flew up to catch up with her.

"Hi Sinxo!" yelled Leida.

Sinxo hovered and turned to greet her. "Hey Leida! You look happy, is training going well?"

Leida caught up and hovered near her. "It's going very well; in fact I just had a run in with a Lizariaous hunting pack!"

"And that is going well because?" Sinxo looked confused.

"Because I outsmarted them!" Leida announced proudly. "Using the training techniques I've been learning!"

"Well that *is* good news. We'll get the better of them yet!" Sinxo smiled, happy for her friend. Leida somersaulted and roared with joy. She was so happy to have finally gotten something right. It was an enormous confidence boost.

Sinxo started playing in the air too and soon both were flying around and showing off. It was so rare for things to actually go well for either of them.

Finally Leida stopped and Sinxo followed. They landed on a lone tree, not so far from the training grounds. Leida had a question.

"Have you heard anything about Mettalika's latest attack?" she asked.

"Why? No, no I haven't...what has she done?"

"Kayto came and told us, Diabloss has gone there now. Apparently Mettalika is holding up some Lizariaouses and a Gryphie too." Leida explained.

"Why a Gryphie?"

"She thinks the Gryphie is in league with the Lizariaouses. Diabloss thinks it's because you rescued Jadariol and Mettalika saw."

Sinxo looked horrified. "I didn't think she was watching when I made off with Jadariol. She was searching with her back to me." She looked at the ground. "Grik" she mumbled, "that means Mettalika is probably after me too..."

"Well she seems to think we are now working with the Lizariaouses to get rid of her" Leida said.

"If only that were true." Sinxo growled. The very thought of what she had seen Mettalika do to poor little

Jadariol made her blood boil. She immediately wished she was stronger, strong enough to fight Mettalika. "She caused this mess. We wouldn't constantly be living in fear if it wasn't for her."

"Diabloss already tried to band together with Zephirak over this but Zephirak wants total control. If it were that easy to just band together and rid ourselves of Mettalika then it would have been done long before now." Leida sighed. They both sat in silence for a while, neither looking at the other, only out over the training grounds in the distance.

"War is coming. The best we can do is train and be ready when the time comes." Leida said solemnly.

Sinxo growled in annoyance. "That's all we ever do, be ready, defend ourselves, back down. I know a lot of us are getting tired of this."

"Then talk to Mystik about it"

"I've tried, all she ever says is I must do my duty which is apprentice healer and not waste my time on a war that may not even happen."

"May not even happen? Of course it will happen! Even I had to accept that." Leida was shocked at Mystik's naivety.

"She keeps reassuring me that healing Jadariol will make Zephirak see sense. If you ask me and not to be disrespectful to my elders but I think she's going a bit in the head. She doesn't think it, she *hopes* it. She keeps her fingers crossed and hopes for the best."

"You do know she thinks this whole fiasco is her fault, right?"

"What, for saving Mettalika? No, she'd be stupid to think that. Mettalika was nothing like she is now before the accident happened. Mystik would never have guessed that would happen; she was saving a life. Anything could have happened; Mettalika may not even have survived the operation, would Mystik have blamed herself for that? I don't think so. She's wiser than that." Sinxo had a lot of faith in her teacher even if she didn't approve of some of her decisions.

Leida shook her head. "Think what you like but Mystik does regret her decision. Even if she doesn't blame herself for all this, she still realises that saving Mettalika was a mistake. Yes, she never would have guessed that would happen but its tearing her up inside to think of it."

Sinxo gave her an odd look. "Did she tell you this?" she asked.

"No, but I know that's how she feels."
"You don't know. You can't know; how could you? You just assume but you don't know." She started to snarl a little.

"I've seen her, seen the worry on her face whenever she hears of an attack. Ask her. If I'm wrong then you can tell me and laugh at me for being presumptuous. If I'm right well then, I'm right."

Sinxo flew off without another word. That had always unnerved her about Leida. She seemed to be able to sense things others couldn't. Not all the time, just sometimes. But it was still unnerving.

She flew back to the forest, landed and walked through the trees, passing young Gryphies at play and a few guards having their lunch break and chatting together, mostly about who was the better fighter or hunter or who had the best way with females in the gathering.

Sinxo reached Mystik's tree. Mystik was inside tending to Jadariol so Sinxo waited for her to finish before she announced her presence.

"Ah, Sinxo, how did this sun cycle's scouting go?" Mystik smiled as she walked up to the young Gryphie.

186

"Pretty good although I heard of another attack. Mettalika is apparently holding up not only a bunch of Lizariaouses but a Gryphie too." Sinxo brought this up to see Mystik's reaction.

Mystik's face clouded with worry but she tried to hide it and returned to her usual serene expression. "I am sure it will be sorted out" she replied and turned to her tree.

"Mystik..." Sinxo ventured.

Mystik looked round. "Yes, my dear?"

"Do you ever blame yourself for all this...the war I mean and how things are now?" Sinxo watched her carefully.

Mystik let her worry and regret show now. "Sometimes one thinks one makes the right decision. When a decision is completely for the good and one thinks nothing bad could ever come of it. I felt pride that sun cycle. That I had saved someone against all the odds, rescued a life. Do you know what it is like to wish you had never done the good thing? It is a horrible feeling. Yes. I do blame myself. For all of this. But I will make it right again. We will heal Jadariol and return him, peace will come again and our two species won't be hateful any more." Mystik brushed a small tear from her cheek. To wish someone had died was an awful feeling but she wished with all her heart that she hadn't saved Mettalika and that she had left her to die. This made her feel corrupt when she had always been so pure and good.

Sinxo didn't even want to venture and suggest what might happen if the peace offering didn't work. She merely replied "I'm sorry, Mystik" bowed her head and turned, walking away slowly.

Mystik watched her leave and sat down. Suddenly she felt so tired.

Chapter 20
Against the World

Diabloss had flown with Kayto and they had arrived near the swamp where Mettalika stood before two very frightened Lizariaouses and a terrified Gryphie. She was flaming the five members of the squad who were trying to persuade her to let them go.

"No! You're all working together, you're all against me. I'll kill, yes I will, I'll kill *all* of you!!!" Mettalika snarled, her eyes burning with fury, her wings spread threateningly and her nostrils flared, billows of smoke rising from them.

"You sound just like Zephirak."

Mettalika looked up and saw Diabloss.

"I'll kill you too! Stop trying to stand in my way. Those who consort with Lizariaous scum deserve to die like them. You notice me now but only when I have to threaten others. Is this what you want? Is this the reason you notice me and ignore me the rest of the time? You want to see me kill don't you Diabloss, otherwise you would notice me more."

"Don't try to place the blame of your errors onto me, Mettalika. You are crazy, being a solitary for so long has made you like this; this has nothing to do with me."

"Oh but it does. You never noticed me before, nothing I did impressed you. It impresses you now though; your squad couldn't defeat me on their own so they had to call you to deal with me." Mettalika's mouth formed a snarled grin of insanity and amusement.

"It doesn't impress me, it disgusts me. You want to impress me? Don't kill any more. Stop being a fool. One sun cycle you will be killed and none of us will care. Not even me."

"Then *you* kill me...any of you!" she looked around at the rest of the squad who were hovering or stood ready nearby.

Kayto spoke up. "We would be murderers like you then. We don't want to be as bad as you, Mettalika."

"No one does! No one dares try to kill me because I am stronger than all of you. You *fear* me, don't you?" she erupted into a spiteful laugh.

Diabloss had had enough. The two Lizariaouses were huddled together, one had been reduced to tears and the Gryphie was trying to hide behind them, even more fearful.

"You like me? Then please me. Let them go" Diabloss said firmly.

Mettalika gave him an odd look. "If I did that, afterwards you would simply leave. I'd have no meal and I doubt you'd respect me. Nice try."

"I would respect you; I'd respect you for doing the right thing."

"Doing the right thing? Like Mystik you mean? It was right for me but it's totally grikked up the rest of you hasn't it? I choose not to do the right thing. The right thing is the *wrong* thing; you of all Gryphies should know that. I'm helping you. I'll kill Zephirak for you! I can end this war. If you wish to be with me that is, Diabloss. Be my mate and I will dispose of your biggest problem." Mettalika grinned and narrowed her eyes at him. She suspected he would say no but there was no harm in trying.

"Right now, *you* are my biggest problem" growled Diabloss.

"Ooh flatterer!" sneered Mettalika.

Diabloss was wound right up now. He wanted to end it, save the youngsters in peril and leave.

189

"What do you say then?" Mettalika smirked and gazed directly into his eyes.

"I say...NO!" Diabloss roared and suddenly leaped on Mettalika, taking her by surprise and knocking her over. The Lizariaouses and the Gryphie fled in terror as soon as they could get past her.

Mettalika, furious now, leaped up and flew at Diabloss's throat. He shielded himself with his wings but her tail whipped in under his legs and tripped him up, the steel vice shaped end of her tail closing on one of his back legs and cutting into it painfully.

Kayto and the others immediately dashed at her, attacking her all at once and forcing her back. Mettalika flamed them but Diabloss had already taken off when he had the chance and was flying away. She didn't follow. Instead she tried to take her temper out on the Gryphie nearest but his comrades butted in and flamed her, biting and clawing at her until she could take it no more. She made her escape but not before she'd taken a trophy with her; half the tail of the Gryphie she had attacked.

Diabloss flew back to the forest. His leg hurt but he put up with it. He needed to land somewhere and check how bad the damage was.

Eventually he found a secluded ledge and landed there to check his leg out. It had a deep gash but nothing too serious and it would heal by itself.

He took this time to compose himself and think about what had just happened. Mettalika was getting worse. He'd never seen her so worked up and crazy like that before and he didn't like it. She was starting to become out of control. Diabloss was starting to feel fear himself now, fear of her temper and personality which was breaking down and beginning to disintegrate. Something else was kicking in, something more sinister.

She was like a Gryphie version of Zephirak and it greatly disturbed Diabloss. He had no idea what her true goal was now. In the beginning it had been revenge but now she killed simply because she got a kick out of it. If she hated Zephirak that much why didn't she just kill him off and get it over with? Because then she would have nothing more to do. Once Zephirak was dead, Mettalika would have no purpose so she killed the other Lizariaouses as an excuse and also to get to Zephirak. Then there was all this stupidity with her wanting him to be her mate. Diabloss was troubled by this even more because he knew if she wanted to, she could kill Leida in an effort to be with him. Except she knew full well that doing that would only make Diabloss hate her more, however the way things were going, she might not stay sane enough to remember that.

Diabloss was angry and confused, wanting to know how to sort everything out in a way that wouldn't have anyone come to harm. But inside he knew Mettalika had to die. It was the only way. Maybe with her dead, Zephirak would give up his stupid ideas of ruling over all the lands. He threw back his head and roared in annoyance and stress.

Leida had remained where she was after Sinxo left. She knew she'd been right about Mystik but she understood that Sinxo wouldn't believe her, since she had so much faith in the wisest of the gathering. She lay down on a large branch and enjoyed the cool air. Soon she heard wings overhead and looked up. It was the squadron who had fought Mettalika. Kayto saw her and alighted nearby while the others flew back to the forest. Leida sat up.

"How did it go?" she asked.

"Not well...not well at all. Mettalika went crazy when she saw Diabloss and took half of Bronro's tail because she couldn't drive Diabloss down. She got him in the leg but I think he's ok. The youngsters escaped luckily. So everyone else was ok." Kayto replied.

Leida looked worried. "Are you sure Diabloss is ok?"

"Yeah he's fine, she got that tail blade thing around his leg and clamped it down, he got a nasty gash but he's fine, he flew away ok at least."

"At least? Then you can't be sure?"

"Well like I said he looked fine to me, he wasn't nursing the leg as he flew. He's a big boy; he can take care of himself." Kayto smiled reassuringly but it didn't work. Leida had taken off to look for Diabloss before Kayto had even finished his sentence.

From the air, Leida let out a few short calls for Diabloss. They echoed across the valleys and plains. Gryphie calls travel a long way. Diabloss heard from his perch on the ledge and called back. Leida soon found him and alighted beside him.

"Are you ok?" she asked, rushing to his side.

Diabloss smiled, thankful for her presence. "Yeah I'm fine; my leg will heal by itself. I guess you heard what happened."

"Well, only that Mettalika took half of Bronro's tail and hurt your leg" She examined his leg carefully and when she realised there was nothing to worry about, she relaxed.

"Yeah, she went a bit, well, actually extremely crazy. I've never seen her like that before, she was starting to get out of control and I knew I had to end it as fast as possible. I'm worried now that if she's left, she'll get worse. She's been a solitary too long and it's affecting her mental state of mind."

Leida looked worried. "In that case I hope I never encounter her again."

"I hope so too" replied Diabloss, fearful for his mate's safety now Mettalika had taken this turn.

**

Back at the forest, Jadariol was being kept company by Lunara. She spent a lot of time with him since she knew from when she'd been ill over the winter time that it was boring being unable to go out and you really need friends to visit and keep you company or you get lonely.

She had also been learning from Mystik how to dress his wounds and give him medicine. Mystik was beginning to think she had a new apprentice on her hands. Lunara was very enthusiastic about helping. Jadariol wasn't walking quite yet, his injuries wouldn't allow it but he was starting to sit up more and was less tired. He also valued Lunara's company. The other young Gryphies were fearful of him and wouldn't visit.

Right now, Lunara was feeding him. She held the bowl up to his muzzle so he could drink. The food was a mix of berries all mushed up together and it was his dessert. His main meal had been a sea vulture, a really large one that a hunter Gryphie had brought back. Jadariol was starting to feel rather full now.

He pushed the bowl away with his nose. "I'm ok now, I don't want any more."

"Ok! Are you sure you're full?" Lunara asked.

"Yes, besides I don't like fruit that much. Lizariaouses are carnivores, we don't normally eat them. You guys eat everything, right?"

"Yes, pretty much...even bugs!" Lunara giggled.

"Eww!" Jadariol pulled a disgusted face.

"Oh come on, we eat meat, that's all bugs are. They're just smaller and wiggly."

"I don't...really wanna hear any more. I might throw up what I've just eaten." Jadariol lay down.

"*You* being made queasy by bugs? That's silly; I bet Lizariaouses do much worse than that. Hey, do you guys tell stories? We do. Late summer moon cycles we sit in the clearing and have a storytelling evening. When it gets colder, we light a fire and sit around it with the flames shining blue on our faces."

"What kind of stories do you tell?" asked Jadariol.

"Mostly ones about what we've been doing that sun cycle or funny things that have happened to us. Some of the soldiers or guards will tell of battles they've won against Lizar...er...other creatures and sometimes the best storytellers will make up stories if we don't have much to tell that moon cycle. Sometimes the stories they make up are scary, about the Moon Wraiths." Lunara explained.

"What are Moon Wraiths?" asked Jadariol, with great interest.

"They're the spirits that haunt the forest at moon cycle. I've heard stories of young Gryphies who have wandered off in the forest at moon cycle and never been seen again. The older Gryphies say the stories aren't true, that they're just made up to scare kittens but I know they're true..." she trailed off.

"How come?" asked Jadariol.

Lunara moved very close to him and whispered; "Because I saw one!"

"You saw a Moon Wraith?" he looked at her with scepticism.

Lunara nodded in excitement. "Yes! A few lunars ago. I snuck out to the waterfall because I'd left something there earlier that sun cycle and it was getting dark when I was coming home. I saw a Moon Wraith moving through the trees a little way away and I stopped and watched it."

"Yeah sure, it could just have been a Gryphie." He didn't believe her.

"It wasn't! It was a Moon Wraith! They look like Gryphies but they have feathered wings, which this one had. And they're black with a blue aura around them, which this had."

"You sure you weren't imagining it?"

Lunara snarled. "I don't imagine things like that."

"I bet you do, your head was full of the stories and you saw a Gryphie or some other creature and thought it was a Moon Wraith."

"Why don't you believe me?" Lunara looked saddened.

"Well there's every possibility you saw one but let's face it, you said yourself that they say these stories are made up to scare kittens." Jadariol had a point.

"Yeah but the idea must have come from somewhere. Whether Moon Wraiths are good or bad, someone must have seen one originally and come up with the idea to tell stories about them." Lunara insisted.

"Well yeah I guess. Or they could have seen something that inspired them to make it into a moon cycle spirit. What do Moon Wraiths do anyway? I mean, wandering around in the forest and never showing your face is pretty boring."

"Some say they watch over us to protect us. Others say they take those lost in the forest and show them a better place, one so good that they never want to return to this existence. And of course others say they kill those lost in the forest and that's why they're never seen again. I like the first reason for them best. Protectors." Lunara looked distant as she imagined powerful moon cycle creatures defending the forest from those wanting to destroy the gathering.

"If they protect then why do you have guards?" asked Jadariol.

"Because the Moon Wraiths can't be expected to do everything. We don't demand anything of them and so they look out for us as a favour because we let them live in our forest."

"Ok, now you're making up your own story for them." Jadariol chuckled.

"Well, do Lizariaouses tell stories?" Lunara asked.

"Yeah, actually we do. Mostly about battles but sometimes we make up stories about how we would kill our enemies. We have several good storytellers and it's mostly them who tell the stories. We relate to things we've done that sun cycle though. Good hunting trips, brave battles, that sort of thing." Jadariol told her.

"Do you have any made up spirits and things?"

"Not really. There is a cursive spirit we place on our enemies but it's not really talked about now. That was from the old times, we just don't believe in things like that any more."

Lunara looked happy though. "But you're not so different from us, we tell stories, so do you and we tell similar ones too. You know, about our sun cycles and battles and things."

"Yeah I suppose we do." Jadariol nodded.

"I wish that stupid Zephirak would give up on the idea of only seeing our differences and see what we have in common more. We never hurt him, he's a fool. What do you think of him?" Lunara noticed that Jadariol's expression had darkened and she guessed he wasn't too keen on his leader either. In reality, Jadariol had been annoyed by her comments about Zephirak.

Jadariol seemed to be battling emotions. He finally replied. "Zephirak is brave; he is a good fighter and our leader because of that."

"Yeah but what do *you* think of him?" asked Lunara.

Jadariol looked as if he really didn't want to answer but Lunara patiently waited. She figured if Zephirak heard stuff said against him that he would punish whoever said it.

"Zephirak is a good and fair leader and has never lead us astray yet. I respect his wishes and all that he stands for. If he wasn't a good leader someone else would have overthrown him."

"He can't hear you you know. It's ok to say stuff against him."

Jadariol snarled. "That is all I have to say."

"Ok, fair enough. But it's important to be yourself."

"I am."

Lunara decided to go back to the Moon Wraiths. "Look, I'll prove Moon Wraiths exist. When you can walk, we'll go sit in the forest one moon cycle and watch for a bit. You'll believe me if you see one, right?"

"I guess."

"Good, then we'll do that!" Lunara had brightened.

Jadariol simply nodded.

Outside, Diabloss and Leida had returned. Diabloss had flown into their tree but Leida had gone through the forest since she wanted a drink at the spring. She walked past the guards and entered the main part of the forest. Sinxo had seen her and took her aside for a word.

"I'm sorry, you were right. About Mystik." Sinxo told her.

"You asked her then?" asked Leida.

"Yes, and she does blame herself" replied Sinxo. I should have known you were right, you are right so often with these things.

"Yeah but not always. I can just sense these things." Leida was taking the compliment humbly.

"Yeah but mostly" insisted Sinxo. "If I need advice in the future I will come to you and I'll listen to you more." She didn't wait for a reply but just walked off. Leida knew she found it hard to admit about Leida being right because it meant Mystik wasn't quite as wise as Sinxo had always believed.

At Mystik's tree, Lunara greeted Leida.

"How is Jadariol doing?" asked Leida.

"He's ok, getting better. Hey, did you know that Lizariaouses tell stories just like we do? But they don't seem to be able to make stuff up as well as us. I mean, like the Moon Wraiths and things."

"Do you still believe those are real?" asked Leida.

"Do you?"

"I asked you first!"

"Yes" replied Lunara, "like I told you before, I saw one that time and I've been..." she lowered her voice, "Trying to get out at moon cycle to look for more but haven't been able to."

"Well, just don't get into trouble, remember what happened last time?" Leida warned.

"I won't wander away like last time; I just wanted to go a little way into the forest to where I was before by the waterfall but ever since what happened in Dyarkroeen, my Mum's been wary of letting me out of her sight."

"And I can't blame her either, I would be too."

Lunara suddenly asked something Leida didn't expect.

"Are you going to have kittens with Diabloss?"

"No, I don't wish to have kittens for now. I'm too much of a free spirit to be tied down raising them and I don't think I'd be much good at it either." Leida smiled.

"But what if Diabloss wants them? Would you have some then?"

"Maybe in the future but he isn't worried. Why these questions all of a sudden?" Leida was starting to think Lunara was asking too many questions.

"Well it's just that if you did have kittens, I'd be friends with them and teach them stuff. I've found out I like teaching things and telling stories. I think that's what I might do when I grow up."

"Well there are lots of younger kittens in the gathering, maybe you should teach them things?"

"At the moment I'm teaching Jadariol. He doesn't seem to have much of an imagination and he wouldn't say anything against Zephirak either, I think he's afraid Zephirak can hear him all the way over here." Lunara was clearly troubled by this.

"Or he might believe in Zephirak and respect him. Youngsters are often quite persuadable like that" smiled Leida.

"I'm not!"

"I never said you were; I said youngsters. Now I'm off to my tree for a rest. See you later, Lunara." Leida climbed up her tree leaving Lunara on her own to think about things.

***

A few sun cycles went by; life for a while was fairly pleasant for the Gryphies. Zephirak was mysteriously silent. In truth he'd been training up his soldiers with the help of Mordred for the oncoming fight with Mettalika. Things were going as planned and Mordred was content with the fact that Zephirak was committing all his attention to this and not to destroying or controlling all of Shernaron.

Mordred was on a lunch break of sorts and he sat with Schaarl near the training grounds. Both were tucking into sea vultures.

"I think this will really work! I have a great feeling about it, Schaarl. Zephirak seems to have changed, he's no longer losing his temper, look how positive he is!" Mordred smiled and they watched Zephirak encouraging his soldiers. Zephirak was happy and standing tall. He had been coming close to going crazy but now he seemed to be back to his old self, almost like he had been before his mate was taken by Mettalika.

Schaarl smiled. "I think this is really great, things will return to peace once the threat of Mettalika has gone. Maybe we can live as we used to again." She nuzzled Mordred and he smiled. These last few sun cycles had been wonderful. However, soon they would have to plan their attack on Mettalika. Mordred was half dreading this in case it was another failure but Zephirak kept reassuring him, much to his surprise, that if they did fail again that training would resume and they would keep on trying. They were spending a couple of lunars of heavy training to make sure all concerned were up to scratch physically and mentally. They wanted to ensure it would go well.

Chapter 21
Hero's Comeuppance

In Shernaron things had also been peaceful. Jadariol's wounds were healing well and Leida's training was going well. Her legs were still her greatest weakness though, she damaged them or came close to damaging them a lot and so it was decided that in battle she would have special armour made for them for protection.

She had told Otuss of her encounter with the Lizariaouses but he'd only told her not to pick fights since she wasn't yet strong enough and she'd end up getting seriously hurt taking risks like that. He also didn't stop calling her "baby".

During training with Diabloss one sun cycle, Leida mentioned about her encounter with the Lizariaouses. She hadn't done so previously because it had slipped her mind back when it had happened; she'd been more concerned with how Diabloss was after his encounter with Mettalika. That morning she had told Otuss which was what brought back the memory of it. She'd been so proud at the time and didn't understand why she had forgotten.

"Diabloss, back when you were fighting Mettalika last, I was also attacked by a pack of Lizariaouses." Leida had stopped flying about for a moment as they were in mid training. Diabloss immediately looked concerned.

"Why didn't you tell me? Are you alright? What did they do to you?"

"I'm fine, I outsmarted them using the techniques I've learned and they didn't have much of a chance. I wasn't scared of them either, I surprised even myself. They ambushed me on the cliff, one even jumped off it after me! But I simply flew up and laughed at them. I'm becoming much better with my confidence and fighting skills." Leida for once looked proud of herself.

Diabloss also looked proud. Now fighting was becoming a heavy part of life, it should be second nature to her to defend herself and it was certainly going well.

"You did great, I wish I could have seen it" he said, pride showing in his voice and expression.

Leida smiled. "Well, next time it happens, you probably will see." She knew there would be a next time, it was inevitable.

"Let's go for a flight" suggested Diabloss. "I want to show you where I patrol so you can get a good idea of what I do from sun cycle to sun cycle. I've never showed you before but now I think you are ready and if it gets dangerous, well, I'd like to see how you protect yourself. I'll be right beside you to defend you though if things go wrong."

Leida for the first time in her life looked excited about the prospect of such an adventure. She was no longer shy and retiring, she was becoming bold and strong. After all if she could put up with Otuss's nagging and lack of respect for her, she could face nearly anything.

They set out for a flight to the patrol areas.

***

Meanwhile, somewhere else in Shernaron, Sinxo was out gathering medicines again. This time it was to restock Mystik's inventory since Jadariol had been going through all the antiseptic and healing herbs pretty fast. Sinxo had a pouch around her neck for gathering what she had found. Right now she was looking for wing wort.

It wasn't just wings that it was useful for and Mystik wanted some for Jadariol's broken leg.

Something moved in the bushes and she stopped, her ears pricking up. She looked around but saw and smelled nothing. Whatever it was, it was either concealing itself well or it was nothing at all. She continued on her way, feeling unnerved and wanting to find the herb and get out of there as fast as possible. Another sound. Sinxo stopped again, sniffing the air with her soft nose and glancing about.

Suddenly a Furmine dashed out from under a bush and ran past her as though it had been taken by surprise. Sinxo wanted to ask what had scared it but it was gone before she could open her mouth to say anything.

She carried on, cautiously. Moments later she found the spot where the wing wort grew. But there was none there. Sinxo looked around. She was sure she'd had it right; this was where it was supposed to be. She sniffed and searched. She could smell the faint scent of it but found nothing. It was almost as if it had been there but someone had picked it all. She knew of somewhere else it grew anyway, a cave which was deeper into the forest past the swamp. It was pretty far though which was why she'd always gathered the herb from this spot. Sinxo sighed and trotted on. She hoped Mystik would appreciate the trouble she was going through to get hold of it.

All around her was eerily quiet, she wasn't quite sure why. She couldn't smell Mettalika though and found that as a blessing. Mettalika reeked of death and blood, a metallic smell from her armour and Sinxo was very surprised at, given the state of Mettalika's armour, that it didn't make more noise. It was hardly well oiled or cared for. It wasn't rusty; it had been created from the finest steel from the steel mountains and didn't rust. That could also be the reason for the fact it didn't creak, even when not cared for properly. Sinxo wandered on, now thinking about how Mettalika thought of herself. Since she didn't care for her appearance any longer, maybe she disliked herself, felt that she was inferior since she had always been a bad fighter and even when she had trained and gotten better no one had ever been that impressed. Sinxo thought Mettalika would make a great soldier and fighter. However when one chooses the path of darkness, they rarely turn back.

Sinxo was about the only Gryphie from the gathering who pitied Mettalika. Leida did too but most of the others disliked or hated her and the rest didn't even think about her since she never affected them in any big way. They all heard stories about her, Mettalika was common knowledge and a large conversational piece around the Forest but most wanted nothing to do with her more than hearing about her all the time.

Sinxo was nearing the cave now. She could see it in the distance and she picked up the pace. Her feet hit wet patches on the ground as the rain had come through the thick trees a little. Everything was still too quiet and she decided to pick up the wing wort and then fly out to gather the rest of the things she needed. It all unnerved her and the cave's black gaping mouth looked foreboding. She stepped up to the entrance and peered in. Nothing but black and the herb grew right at the back of the cave. She went in, using her nose to sniff it out. She'd picked up the scent and soon found it, gathering it in the darkness.

Once she had it all, she turned to leave…but her path was blocked by something and the light from the entrance was blotted out.

"H...hello?" Sinxo padded forward a bit, reaching out with a hand to see what was covering her path.

Suddenly it hit her; a rusty bloody smell. She drew back immediately and quivered. "Mettalika." That wasn't a question, it was a statement.

Cruel laughter filled the cave. "You let him escape and now you will make up for it."

Sinxo knew this was about Jadariol. "He was just a kid. You broke his leg and really hurt him; I couldn't just stand there and watch you do that."

"You shouldn't have interfered. It only proves my suspicions are correct. And now you will pay for what you did." Mettalika spat maliciously.

"What suspicions? That hurting youngsters is bad? That was why I saved him. He was little; he didn't deserve to be treated like that, through the fault of the others. This war is nothing to do with our youngsters; it's between the adults of the territories." Sinxo surprised herself at how she was standing up and not cowering in fear. Mettalika found this amusing since she was at an advantage and Sinxo wasn't.

"No, my suspicions are that the Gryphies and Lizariaouses are working together to rid the territories of *me*. You saved him; a Gryphie would never save a Lizariaous and that proves I am correct with my assumption. It started with them hunting us, then when you all found out how strong I was, you all felt threatened by me and decided to team up. I'm not stupid. You're all out to get me."

"You *are* stupid if you believe that to be true. This isn't about you or who's against you. There is a WAR going to start soon between the Gryphies and Lizariaouses because of a stupid decision that was made seasons ago. This has gone beyond you Mettalika. You are one Gryphie, we're gunna have the entire Lizariaous army on our backs soon unless something is done to restore peace to the territories. None of us want war. It brings hatred, death and destruction. However you did start it. Zephirak wouldn't be so vengeful on us all if you hadn't killed his mate. Then again if he was better at forgiving, this also wouldn't be happening. You are nothing in this; it has spiralled out of control now." Sinxo growled.

Mettalika suddenly swiped a steel clawed hand at Sinxo, tearing into her side. "I am EVERYTHING in this. You are trying to deceive me. Don't use Zephirak as an excuse, Sinxo. If you were really at war with the Lizariaouses then you would be glad I wanted to rid the world of that little vermin youngster."

Sinxo had fallen on her side and tried to get up now, gritting her teeth in pain. Mettalika's steel claws went deeper than regular Gryphie claws; far deeper.

"You're grikking deluded Mettalika. You've been a solitary far too long and it's having its effect on you now. You won't even listen to reason. I *told* you, it wasn't that I was trying to save a Lizariaous, I was trying to save an innocent youngster who has nothing to do with our fighting." Sinxo was panting softly from the effort of trying to stand.

"Oh you are so blind! That kid was probably the son of some soldier. They train them up to kill us. One less youngster to be trained is a good thing. He wandered into my area. It wasn't like I went out and looked for him although that wouldn't be a bad idea."

"No, you didn't just want to kill him, you wanted to make him suffer. Make him suffer for something his parents and leader did. Not him. You tortured him. A simple blow to the neck or slice of the stomach and he'd be dead but no, you weren't happy with making it fast, you broke his legs and mocked him. You disgust me. I

206

feel pity for you. You're a sad pathetic creature with a poisoned heart and no amount of armour or training will fix you. You're blind, you only see things your way and don't listen to others. You could have rejoined the gathering, been a part of the battle squadron but instead you've chosen this existence and it will be your undoing." Sinxo's eyes narrowed and she stood, snarling.

Mettalika laughed. "You have a lot of guts saying things like that to me considering your current situation. You have two options. Join me and I'll spare your life. If you think it's so bad being a solitary then I invite you to become a part of my gathering. If not, then I'll kill you here and now."

"Your gathering? You think everyone's against you. Why would you even trust me enough to let me join?"

"Because if you did, you would be with me, you wouldn't be allowed to return to the Forest and I would expect you to kill Lizariaous scum with me. If we recruit others, we can wipe them all out. Rid the territories of the Lizariaouses and this "war" as you call it, would be over."

"I think even less of you than I did before, if that's even possible" snarled Sinxo. "I would rather die than join you. And if you kill me, the rest of the Gryphies will find out and they'll hunt you down like a forest deer. Up until now you haven't killed a fellow Gryphie. If you do, then you are no better than Zephirak. So go ahead, kill me. You will regret it for the rest of your short and pathetic life."

Mettalika was really angry now, she hated being shot down and the fact Sinxo had compared her to her most hated enemy angered her even more. She leaped on Sinxo, slamming her to the ground and raking her steel claws along the Gryphie's body. Sinxo screamed out distress calls but no one heard. This had been an ambush, she realised it now. Mettalika had picked all the wing wort, forcing her to go to the cave instead. Deeper into the forest where no one could hear the attack. Since she'd been cornered in the cave there was no point talking nice to Mettalika, she knew she was as good as dead or at least severely injured and Mettalika never gave in to bargaining or sweet talking. Sinxo tried to fight back but kept hitting armour and only made the connection to Mettalika's body once. It was useless. Mettalika sank her teeth into one of Sinxo's wings, pulling her head up and breaking it with a crack. Sinxo screamed and tried to bite back but Mettalika's helmet stopped her. Her wings were already torn to shreds beyond repair from Mettalika's steel claws. She tried to go for Mettalika's neck, the weak point, but Mettalika's jaws closed on her own neck and started to crush it. Sinxo's screams were choked off as blood poured into her mouth and spilled out onto the cave floor. Her struggling became weaker, her head felt like it was about to explode. Mettalika had hit a major artery in her neck and she was drowning on her own bloody fluids.

Mettalika pulled back to watch her die, a sick expression of satisfaction on her face. No one mattered to her any more. Gryphie or Lizariaous, they were all scum to be destroyed and they were all out to get her, to stop her from cleansing the territories of their disease. Now she was a lone killer. Anyone who crossed her path would die, there was no doubt.

Sinxo's vision became blurred as she slowly started to black out. She couldn't move her legs and her wings had been long since broken and shattered. Her eyes rolled about, odd shapes coming into focus. She saw what she thought to be her wing, laying far too far away for it to still be connected to her body. Tears ran down her muddy cheeks. Bloody tears. She saw Mettalika vaguely sitting back watching her and tried to reach out a hand in one last desperate effort for mercy. The image of Mettalika did nothing to respond. Things started swirling into other things as hallucinations set in from loss of blood. Mystik's face appeared. Disconnected, floating in nothingness. It spoke, the mouth dispersing and reforming as it did so.

"You died with honour; standing up for what you believe is true. Take flight Sinxo, take flight and soar." Sinxo's hearing was getting worse; a buzzing, a loud buzzing in her ears. She blinked; the fluid of her eyes filling with blood and then draining and her whole body relaxed. She glanced up at Mettalika one more time before her eyes closed forever.

Meanwhile, Diabloss and Leida were oblivious to all this. Diabloss was showing Leida a bird's eye view of the areas he patrolled. Trees and clearings passed them as they flew.

"So where does she normally hang out?" asked Leida.

"The swamp mostly" Diabloss replied. "But she's lately had the confidence to wander out in the open. Sometimes I see packs of Lizariaouses come across her. Sometimes they attack but mostly they run on sight. She always takes at least one life if they attack her and I think most of them leave her alone now. I haven't seen a large hunting pack go out after her for some time. It makes me think the Lizariaouses have given up going after her."

"Or they could be training up to launch a large attack?" suggested Leida.

"Maybe" replied Diabloss.

"Do you ever fly over Dyarkroeen these sun cycles?" Leida asked.

"No not any more. We stopped flying over their territory a few lunars back, since after this all started; they tend to fire needles at you if you get too close. They have guards posted here and there and the closer you fly to the more populated areas, the more needles fly at you. I could fly high enough for them not to hit me but they're always watching the skies in case Mettalika goes in for an aerial attack I suppose and some of them can shoot higher than others. They must have been training for that. One of my soldiers said he flew over Dyarkroeen high enough for the needles not to hit him and one nearly did. He was surprised and shocked at how high this Lizariaous could shoot. So we don't go there now much. Not unless we fly above the clouds but unless there's low cloud, at that height you can't see much anyway."

"Well it's pretty cloudy this sun cycle and misty too; could we fly over and have a look? I'm curious to see what they're up to. They've been so quiet these last few sun cycles." Leida gave Diabloss her patented pleading look, the one that usually made him say yes to her question. This sun cycle was no different.

"Ok, well yeah I admit I've been a little curious too and this is the first sun cycle in a long time that it's been so rainy and misty. Let's go!" Diabloss suddenly swept his wings up in a large motion and flew up higher. Leida followed, laughing, enjoying the prospect of some kind of adventure that was a little risky but also safe enough at the same time.

They soon crossed the border into Dyarkroeen. Leida saw the little soldiers down below, constantly on guard at the edge of their territory. They all looked so small from up here. She and Diabloss weaved in and out of the clouds, keeping above them as much as they could. Rain pelted them more the higher they went and they had to be careful not to get too waterlogged which would hinder their flying.

Leida looked down as she flew, keeping an eye open for anything suspicious. Diabloss did the same. They didn't talk much in case the Lizariaouses below heard them although it wouldn't have mattered much since the sound of the rain was nearly deafening anyway.

They flew over the training grounds and saw the setup with the cave cat tied up and the sea vulture on the rope for target practise. Leida flew closer to Diabloss and yelled above the rain.

"Hey, what do you think those are?" she pointed to the two creatures.

"I have no idea. Maybe they're keeping food nearby so they don't have to go out hunting in this weather?"

"Hmm, maybe…" Leida chanced to go down a little for a closer look. Diabloss warned her not to in case she flew low enough for the Lizariaouses below to see her form as that of a Gryphie and not just a passing bird.

She flew low enough to see the soldiers training and work out what they were doing. She saw them fire needles at the sea vulture as it flew about trying to avoid them, squawking. It didn't seem fair they had tied their food up so it was easier to hit. Then it occurred to her that they could be using it for target practise. She watched a little more and saw this was the reason. So they *had* been training. She guessed this was why they were so quiet. She flew back up with Diabloss and they hovered to talk.

"Well it looks like they're training. Not just training either, it must be pretty intense; they're rushing about and using the sea vulture for target practise. Also, training in the rain without taking breaks until it's passed, that must mean the training is important for something."

Diabloss nodded and pondered the situation. "Then what could they be training for? I can only imagine it's either to fight us or fight Mettalika."

"Yeah it must be for something like that. I can't think that they'd be training all weather for something less important." Leida looked back down at them again. "They would have a bit of an advantage if they attacked Mettalika in the rain though, her fire wouldn't be as powerful with all the water around."

"Yes, I wonder if that's occurred to them yet." Diabloss thought carefully about it. "Hmm, but what if they attack the Forest when it's raining. Our fire is our greatest asset against them; it's what helps us the most; that and our wings of course. Let's hope they're too stupid to think of that." He looked concerned now and wondered why he'd never thought of that either. Then again it didn't rain much. Only a few times a lunar; which meant that it was unlikely the Lizariaouses would wait if they wanted to do that. They weren't known for their patience. Rainfalls, because they were so scarce, were always heavy when they did happen and often carried on all sun cycle and way into the time after the sun had set.

"Come on Leida, we must call a meeting over this. I think it's important enough for the whole gathering to be warned about." Diabloss swung round and headed back towards Shernaron. Leida followed. Things were taking a more interesting but maybe worse turn it seemed.

Back in the cave, Mettalika was devouring Sinxo with much relish. She figured she didn't want the others to know Sinxo was dead. It may be more interesting if they thought she'd been kidnapped by the Lizariaouses or only assumed she was dead. Without proof, one is never sure and so doesn't feel confident with what they know. Mettalika found the taste of Gryphie to be milder and tenderer than the tough Lizariaouses she was used to eating. She quite liked it. This would not be the last Gryphie death she would deal.

Chapter 22
The Meeting

Diabloss and Leida had reached the Forest again and decided to walk through to the main living area for the gathering. They were soaked through and flying was becoming an effort.

"There is a meeting going to be held" Diabloss told the guards. "Listen in on it but keep your guard up." The guards nodded and smiled at Leida as she and Diabloss passed. They were good natured although brutal in battle.

Diabloss headed to Mystik's tree to tell her and Leida called out to all the Gryphies in the Forest that they should attend the meeting which would happen immediately. Some complained since they had been staying in due to the weather but Leida assured them the meeting would be held under Mystik's big old tree with its evergreen leaves that would shelter them all. So they all arrived and crowded under the tree. Mystik sat at the entrance. Jadariol hadn't been invited and he was at the back on his little bed dozing lightly.

"Is everyone here?" asked Diabloss.

"Sinxo hasn't returned from gathering medicines yet" Mystik spoke up.

"Well we don't know when she will return so I won't wait for her, you can tell her all I'm about to say when she gets back. What I have to say is important and it affects all of us." Some of the Gryphies looked worried at this. "Don't look so worried" continued Diabloss, "It's only a warning and a little heads up on what the Lizariaouses are doing and why they've been so quiet these last few sun cycles."

Everyone looked around at everyone else, seemingly hoping for reassurance from someone. Even though they had good defences, being naturally peaceful, most of them wanted to stay out of fights and wished for all the world that there would be an agreement before a war started. Some of the kittens shifted about and they were scolded lightly by their parents. When all was quiet again, Diabloss continued.

"Now, Leida and I flew over Dyarkroeen earlier and we saw they are training soldiers heavily for something. They were using prey creatures for target practise and training in the rain which meant it was intensive. They don't value being out in the rain any more than we do. This made my mate and I think that maybe they might think of attacking us during a storm when we have less defences and our fire is weakened. Now don't get worried, I doubt they'll think of that." He looked around and Gryphies were muttering to each other doubtfully. A whole new dimension of foreboding had been suggested to them now and their confidence was a little dampened.

"It doesn't rain often, I doubt that if they wanted to attack, they would wait for it to rain anyway but I wanted to warn all of you. It's not like Zephirak to train up as many soldiers as we saw being trained all at once. They must be planning something. Now, personally I think they're training to go after Mettalika. In which case all to the good. Let them kill her for us."

"Yeah! She deserves to die for what she did to Jadariol!" Lunara yelled suddenly. Shen rebuked her swiftly. "Quiet! You sound like a Lizariaous speaking like that!" Lunara mooched and looked at her feet, a mixture of annoyance at being told off and defiance because she wanted her anger to be heard.

Diabloss smiled a little. Then he looked serious. "See the effect this is having on our kittens? They are starting to hate Mettalika and Lizariaouses for what they are doing to us."

"Well what do we do about it?" another Gryphie spoke up.

"Yes, do we sit around and defend ourselves as we have always done or do we go out and get them before they get us?" someone else said.

"We will train, we will keep an eye on the Lizariaouses and if need be, we will fight for our honour and freedom. We will not go out picking fights though. We want them to know that whatever they do in their own territory is up to them but we will not have them hunting and slaying us for food or any other purpose. We will threaten them and continue to do so until we either reach an agreement to leave each other alone or stay out of each others' way." Diabloss told them.

"How about reasoning with them?" asked Shen.

"That is where the young Lizariaous comes into play" said Mystik. "He will be a peace offering when he has recovered."

"What if they don't agree to peace?" asked Shen. "I don't want Lunara put at risk again. I never thought this would affect our kittens since they are always close by but ever since that run in she had with Zephirak, I have feared for her life and the other kittens of the gathering too. We cannot allow this to get out of hand any more than it already has."

"I agree" replied Diabloss before Mystik could speak again. "And it won't, we will make sure of that. They may attack us elsewhere but we will ensure they do not come into this part of the Forest where we live. If you keep your kittens with you, there will be no risk to them. As for when they are taught and learn to fly, the training grounds have never been infiltrated by Lizariaouses and if they tried, they would have Strassor to answer to."

"Aye that's right!" Strassor sat up and snarled. "And I won't be goin' easy on 'em neither! Nor will my sons!"

216

Otuss and Odax snarled.

"I've killed Lizariaouses before, they aren't that hard to destroy" snarled Otuss. "We'll have no problem with them. And if it did come to a war, I'll take a lot of 'em with me before I die."

"Hopefully it won't come to war, Otuss. We hope to stop this before it really gets out of hand." Diabloss replied.

"It has *already* gotten out of hand. They are training special troops to kill us now" growled Otuss.

"No, we believe they are training to go after Mettalika." Diabloss corrected him.

"It won't end with her though will it. We'll be next. Once they see they can destroy her, the rest of the gathering will be easy for them to bring down." Otuss's face was dark.

"We're hoping it won't come to that" reiterated Diabloss.

"Why don't we take them down ourselves. If you think they'll agree to a truce, you're out of your mind." Otuss challenged. Strassor warned him to shut up and show some respect. Otuss just snarled in defiance but obeyed his father.

"I'm not saying they'll agree to a truce. In fact I tried to reason with Zephirak some lunars ago and he wouldn't have any of it. But Jadariol, the young Lizariaous is our last chance. If they don't accept him then they've as good as declared war anyway. I'd like if we only attacked them in defence but I know for a fact there are some in our gathering, such as you Otuss, who would go out and attack without provocation. That is up to you and it is out of my hands though I would prefer that you didn't do it." Diabloss mostly focused on Otuss as he spoke.

Strassor sat up to his full height. "My sons will do whatever I be wishin' 'em to do. They go against you; that means they'll be goin' against me too. Yeh hear that Otuss? So if yeh wanna keep me happy, I suggest you be listenin' to Diabloss."

Otuss grumbled but nodded. Leida looked quite pleased he'd been cut down like that.

Kayto spoke up. "Sir, why don't we kill Zephirak? With him gone, the other Lizariaouses won't bother with the war. The only one with a real problem is him."

Diabloss sighed. "I've thought of that. It wouldn't work. Chances are there are others who see his way of thinking as the only way. We can't hope to think that they *all* act as he tells them to out of fear. No, there will be some who will carry on his work for him and will be deeply angered at his death. It may make things worse."

"Ha, that's hardly likely sir, and if there are others, there won't be many of them" Kayto pointed out.

"Don't be so sure of that. It's mostly wishful thinking that we assume Zephirak has them all under his control simply because they fear him. He has many soldiers who are close to him, I've seen them in battle and some of them fight in his name. They wouldn't do that if they were acting out under fear of him. They would do it because they *have* to; these guys do it because they *want* to." Diabloss stated.

Kayto was defeated and lay back down.

"So what is our plan of action?" asked Mystik.

"Well, we keep on our guard. When Jadariol gets better, the squadron and I will return him to Dyarkroeen. Any Lizariaouses who attack us whether in hunting packs or for other reasons, you have my permission to kill them if it comes to that. We need to show them we mean business and won't take it any more. No more running, however no fighting in battles you know you

218

won't win; that will be another point to them. And no looking for fights" he stared pointedly at Otuss. "I don't want to hear that you were "ambushed" when in fact you went out *looking* for Lizariaouses to kill. I will not have us sink to their level of looking to kill others because we will have all out anarchy on our hands, I can assure you of that."

The rest of the gathering nodded in agreement and it was settled that that was what they would do.

"Most importantly" Diabloss continued, "make sure you are trained in at least some fighting skills. Strassor and his team of trainers will be glad to teach you anything you need to know. You must at least be able to defend yourselves enough to get away from the danger. This means I want *all* of you to go in for at least a little training. If you do not, well that is up to you but don't expect anyone to rush in and save you. Of course if anyone sees a fellow Gryphie being attacked, if you can, go to help them or send out a distress call. We're all in this together."

"Does that mean the kittens must train too? Lunara has only just learnt how to fly confidently." Shen spoke up.

"Yes" replied Strassor. "I be wantin' all kittens, once they be finished their flight trainin' ta come ter me and I'll teach 'em basic defence. If they want ter continue trainin' more after that, then that is up ter them."

"But what if we don't want our kittens to become cold hearted killers and hurt others?" asked Shen.

"Then next time your kitten has a run in with a Lizariaous; that could be the *last* time." Odax said firmly.

Shen looked at Lunara and sighed. She didn't want her sweet little daughter to grow up and kill or hurt others but desperate times called for desperate measures. Lunara looked determined; she didn't want to see anyone hurt like Jadariol had been but she wanted to have some kind of chance if she ever came up against Lizariaouses again.

"I want to learn" Lunara said quietly.

"Then you shall" replied Shen.

"Ok, everyone, now anyone got any questions before I call this meeting to an end?" Diabloss surveyed the gathering before him sheltering under the big old tree. Some looked confident and determined, others scared. Some looked worried and some looked solemn. He'd never seen such a wide variety of moods or expressions and noticed that not one was a happy or positive face. Still, it couldn't be expected really.

No one spoke up. It had put a downer on the whole gathering and they all just seemed to want to get back to their trees and mull it all over.

"Very well" said Diabloss after a while, "You may now all return to your trees. Thank you for coming and please bear in mind all that has taken place in this meeting."

They all, most of them gratefully, got up and went off home.

Diabloss caught Strassor before he left.

"I hope you don't mind all this extra work for you and your team" he said.

Strassor smiled warmly. "Not at all! If I can be helpin' train others ter defend us and win this, I'm all fer it!"

"Thank you old friend, I really hope we can win this. For the sake of me, my mate and the whole gathering. Those faces I saw in the meeting, so many of them looked like their spirits were about to break. So many looked sad and worried."

"I know I saw it too. But what can yeh expect? Still, keep positive." Strassor patted Diabloss on the back and walked off, following his two sons who were walking ahead, talking about the events of the meeting. Odax seemed wiser, Otuss was merely pointing out what he would do to any Lizariaous who dared to attack him.

Diabloss shook his head with a small smile and returned to Leida outside the tree. She was sat with Mystik now. Mystik was concerned about why Sinxo hadn't returned; it was nearly moon cycle.

"Don't worry, she's probably taking shelter from the rain" suggested Leida.

Mystik still looked concerned. "Well I hope she will return soon. It will get dark and with things the way they are, I don't want her to be at any risk. I know when I ask her to collect herbs; she tends to not return unless she has found all of them. If she has trouble finding any then she will stay out until she does. She is very attentive about her work."

"Well if she isn't back by the middle of the next sun cycle then I will get Diabloss to send out a scout party for her. I'm sure she's just sheltering from the rain though. None of us like it very much and if it risks her getting waterlogged then I've no doubt she's keeping dry." Leida replied.

Mystik nodded and returned to her tree. Leida joined Diabloss and told him about Sinxo and that Mystik was worried.

"She's resourceful that Sinxo, she'll be back tomorrow. She's been known to stay out for three sun cycles before when what she needed to collect was far away." Diabloss looked calm about it at least.

"Yes but that was before the Lizariaous rebellion" replied Leida.

Diabloss pondered the situation, neither of them suspected it could be Mettalika's work as she had never harmed a Gryphie before, only threatened them and even then not that often.

"I have a bad feeling" continued Leida. "I don't think we will see Sinxo again."

Diabloss looked a little surprised. "Now don't talk like that, that's just your worry showing. We'll see her again. She'll fly home if she's a long way away."

"I just can't picture in my mind meeting her again." Leida looked at her feet and her ears laid back sadly.

Now Diabloss looked concerned. Leida's senses weren't often wrong and she did look pretty convinced this time was no different. He thought about Sinxo and what might keep her out so long. Ever since the problems had started, she had worked faster to gather the herbs and medicines to ensure she wouldn't have to stay out any longer than was needed. She could have been held up though he doubted it was by Zephirak. Maybe a hunting pack had caught up to her and ambushed her, weakened by the rain so she wouldn't have had much fire to fight back with. If they'd damaged her wings too... He didn't want to think about that.

Leida had settled down now and was staring out of the large hole in the front of the tree at the rain, watching it splash off the leaves and onto the ground. She was deep in thought about her friend. Diabloss settled down beside her and curled his tail around her, placing one wing over her like a blanket for security and comfort. Leida rested her head on him and sighed.

"I hope it will be over soon" she said quietly.

The next sun cycle, the rain had stopped and it was hot and sunny. It was a little humid too. Leida woke and stretched a little; as much as she could in the tree where there was little room to stretch out her wings. Diabloss was still asleep. Leida smiled and nuzzled him, then rested her head on her forelegs and gazed out at the sun. Hmm, this sun cycle was a nice one. She wasn't thinking of Sinxo now, she was celebrating a fresh new sun cycle and the lovely weather that came with it. She sighed and suddenly saw something appear over the edge of the tree's entrance hole. It was small and lilac. It was a nose. Lunara's nose. Leida lifted her head and watched it sniffing around to see who was up in the tree. She was soon followed by her best friend, Hiryasis. Leida wasn't sure what kind of game they were playing.

"I can see you, you know" said Leida quietly. Lunara giggled and Hiryasis clambered in.

"Hey Hiry! Don't leave me hanging here!" yelled Lunara.

"Quiet! Diabloss is sleeping!" Leida snapped in a whisper. Lunara ducked down and clambered in quietly.

"Sorry" she replied sheepishly.

"So what brings you two up here? Playing hide and seek?" asked Leida.

"No" replied Hiryasis, "I'm trying to get Lunara to *do* something instead of hang around with that creepy Lizariaous.

"He's not creepy!" yelled Lunara.

"Quiet!!" scolded Leida. Lunara looked sheepish again.

"Well I think he's creepy. He keeps looking at me weird whenever he sees me and he sits in Mystik's tree like he's some kinda king."

Lunara gasped. "He does *not!*"

Hiryasis looked indignant. "He does! I don't like him and I don't think you should be hanging around with him. I don't wanna play with him and I can't play with you when you're with him."

"You could, just get over your stupid dislike for him. He's done nothing to you and it's wrong to accuse him of something others of his kind have done and not him." Lunara growled.

"Hey, hey! What's all this arguing…" Diabloss had woken up and was looking at them sleepily.

"Now see what you've done, I told you two to be quiet!" Leida frowned at the kittens and they both hurriedly spread their wings and took off, leaping out of the tree, gliding to the ground and running off still arguing.

Leida shook her head. "Seems Hiryasis is jealous his best friend has a new friend."

"A new *Lizariaous* friend" said Diabloss.

"Once again I wish we all could put aside our differences like Lunara and Jadariol" said Leida.

"Well, it seems we can't and neither can the other youngsters." Diabloss sat up as he spoke and yawned. "Up for some breakfast?"

"I always am!" Leida laughed and they left the tree and flew over the forest in search of breakfast.

Meanwhile on the ground, Lunara and Hiryasis had separated; Hiry being called for his breakfast. They had gotten over their argument when Lunara said that when Jadariol was better he could join in with their games and they could all play together. She told Hiryasis that Jadariol was probably grumpy and untrusting because he was in pain and surrounded by those he didn't know. So he'd agreed to try making friends with Jadariol when he was a bit better.

Lunara headed over to see Jadariol now. He was lying in the tree on his little bed eating a forest deer one of the guards had brought back for him. He seemed happy with this. Lizariaouses have bigger appetites than Gryphies.

"Hey Jaddy!" Lunara called brightly as she entered.

"What have I told you about calling me that?" growled Jadariol.

Lunara just shrugged and asked how he was feeling, to which Jadariol replied that he was feeling in much less pain but the medicine that was needed for replacing the dressings on his wounds hadn't arrived and without it they would go bad and not heal right or fast.

Lunara explained that Sinxo the gatherer hadn't returned with the replacement medicines and herbs.

"Why not? I need them or I might not be able to walk again. Why can't she hurry up? Stupid Gryphie, useless creature!"

"Hey! Sinxo is my friend, don't talk badly about her, she's a great gatherer. She even gave me a real Lizariaous claw once!"

Jadariol growled. "What, did she kill a Lizariaous for it then?" he asked although he knew the answer already.

"No of course not! It was the outer layer of a claw or one that had been shed or something, not one that was taken off a Lizariaouses' foot, remember, I had it when we met. Gryphies don't hunt Lizariaouses!" Lunara looked shocked at the very thought.

Jadariol laughed. "I know, I was only joking" he said.

"Didn't sound like it" grumbled Lunara.

"Pah! You obviously tell different jokes then" replied Jadariol.

"Yeah we do" Lunara left it at that. She was going to say that Gryphie jokes were funnier but decided not to.

"So when will you be ready to walk?" she asked instead.

"Mystik told me that when Sinxo comes back with the new herbs and she's replaced my dressings; I can try to stand on my feet a little to see how strong I am." Jadariol looked happier about this. "So she'd better hurry up" he added.

"I'll go see Mystik and see where Sinxo is" said Lunara. She rushed out to look for Mystik. She found Mystik at the top of her tree looking out over Shernaron.

"Mystik! Is Sinxo back yet?" Lunara asked, flying carefully up and landing next to the old Gryphie.

Mystik shook her head slowly, staring out over their territory still. "Since this trouble started, Sinxo has always returned promptly. I worry about her being so late."

Lunara watched too, then got bored and spread her wings. "Jadariol really needs those herbs" she said.

"I know, which makes it all the more important that Sinxo returns fast. This sun cycle is hot and humid and there are more bugs about then, more flies, more a chance for disease to take hold if they are allowed near the wounds and if the wounds aren't clean they will be attracted by the smell." Mystik was looking more anxious with every word.

"I'll go back and tell him she isn't back yet" said Lunara and flew off, Mystik didn't reply, just kept her quiet vigil over the Forest and valleys beyond.

Lunara returned to Jadariol. He had finished the forest deer now and was lying down once again, watching out of the entrance to Mystik's tree. He saw Lunara before she saw him.

"Well? Is she back yet?"

"No, she's not back yet. Mystik looks pretty worried. She's worried about both Sinxo not returning and your wounds going bad." Lunara sat beside him and sighed.

"And I thought Lizariaouses did a bad job as healers" murmured Jadariol.

"Hey, it's not Mystik's fault. Maybe Sinxo has run into some Lizariaouses and is hiding from them."

"How do you know it's not that murderous Mettalika who killed my mother. She could be killing your kind now too" growled Jadariol.

"No, she's horrible and all but she's not that horrible" replied Lunara with confidence. "She won't hurt us."

Jadariol just snorted and rested his head on his paws.

The middle of the sun cycle arrived and still no Sinxo. Jadariol and Lunara were occupying themselves by playing a game Lunara was teaching Jadariol called Which One. It was a game in which one would have two items, small enough to be covered by a hand or paw and place them under their paws. They could either both be under one paw or one under each and it was the task of the other player to guess which it was. Lunara had chosen two rock pebbles which were a little too big for her hands. So Jadariol could easily see which hand they were under because one would be slightly larger than the other; the one holding the pebbles was the larger and when she had them both in one hand it was even easier. She couldn't understand how Jadariol was able to get it right nearly every time. She figured he'd played before and wasn't letting on.

Jadariol thought he'd have a go although it was difficult for him but he had an idea that when he was better he could hide them under his back paws too and make the game harder since Lizariaouses have opposable thumbs on their back feet as well as their front and he could conceal them easily.

Lunara thought his ideas to improve the game were pretty good. She was looking forward to him recovering but also would be sad about it since then he would have to go back home again and she wasn't sure if she would see him after that.

Mystik hadn't returned the whole time she and he were waiting. Diabloss had returned though. Leida was out training so Diabloss took the chance to fly back to the Forest and see if Sinxo had come back yet. He saw Mystik still sat in her tree upon his return and knew the answer even before he asked though.

"She isn't back is she?" he asked as he alighted near Mystik. The top of the tree was vast and easily held them both.

"No, I'm afraid not. I haven't seen her, not even a flash of her orange and black fur; she is not hard to miss but I have seen nothing." Mystik sighed and hung her head.

"I'll get the squadron out searching for her" said Diabloss. "They'll find her if she's out there."

"It is not just her I need, I also need the herbs and medicines she was sent out to collect. If I do not get them soon, Jadariol's wounds may go bad, he needs his dressing changed."

"Well first we'll search. You can tell Tranzoss the herbs you need if you like. She is my best female fighter but she is also good at gathering and scouting so she won't have a problem finding the things you want. I'll send her round." Diabloss looked at Mystik for confirmation and the old Gryphie nodded solemnly. Diabloss spread his mighty wings and flew up and off into the sky. Mystik stayed where she was. She had flown up there after her morning meal and hadn't left that spot since. She intended to stay and keep watch for as long as it took.

Soon a large and lithe black and teal Gryphie arrived.

"Tranzoss at your service Mystik!" she said brightly and stood to attention, awaiting orders. She was highly trained and got the job done when needed, no questions asked.

Mystik looked at her slowly and sighed again, then told her what needed to be collected. She only told her what was needed to keep replenishing Jadariol's dressings for the next lunar.

Tranzoss nodded and flew off before Mystik could tell her to fetch a carrying pouch to put the herbs in. Tranzoss was a bit of a live wire. She was the kind of Gryphie who was happiest on the move and hated when things were slow or when she had no orders. Sun cycles off were not in her vocabulary, she worked every single sun cycle she could, hardly any breaks; her wild metabolism wouldn't allow her much rest. She was up as soon as the sun rose and asleep when the moon rose. She was also very fast and efficient. Diabloss had chosen wisely for someone to collect the medicines. However she wasn't Sinxo with her young and happy go lucky outlook, one who always had time for everyone; a training assistant to Mystik. That was another reason Mystik was so worried. Sinxo was her student; she was doing extremely well on the road to becoming the gathering's next wise one. When Mystik retired; Sinxo would take over. Mystik had been proud of Lunara though too, her caring for Jadariol, feeding him and keeping him company really showed that the gap between the two species could be bridged even if for now it was done simply by youngsters.

Meanwhile, Diabloss, Kayto and a few of the other members of the squadron were out looking around. Most of the squadron members had keen eyesight and could see pretty far. They flew over the forest and looked around searching meticulously. They called out to each other every so often to alert the others as to how they were doing. No sign of Sinxo had been found so far though. Some were searching on the ground. Kayto was one of these. He was a good and thorough searcher even when running, which was what he was doing now. He was searching all around where he knew Sinxo would normally gather herbs. He found the place where the wing wort grew and saw it had all been picked. He assumed Sinxo had been there and picked it. He wasn't aware that it also grew elsewhere and it wasn't Sinxo who had picked the ones growing where Kayto was now. He carried on his search but found nothing. He wandered right up as far as the cave where Sinxo had met her death and as luck would have it, he found her gathering pouch on the ground. He picked it up, slung it over his shoulder and went into the cave. It was dark and murky and smelled of damp and something else. Blood. The steel smell of blood wafted into his nostrils as he sniffed. However it was only the smell it seemed; there was nothing on the ground, no redness anywhere or a corpse or anything else for that matter. It was just a smell. Little did he know he was standing on the very spot that Sinxo had died. Mettalika had scraped earth over the mess and blood, walking around on it, making sure it was patted down properly so it seemed there was nothing unusual there. That, coupled with the darkness, also ensured that whoever went in there would not suspect. There were no bones either; Mettalika had eaten the smaller ones and the larger ones she had carried off elsewhere. She was certainly good at covering up where she had been.

Kayto wandered back out again and carried on his search. He didn't call for Sinxo; he didn't want anyone to know he was there either. He had already been spotted though. Mettalika was hanging about in that area out of curiosity that someone might come looking for Sinxo and she had been right. She didn't reveal her position though, she wasn't stupid. She just watched carefully. Kayto left the area after one last look around.

Kayto returned to Diabloss with the carrying pouch. Diabloss left the rest of the squad still searching and took the pouch back to Mystik. He knew this almost certainly proved that Sinxo had died or perhaps was being held prisoner by Zephirak as Leida had been but the latter he doubted since Sinxo had no importance to the Lizariaouses.

As soon as Mystik saw the pouch, her face clouded over and she started to sob. She knew that it was likely Sinxo was dead.

Diabloss comforted her.

"She might still be out there you know. Maybe the Lizariaouses have her and she left the pouch behind as a clue for us to find her." Diabloss suggested.

"That is wishful thinking" sobbed Mystik "and you know it."

"Well, maybe. But we can hope can't we?" Diabloss tried to smile but Leida's words of the fact she thought she wouldn't see Sinxo again rang loud in his ears.

Mystik took the pouch and flew down from the tree, going inside and attending to Jadariol.

"Oh, Sinxo is back!" yelled Lunara brightly. But then she saw Mystik's face. "Oh, what's wrong? Is Sinxo hurt? Was she attacked?"

"No my dear, she isn't coming back" Mystik said quietly and went about her business crushing up herbs and mixing them for the new dressings.

Lunara felt sick inside. She just sat down unable to speak. No one she was friends with had ever been killed before. Tears ran down her face in silence but she couldn't speak. For once the little Gryphie was lost for words.

Jadariol just lay there and didn't say anything. He didn't know what to say either. He thought he didn't really care but there was something still upsetting about it. Sinxo had saved his life after all. Did he care about a Gryphie? He regretted his mood earlier and calling Sinxo useless. He just rested his head on his paws and watched Mystik while he listened to Lunara's quiet sobbing. This was not a scene he was used to. Lizariaouses never cried unless they were very very young. He and his friends were all too old to cry when they got hurt or heard of someone being killed by Mettalika. Plus no one gave them sympathy. He was interested to see now how seemingly Mystik wasn't comforting Lunara. Mystik was more concerned with getting done the job in hand and that was changing Jadariol's dressings. He held still as she worked to remove the old ones and put on new fresh ones. The new ones smelled nice, kind of spicy. Jadariol liked the smell of the herbs and it made him feel fresh and clean again.

When Mystik was done, she went about placing the other herbs and medicines from the pouch in the correct crevices around the tree. They stored well in the big old tree since the trunk and around it was kept dry by its evergreen leaves. Jadariol didn't know how to comfort someone so he sat now, simply watching Lunara crying with interest.

Mystik noticed this and walked up to him slowly, whispering in his ear.

"Offer her comfort. She is your friend and needs you."

Jadariol gave Mystik a look of complete confusion. He had no idea how to comfort someone. He gave it a go anyway.

"Hey Lunara...umm...you have plenty more friends, it's not the end of the world you know."

Lunara's eyes widened, she stared at him and then ran out of the tree crying harder.

Jadariol shrugged. "Did I say something wrong?"

"Well, yes you did. Friends are important. It is not how many you have although having a lot of them is good; each one means something special to you. Although Lunara has many friends like you and Hiryasis, no one is Sinxo and no one can replace her." Mystik explained.

"But where I come from if a friend dies in battle, which Sinxo must have done, we are proud and happy and we forget about it by hanging around with our other friends." Jadariol still didn't get it.

"Well, if Lunara comes back in upset, try saying something like "Sinxo will be greatly missed; she saved my life and I know she cared about you. She might have gone but she will live on in your heart through all the happy memories you have of her."" Mystik smiled.

Jadariol didn't. "How will I remember that?"

"Well you just say what is in your heart" said Mystik.

"I did and it was wrong" mooched Jadariol.

"How do you feel about it? Are you sad the one who saved your life is dead?" asked Mystik.

"Like I said she probably died in battle so I'm proud she died fighting. She might have been saving someone else even." Jadariol said, shifting his weight because he couldn't sit up any more and had to lie down again.

"That's true but we are sensitive creatures and although it is good that someone dies fighting for what they believe is good and true or even fighting for their loved ones; it is still sad because they are gone forever and we won't see them again. We will miss them and that is what hurts. Never seeing their smile or hearing their voice again. Do you understand?"

Jadariol shrugged again. "You're different from us. We don't see it that way. If we got depressed whenever one of us died then we'd be sad all the time."

Mystik was, as she had been many other times, amazed at some of the strangely wise sounding things that youngsters could say. She nodded.

"Yes, that is a good point. Just please either don't say anything at all when Lunara returns or try to remember to say what I told you or something similar to it."

Jadariol nodded and rattled his needles a little as a small pain shot up his hind leg.

Mystik left to make sure Lunara was ok.

Jadariol rested his head on his paws and closed his eyes. Gryphies sure were strange to him.

Chapter 23
First Steps

The squadron hadn't found any sign of Sinxo at all. It was like she had disappeared into thin air. Diabloss suspected she had been killed by Lizariaouses and then taken back to Dyarkroeen but because no blood or sign of a struggle had been found, he was inclined to think that maybe they had taken her back to use as a live target for that training he and Leida had seen them doing the previous sun cycle.

So he went off to have a check. He flew up high over Dyarkroeen and looked around. Sure enough they were training again. He could see the tiny forms of Zephirak and Mordred commanding the soldiers who, worryingly to Diabloss, seemed to be doing a very good job.

But he couldn't see Sinxo or anything even remotely resembling a Gryphie. He saw some sea vultures and a cave cat but that was it. The cave cat met its demise as he watched.

Diabloss returned over the Outlands and back to Shernaron. There he met Kayto and Tranzoss. Kayto had told Tranzoss about the pouch so her herbs weren't needed but she decided to take them back anyway since she had gone to the trouble of getting them.

"I couldn't find any wing wort though" she told Diabloss.

"Oh I think I saw some of that in the cave I was in" Kayto replied. "There wasn't any in the usual place but there was some in the cave near where I found the pouch."

"Then there will be some in the pouch I've no doubt. But that is interesting" said Diabloss.

"Why?" asked Kayto.

"Because she had to go further out to get the wing wort. It could have been a trap. If there was a struggle, that's where she would have dropped the pouch. I wonder if a hunting pack of Lizariaouses have been doing their research and knew she would visit there."

"That's awfully farfetched Sir" replied Tranzoss. "What Lizariaous would have the brain power to actually lie in wait for a Gryphie or ambush one?"

"Well they've tried it a few times with Mettalika, I know that. If they have a lot of taste for us, they might find easier ways to catch us; ways in which we would have more trouble escaping." Diabloss looked thoughtful.

"I still don't think that's the case Sir. I mean, Sinxo could have been running from them and dropped the pouch. She could have come from somewhere else and run a long way." Tranzoss argued.

"Well there wasn't a sign of a struggle there" put in Kayto, "so I don't think she was caught round there anyway. She probably dropped the pouch because it hindered her movements and hoped to be faster without it. The Lizariaouses wouldn't bother with it so there it lay until I found it. It was just lucky it hadn't got wet from the rain."

"The rain! Was it inside the cave or out?" asked Diabloss.

"It was outside" replied Kayto.

"Then in that case, she must have lost it this sun cycle! If she lost it last sun cycle it would have gotten wet. So I think she took shelter in the cave for the moon cycle and was just heading out this morning when a pack found her and chased her. She could have been holding the pouch in her mouth about to put it on and then dropped it and fled when she saw them." Diabloss was thinking it through now.

"Hmm, true. She could have run a little way and then they caught her but I checked all around. Wait…the cave smelled of fresh blood." Kayto thought back. "But there was no sign of a struggle in there though."

"It's all so weird. At any rate, I'm pretty sure she's dead." Diabloss looked thoughtful again. This was starting to get serious now; members of their own, important members had started being picked off. Mystik knew that Sinxo was dead even without hard evidence.

"Well, we can't change it. She was taken by Lizariaouses somehow and we'll never be able to get her back. They took her back to Dyarkroeen so the body won't be found. I'll fly back to the Forest and spread the word. We must all be extra careful, now more than ever. I'll call another meeting." Diabloss and Tranzoss made their way back to the Forest. Kayto carried on keeping an eye out for a body a while longer.

"Sir, you don't suppose, I mean, has it ever occurred to you that Mettalika did it?" asked Tranzoss as they flew along.

"It did. But then again she's never been known to kill a Gryphie. I don't think even she would. I'm pretty sure it's the Lizariaouses."

"I dunno, Sir…something about this doesn't quite add up."

"Then think on it and get back to me. Sound out for a meeting to be held." Diabloss replied and started roaring out his message to gather everyone under Mystik's tree for a new meeting. Tranzoss joined in.

Back in Mystik's tree, Jadariol hadn't seen Lunara since his unfortunate attempt at comforting her. He was sure she'd call round. Mystik had left again. He sat up carefully, the herbs were working their magic well and he was feeling stronger every sun cycle. He tried to put some weight on his front leg and winced. He'd always been taught not to fear pain, to put up with pain and never ever to show he was in pain. So he eased himself onto his feet. He held his injured legs carefully, resting more weight on his good ones. Hmm, it seemed ok though it did hurt. Next for some steps. Jadariol tried to put weight on his injured front leg as he attempted to walk. He gritted his teeth and snarled. It hurt a lot. He limped forward a little way before collapsing and pulling himself back to his bed. This wasn't fun. He started to feel anger for Mettalika for what she had done. He lay down and mooched.

Then he heard the calling out for a meeting. He had no idea what it meant since he didn't understand Gryphie roars or sounds. Maybe something was wrong. He looked out of the entrance to the tree from where he lay and saw Gryphies gathering under the tree. So, they were having another meeting. He yawned; it was none of his concern anyway.

Outside, Leida and Mystik joined the others. Diabloss and Tranzoss alighted and Tranzoss gave Mystik the herbs she had picked up. Other Gryphies sat around, some curious, some annoyed at being disturbed from their various activities. Otuss and Odax were there as well as Strassor and a whole troupe of Gryphies they had been in the middle of training; young and old. A lot of Gryphies had listened to the previous moon cycle's meeting and taken to heart what had been said. They and their kittens were getting trained up for basic defence.

"Ok everyone; you're probably wondering why I called another meeting so soon after the first one" said Diabloss. A lot of Gryphies nodded, disgruntled.

"Sinxo, one of our Forest's Gryphies was not at last moon cycle's meeting. She was being killed by

238

Lizariaouses." He paused, letting this sink in and watching the reactions it got. Most were of shock.

"Yes, which is why I called this meeting. From now on we stick to the Forest. No one is to allow their kittens beyond the edge of the Forest. No one is to stray into the Outlands. From now on only soldiers and members of my squad are allowed to venture out. We can't lose any more of us. Now we are taking a stand. If they want us, they come to us but if they do, they won't be returning to Dyarkroeen. All Lizariaouses venturing into this forest will be killed on sight. We will train, we will work up our strength in the next few sun cycles and lunars and we will be a force to be reckoned with. I for one have had it with living in fear from Lizariaouses. We'll give them the chance to leave us alone or be killed. If they still wish to fight then I will enlist the help of my cousin, Iseera and the Gryphies from the metal mountains. They will make us armour and help us in the fight. If the Lizariaouses still won't quit, then I will call in the help of the Deamons." He paused again. Now some members of the gathering looked nervous. Deamons were deadly and hated to be disturbed themselves. Bringing them into the battle worried the gathering.

"Sinxo won't have died in vain! We will stop this fight with any means necessary and if that means taking a squad to Dyarkroeen and taking out Zephirak then so be it." The last three words he snarled out with malice and took off into the sky to round up his squad, leaving everyone else sat there looking somewhat perplexed, fearful and angry. Gryphies muttered to each other as they left.

Leida joined Strassor; it was her turn to train now. Otuss walked behind her talking to Odax.

"Yer mate sounds pretty riled up" Strassor remarked.

"Yeah, well you can't blame him" replied Leida. "He has a lot of pressure on him. We are a small gathering; another reason why I think Zephirak wants to target us first. He thinks we have minimal defences and few contacts besides the forest we live in. Well, Zephirak will be in for a shock."

"That be very true, if he wants ter mess with us, we'll put up a fight before goin' down" said Strassor grimly.

"Before goin' down? We aint goin' down!" Otuss butted in. "We'll train up and kill the lot of them. Diabloss is giving them too many chances. We've tried it his way, now we'll take them before they take us!"

Strassor stopped in his tracks. "No. That doesn't help anyone. We want as few casualties as possible."

Otuss snarled. "Father, thinking like that is grikking stupid. Do *they* want as few casualties as possible? No! Do Lizariaouses have standards or morals? No! So why the grik should we? Tell me that."

"Because," Strassor shoved his muzzle at Otuss's, "WE are not sinking to their level."

Otuss replied with a fiery snort. "Come on, baby, let's go train you for your death." He grabbed Leida's tail unceremoniously and marched off with her following.

Odax stood beside his father, watching them go. "Father, I don't think we'll be able to keep him under control much longer. Otuss lives to fight. He won't stop until he's torn out every throat in Dyarkroeen. I think he's going to recruit like-minded Gryphies and it worries me."

"Ay yer right, I thought of that too. But there's nothin' we can do if he does. We can only hope he'll learn from his own mistakes. I hate ter see a son of mine go that way."

"I feel partially responsible. I am his older brother and I feel I wasn't a very good influence on him, even though I tried to show him the ways of good." Odax sighed.

"Ah, he'dve turned that way however yeh taught him. He be just reckless like that." Strassor shook his head. "Come on; let's be gettin' back to the training fields."

The two of them headed back together.

Meanwhile Leida and Otuss had nearly reached the grounds.

"You remind me of someone you know?" Leida spoke up as they reached the edge of the grounds.

"And who is that?" asked Otuss.

"Well…in a way, Zephirak." She replied.

"What?" Otuss turned to her and the unpleasant anger in his face was obvious.

"Well, he lets his anger control him instead of his mind and common sense. You're heading that way, Otuss." She could see the anger rise in Otuss's face and body language and the snarl on his lips grew.

"You grikking moron! How dare you compare me to him. I'm gunna show you to treat your masters with respect!" And he lunged for her.

Leida dodged, her dodging abilities had vastly improved even though they had been good to begin with.

"Yeah? I overcame a whole pack of Lizariaouses but did I get any of your respect for that? No! Maybe you should pay more attention to how I am learning and growing and do your job better." Leida was in the sky now. She'd had it up to here with Otuss's attitude and not getting any recognition for her hard work or any praise. She freewheeled and spun around, showing off her skills, letting him know that he'd have a fight on his hands if he challenged her.

Otuss frowned and followed her, snarling. He shot up in the sky and blasted her with his fire. Leida dodged again.

"You can't dodge all your life, fight back baby!!"

"Don't call me baby!" yelled Leida and blasted him in the face with her flames. He tried to cover his face with his wings but trying to fly at the same time was hard so he flew out of the way, muttering expletives and cursing her.

"I've grown now, in case you hadn't noticed. I'm not the shy Gryphie, the rubbish fighter I was before!" But her talking cost her dear because Otuss flew up behind her and lunged at her, grabbing one of her wings and preparing to take it out.

"You talk too much, baby. No grikking talking in battle"

"Yeah? And no grikking swearing either!" Leida roared as she twisted herself around, risking her wing but at the same time thrashing up with a hind foot and digging it into Otuss's belly. He yelped in pain and let go of her wing. Leida kept on flying at him now, kicking out with her hind legs, hitting him each time. However, one kick she didn't judge and he managed to slash her leg with his claws. She cried out and fell back. Now Otuss was really angry and in hot pursuit, flaming her and roaring. Time for talk was over, their instincts took hold. Leida tried to hold her injured leg close but found it difficult and painful. Now her only choice was to take out one of Otuss's wings. She kept flying straight and then suddenly veered up, taking him by surprise just long enough to fly around and over him, kicking out at his wing and hitting it dead on. She could easily have torn it with her claws but she didn't want to render him completely defenceless. A torn wing takes a long time to heal and if the damage is bad enough, sometimes doesn't heal at all. At the same time her tail hooked round his and pulled him back so she could grab his other wing and bend it back painfully. She heard the muscles in it click and let go, leaving him to crash to the ground below, one wing bleeding and the other nearly broken. She landed nearby, ready to take off at any moment and yelping at her hurt leg.

Otuss sat up, panting and examining his wings. Then he looked at Leida and oddly, smiled. He stood and she prepared to fly away.

"Well done, Leida. You successfully brought me down."

"What?" was all Leida could say. It had all been a test?

"You really pissed me off back there but you defended yourself well and defeated me. My teaching of you is over. You pass. You are now a fighter and can go on honing your skills by yourself." He came and offered her his hand. She took it and he shook it firmly.

"Well done, Leida. You graduated!"

Leida smiled and went a little pink. She still found compliments, although nice, difficult to take. She noticed with satisfaction that he no longer called her "baby". Now she did have his respect. It took her mind back to when they first met. Their first encounter had been a test too. She should have suspected it but to her, now, everything was to be taken seriously.

"So no more lessons?" she asked, to be sure.

"No more lessons. Your training is complete. Now, fly, and keep the fire burning Leida." Otuss replied with a smile. He bowed his head to her, she reciprocated and he galloped off to find more students in need of his teaching.

Leida took to the air, happy and feeling achievement. She was happy she wouldn't have his grumpy demeanour to deal with each sun cycle and she was glad she'd managed to train up to something that could protect itself in the face of danger. She'd never been able to do that before. She flew off to find Diabloss.

Back in the Forest, Lunara and her mother were having a talk. Lunara had been training early that sun cycle and she was doing well. Strassor was training her and a group of others. She had passed her flying test and was moving into basic defence like Leida had done, except on a smaller scale reserved for kittens.

"Now, I want you to promise me to stay in the Forest. You heard what Diabloss said. I don't want you leaving at all. I want you and your friends to be within sight distance of adults in the Forest. And I don't want you hanging around with that young Lizariaous any more."

"But he's my friend!" Lunara objected.

"I don't care; you have lots of other friends, ones of your own species. You don't need to be hanging around with him. I don't want you going in Mystik's tree any more to see him." Shen told her.

"But I'm helping him. Without me, he'd be depressed and lonely. Besides Mystik needs my help too, without Sinxo, she doesn't have an assistant and she needs help around with healing and making medicine." Lunara was obstinate.

"She can find someone older, an adult or a young adult, to help her. She doesn't need a young kitten getting in her way. Also, you wanted to train, you must do your homework and concentrate on your training."

"But Mum, that's not fair! Mystik said I was a great help and that Jadariol needs me" cried Lunara.

"He needs *no one*, Lunara. He is a Lizariaous, they aren't like us. He'll be fine on his own. You are forbidden from interacting with him."

"He's just a youngster like me. I see a lot of things we both share. His mother was killed by Mettalika. Besides, Sinxo saved him for a reason; I want to honour her death by looking after him. When he's better, he can leave and I promise I'll never see him again." Lunara was close to tears now.

"You are not playing with him and that's final. And if you argue about it, you will be grounded to your tree and not allowed to leave even to play with your real friends!" Shen snarled at her, getting annoyed at her daughter's resistance. Lunara simply snarled back and climbed to the top of the tree to drown her sorrows in tears.

Meanwhile, Jadariol was wondering why he hadn't seen Lunara since his unfortunate comfort offering. He wasn't especially worried, he was just curious. Mystik was mixing medicines at the back of the tree.

"Mystik, have you seen Lunara?" he asked.

"She was at the meeting with her mother but I haven't seen her since. I think before the meeting she was training." Mystik replied, grinding up some wing wort with some asha herbs.

"Training?" asked Jadariol.

"Yes, all Gryphies are training in self defence now. There is a war coming and we must be prepared. But that is nothing for you to worry about."

"Ok" was the one word reply as Jadariol rested his head on his paws and thought about that.

Later, Tranzoss came in to see how Mystik was doing.

"Did I get enough herbs?" she asked.

"Yes, thank you my dear. These will last a good long time." Mystik was still busy mixing, preparing and

245

preserving medicines. She knew that if the war broke out soon, she would need a good stock of them. She looked at her inventory.

"Actually, could you gather me some blood wort, heart herbs and grass bane? Then I think I will have enough."

"Yes Sir!" Tranzoss stood to attention and saluted rather clumsily since the tree, although large, would not permit much movement of wings and Tranzoss was a big female, the largest in the gathering. She was nearly as large as Diabloss.

"Just call me Mystik, dear" replied Mystik with a smile and carried on her work.

Tranzoss nodded and headed out of the tree. On the way, she looked down at Jadariol and snarled slightly. The look said "I have killed many of your kind and many more will fall if they dare come up against me in this war." She then snorted a flame and walked out. The snort said "And I don't trust you any more than the others of your kind."

Jadariol didn't have to have a deep understanding of Gryphie actions and body language to understand some things that are universal. He swallowed and stared at the ground.

Leida had paused for a rest on the cliffs. She'd forgotten about her injured leg in her excitement of graduating. She looked out to sea and remembered how she defended herself against the pack of Lizariaouses who had attacked her. She sighed. She was confident now, she had grown and learnt and she was no longer shy or for the most part, afraid. She sat up proudly and swished her tail. She couldn't wait to tell Diabloss but so far she hadn't found him. For a while she rested and then saw movement further down the cliff towards the sea. It was Tranzoss looking for grass bane. Grass bane grew near salt water; the only place it grew. Tranzoss found what she was looking for and moved away. Leida called out to her and she flew up, alighting beside the blue Gryphie.

"Yes?" she asked, recognising it as Diabloss's mate. Otherwise it was unlikely she would have allowed herself to be broken from the task at hand.

"Have you seen Diabloss? I've looked for him everywhere." Leida smiled after speaking.

Tranzoss looked at her. "No" she said, "I haven't. He left the meeting and I haven't seen him since. I think he went to round up the squad. I'm on herb gathering duties." She sighed. Herb gathering was not a soldier's work. How had she gotten roped into this again?

"Oh, ok. I just wanted to tell him I've passed the final test in my fight training and Otuss graduated me."

"Hey, well done! You'll soon be in with us big leaguers!" Tranzoss grinned.

"Well, I won't be as strong as you guys, I mean, look at you! You're the best of the best. I'm only really starting." Leida scanned Tranzoss with her lean build and powerful muscles. She was the picture of fighting perfection; well trained and well conditioned.

"Strength ain't everything. I specialise mostly in agility as a lot of the females in the squad do. Actually…all four of us do. The males are the brute strength. We females, not being as strong, have to turn the enemy's strength against them by using agility. If you're good at dodging, flying, using fire in a sneaky way, thinking on your feet or wings, there's no problem." Tranzoss explained.

"Well I'm good at dodging but I'm no good at thinking. I act too soon quite often"

"Ah you'll learn. I did. I gotta get back to work now, k?" Tranzoss stood and spread her mighty wings, the sunlight shining off her glossy mane.

"Ok, well, thanks. And if you see Diabloss, can you let him know I'm looking for him?"

"Sure thing, see you" and with one sweep of her wings, Tranzoss took off and flew back towards Shernaron. Leida stayed where she was. Another sun cycle was ending. She flew back to the Forest. Diabloss may not be back until late so she caught herself a forest deer on the way and took it home to eat.

Chapter 24
Building the Troops

In Dyarkroeen, Zephirak was proud of the improvements his soldiers were making. He was also proud of Mordred, who had his trust and respect back.

Mordred and Schaarl were still concerned about the whole plan not working; either they couldn't kill Mettalika and Zephirak went after the Gryphies or he simply killed her and went after them anyway. However their doubts fell as Zephirak's enthusiasm rose.

The soldiers had trained hard for the past lunar and things were going really well. They were now a pack of advanced killing machines. None of them were clumsy and they were all fully trained in combat. Even Croter and Zarkiz were doing better. Now the plans to assemble the troops and move in on Mettalika were being organised.

Zephirak sat in his cavern early the following sun cycle, with Mordred and Karnos.

"Ok, we've got the power. Now to put it into action. We've only got one shot at this so we'd better make it good. If you two fail to get the troops in order and destroy her, I will degrade both of you. I haven't decided on whether or not I'll take your lives yet so that can be a nice little surprise if you fail, depending on how angry I am." The other two stole glances at each other in worry.

"But I'm confident it will go smoothly. As you know, I will be accompanying you to deal the final blow. I want her held down, secured and killed in a timely fashion. There will be no talking, taunting, anything else. Given her strength, I would rather kill her fast than spend time making it so I felt good and risking her escaping."

"How about we injure her so badly she can't move, she's immobilised and can't escape? Then you can

taunt her, degrade her and kill her like she deserves"
suggested Karnos.

"No, we're doing this my way. I suggest you keep
your suggestions, however useful they may be, to
yourself." Zephirak snapped. Mordred suspected that he
was discouraging this in case Zephirak changed his
mind. Mordred knew how much Zephirak wanted to
humiliate the Gryphie he hated above all others. He was
wise and kept quiet though.

"Now, Mordred, you should have been planning the
ambush. What are your ideas for how we're going to
initiate this?" Zephirak's red eyes bored into Mordred.
Any lesser Lizariaous, put on the spot like that, would
have crumbled but Mordred was used to it and it rarely
fazed him now; unless his leader was angry that is.

"Well, from what we've been able to work out
through observance, and might I add that recently we've
been watching her undetected every so often, trying to
work out her routine without making her suspicious, is
that she has no discernable routine. Now, before you
start getting worried, we do realise she has to go to
water to drink. There are springs and there is the marsh.
We can't block off any of these and force her to drink at
a particular one, nor can we set a trap. She would know.
I thought about setting up various sentries around the
areas she is in a lot but then she would still know. So, I
came to this conclusion. She attacks hunting packs. We
all know this from experience. So we send out a pack.
But not a hunting pack, a pack of advanced soldiers.
When she attacks, all soldiers in the areas around will
sound the alert. She'll only think they're calling for help
because a pack is in trouble. Then we all move in on
her, surround her from all sides. Climb trees and launch
ourselves on her if possible." The last part was meant to

be a joke but Zephirak nodded, seriously. He hung on Mordred's every word.

Mordred continued. "Sir, you can watch the action from a safe distance. When we have her pinned, one of us will give the signal and you come in and kill her. By this time hopefully, we will have destroyed at least one of her wings so she can't fly away."

"She wouldn't. I haven't seen her back down from a fight, especially if she is still capable of killing. She may flee once she knows she's lost but we won't give her that option. When the fight starts, send the signal, get more soldiers in, surround the area. If Gryphies come in and try to help, kill them. Nothing will stop this. Nothing will stop her death. I will make sure of that" snarled Zephirak. "She will PAY!" he roared out the last word, making Karnos jump a little.

Zephirak grinned, showing off his sickle like teeth. "This will be a great sun cycle for all our kind. We will bring that Gryphie down once and for all. Now, when to do it. I know you need to run the troops through their paces on the plan. Also, one of my soldiers rightly pointed out to me that rain makes Gryphies weaker, since they have trouble breathing fire when it's wet. However I don't think that Mettalika will be affected by rain. The worst thing about her isn't her fire, it's that damned armour. If it wasn't fused to her body, we could have removed it easily. But we will go with what you suggested, Mordred. Well done."

Mordred saluted in respect.

"Both of you; go out and assemble the troops. Call a meeting; make sure everyone knows what to do and how to do it. Mettalika will not see the next season!" Zephirak laughed triumphantly.

Mordred and Karnos saluted and bounded out to do their tasks.

Behind them, Zephirak's laugh had dissolved into cruel chuckles of delight and glee. It was finally going to happen. No longer would Lizariaouses fall at the claws of Mettalika. He would finally have his revenge.

Leida was sat under her tree, eating the forest deer and thinking how happy Diabloss would be when he heard she had graduated. She watched Mystik's tree as she ate, since it was opposite to hers. The forest was its usual hubbub of activity; it seemed like everyone had decided to be more positive and try to ignore the impending war for now. There were a few subtle differences to normal though. Instead of playing, youngsters were doing their homework; training. It was odd to see kittens learning out of training time. Leida watched them working out their attack and defence techniques, it was quite different to play fighting; it was done with an intelligent intent and thought.

Out of the corner of her eye, she spotted Lunara with Hiryasis. They didn't seem to be training or having fun, they were just sat talking and Hiry soon walked away and left her on her own. She looked downtrodden and headed for her tree, the way she held her body showing off how she was feeling. Head down, tail down, wings drooping. Leida wondered if they had had a falling out.

Suddenly a gust of air beside her made her jump. Diabloss had just bounded in, hungry and eager for something to eat. He greeted her with a nuzzle and tucked in to the forest deer with relish.

"Mmm, this is a good one you caught honey!" he smiled with his mouth full. Leida smiled back, regaining her composure since he had made her jump by bounding in like that.

"I have wonderful news as well, I can't wait to tell you Diabloss" she beamed. He listened, thinking she would reveal what it was but she said nothing else until he had finished his meal.

"Well? What is it then? The war is over? Zephirak quit?"

She chuckled. "If only. No, sadly nothing as exciting or good as that. Actually I graduated from my training! Otuss passed me."

Diabloss smiled widely, hugging her tightly to him. "I think that's nearly as good. I'm so proud of you! You've matured and become a proper member of the Forest."

"And...I wasn't before?" Leida spoke muffled as he had her squished up against him in his strong bear like hug.

Diabloss released her. "You always were. You will always be special to me, no matter how you are and what you do. That is the Leida I fell in love with and that is what makes you unique and special. But when we first met, you were so shy and retiring. You ran at the slightest notion of danger and you wouldn't say "boo" to a Lizariaous. Now look at you! Otuss must have been impressed with you to graduate you so suddenly."

"Well...I kinda insulted him. I said he reminded me of Zephirak because he wanted to go in and kill the Lizariaouses before they killed us first. Then he got angry at me and attacked me so I defended myself. I'd already had that run in with the Lizariaous hunting pack, not that he ever acknowledged that or gave me any respect or praise for it. I was angry about that too. He never respected me, he called me "baby" and he just made me feel awful all the time." She sighed.

"That's just how he works. He doesn't respect anyone unless they prove themselves" explained Diabloss.

"I don't think he even respects you. It makes me angry that he seems to think you're a fool." Leida snarled at this, it really did annoy her how Otuss had nearly no respect for anyone.

"Most of the stuff he says, he says to be big, that's all. He'd never ever even think of coming up against me or picking a fight with me. I am a little concerned about him however, I'm not sure how many others have his view of this whole affair but if he recruits other Gryphies and they do go into Dyarkroeen to attack the Lizariaouses, then it will definitely start this war. Strassor won't be able to stop him, nor Odax. It really troubles me. I don't know if he is trying to prove something or whether he feels he hasn't had enough of the action. But whatever it is, I think I should have a word with him about it and see if he'll change his mind."

"I don't know. I saw how he acted at the meeting too. In fact a small part of me thought he graduated me just to get rid of me and get on with his own plans." Leida looked downhearted at this.

"No, he wouldn't graduate you unless he knew you were ready. Otuss might have his own strong views on things but he likes to get the job done and he will. Whatever he wants to do personally, it always comes after his work. That is one redeeming quality about him at least." Diabloss explained.

"Umm, does he have many redeeming qualities? Because I never saw that many when we were training."

"He does. He is strong, fiercely loyal, attentive to his work, courageous and a good trainer. But he lives for the fight a little too much. It's his life and he has a bloodlust running through him. It is his weakness. Strassor tried to train it out of him but he was badly bullied when he was a kitten, due to his funny looks and crooked teeth. One sun cycle he had enough of it and fought back, he never stopped after that. He has often been mocked for being a Lizariaous look alike. I'm sure you've heard that joke running around the forest."

"Oh yes, I have and until I met him, I wasn't sure what the others were on about when they referred to him as that. I knew once I saw him though." Leida smiled a little. "Then it matches his personality."

Diabloss nodded. "But as I say, he would never graduate you if he didn't think you were now a worthy fighter or a worthy opponent."

"I don't think he thinks I'm a worthy opponent, I wouldn't be able to do any lasting damage to him or put him in his place properly. Nor would I want to. I've never liked him but I don't wish bad things on him."

"Out of interest, what *did* you do to him when you fought and he passed you?" asked Diabloss, curious now. He wanted to see what his mate was capable of.

"I damaged his wings; I think I strained one and the other I damaged. He bled but I didn't make it so bad that he couldn't fly or that it wouldn't heal fairly fast" she told him.

"But *could* you have done? Could you have put him right out of action?"

"Well, yes, I could have…but why would I want to?"

"The very fact it was in your power to really do some damage and that you could have inflicted that makes you very skilled indeed and it also means you are learning well. So, well done Leida. Who knows, maybe you'll be on my squadron one sun cycle?" Diabloss smiled proud of her.

"Well I don't know about that. Tranzoss said something similar earlier." Leida chuckled, feeling proud of herself.

"There you go then! She doesn't give that kind of compliment to just anyone. Let's go for a flight and you can show me some of your skills." Diabloss stood up and stretched. Leida smiled and followed.

As they headed out of the forest, they were watched by Mystik. She smiled. She was secretly proud of shy, quiet Leida, blossoming into a fully fledged fighter with the ability to defend herself correctly. Mystik had always been fond of her and knew that there was something special about her. She didn't want anything to happen to her and now she knew that Leida would be safe, or at least safer than she used to be. Mystik loved seeing members of the gathering grow and improve in the various aspects of their lives. She sighed as she thought of Sinxo. Her trainee assistant. She missed her horribly. Even Lunara hadn't returned after Jadariol's unfortunate comfort words. She was worried it had upset the little Gryphie a lot more than she cared to mention so Mystik went to Shen's tree and called up to see if anyone was there.

In due course, Shen poked her head out from the large hole in the tree trunk.

"Oh, hi Mystik! What brings you here?" Shen climbed down and greeted her.

"I was wondering if Lunara is ok" replied Mystik.

"She was out playing with her friends. She did come back not long ago I think. She never spoke though; she just went up to her hollow. Shall I call her? Has she been bad?" Shen's face clouded over at the prospect of Lunara misbehaving.

"Oh no! It's just that I have not seen her for a while, I was wondering if she was ok and Jadariol is missing her."

As soon as Mystik mentioned Jadariol, Shen's expression hardened. "She is not to play with him any more. He is a Lizariaous, a bad influence and a nuisance. I forbade her to have anything else to do with him so she won't be around to visit him."

Mystik looked sad at this. "But she is his only friend. He has no one else and she has been helping him so much and so well. She is learning how to care for another and look after them. Not only that but she is learning to put aside her differences and look after someone who normally would have been left to die."

"She is not to play with him any more." Shen stood defiant, the mane along her neck stiffening as she became irritated.

"But she is bridging the gap, don't you see? Maybe if we were all more tolerant of each other, things wouldn't be this bad. It is individuals like you who mark all Lizariaouses with the same spot, who make peace impossible." Mystik pleaded.

Shen wouldn't move. "She is *my* kitten and I can do as I wish. I consider it dangerous for her to hang around with one of them. That is my decision."

"Even if it hurts her and him in the process?" asked Mystik.

"They can't get hurt. They're evil." Shen replied.

Mystik frowned. "So, you would stop your kitten showing compassion to someone less fortunate than herself? Whether it is one of them or one of us, caring for someone bridges every gap. You have a wonderful kitten, who will go on to do great things because of her pure heart and lack of prejudice and yet you encourage her to hate. I am ashamed of you, Shen. It is not her, or him, but *you* who needs to change."

Shen snorted. "I don't encourage her to hate. I encourage her to be careful. You have never had kittens, what would you know?" And she turned and climbed back up her tree with a disrespectful flick of her tail.

Mystik stood a moment, taken aback and upset. It had never been her fault she had been unable to have kittens.

She called up after Shen. "If you had given Lunara a chance, she would have been my new assistant. She has great potential." There was no reply. Mystik sighed sadly and wandered back to her tree. There was so much hate already, why were some of the gathering encouraging it in their youngsters? She could understand that Shen was worried about her kitten but no harm could come of it and she and Jadariol had been getting on so well.

Back in Mystik's tree, Jadariol had grown very bored without Lunara to talk to. Lunara had been there most of the time with him and now he hadn't seen her for a long while. He also felt he'd upset her. He wasn't sure why that mattered to him. He focused himself on walking or at least standing, to take his mind off it. His legs felt stiff from lack of use and he struggled at first. Then he found he could stand on his two undamaged legs and hobble a bit but he soon had to sit down. It was a start at least.

Mystik returned and saw him trying to walk. "Now Jadariol, don't over exert yourself dear. The bone is healing nicely but it won't if you try to put any weight on it." She ushered him back to his bed.

"It would be best if you just try sitting and standing here, but don't try to walk just yet."

Jadariol mooched and grumbled. "Where's Lunara? I want to play "Which One?" with her."

"She won't be visiting you any more. Her mother forbids it. You will have to make do with me for company I am afraid." Mystik told him.

Jadariol clearly didn't like the idea of this. "Well, tell her mother to let her see me. What is her problem huh?"

"I tried, her mother says no. Now, just rest and get some sleep, it will be moon cycle soon."

Jadariol growled in annoyance. Why didn't Gryphies go against their parents like Lizariaouses did? Then again, if the punishment was as bad as what Lizariaous youngsters got, maybe that was why they did as they were told. He lay down, feeling put out.

Lunara had overheard the conversation between her mother and Mystik and she curled up and sobbed over the fact that Shen wouldn't let her see Jadariol, even though Mystik had asked. She hoped Mystik would ask and be able to persuade her mother to relent but this wasn't happening. Lunara sighed.

Moon cycle was drawing in fast now and Diabloss and Leida were out on the cliffs, watching the sun set, cuddled together happily. Leida felt proud of herself for once in her life and Diabloss did too. He felt he had made the right decision all those seasons ago when he chose Leida over the more powerful but equally as bitter Mettalika. He was worried more than ever about how things were going in the Forest though. The training was going well, nearly every member of the gathering was training up to fight but there were strong emotions and strong feelings among them all. Kayto had told him that there were a lot of mixed feelings. Most of them didn't want to fight but would if they had to and so they trained. Some wanted to move away but knew they didn't really have anywhere else to go and the Gryphie loyalty to gathering and homeland wouldn't permit them to leave for long; they would always return when needed, they knew that. And there were the odd few who wanted to go on the offensive. These were the ones Diabloss was particularly worried about. If a war started full on, it would undoubtedly be those who caused it. He still, maybe foolishly, hoped that it would blow over once Mettalika was dead. He knew the Lizariaouses were planning to kill her and that was another reason all Gryphies were confined to the Forest now. He didn't want anyone getting in the way of that. Did he care that she was going to die? A part of him did. But a larger part of him knew that if she died, one life taken, hundreds could be saved. He rested his head on top of Leida's and murred in his throat to her, comfortingly. It was a rare moment he was relaxed like this. She was murring back to him and he lay his ears back and enjoyed the soft sound. It was times like this that made it all worth it. The fighting, the worry. If he could still have a small amount of happiness with his mate, he would keep going. He was fairly certain she felt the same too. He could feel her love for him and now he knew she could defend herself, he felt more confident, not needing to worry about her as much. They had flown around and he could see her skills as they trained. Seeing it for himself, he knew that Otuss had graduated her with good reason. Diabloss felt satisfaction as the sun set, turning the sky golden. They would win this war.

Chapter 25
The Moon Wraith Mystery

Over the next few sun cycles, things went as they normally did. Training, talking, no more meetings were held but everyone knew where they stood. Leida went out with Stervia, one of the squadron females. Stervia taught Leida a few more techniques and she learned fast now she had the hang of the general ideas. Stervia was impressed with Leida's attentiveness to detail and now she was actually thinking on her wings. She was able to work out things and act swiftly; overcoming almost everything Stervia threw at her.

Diabloss kept an eye on the Lizariaouses with some of the soldiers. It was worth keeping an eye on them just in case they tried anything. They didn't though; they were quiet and carried on as normal. They found Gryphies hard to hunt because they had all been forbidden to leave the main living area of the Forest. So the Lizariaouses hunted forest deer, like they used to. Wandering Gryphies from other places were easy targets though and because they wandered nearby, the Lizariaouses didn't suspect or think about why none of the Forest Gryphies were around. Not that they could really differentiate them anyway.

Jadariol's condition continued to improve, though now without Lunara's help. He busied himself trying to walk and building his strength. Mystik fed him herbs that would help him heal faster and his bones grow back stronger. He was doing very well and could make it to the front entrance of the tree now. He limped around in circles inside, finding this new freedom to be very refreshing. He had missed it so much in the time he'd been unable to walk.

Lunara hung around with her other friends, though she dearly wanted to see Jadariol. She sometimes saw him walk to the entrance of the tree but she kept out of his vision and didn't speak to him. Even looking at him made her sad inside, like a sick feeling of missing him and the fun they had had. It was interesting hanging around with him because he was different. He had different views, told different jokes and generally behaved differently too. But she did as her mother told her. Hiryasis had tried particularly hard to cheer her up. He secretly liked that her mother had made the decision not to let Lunara hang around with Jadariol so he was perky and positive about it and tried to make Lunara as such, too.

Mystik also missed having Lunara around. She would be allowed to go back and help Mystik after Jadariol was better and had been taken back to Dyarkroeen. Mystik was glad about this but still sad the little Lizariaous now had no one to keep him company except her. Mystik was wise but she was no kitten and she was no substitute for Lunara. So instead, she would sit down and tell Jadariol stories she thought he might find interesting. Stories of battles and heroics. He did enjoy them but he couldn't relate to them because they were about Gryphies and invariably, he fell asleep while she told them. She made a note not to tell him stories before bed, but during the sun cycle instead, when there would be less of a chance of him falling asleep.

Strassor, Odax and Otuss trained their classes hard every sun cycle. Otuss however, had been secretly gathering together other like-minded Gryphies who wanted to infiltrate the Lizariaous colony and kill Zephirak and anyone else who was on his side. Since things were moving so slowly and because of the death of Sinxo as well, they decided that they would speed things up and put a stop to this. Without anyone else knowing. They would leave one moon cycle and make their move.

Strassor and Odax were pleasantly unaware of this. Otuss wasn't good at covering things up but miraculously, he had managed to hide his plans from them. He just had to keep in mind to be calm and controlled with it when he was around them. He pretended to be more concerned with training the other Gryphies.

Over in Dyarkroeen though, things were getting well underway. It was taking some time because everyone involved had to be completely sure of what they were doing, there was no room for mistakes. They had one shot at this. If they failed, they may all end up dead or seriously wounded. Also, Mettalika would know for the future what to look out for and they would never be able to catch her again. So everything had to be explored and planned with precise accuracy. From the ambush to the immobilization to the final killing blow, everything had to be perfect. Mordred was ensuring this. He did not want this to go wrong. It would ruin any hopes for peace they might have. Schaarl was equally as confident but also as wary.

Croter and Zarkiz were no longer simply bone headed guards, they had transformed into soldiers, able to take on all obstacles and overcome them. Karnos was commanding half the soldiers, Mordred the other half and Zephirak was overseeing all of it. They would be ready to put their plan into action in a couple of sun cycles and bring down Mettalika, putting an end to all their troubles and fears of being hunted by her. A few more double checks on the plan of attack and they would be completely ready.

***

It was afternoon in Shernaron and Jadariol was limping around in Mystik's tree as he usually did every few hours. He heard the sound of young Gryphies playing outside and he was reminded of Lunara. Where was she anyway? Even though Mystik had told him her mother had forbidden her to see him, he still thought she might pass by and say hi to him in the tree or something. He limped to the entrance and sat down for the first time just outside the tree. A couple of kittens saw him and squealed, running away. He rolled his eyes and snorted. Silly kittens. Once again he thought Gryphies were stupid to be so afraid. He often forgot how scared he had been in the claws of Mettalika. He sat in the sun that streamed down through the leaves of the tree and watched. He yawned and lay down; sitting up for too long was still an effort. He had no idea which tree Lunara lived in. Living in trees was also weird to him. Who wants to live up high when they can live in a nice dark cave on the ground? He kept an eye out for Lunara. He didn't want to wander away from the tree because he wasn't sure how big the Forest was or if he could find his way back again in his condition. Most of the kittens saw him and kept away. Some watched him from afar but none of them spoke to him. They had all heard of him and that he was there but they had also heard rumours started by other youngsters that he ate kittens and that he had a bad temper and could attack at any moment. These rumours of course had gotten bigger and more unbelievable the more they went around, some even coming out with silly things like he was Zephirak's son and that he had already eaten kittens behind Mystik's back. Jadariol felt a bit left out that no one was talking to him and when they looked at him, it was out of fear; that they hoped he'd stay where he was and not come after them.

Out of the corner of his eye, he saw something in the bushes. It was Lunara, Hiryasis and some other kittens. His ears perked up and he watched, hoping she would see him and come over to talk to him. She didn't though, she was training with them. Then Jadariol heard Shen calling her and he watched as she left the group and returned to her tree for a meal. Ah, so that's where she lives! He felt satisfied with that and kept watching. Shen left the tree. She was going to the spring to get some water. She headed out of the clearing and into the Forest. Jadariol sat up. Lunara was sat inside the tree eating a sea vulture.

So, with some difficulty, Jadariol stood and limped to her tree slowly. Other youngsters ran from him as he passed but he ignored their silliness.

Lunara had nearly finished her sea vulture and didn't notice him approach. His voice interrupted her meal.

"Hey, Lunara. Err...Sinxo will live inside you to the end of time and look at you doing things you know" he said clumsily.

Lunara looked up. "Jadariol?"

"Yeah, I just came to tell you that Sinxo will be inside you forever...or...or something...you know?" He paused as she came up to him, nuzzling him under the chin. He wasn't sure what she was doing. She was happy to see him and even happier to see he was walking. She nuzzled him out of joy and friendship but Jadariol knew little of these, and less of the latter of course. He wobbled and sat down on his rump.

"I'm so happy to see you! Mum won't let me visit you any more" she looked downhearted and miserable about this. "I wanted to come and see you but I don't wanna make Mum mad and disobey her so I kept away. How are you feeling? You seem to be getting better. You aren't overdoing it are you? Are the herbs working well? How long have you been walking?" she had so many questions.

Jadariol answered them all. "I'm feeling better, no I'm not overdoing it, yes they are and a few sun cycles. Ever since you stopped visiting, I got bored and started walking. At first I thought you stopped visiting because of what I said about Sinxo. I can't comfort very well."

"Oh it's ok. I still miss her greatly but the thought was there so I know you meant it in a kind way even though it came out wrong" replied Lunara.

"Hey, where's your mother gone?" asked Jadariol.

"She went to get some water" said Lunara. "She'll be back soon but don't worry; I can go after I've finished my meal, which I have now." She smiled happily and trotted about playfully. Jadariol sat and watched her.

"Come on, let's go somewhere else before Mum gets back and finds you outside our tree" said Lunara and walked backwards, smiling at him. Straight into the legs of her mother.

"Go where?" asked Shen. Lunara spun round, squealed and made for the tree but Shen grabbed her tail.

Jadariol watched with interest.

"What did I tell you, Lunara?"

"You told me I can't visit him or hang around with him. But he's visiting me. You never said anything about that." Lunara smiled sheepishly and looked up at her mother.

Shen looked at Jadariol, expecting him to say something but he said nothing. He didn't stand up for his friend, nor did he make a fuss. He just looked at her. A Lizariaous youngster would have been bitten or cuffed around the head, then sent straight to his cave. Jadariol found it interesting how Gryphies didn't seem to immediately use violence on their youngsters.

"You came to visit did you?" asked Shen.

"Yeah" replied Jadariol. "To show Lunara how I'm getting better."

"What is she to you?" asked Shen.

"What?" Jadariol put his head on one side, puzzled.

"What is she to you?" repeated Shen. She wanted to know if Lizariaouses knew what friends were.

"I dunno, a friend I guess. She's helped me get better and stuff."

"Hmm..." Shen still didn't trust him but she was a little surprised he would make the effort to actually visit Lunara. She had never expected an injured Lizariaous to go out of his way to see a Gryphie he considered to be "a friend".

Shen let go of Lunara's tail. "Ok, if you want to play with him, you can" she sighed.

Lunara's eyes grew wide and excited. "Really? You really don't mind?"

"I will reserve my judgement but only because Mystik says we should "bridge the gap" between our species. If you can help him then it's one more step towards mutual peace between us."

Lunara jumped for joy and beckoned to Jadariol to follow her, which he did slowly.

Shen watched them go and felt a strange feeling. She had never seen a Lizariaous and a Gryphie on such good terms, even before the whole incident with Mettalika happened. The two species lived in toleration of each other but rarely interacted at all. She climbed back up her tree again.

Lunara and Jadariol joined Lunara's other friends. Most of them looked scared of him.

"This is Jadariol! Don't be scared, he's one of my best friends and he wants to be your friend too." Lunara said, brightly.

Jadariol wasn't all that bothered about making friends with the others but he attempted a smile and sat down, getting tired again.

Hiryasis looked him over, he was still unsure of him and didn't really want Lunara hanging around with him but he'd promised to try and make friends when the time came so he kept his word.

"I'm Hiryasis. My friends call me Hiry but you can call me Hiryasis" he said. Jadariol just looked at him.

"That's nice" he replied.

"Not very talkative is he?" Hiry said privately to Lunara.

"Oh I think he's shy" replied Lunara with a giggle.

The others introduced themselves to Jadariol. There were three others, Kammy, Hevia and Zephyr.

Now they had to work out a game they could all play happily, even with Jadariol's injuries. They decided on hide and seek. So Jadariol could just sit somewhere until he was found. He found it boring after a while and went back to Mystik's tree.

Later, Lunara popped in.

"Wow, this is a great hiding spot. We found everyone else and we've been looking for you for ages! You win!"

"I got bored and came back here" replied Jadariol. "Your friends aren't very good seekers now are they?"

"Well, you did choose a hiding place that was out of the area you were at. We all thought you were around hidden in a bush or something." Lunara sat down next to him and asked him how he was feeling. Jadariol adjusted himself on his bed and yawned.

"Tired really. I'm gunna take a nap I think."

"Ok, well, I'll come visit later. See you!" Lunara bounded out of the tree, happy that the introduction to her friends had gone well.

Jadariol rested his head on his paws and sighed. Gryphie youngsters were so much different from the ones he was used to hanging around with. Lizariaouses liked to play fight mostly. And when they played hide and seek, they didn't just find the hidden ones, the hidden ones had to fight them and defend themselves to see if they would be able to help the seekers find the other hidden ones. All Lizariaous games resulted in some kind of fight. Many Lizariaouses got their scars when they were youngsters. Those who didn't were considered to be bad fighters if they stayed out of childhood battles. Jadariol yawned and fell asleep.

Outside, Lunara had returned to her friends and was asking them all what they thought of him.

"He's boring. He doesn't do or say much" said Kammy.

"I liked him" said Zephyr, "it's not his fault he doesn't do much, Mettalika attacked him remember?"

"Oh yeah" said Kammy, "I forgot about that."

"You'd forget your own wings if they weren't attached" laughed Hevia. "I thought he was ok. I don't think he'll play with us much though; he just seemed bored with it all. I bet they play different games in Dyarkroeen."

"If they even live to grow up" muttered Hiryasis.

Lunara poked him and scowled, "don't be so mean to him! He has no friends; I don't even think he has friends where he lives. Then again, I did see him with some others when I went to Dyarkroeen. I wonder if they miss him." She looked thoughtful.

"I doubt it. They don't feel things like that" snorted Hiryasis.

269

"Hey, would you shut up about it! He feels pain and sadness. I saw him after Mettalika hurt him and he looked as scared as any of us would be" growled Lunara.

Hiryasis knew he was fighting a losing battle and he shut up about it.

They chatted and played some more.

Later, Lunara visited Jadariol again. Mystik was there this time; she was putting a fresh dressing on one of his legs.

"Hold still dear, this won't take long."

Jadariol struggled a bit; he was getting tired of the new dressings being put on. Since his legs were a bit better, he had to hold them up for Mystik and when he did it for a long time, it became a pain to do and they got tired. Previously, she had held them herself and applied the dressing, which had been much more difficult. But they were healing very well. To begin with, he had had the dressing changed frequently. Now it was down to once a sun cycle. He was supposed to have it in the morning but this morning, Mystik had been out hunting and it had taken her longer than usual to catch her meal. She had been catching a forest deer and sharing it with Jadariol. It saved having to catch two meals, since she was not as young as she had once been.

Lunara sat patiently and waited for Mystik to finish.

"Lunara, could you please come and hold up Jadariol's back leg, he is struggling with it now and keeps relaxing it" said Mystik.

Lunara obliged and soon the dressings were applied again.

"Thank grik that's over" grumbled Jadariol.

"Now now, there's no need for language like that" scolded Mystik with a frown.

"Sorry." Jadariol said and sighed. Swearing was never frowned upon back home. Once again he thought Gryphies were weird.

Lunara sprung up to him excitedly.

"Jaddy!! Guess what? There will be a story telling this moon cycle and we can look for Moon Wraiths!"

"Really? And don't call me Jaddy!"

"Sorry, it's just exciting. Now I can prove to you they actually exist!" squealed Lunara.

"Well it sounds cool. I can't walk far though" replied Jadariol.

"No need to walk that far, we just make our way into the Forest a little way and keep our eye out for them."

"What do they look like?" asked Jadariol, curious now.

"I told you before, they're like Gryphies but with feathered wings and they're black with a blue aura around them! I've only seen one but hopefully this moon cycle, that will become two." Lunara hopped about. "It was around this time last season that I saw one so I reckon I could see another this moon cycle and you will too!"

"Well, if you're sure. There are a lot of weird creatures around anyway, I know, cos we catch a good few of them to eat."

"You can't eat Moon Wraiths though cos they're sacred. I heard if you eat one, you die a horrible painful death and your gathering will be cursed forever!" Lunara looked scared at this.

"Yeah, sure. I've never heard of that happening before." Jadariol snorted and lay down. "But I'll come with you and see for myself."

Lunara nodded and told him she would be back at moon rising.

At moon rising, everyone was either preparing to go to the story telling or in their trees settling down for the moon cycle with their loved ones. This story telling, Mystik was attending since she always had something wise to say or a story with a moral to speak of. Odax was also there, although Otuss was unusually absent. He liked the story tellings but lately he hadn't shown up to them or been seen outside of training time when he was teaching.

Leida was there too, although Diabloss wasn't. He was out with the squad. Leida had tried to persuade Tranzoss to join in but she had been too busy to attend, plus she wasn't that good at sitting and listening. She needed to be busying herself with things she considered to be of worth and use. Leida also wanted to keep an eye out for things happening around the Forest, since the previous moon cycle she had heard faint noises. She wasn't sure if she believed in Moon Wraiths and if they were the reason but she was always curious about these things so although she sat with the other Gryphies, she kept one eye on their surroundings and her wits about her.

Lunara joined the little group. There were about 15 Gryphies attending that moon cycle by the light of the Glowbugs. Syrup had been spread on some of the trees for the bugs to feed on to ensure they would stay there and light the area. They were very useful when it was dark.

Lunara saw Jadariol sat with Mystik and went over to see him.

"Are you ready for this?" she asked with a devious grin.

"Yeah, let's see if they actually exist" he replied. In truth, he was pretty excited about it himself but he wouldn't let it show. Excitement was a form of weakness.

The first story was being told by Conosza. He was a large blue Gryphie with an odd accent. Some of the others often couldn't understand what he was saying so they had to pretend to understand his story. He was telling the story of the SilvaGryphie. She was like the Gryphie equivalent to a legendary hero. It was said that the SilvaGryphie was the first Gryphie to land in Shernaron and she brought others there too. They all looked up to her because she was their leader. However, some treated her like a God and worshipped her. She didn't like this and banished them, saying "I am not a God, I am simply a Gryphie, like everyone else and I do not deserve worship. I lead you because I want to see you happy and do what is best for all of us. In seeing you happy, I am happy too." Those who were banished thought she was ungrateful and decided to overthrow her, take over and banish her instead. However, there was a flash of bright light when they attacked her and none of them were ever seen again. Some say they were struck by lightning as they made to attack her, some say she could use magic and made them disappear. And some say she actually was a God in Gryphie disguise, being tired of being worshipped and choosing to live life as a mortal. Whatever the reason, the SilvaGryphie is a legend and a good influence on all kittens for them to be true, loyal and pure of heart like she was, with her motto "If you make those around you happy, you will gain true happiness yourself."

Oddly enough, while everyone was listening to Conosza's story with difficulty and trying to politely hide the fact they understood hardly any of his words, Jadariol listened intently, understanding every last syllable of it.

Lunara saw this. "Wow, you can understand him?"

"Yeah, it's a Dyarkroeen dialect, or at least, from around our territory. He must have either come from there when we started hunting you guys or he's been hanging out too long with other Gryphies from around there." Jadariol replied.

"There are Gryphies there?" Lunara hadn't realised that.

"Yeah, you're lots of places. He will have come from the borders of our territory, not actually in it. The soldiers tend to kill any Gryphies who wander in. I know there were a few colonies around about there, they've all gone now though."

"Hmm, actually he is new to the Forest. I bet he moved here from one of those gatherings." Lunara looked thoughtful and then snarled, angry that the Lizariaouses pushed Gryphies out of their homes as well as hunting them. It never occurred to her that maybe the Gryphies wouldn't want to live near Lizariaouses just in case they were attacked and actually left without being pushed out. When the trouble first started, they stayed but as it got worse they decided it would be safe to move away.

Jadariol thought Lunara wasn't that smart if she didn't even know where all the other gatherings were. He knew where all the Lizariaous colonies were, since he had started training to be a soldier, he had to know these things. Gryphies had no need to train their kittens up to be like that and so most of them had their birthplace, sometimes moved to other places, but rarely knew where all the other gatherings were.

The story had finished now and the next Gryphie started hers.

Lunara tapped Jadariol and beckoned him to follow her. He stood up quietly and shakily, Mystik didn't notice, and he followed Lunara to the edge of the clearing. It was darker here now they were away from most of the Glowbugs. They both peered into the trees.

"How far in did you see it?" asked Jadariol.

"Not far, it was wandering around…well, I'll show you!" Lunara padded into the bushes and Jadariol slowly followed, making sure he trod carefully and silently. Not that anyone else noticed their disappearance, since they were all engrossed in the story that the female Gryphie was now telling them. It was about the metal mountains and how they came to be. There were the metal mountains and steel mountains and these were collectively known as the high mountains, both of which had gatherings of Gryphies around. Jadariol listened a little as he and Lunara headed into the Forest.

They didn't go far though and Lunara crouched down in the bushes.

"I saw it over there." She pointed to a small clearing. "It passed through that area and went off into the Forest. Maybe it came for a drink or something. Whatever the reason, it was a beautiful creature and I want to see it again." She sounded excited. Jadariol sat next to her and then lay down. Well at least finding a Moon Wraith was something he could sit down to do.

For a long while, they sat and just kept watch quietly. Neither said a word. Jadariol wasn't sure how long she had waited before she saw it last time and Lunara didn't want to speak in case it heard them.

Jadariol started to nod off to sleep. Lunara yawned too. She had no idea how long it had been since they arrived and a part of her wondered if the others might be getting worried about them or if they had been missed at all. If they were missed, it was likely either some would go and look for them or the whole story meeting would be called off to search, what with the threat of Lizariaouses infiltrating the Forest.

Lunara's eyes kept closing and she jumped awake each time. Her vision became blurry from needing to sleep. She saw something shining in the distance. She thought it was a Glowbug but found it got bigger as it got closer. Not taking her eyes off it, she nudged Jadariol who awoke with a jump and started to speak but Lunara cut him off and pointed at the light.

It was a faint blue aura and it was getting closer. Both of them sat bolt upright and stared now. This was it! A Moon Wraith. Lunara couldn't believe her luck. Jadariol couldn't believe it was actually true and they really did exist. As it neared, the light stopped growing. Actually, it was pretty small. Disappointingly small in fact. Not as big as the one Lunara had seen before.

It trotted past them. It was a Furmine with some Glowbugs on a syrup covered stick.

"That's your Moon Wraith?? That's bad…really bad Lunara." Jadariol snorted and stood up. "Come on, this has been a waste of time. I thought I'd see something awesome. All I see is a Furmine taking a moontime stroll."

"But that wasn't what I saw last time! It was bigger, it wasn't a Furmine, it was a Moon Wraith! Like a Gryphie but not as big as a Gryphie and it glowed. It wasn't that…I'm not lying, Jadariol." Lunara started sobbing a little at the fact he didn't believe her and also at the fact she had got excited and then been disappointed.

"Oh sure. Well, maybe you were tired when you saw it and you mistook that for a Moon Wraith. It's an easy mistake to make when you're tired. Can we go back now? I wanna hear the rest of those stories and I'm bored." Jadariol turned to go.

Lunara but sat hunched over and staring at the ground. "But...I *did* see one."

"Ok, so you saw one. I don't care, let's go back." Jadariol was starting to get annoyed that she wasn't following and his back leg was hurting him.

"Ok, we'll go back" sighed Lunara and took one last look at the small clearing the Furmine had come from. Her gaze travelled around and then she saw something glow. She blinked, thinking it was another Furmine and turned to go. But the glow was much bigger this time.

"Jadariol?"

"What? What is it now?" Jadariol turned and looked in the direction Lunara was pointing. Then he stared. This *was* much bigger than the previous glow had been. They both stared and out of the trees wandered a Moon Wraith. It was like a Gryphie but a little smaller and had feathery wings. It was dark and a pale blue aura shone off it, giving it the glow. It looked around, didn't see them and went up to a tree, looking up into the leaves. Lunara beamed at Jadariol but Jadariol just looked unimpressed. This puzzled her.

"It's a Grypher" he said.

"A what?" she asked.

"A Grypher. They're like Gryphies but rarer and they don't talk. My Dad caught one once. You don't see them very much though. Grown-ups probably know about them, even if you don't. That's not a wraith thing though." Jadariol explained.

Lunara looked at him, suddenly the thought of the Moon Wraith actually being a subspecies of Gryphie put a dampener on the whole thing.

"You're making that up! There aren't things like Gryphies that don't talk."

"No I'm not! You got the mountain Gryphies, the forest Gryphies, the Daemon Gryphies and the

Gryphers. But the Gryphers are too dumb to talk; they haven't evolved like the rest of you did. Dad told me, when he caught it" stated Jadariol.

Lunara just stared at the "Moon Wraith" as it sniffed the tree and wandered towards them. It really was beautiful but the air of mystery had gone. Lunara half wished she hadn't shown one to Jadariol. There was no magic or mystery now that there was an answer to what they were. She still watched quietly though, so as not to scare it. She had no idea if it would be scared or not or if it would try to eat them or something. Jadariol watched it too. Even though he knew what it was, the only one he had ever seen had been dead, so seeing a live one was interesting to him as well.

The Grypher wandered past them, turned a corner round a tree and was gone, only the faint glow of its passing remained.

"Well, they're still cool. Maybe I can come and watch them or make friends with one. Do you know if they eat Gryphies?" asked Lunara.

"Na, Dad said they only eat small things, you're bigger than they are so they wouldn't eat you anyway. I bet a Gryphie could easily kill a Grypher, they look weak. Wanna go back now?"

Lunara nodded and they headed back to the clearing, where Mystik was sharing her story with them. It was about Sinxo and all the funny and touching things she had done in her life.

Lunara and Jadariol sat back down quietly but Leida had seen them leave and whispered to them.

"So, where did you guys go off to then?" she asked.

Lunara looked shocked and worried. "Err...we needed to go...umm well you know, to relieve ourselves of our waste food."

"Sure you did. You weren't looking for Moon Wraiths again, were you? You were gone awfully long for merely relieving yourselves."

"If we did go looking for Moon Wraiths, would you tell on us?" asked Lunara.

"You know I wouldn't. So long as you stay out of trouble and don't get Jadariol into trouble. Don't forget, even though he can walk a little better, it doesn't mean that he has the same energy as you have just yet. Don't take him too far away because he may not be able to walk back and that would upset and stress him." Leida warned.

Lunara nodded and apologised. Jadariol was busy listening to the story. Lunara noticed that he enjoyed the stories and listened carefully to them. She thought maybe it was because they contained more stuff than just fighting or killing all the time but it was mostly because he'd grown to enjoy them because Mystik had told him so many.

Soon though, the story telling was over and they all headed back to their trees. Lunara said bye to Jadariol and Mystik took Jadariol back to the big old tree they shared.

"Did you enjoy the stories, my dear?" she asked him.

Jadariol nodded. "Yeah, they were interesting. I liked the one about the SilvaGryphie best, it sounds interesting."

"You could understand Conosza's speech? That is impressive. He moved here recently and has not been able to make many friends because no one can understand what he is saying to them. Even I struggle and I can understand quite a few different dialects."

Jadariol shrugged. "I dunno; I just listened" he replied and settled down on his bed for the moon cycle.

279

Mystik checked his dressings and padded over to her bed at the back of the tree, settling down too.

Over in Leida's tree, Diabloss had returned and she was telling him to keep an ear open for the strange noises that she had heard last moon cycle.

"What kind of noises?" he asked.

"I heard rustling and what I thought to be low voices."

"It's probably Furmines. I wouldn't worry about it" said Diabloss and he pulled her close, getting comfortable and closing his eyes. Leida closed hers too but later on that moon cycle, she heard the noises again. Furmines were known to be noisy and be active at all times of the moon cycle or sun cycle, she figured Diabloss was right and put it down to that, falling asleep against him.

Chapter 26
Into Action

Over in Dyarkroeen, plans had been set. It was arranged for the soldiers to go out the following sunrise and find where Mettalika was. Attacking her soon after sunrise would be the best idea, they worked out. That way, everyone would have the energy to fight her, having got up fit and ready for the new sun cycle.

That moon cycle, while Lunara and Jadariol were in the Forest hunting Moon Wraiths, Mordred and Schaarl were in their cave talking about the events of the next sun cycle. Schaarl was worried for Mordred's safety.

"If she hurts or kills you, I don't know what I'd do" she muttered, nuzzling her mate.

Mordred put a paw on her shoulder and reassured her.

"It will be fine; we know what we're doing. We will bring her down and it will end this stupid war. Things will go back to how they were before and there will be no more fighting. Zephirak is confident and happy about this plan and when he is happy, you can be pretty sure that it will go well and work out."

"But what if it doesn't? What if they don't have her properly pinned and she kills Zephirak?" asked Schaarl with concern. "Then she might kill the rest of you for good measure."

"If she kills Zephirak, to be honest, I don't care. One of them has to die. He is as corrupt as she is, they suit each other. If she kills him, I doubt she would come after the rest of us since she would be tired from the fighting and there would be too many of us in any case. We will definitely get her, Schaarl. This will be our sun cycle of victory! Trust me, we have it all worked out. Nothing will stop us."

"But Zephirak will probably still hate Gryphies, he may even still keep on killing them. Some of us have a taste for them now." Schaarl still didn't believe that things would be ok, even after Mettalika's death.

"Look, if he still wants to kill them, we can't do much about it. I'm pretty sure as I've told you before, that he won't want to control them all. Even if he feels like that now, after Mettalika is dead, I am pretty sure his mind will change and he won't go after the others. Funny things can happen you know, to change minds." Mordred assured her.

"I only hope you're right" she replied and closed her eyes with a sigh.

This would be the sun cycle it all ended and the impending war would be forgotten.

The next sun cycle dawned and Mordred was up early. He woke Schaarl up to say goodbye to her. She nuzzled him, crying a little, terrified for him and he left her stood at the entrance to their cave, her face clouded with worry and fear. He hated that being perhaps the last expression he would ever see on her face. Even though he wanted to be confident that it would go well, this was Mettalika they were ambushing, not just any rogue Gryphie. And she would not go down without a fight and a lot of bloodshed. Mordred tried not to think about it and headed to Zephirak's cavern for the meeting they were having before assembling the soldiers and heading out.

Karnos and Croter were already there. Mordred wondered why Croter was there.

Zephirak sat on the large stone that Leida had once been bound upon.

"You're late" he said.

"Sorry, Sir, I was making sure I was ready, one hundred percent, for what we are about to do!" Mordred saluted. In reality he was late because he had been saying goodbye to Schaarl but he didn't want to mention mates around Zephirak.

"Well then sit down and listen up" said Zephirak with a dangerous snarl.

"This is the sun cycle! This is when we will bring down the Gryphie who has caused us pain and misery for far too long. You know what you must do. I am proud of all of you. Mordred, leader of soldier pack one, Karnos, leader of soldier pack two and Croter, leader of soldier pack three, you are the keys to this mission. You are the ones who will help it succeed the most with your organisation and skill. Make sure the soldiers are all in the right places at the right time, keep in contact with each other, use your second in commands wisely to help you and above all, don't fail. Because we all know what happens to failures, don't we? They will either get reduced to being workers or I will kill them. We will not fail this time. Lizariaouses! Show your strength! Never back down and grind her to the ground! She will feel every ounce of fear and pain she's put us through and she will feel my wrath. This is the sun cycle Mettalika dies!" He roared loudly and powerfully. Mordred, Karnos and Croter joined in, their roars echoing around the cavern and out through the hole in the roof of it.

Outside, the soldiers were ready and waiting to go out in their various packs and scout about for Mettalika. They would be outposted around the swamp area where the trees and foliage was dense and she would have trouble spreading her wings. Gryphies and Lizariaouses are all around the same size but without huge wings to hinder them, Lizariaouses have the advantage in such a place.

283

The plan was that three packs, each lead by Mordred, Karnos and Croter would go into the swamp and the area around, hide in places they expected Mettalika would go such as the places she drank or caught her prey and hide there until she came along. They would all leap out, roaring, causing as much noise as they possibly could to alert all the other Lizariaouses, who would in turn roar from their hiding places as they went to aid the pack who had Mettalika, passing the message along until they were all alerted. Each pack had five soldiers and the leader. The backup soldiers were about thirty. So altogether, around fifty of them as well as Zephirak were to attack her. One Gryphie had no chance against them.

In the ranks outside Zephirak's cavern, Zarkiz was a little annoyed Croter had been chosen as a leader and not him.

"I'm as good as him" he told Rondo, a rather chunky Lizariaous soldier who was stood next to him. Rondo ignored him, his mind focused on the plan ahead. In fact, only Zarkiz was moaning about his situation. If any of the others had any qualms about who was leading the packs, they certainly didn't let on.

"You think I did as good as Croter right?" Zarkiz asked Rondo. Rondo just glanced at him and snarled a little, warning him to shut up about it.

"Just answer, yes or no." Zarkiz looked pleadingly at him.

"Shut the grik up and get focused or this will be the sun cycle you die as well as Mettalika" he growled and moved up the rank a bit so Zarkiz could no longer speak to him. Zarkiz looked crestfallen and sighed. He could have been a great leader; he'd grown so much from being a mere guard. He resolved to do the best damn job he could in this plan. None of the soldiers were shifting about; none of them looked in the least worried. They were a violent species and battles were a way of life for them. The fact they were going up against probably one of the strongest and most feared creatures in both the territories didn't seem to really hit in on them. They were as warlike as the Gryphies were peaceful. Also, they had been so convinced this would work that none of them had any doubt about it at all. In fact, a lot of them had been talking to each other over the course of the training if Mettalika's armour could be used as spare parts or re-used as armour again. It had become pretty much legendary, some thought the armour gave her special powers and they wanted to wear it and see if it had the same effect on them. It never really occurred to them that armour is useless without the training and experience of the creature wearing it.

They immediately stood to attention as Zephirak walked proudly out of the cavern, flanked by Mordred, Karnos and Croter.

"Alright, time to prove you're not useless stinking layabouts!" Zephirak yelled. "This sun cycle you will bring her down! Now go! The next time I see you, I want to see her crushed beneath you and ready to be dispensed. Is this clear?"

The soldiers saluted and answered as one; "YES SIR!"

Zephirak nodded and smiled at them. "Then GO!" and he roared as the three leaders assembled their own packs and headed out, followed by the other thirty soldiers behind, marching in formation. They would split up as they left the residential area of Dyarkroeen so they would not be conspicuous.

Mordred's pack went first, then Karnos and then Croter. Zarkiz was not in Croter's pack, he had refused to be allocated into that one. He was in Mordred's. Rondo was in the same pack.

As they moved along, no one spoke. They all knew exactly when the packs would split and where each one would be outposted. Zephirak and Mordred had arranged the whole plan with precise accuracy. Nothing would go wrong. Nothing *could* go wrong.

As they left the caves in the distance and reached the Outlands, they split up, heading out a large distance away from each other. The thirty split into two packs of fifteen, one even wandered onto the border of Shernaron, looking for all the world like several hunting packs that had for some reason regrouped. If a passer-by saw them, they would probably assume the packs were grouped together for protection because Mettalika was around. It wasn't unheard of for this to happen.

The swamp was closer to Shernaron than Dyarkroeen. For this reason, Mettalika hung out there a lot. She actually lived for the most part in Shernaron. The swamp was one of the Lizariaouses main hunting grounds and that was why she spent so much time there; to pick off hunting packs while they were out getting meals. She found this the easiest way. Also, the swamp was pretty much neutral territory. Even before the whole ordeal with the food shortage, if either of the two species wandered into the other's territory, it was considered to be a threat and they were chased off. So, they lived in toleration of one another, neither one causing trouble for the other. It was also considered more of a threat when a Lizariaous was caught in Shernaron, especially if they weren't just passing through. This pack of fifteen kept a low profile, stating that they were on their way through and would not hunt. Body language told a lot but it was not unknown of course, for the language to be faked and an attack suddenly made, so if this pack was found, they would be treated as a threat by default. They were headed for the swamp through Shernaron.

The other pack of fifteen went right out around the Outlands and to the other side of the swamp, so they could move in from the other side.

Mordred's pack stationed themselves by one of the murky ponds Mettalika often drank from when she was in the area. Karnos's pack stationed themselves near one of the hunting grounds in the swamp and Croter's pack was stationed by the other pond. They all concealed themselves well in large bushes and a couple even hid in the water and in the tall swamp grass, so they could leap out when Mettalika had a drink.

Zephirak had followed behind the thirty back up soldiers and was with the pack that had gone wide around the Outlands to the other side of the swamp. They surrounded him in case Mettalika found them and attacked. The best prize she could ever hope for was Zephirak but even she wasn't stupid enough to actually go into Dyarkroeen and kill him now she was so notorious. He had however, maybe foolishly, wandered around by himself when he had been called to see something or check on Mettalika's whereabouts but this wasn't often. Right now he needed the protection.

They concealed themselves and waited for the signal, likewise, the other pack that was on the Shernaron side of the swamp. If any of them saw her, they would bound into action. They were dotted all over and since the scout they had sent out at sunrise had returned and told them she was in the swamp, there wasn't much chance she could leave without being ambushed.

Mettalika had been up early that morning and had headed into the swamp to find something to eat, which she had; a swamp cat. They were like the cave cats but of course, lived in the swamp. She had toyed with it for a while, grown bored, killed it and settled for a nap which was how the scout found her without being detected. She was sleeping in some dry reeds, concealed nicely despite her shining steel and red fur. She had no idea that she was slowly being surrounded and later, woke up feeling thirsty and a little hungry again. She yawned and stretched, standing up and sniffing the air. She smelled the faint smell of something under the stench of the swamp but couldn't make out what it was except that it was everywhere. She scratched her side and wandered in the direction of one of the pools. It was pretty quiet and she found this unusual. Still, no one came into the swamp much except hunting packs of Lizariaouses and she kept her eye on the world around her. A few frogs and toads croaked from unseen places, breaking the silence. By now all the soldiers were settled in their positions and the wildlife had started to resume its activities.

Mettalika headed for one of the pools, the larger one and by chance, the one with a soldier concealed in the water. He watched her as she came to the edge to drink. It was a little way away from him and he started to move slowly towards her, so he wouldn't miss when he jumped out at her. She started to drink and he drifted through the water towards her, his needles flat along his spine so they wouldn't give him away. Her ears twitched and he paused. She didn't look up so he carried on, breathing through a small, hollow reed. He couldn't move too fast because it would make him out of breath and it was already hard enough to breathe through such a small and inconspicuous thing. He saw the ripples she made as she drank and headed for that, slowly and carefully.

Suddenly, he felt a huge weight on him and the crashing of the water around him as something landed on him, forcing him down. He panicked, breathing in a noseful of water, it flooded his lungs and he choked, flailing and suffocating almost instantly. His body lay still underneath whatever had pushed it down. Mettalika had noticed him and had been listening to how close the movements of the water were getting to her. She had no reason to look up, her ears were her eyes. She dragged the unfortunate soldier out of the water. He had become unwitting bait for the whole thing to now effectively unfold.

Mettalika thought it was very odd that a Lizariaous would be hiding in the pool. He could have been hunting but she doubted it and it put her defences up. Still, at least now she had a more filling meal. She decided to drag him to a more private place and eat him. She passed under some trees that contained soldiers hidden in the branches. One nodded to the other. Now was the time. She wasn't on guard, she was pulling along a sizeable meal and their anger at her killing one of their comrades would only make them stronger. The other snarled, the first snarled, they took aim and lunged at her from out of the tree. As they moved, the leaves rustled, alerting her to their presence and she looked up just in time to see them leap at her, claws gripping the air like talons, needles rattling, horrific snarls on their muzzles and eyes burning with hatred and anger.

Mettalika flamed them, right in the faces. They had to close their eyes so their landing was bad. One missed her completely, while the other landed on her tail and was swiftly knocked to one side by it. The one who missed roared and called for backup. They were part of

Croter's pack. Croter and the other three soldiers roared too, rushing in from their hiding places. Over at the other pool and the hunting grounds, the soldiers roared in turn, alerting each other and the other thirty soldiers who were dotted around let their calls out. The swamp was alive with Lizariaous voices. Mettalika was deafened by them and roared herself, in anger and defiance, showing that she had no fear. The dead soldier was forgotten as she viciously lunged at her aerial attackers. Her wings shielded her and they shot needles at her, most of them bounced off her armour though.

"You fools! You thought you could take *me* on? Have they taught you nothing in Dyarkroeen?" Mettalika lunged at one soldier and he tried to dodge but the trees and mud didn't give him much room to move. She flamed him relentlessly as the other soldier tried to grab her wings. Croter and the other three soldiers bounded in and attacked. She had one soldier cornered and lunged her muzzle down, snapping his neck as another who flew at her tail had his stomach sliced open for his troubles. Croter looked around in fear. Two were down already. He had never seen her in action like this and it was far worse than he had thought. Her steel claws bought another soldier to his death but luckily, backup had arrived and Mordred's pack was there. Mettalika violently head butted another soldier, the long spike on her helmet piercing his stomach and killing him instantly. She tossed the body to one side and defended herself against a female soldier who had clawed her un-armoured back leg. Mettalika kicked out at her with her other, steel clawed foot, slashing her across the chest and forcing her back. Karnos's pack had arrived now and they were piling in on her, working as a unit, as one organised group.

Mettalika kept her wings as much out of harm's way as she could, flaming the attacking soldiers and smacking away needles with her wings as her legs worked on killing. The two packs of fifteen had arrived now, she was completely surrounded, being attacked by six soldiers at a time, who, once pushed back, would take a rest while others waiting at the side would jump in and resume the fighting. The idea was that they would either seriously injure her or wear her out. She fought with tenacity though. Zephirak and two soldiers flanking him waited out of sight for the finale.

One soldier managed to get under Mettalika and her claws gripped the edge of Mettalika's steel chest plate as she attempted to rip it off. Mettalika screamed in discomfort since the steel was fused to her flesh. She lunged her head down at the soldier's neck and slashed the body with her steel claws. The biggest mistake a soldier could do was actually get underneath her.

Mordred took his turn now, he had climbed up a tree overhead and he launched himself on her back, holding on with his claws and biting down on one of her wings. Breaking these was the most important thing and since no one had been able to get near them from the ground, he had decided to try from above. Since they were held up, they were hard to land on. He managed to get between them and hold onto her back, pulling the wing out with his muzzle. She snarled in sheer, unadulterated rage; there was still no fear even with so many attackers. She was full of hatred and the lust for blood and revenge. In her mind, she would kill each and every one of these foolish Lizariaouses and revel in her victory afterwards.

Mordred held on as she struggled and tried to knock him off with her other wing. This gave Karnos a good opportunity to grab the wing Mordred had hold of since movement of that one was hindered and the wing was lowered. He pounced on it, tearing into it and pulling on the fingers as Mordred twisted his head and snapped it at the arm.

Mettalika screamed. It was a horrible sound, it filled the swamp. It was the sound of sheer anger and hate. In one huge, powerful movement, she threw Mordred off her, his claws taking a good chunk of her back as he fell. Karnos was next. She lunged at him in a rage and he took one last slash at her wing and backed off as another couple of soldiers flew at her.

She was panting but her adrenaline was flowing and her anger made her stronger. Her aim was getting worse though as her body tired. Not that it mattered much since it seemed wherever she struck out, she hit a soldier. The whole swamp was boiling hot now from Mettalika's fire. She was dragging her broken wing; it hindered her but not too badly.

Mordred and Karnos rested together, watching the continuing battle.

"We're beating her! I don't believe it but she's actually weakening. She'll be down soon" remarked Karnos.

"Just as we planned" replied Mordred, watching carefully. They needed to take out her other wing now, to ensure if she did decide to flee, that she couldn't get far by attempting to fly. Her other wing had a small steel claw on but it shouldn't be too much of a problem.

She had killed a good few of the soldiers and damaged most of the others. A few highly skilled ones were a force to be reckoned with and she found that to her dismay, there were several that she couldn't hit; they were just too fast. These guys were trained well and Mettalika knew she had been ambushed. A small part of her also knew that she was in a lot of trouble. This was pushed to the back; however, her anger took precedence now. Her body ached; blood flowed from several deep wounds on her exposed areas such as her thighs and the un-armoured right back leg. And still they kept coming! More and more! She suspected that the entire population of Dyarkroeen was trying to kill her. This only made her more determined though. If they wanted a fight, she would destroy them all. And after this, she would destroy Zephirak. Now she hated them so much, she no longer cared about being wary about going into Dyarkroeen. If they came to her to kill her, she would go to them to kill him. Her violet eyes raged with her inner fire as more blue flames erupted from her mouth, sending the current attacking soldiers scattering, only to be replaced with a new pack, freshly rested from their last attack.

In his hiding place, Zephirak grinned maliciously. This was wonderful! His mortal enemy was slowly being destroyed before his very eyes and he got to watch. He had waited seasons for this to happen; now his dream was becoming a reality and soon he would be able to give that killing blow. She would die at his teeth. He chuckled and watched, everything else lost to him; his only focus was on her and how she was being brought down.

Mordred and Karnos planned their next move. This time, Karnos would climb up the tree and drop on her. Nearby, Zarkiz overheard.

"Hey! I'll do it. Let me climb up and take out her other wing, you two attack it from the ground" he suggested, creeping over.

Karnos questioned him over this.

"Because I want to prove my worth. I'll make them regret not letting me be a pack leader and choosing Croter over me."

293

"Very well" replied Mordred. "Prove your worth like a soldier. Now go!"

Zarkiz ran off, climbing up the tree as Mordred and Karnos readied themselves, ready to lunge at Mettalika at the same time as Zarkiz fell.

With a great roar, he leaped from the tree; claws outstretched and flew at her. In a split second, Mettalika turned her head, flipped her whole body onto her back and grabbed him as he fell on her, her claws slicing through him, gutting him as she tore his throat out with her teeth and tossed him to one side, resuming the battle with the other soldiers.

Mordred and Karnos stopped in their tracks when they saw this happen. They never expected it.

"That could have been me" murmured Karnos. Mordred shivered. This may be the last battle of his life and now he was fearful, the image of the event that had just occurred, imprinted on his vision. He shook it off and roared to Karnos to follow him. If his life was taken in the battle that ended this foolish feuding, then it would be worth it. He thought of Schaarl, he thought of his home, the young Lizariaouses, the blue Gryphie he had helped all those lunars ago, the pointless fighting, seeing the soldiers returning with a Gryphie meal, Zephirak trying to trick Leida into eating her own kind and the anger inside him grew. If killing Mettalika meant this would all be over, then so be it.

Mordred roared, Karnos joined him and together they rushed at Mettalika, going for her other wing relentlessly while the other soldiers distracted her teeth and claws with themselves.

They both got a grip on it in their teeth at the same time, pulling the membrane apart in different directions and breaking it as the finger bones cracked and split. Mettalika screamed in anger and tried to move her head round to reach them and bite but every time she did, she left her neck exposed and had to turn to the attacking soldiers again to make sure they didn't get a grip on her. In the end, she ignored the pain and the attacks on her wings; they were useless now in any case so it mattered not if they were destroyed completely. She knew as soon as the membrane ripped that she wouldn't be able to fly any longer.

Mordred and Karnos's muzzles were bloody and they had gone into a frenzy now Mettalika was ignoring them. They were trying to get her attention so the other soldiers could bring her down and hold her ready for Zephirak.

"Come on, monstrosity to our existence! Freak of metal and flesh! Feel our anger!" growled Karnos through gritted teeth, still with his jaws clamped onto her wing.

Mettalika snarled at him. "How dare you, Lizariaous scum! I will kill all of you and then I will go to your territory and destroy your worthless leader. You have started something you will wish you hadn't." The pain was numb now, she ignored it. She couldn't move her wings at all.

"Come on then, kill us and more will come and more after them! You won't defeat us and you will wish you never messed with us!" growled Mordred.

"Yes" put in Karnos, "you should have stayed in Shernaron and accepted that you were lucky you survived that pack attack when you were little and just kept to yourself like a good little meal creature." Meal creature was the term used for a prey animal, one that was commonly hunted by the predators of either side.

"What did you call me?" Mettalika's eyes grew wide and she snarled.

"A good for nothing, worthless little meal creature" replied Karnos mockingly. "You were born to be killed. Something went wrong but now fate is taking its turn and what was supposed to happen all those seasons ago is happening now, just as it should." Karnos chuckled. He and Mordred still had hold of her wing and they were speaking through their teeth.

Mettalika roared in anger and flamed them. They shut their eyes and held on but the distraction was a cue for the other soldiers to attack from all sides, each taking a part of her and working to either damage it or hold it there. Two had her tail, one for each of her back legs. They pulled them out painfully and she realised what was going on and started to struggle. She roared and screeched, realising with a horrible feeling of finality that the soldiers were winning. They had her tail firmly pinned and without the use of her wings to fend them off, she could no longer keep them off her back. Croter pounced onto her back, as did Rondo, both of them digging their claws in and pinning her to the ground. Her front legs scrabbled about and she attempted to thrash around but it didn't work.

Croter and Rondo forced her against the ground, pressing down hard. She was on her belly now, she couldn't move her head very well since her chin was pressed into the mud so that put her helmet spike out of commission.

"LIZARIAOUS SCUM!" she screamed. "I'll kill all of you!" She now had a soldier sat on each back leg, holding it down, two on her tail and two on her back and she couldn't move.

"No" a voice said smugly. "*We* will kill *you*." It was Zephirak, a large soldier either side of him, strutting proudly up to Mettalika.

"Ah, I have waited a long time to do this. Zelle, the helmet. Remove it." Zephirak motioned to one of the soldiers beside him, who gripped the spike of Mettalika's helmet in his claws and pulled. It didn't budge though.

"It's fused to her, Sir." Zelle said with a shrug of his claws.

"Well then you'll just have to pull the spike forward and keep it there when the time comes" said Zephirak, annoyed a little, since the spike would hinder his killing bite but at the same time happy with the fact that it could act as a lever to keep her head forward and her neck exposed.

Mettalika panted, staring defiantly at Zephirak, blood caking her mouth, the mud beneath her reddened by the battle.

"This is the sun cycle where you die. This is where it ends. I wasn't going to allow you any last words but I'll be gallant and relent. So, any last words? Not that it matters of course; I just wanted to hear your rage at being defeated by me. I bet you never thought we were capable of bringing you down." He sneered at her, moving his face close to hers but just far enough away that she couldn't reach him if she snapped at him.

Mettalika struggled; Zephirak was so close, she could smell him and she wanted to destroy him but she was completely immobilised.

"I hate you; you and your kind are a plague on these lands. You will fall, not now but in the future. My spirit will come back and ensure it. I will ensure your demise, Lizariaous scum, ALL of you. There will be others who will follow in my footsteps, kill enough of us and we will retaliate. We will come with armour and determination and drive you away or destroy you. It won't end with me and you are a fool to think it will. But you know what? You know what I enjoyed the most about this whole feud, this whole thing? Hmm? Do you? The thing I enjoyed most, that I will *never* forget is the look on your pregnant mate's face when I killed her, Zephirak. The look of horror and fear as she died. And her cry of pain. I killed her to ensure you would not have an heir to your empire of scum. I should have taken the unborn youngster as a prize really. I bet it would have tasted *really* good." She started to laugh, gargled, bloody laughs but laughs nonetheless. She was a crazy solitary with a lust for blood and no companions.

Zephirak was seething. "Zelle, pull the spike forward" he commanded and Zelle obliged, pulling Mettalika's helmet forward, which in turn pulled her head forward, exposing the back of her neck.

Zephirak advanced on her, his red eyes flaming with rage and hatred. She had mocked the murder of his beloved mate, Salvariss and now she would pay the price.

Mettalika was struggling but couldn't lift her head. Her eyes flashed wildly about, in a slight panic now. Zephirak placed a paw on each of her shoulders and looked down at her neck.

"This is the last voice you will ever hear and these are the last words you will ever hear. *You* are the worthless scum, Mettalika. You were saved just to die again. Now you will know the feeling and I hope your spirit will burn in darkness because you lived your life in vain." And with that, Zephirak lunged his head down on Mettalika's neck, clamping his teeth down; tearing through arteries and tendons, right through to the bone and breaking it clean in two, snapping her neck and her life source. Mettalika's struggles became weak as he bit down, her body falling limp as he crunched through the bones.

Zephirak threw back his head and gave an earth shattering roar of triumph. The soldiers joined in. They roared to honour their dead, the survival of their kind and above all, the end of Mettalika's reign of terror over them.

Mordred's roar was one of the loudest of them all. It was finally over! No more worrying about running into Mettalika, no more threat of war, no more unpredictability with Zephirak. He had survived with minimal damage and they had come out the victors. Now he could raise a family with Schaarl into a world where they wouldn't be afraid to let their youngsters out to play. They had brought her down! The plan had worked! Finally, it was over, finally things could go back to how they were before.

The rest of the soldiers roared in triumph and pride. Those who had died had fought well and those who lived could return to Dyarkroeen with their heads held high and the body of their enemy on their shoulders.

Their roars echoed through the swamp as the sun climbed high in the sky. The plan had paid off, they had triumphed.

Chapter 27
Universal Celebrations

In nearby Shernaron, the noise had been heard. Both the noise when the Lizariaouses first ambushed Mettalika and the noise of the battle's end.

It didn't reach the Forest but those near the swamp heard it and listened. They didn't attempt to go closer though, they knew it was probably something to do with Mettalika and in affairs like that, they preferred to stay out of it.

Leida and Stervia were nearby. They were having a break and catching a forest deer. As they sat down to eat it, they heard the commotion.

"I wonder what all the fuss is about" said Stervia, with her mouth full.

Leida shrugged. "I don't know and I'm not sure that I care. I don't want any part of it. If it's to do with Mettalika, I'm staying well away." She carried on eating but they stayed in the area, curiosity getting the better of them. After the second lot of roars, Stervia remarked that it sounded like a battle had been won.

"The first chorus was because they were calling for backup. Now it seems the battle has been won" she explained.

Leida listened. "It's coming from the swamp. Maybe we could go closer now it seems to be over?"

"Good idea. We can work on your stealth as we go" said Stervia.

So they headed towards the swamp swiftly, so they would still catch what was going on and it wouldn't all be over by the time they got there.

They hid themselves away well when they reached the swamp. The place was covered in dead bodies from the soldiers who had met their fate at Mettalika's claws.

There were about twenty, maybe more lying in the pool or the tall grass. Leida felt sick. She had never seen so much carnage.

Stervia sniffed the air. Over the stench of the swamp, she smelled Gryphie blood among the Lizariaous blood.

"They fought a Gryphie here" she said.

Leida's eyes grew wide. She suddenly feared for Diabloss's life. It looked as though it had been a tough battle judging by the amount of dead soldiers lying around. She started to panic, looking around, then sniffing, trying to get the scent of which direction they left in.

"What's up?" asked Stervia.

"I...I think they killed Diabloss!" Leida yelled. "Help me find which way they went!" Together, they followed the trail of the remaining Lizariaouses as they left the swamp. They found the path they took and followed it to the edge of the Outlands. There, they scanned the area and saw them heading towards Dyarkroeen in the distance. Leida wanted to follow them but Stervia warned her that if they went by foot, they would surely be seen and maybe attacked, though, judging by the state the Lizariaouses were probably in, that was unlikely.

So they took to the air and flew overhead, high enough that they wouldn't be seen but low enough that they had a good view of the group below.

Stervia was going to suggest that maybe it wasn't Diabloss they had killed but even she doubted and it never even occurred to her that it was in fact, Mettalika. To most of the Gryphies, Mettalika was immortal and couldn't be killed because she actively went out and hunted Lizariaouses which was in itself, a very dangerous thing to do. A Lizariaous was always a match for a Gryphie. Her armour had only increased the idea that she had some kind of powers. They had a similar view of this as some of the Lizariaouses.

The two of them flew over the Outlands, looking down on the travelling pack of Lizariaouses. Leida wanted to fly closer but Stervia told her not to.

"Hey…it's not green like Diabloss" remarked Stervia.

"Of course it isn't, it's covered in blood" Leida shuddered on the last word. "Look at the wings, they're almost torn off."

Stervia looked harder. "I don't think it's Diabloss. It's big enough to be a male though. Wait, there's something shining, it keeps catching the sun. Leida! Look! It can't be! I think…it's…yes, it's Mettalika! They've killed Mettalika!"

"No way! Mettalika?" Leida flew a little closer and saw the spiked helmet and the armoured tail. "It is! I can't believe it!"

The two of them followed for a way, wanting to get a good long look, wanting to be sure that it wasn't a trick of the eyes or the light. But it was without a shadow of a doubt, Mettalika.

Excited, they both flew off to find Diabloss. He was with his squadron on the cliffs. They were hunting sea vultures for some of the kittens. Kittens are generally raised on sea vultures because they are sizeable but not too big and easy for the little ones to handle. Sometimes they are brought back alive so they can be hunted but mostly they are killed and taken back for a meal. These ones were killed. They were easy for the Gryphies to catch and they already had a good pile of them. The male Gryphies or the squadron hunted so the mothers could stay home and look after their young kittens. Mothers would go out and hunt while kittens were either training or in flying lessons though.

Leida called to Diabloss as she and Stervia landed on the cliff. He flew over.

"Diabloss! The Lizariaouses have killed Mettalika! We saw them taking the body back to Dyarkroeen" she told him excitedly.

"Are you serious? She's actually dead?" Diabloss knew his mate wouldn't lie about such a thing but he still couldn't believe his ears, it had to sink in first.

"Yes, they fought in the swamp. Leida and I were training nearby when we heard the call for help. A long while later there was a victory call so we thought we would go closer for a better look. She's killed about twenty or so soldiers, they're all laid out like a dead field in the swamp near the largest pool. Blood everywhere. So we tracked the leaving pack and saw they had her body with them. She's definitely dead, sir, there is no doubt of that at all. We did an aerial track. We followed them nearly all the way back to Dyarkroeen across the Outlands. I have no idea how they brought her down. Numbers I guess, it's the only way they could have."

"Was Zephirak there?" asked Diabloss.

"Yes, he was leading them. Maybe he killed her himself" replied Leida.

"No, he wouldn't have been able to bring her down without help. I imagine he watched as they killed her or something. That was what they were training for all those sun cycles that Leida and I saw when we went over to Dyarkroeen to check out what was going on." Diabloss took to the sky.

"I'm going to see for myself" he said, flying up high.

"They're probably back home by now" called Leida.

"Yes, but I can go over to their territory and see if I can see for myself. I won't be seen, I'll be back soon." And he flew off towards Dyarkroeen.

Leida wanted to go too but didn't offer since if two of them went, it might be more conspicuous.

When they saw Diabloss leave, the rest of the squad landed and wondered why.

"Mettalika is dead. She fell to the Lizariaouses" explained Leida.

Tranzoss beamed. "Really? Well that is good news! A meeting must be called."

"Wait till Diabloss gets back" replied Leida, "I think he may want to tell everyone himself. If you called it now, then everyone would be waiting around for him to return and who knows how long that will be."

Tranzoss nodded. Leida was getting wiser and more thoughtful these sun cycles.

Diabloss had made it to Dyarkroeen and had nearly reached the residential area with its caves and Lizariaous families. The training ground was empty and he soon saw that all the Lizariaouses were gathered by Zephirak's cavern as he showed off their prize. He stood outside the cavern with Mettalika's body on a rock in front of him. Diabloss landed in a lone tree nearby and listened.

"...great sun cycle for us all! She fell at my teeth and will never hunt or terrorise us again!" Zephirak said mightily. He took hold of the spike on her helmet in a paw and pulled, raising her head.

"Look at the face of our enemy! Look and see that despite her armour, she is just a worthless creature; she can be killed like any of us can. She wasn't meant to live in the first place and now we have corrected the mistake we made all those seasons ago. Roar with victory, fellow Lizariaouses!!"

The whole population of Dyarkroeen roared as one at the face of their enemy. They roared with pride, anger, happiness, vengeance and victory.

"I brought her down. I killed her! I proved that she could be killed!" roared Zephirak. And the others roared for him now. They didn't know it was the soldiers who had brought her down really. In their eyes, Zephirak was a mighty hero, capable of great destruction now that Mettalika was dead. None of his soldiers spoke or corrected him on what he said. They were in formation either side of the rock her body lay on. They stood completely to attention while everyone else roared; their faces solemn. Mordred thought it was disgusting that Zephirak appeared to be taking all the credit for himself but as long as he was happy, there was no threat of his awful temper.

When the roars had died down, Zephirak looked pleased and proud. He stood there, revelling in the death of the one who had killed his precious mate, Salvariss.

Diabloss shook his head with disapproval. Still, if it meant that this whole thing was over then so be it and that was a good thing. He left Zephirak to revel in his victory and flew back to Shernaron. On the way, he stopped off at the swamp to see the full extent of the damage that Zephirak and his soldiers had done. The place was littered with bodies and torn off bits of Mettalika's wings. Diabloss felt sad as well as relieved. Whatever happened, it must have been a long and bloody battle for her. He stopped a while and just surveyed it all.

Some of the bodies had partially sunk into the mud. Diabloss sighed. He wondered how she had died. He knew she wouldn't have backed down but once she knew she was helpless and wouldn't survive, he wondered what went through her head then; what her last thoughts were.

Finally, unable to look any more, he climbed up a tree and took to the sky once again. Time to call a meeting and tell everyone.

Back in Shernaron, Leida and Stervia had returned to the Forest and were slowly telling others that Mettalika was dead. Leida went and told Mystik. She was changing Jadariol's dressings and had just finished when Leida walked in.

"Mystik, I have big news! The Lizariaouses have killed Mettalika."

Mystik looked at Leida as though she was a stranger; the news wasn't even registered until it had sunk in. She just stood, speechless.

Jadariol grinned. "Well good I say! She killed my mother and deserves to die. I hope they tore her apart!"

This snapped Mystik back into reality.

"Jadariol! She wasn't evil, just confused." Mystik still refused to see of Mettalika as anything other than a poor lost solitary who was the way she was because of rejection. Or at least, that was how she wanted to see it, however she really felt.

"So? She needed to die, it was a requirement" replied Jadariol spitefully. Even though he was a youngster, he was still a Lizariaous and had the same views as the rest of them.

Mystik gestured to Leida to follow and they went and perched at the top of her tree away from Jadariol.

"Somehow, I fear Jadariol is right. It *was* a requirement for Mettalika's life to be taken" sighed Mystik.

Leida explained what had happened and that Diabloss was out seeing for himself. Mystik listened carefully. Afterwards, a small smile came to her face. It was not a smile of joy or happiness, just of ease and relief. Now this whole affair would be over. They would return Jadariol when he was better and show that they were sorry and the deaths the Lizariaouses had caused were forgiven.

Leida and Mystik looked out across the Forest and over to the mountains, both of them silent but both feeling calm. Soon, they saw Diabloss return, he was calling for a meeting. They called too and Gryphies from all around flew to the clearing where Mystik's tree was and the normal meeting place. Diabloss called out that this meeting was important and that it brought great news that would benefit everyone. So, the whole gathering grouped together under the big old tree to hear it.

Leida and Mystik joined them and Diabloss sat before them to announce what he had to say.

Strassor, Otuss and Odax, Lunara, Shen and everyone else were eager to know what was going on. Diabloss began.

"My mate and Stervia were out near the swamp earlier this sun cycle and they heard a fight going on. After they heard the victory call, they went to see what had taken place and what they saw was a sight of relief to both of them and all of us. The Lizariaouses have killed Mettalika. A huge pack of them overpowered her and I saw for myself that they have her body back in Dyarkroeen. Mettalika is dead. She will no longer kill Lizariaouses and as a result, Zephirak will no longer want to destroy us or kill our kind. It is over!"

Otuss interrupted him rudely. "Here, how do you know it's over? You *assume* that this is correct. Sure, she won't be killing them any more but they have a taste for us now, they'll still kill us. Sure they've gotten rid of her but that's not to stop them just carrying on. You know how greedy Zephirak is."

"He's had his vengeance, Otuss. She killed his mate and now he has killed her. Payback has been received. Yes, I admit they probably will kill us still sometimes but there won't be any war now."

"And you're gunna just let him kill us huh? You're gunna stand back while they still carry on what they've been doing all this time? You don't deserve your position, Diabloss. You are a fool and you are leading everyone into anarchy by insisting that we remain peaceful." Otuss argued back. A few other voices spoke up in agreement.

"No, training will still continue. That way, if they try to hunt us, we can defend ourselves. Once they realise they are no longer a match for us, they will stop hunting us" stated Diabloss. A few voices also agreed.

Otuss thought about this. It made sense. "Very well. But if a war still breaks out and Zephirak's thirst for our blood still isn't satiated, I am holding you responsible and I will take matters into my own hands. I will also never listen to you again." Otuss growled deeply.

"As you wish, Otuss. But I think if we defend ourselves when they attack and become better at fighting instead of backing down like we have always done, then they will see we are a force to be reckoned with." Diabloss respected others' opinions even if he didn't agree with them. In his mind, Otuss was trying to get the Lizariaouses before they got him it seemed and that would only encourage a war.

"Anyway, now Mettalika is dead, we can rest a bit easier. She was no real threat to us but she was only causing more tension with the Lizariaouses, tension that we don't need. All the same, don't let your kittens out of the Forest, it is unadvisable to go into the Outlands still, if you have friends from other places and wish to travel and visit them, try to keep it to a minimum. And everyone, train well! Train hard! Let your fire burn. We're not out of the hole yet but it is a start and I think things will get better from now on!" Diabloss smiled at them. This time, they didn't all look downhearted and broken spirited; they looked hopeful and it was only really Otuss who looked out of place with his disrespectful, slightly smug snarl. It told Diabloss "I'm right, you're wrong and soon you will be proved wrong." Diabloss ignored it.

"Meeting over" he said and joined Leida. Everyone else dispersed, chatting amongst themselves and wandering back to their trees or into the Forest.

Strassor and Odax walked together while Otuss stalked off ahead, by himself.

Leida nuzzled Diabloss. "Maybe this is the beginning of a bright future" she said quietly.

"I really hope so. Otuss troubles me. If a war breaks out because of him, I'm not sure what I'd do and I know I'd do something I will regret later. I'd certainly never forgive him."

"What would you do?" asked Leida.

"I would banish him and all associated with him. If they want to go in there and kill off Zephirak or something then I can't stop it but I can stop the rest of us being a part of it."

"Even if it was just them who went in, Zephirak would accuse all of us. He hates us all for what one of us did and I don't think anything would ever change that." Leida sighed and lowered her head, her ears back. "I worry every sun cycle about what will happen. I just want to have a sun cycle when I am completely happy with nothing to worry about, like it used to be. Sure I'm happy but never completely; there is always a cloud darkening my sky."

Diabloss hugged her to him. "Like I said, this is a start. It should hopefully be the start of the end of this stupidity. Remember the Furmines' war against the QuadraFelieons because they kept raiding the Furmines' nests? They fought for so long that they forgot what they were fighting about. It won't be like that with this though. It will stop soon."

"You can't promise that though. This has already been going on for seasons. Admittedly it's only been a small quarrel with Mettalika killing Lizariaouses and Zephirak angry about his mate but remember when they kidnapped me? That was when the full severity of it started to show; what it was beneath the surface. It's been boiling up and slowly getting worse. I'd like to think though that, like you, this is the start of the end of this feud. Maybe that will give us strength but we will only know with time."

"Yes, only with time" replied Diabloss. And he hoped that time would prove that things can be overcome and put aside.

There was great celebration in Dyarkroeen. Zephirak was being heralded as a hero and he was in his element. Meat had been gotten out of the reserves caves and everyone was having a huge feast and a social gathering to celebrate the death of their enemy.

Croter was a little upset about Zarkiz's death. Rondo told him what Zarkiz's last words were concerning Croter and Croter was hurt by it.

"It's not my fault I was made a leader, Zephirak made me that, I never asked for it. But Zarkiz died bravely fighting, I suppose that's what matters." The two had been close friends as well as guards and they had a strong bond but in the way of the Lizariaous, Croter heralded him as a brave fighter and let go.

310

Mordred and Schaarl were both happily enjoying their meal, Mordred telling her all about the battle and how it ended.

"I should have known he would still boast at her when he killed her, Zephirak can never resist, can he?" Schaarl snorted.

Mordred shrugged. "It doesn't matter now. She's dead, she never escaped when we held her down and Zephirak got to mock her and get it out of his system. It's over! This whole stupid grikking thing is over and I can safely say that I'm happy it is. Maybe Zeph will take a new mate. That should keep his mind off it."

"Maybe you could help? Set him up with someone?" suggested Schaarl.

"Maybe not" said Mordred. "I don't think mentioning mates around him is a good idea at all. I could perhaps do it secretly though. You know, send a female to him or get her to show interest. I know some of the females are interested in him but are too afraid to tell him since he has not made it clear that he is looking for another one."

"That's because he isn't. He's shown no interest in females. He's been too wrapped up in this whole vengeance thing. But yeah, you're right, now that Mettalika is dead maybe he'll relax more. It's worth a try." Schaarl approved so long as Mordred did it carefully.

"Mordred nodded. "I'll give it a few sun cycles and in that time I'll look around for anyone who would be interested in him, find someone I think he would like and tell her very clearly what she should and shouldn't do around him. After she's learnt, I can send her to him. But I'll do it subtly. So that she bumps into him or something, you know, by accident. That would work and then they could get to know each other, start showing interest in each other and soon he will have a mate as wonderful as you, Schaarl."

Schaarl blushed. "Oh Mordred" she tapped him on the nose and smiled. Mordred grinned. Even with the scar Zephirak had inflicted on him, she still thought he was the most handsome Lizariaous in the whole of Dyarkroeen.

Zephirak meanwhile, was telling a bunch of younger Lizariaouses about how to attack and kill correctly. They hung on his every word. Now, after his lie about bringing Mettalika down singlehandedly, they all wanted to grow up to be just like him. The usual thing youngsters do when they see someone they admire. Zephirak loved the attention and no one had seen him in a mood this good since his mate was still alive and he had announced they were going to have a baby.

The soldiers were all at ease now and talking about the fight, sharing their experiences and what each of them had done in the battle.

"Cor, didja see 'er take out Zarkiz like that? Wowzas, that were some guttin'!" said a soldier with a heavy accent.

"I asked to have the tail if they decide to take apart the body. That tail could be made into a good weapon" said another.

"Well you'll have a hard time. The tail and helmet will belong to Zephirak. He's keeping those and he said we could have the rest of the armour. Mordred's having the spiked leg cuff though." A third told them.

"Well then I want 'er front claws, I could put 'em to gud use as a tool when digging" said the first one.

"You're not going to remain a soldier?" asked the second.

"Nope" replied the first. "Too much 'ard work. I were happiest diggin' an' that's what I'll go back to."

The others thought fair enough and some more came over to chat. Youngsters ran around, most blissfully unaware of the event that had taken place but their parents felt relieved that their kids could now wander about without fear of being killed and eaten.

The body remained on the stone. Zephirak was also to have her body. He said it would be the best meal he would ever eat. Soon the armour would be salvaged and put to use but for now, she remained on the stone so that whoever wished, could go and have a look. This was popular with the youngsters; they were all very interested in seeing. Most had never seen a Gryphie up close before and they stared and poked her. No one told them off for touching. It was not like Lizariaouses to disapprove of their youngsters touching dead bodies, given what their staple diet was. One played with her tail.

"Hey, this is cool! Hey, look at this! Wow it's so sharp" he yelled. His friends gathered round and had a look too.

"I wonder if they're all like this" one pondered.

"Nah, this one was like a mega Gryphie! Lord Zephirak has been hunting her for ages. She must have been a great warrior, maybe the leader of her pack. I bet they'll elect a new leader and that one will wear armour like this."

"It's so cool! I wonder if we can have armour made like this. I want a spiked helmet!"

"Hey, let's go ask our parents, they could tell us where to get some!" and they ran off laughing.

The celebrations lasted the rest of the sun cycle and into the moon cycle. They ate lots, talked lots, played lots and celebrated, finally going to their caves full and happy when it was time to sleep.

Zephirak pulled the body into his cavern. He would eat around the armour and have it cleaned the following sun cycle and allocated to whoever wanted it. He had chosen the best parts himself and Mordred had chosen the cuff. The rest, well whoever wanted it could fight over it; Zephirak had what he wanted.

He took one last look at the face of the fallen Gryphie before he had his meal.

"You lose" he said simply and began to eat.

***

Leida slept peacefully until a sound woke her from her slumber. She lifted her head and looked around, wondering what it was. She listened. It was coming from the edge of the Forest or the edge of the clearing at least. It sounded like low voices. She listened more. Yes, definitely voices but she couldn't work out what they were saying. She yawned. Probably someone had gone to get a drink or some kitten was having trouble sleeping so it had gone to tell a friend. She closed her eyes and drifted off to sleep again.

A while later she was running through the Forest, faceless creatures hot on her tail. She screamed and yelled but no one came to help. They were appearing from all around, eyes watching her and voices, those voices she heard before. They were closing in on her and she couldn't escape. Leida, panic stricken, kept on going. She was headed nowhere though, the Forest went on forever in darkness. She cried out, called for help over and over but no one heard; no one came to help. The words kept repeating; she had heard them before somewhere.

"Danger, danger, danger in the darkness!" Over and over in her head these words rang out. She panted, she ran, she got nowhere and all the time, these voices mocked her. Danger in the darkness!

Suddenly her eyes flashed open and she sat up, panting. It had been a dream. And she knew where the words came from; a dream she had had a long while ago soon after she had been kidnapped.

Her quick movements woke Diabloss up too and he saw how terrified she looked.

"Leida, what's wrong?" he asked and he was by her side instantly, wondering if she had had a funny turn or something.

Leida's eyes were wide with fear.

"I had one of those dreams again like the one I had after Zephirak kidnapped me."

"What dreams? Like that moonmare where you were trapped somewhere and creatures were closing in on you?" asked Diabloss.

"Yes, except this time I was running through the Forest and they were chasing me. They were chanting "Danger in the darkness" over and over. Before when I had it, the words came to me as a warning but now they were openly mocking me. I heard voices before I fell asleep. I think it was to do with that." Leida explained.

"Voices? When did you hear voices?" asked Diabloss.

"I woke up and heard them down below somewhere, at the edge of the trees. I think someone had gone to get a drink or some kittens were playing around but it sure influenced my dreams. Usually when we go to sleep, we sleep for the rest of the moon cycle; it was just unusual, that's all."

Diabloss shrugged and yawned. "Well in that case we had better go back to sleep. There's still a lot of the moon cycle left and we don't want to be tired tomorrow. Aren't you going on a scouting outing with Stervia?"

"Yes, I need to be rested for that, we're going quite a way, to the high mountains."

"Then you might see my cousin, Iseera. I saw her a few lunars back but I doubt she will have heard about Mettalika being killed." Diabloss yawned again and lay down, resting his head on his arms and curling his tail around Leida. She snuggled against him and rested her head too. She didn't want to go to sleep, though. Diabloss had already started to nod off. Soon, Leida fell asleep despite herself. She fell into a pleasant dream this time, of flying to the high mountains and having a race with one of the Gryphies there. Mordred was in the dream too, he was walking around but never spoke to Leida or the other Gryphie; he was just there. Leida wasn't sure why but he kept smiling at her. She and her friend flew away from him and the dream turned into something else she didn't recall when she awoke the following sunrise.

Chapter 28
The High Mountains

For the next few sun cycles, things were relaxed. Without Mettalika there, Diabloss's patrols were fewer and he noticed that there were less attacks from Lizariaouses. It had gone back to how it had been seasons ago; the Gryphies only being hunted when they were near to Dyarkroeen, so they knew to keep away.

Something had come up with Stervia's mate, so she and Leida didn't go to the high mountains for a couple of sun cycles. When the sunrise came for them to leave, Stervia was at Diabloss and Leida's tree bright and early, climbing up and calling for Leida to wake up. Leida hadn't realised that she would arrive before she even had a chance to get a meal.

"We can get one on the way, come on! If we don't start early, we'll never be back before sunset, it's quite a flight!

Leida complained a little but Stervia insisted it was all to do with long flight training and strengthening of wings.

"But there probably won't be a war now." Leida stated.

"So? What makes you so sure? Don't trust 'em, Leida! You might not think it but when Zephirak gets bored enough, he may still come after us. I wouldn't trust a Lizariaous further than I could throw one and that isn't far, I can tell you. So let's go, we can get a meal on the way. I've eaten already."

"I don't like flying on an empty stomach" replied Leida.

"Then we'll get one near the beginning of our journey. Come on!" Stervia was already on her way to the top of the tree to take off.

Diabloss smiled and nuzzled Leida. "Off you go and take care."

Leida sighed and nuzzled back before heading up the tree and taking to the sky with Stervia.

The weather was mild this sun cycle and it was fairly warm too. It was a nice sun cycle to fly and they glided over the Forest. Stervia spotted a forest deer and pointed it out to Leida, who swooped down for the kill.

As Leida ate, Stervia shifted about in boredom.

"So, why did you want us to go to the high mountains? Was it just for training?" asked Leida.

"No, not really. Diabloss told me you'd never been before so I thought it would be fun to take you there. It's good to travel places and get a good idea of our territory. There is a lot more to it than the forest we live in. The steel and metal mountains have Gryphies who look a little different to us and beyond the high mountains, the Dark Plains, domain of the Deamon Gryphies. Then there are the Sky Gryphies who live most of their life in the air and live on high outcrops and some say a floating island in the clouds. I dunno if that's true though. I've seen the Sky Gryphies; they're blue and white like the sky and clouds. They are rare to spot though because their fur shines different shades so they blend in with the sky no matter what the weather is like. I've only ever seen them fly overhead. They can fly at higher altitudes than we can, so it's hard to get into contact with them unless you call to them. The Gryphies of the high mountains are strong and they are workers. Zephirak's rage only hit us since we are closest but I've no doubt that if a war did break out, it would spread and involve everyone." Stervia explained.

Leida was nearly finished with her meal. She had always been curious and interested in these things but never thought much about what was outside of her immediate area in the Forest.

"So, are there other clans of Lizariaouses too, like there are with us?" she asked.

"Yeah, there are. They aren't so spread out though. There's the residential area where Zephirak's cave is and the caves of others by their mountains. Then, further out there are more caves. Really, since they live in caves, they don't have our kind of freedom. We can live in trees, mountains, caves, in the forest, even the swamp, but Lizariaouses can only really live in caves and mountains and even then, only the smaller mountains. Is it any wonder they are so jealous of us? We can fly as well and I think all these seasons, through time, through the ages, they have secretly held a great jealousy of us. It's a war just waiting to happen. We are peaceful, they are not. The Deamon Gryphies are warlike but they are also mysterious and don't get involved with our affairs. This makes most of the Gryphies fear them. We have no idea what kind of power they have because they keep it so well hidden. Diabloss's mother was a Deamon Gryphie. This had made him even stronger with that blood in him. It's extremely rare for a Deamon to take a pureblood mate though. She would have killed anyone and anything to defend him though. Her gathering didn't really approve and they sent her to live in the Forest with him, since living in the Dark Plains would…I dunno, mess him up or something. It's all so vague with those guys. They don't tolerate purebloods staying around for long. Diabloss could go and live with them because he has Deamon blood. He couldn't take you though. They completely isolate themselves and I think that is why they are like they are. I think they're close minded personally but I'd never mess with one. You think Diabloss is powerful, you should see a fully grown pure Deamon male. I shudder to think of those. Not even Zephirak would mess with one of them!" Stervia smirked a little at the thought of Zephirak going up against a Deamon Gryphie male. He wouldn't have a hope.

"So really, we have us and then three subspecies from the mountains, sky and Dark Plains" said Leida, stretching her wings.

"Four really, but we don't count Gryphers since they cannot speak and they act like animals. They're a quiet breed who live in the Forest but it's very rare to spot those either. They never evolved with the rest of us. I think they're cute in a way but we don't speak of them much because to most of us, they're on the same level as forest deer, cave cats, sea vultures and ground birds. We don't hunt them though. Even little Furmines are higher on the evolutionary scale since they can talk. I somehow don't like hunting things that can plead for mercy. Some Gryphies like the taste of a Furmine though. I reckon that's what Mettalika lived on mostly when she couldn't get Lizariaous." Stervia shuddered. "It probably amused her to hear it scream not to be killed."

Leida snarled as they took to the sky again. "I hate to say it but I'm glad she's gone. She wasn't meant to live, what she did proved that. Then again I've never met a nice Lizariaous. Well, apart from Jadariol. He's ok but then he's a youngster and easily influenced. I hope when we return him, he will make the others understand that we only want peace."

Stervia nodded and Leida looked thoughtful.

"Actually, when I was kidnapped, there was a kind Lizariaous who wasn't hostile like the others. I can't remember his name. He was grey with red scales and a blue crest. He told me things, although horrible, they were helpful."

"Hmm, I think he's a higher ranker. Let's see if I can remember. He hangs around with Zephirak a lot. Hmm…now what was his name. I know some of their names since I do a lot of scouting and such. I think it was Morris…no, Mordy…Mordred. Yes, Mordred. He's Zephirak's main advisor. You were lucky to get on the good side of one so close to Zephirak."

"He seemed to think what his master was doing was wrong, so we know some of them don't approve" replied Leida.

"Of course they don't. Not everyone agrees about this whole thing. I mean, look at Otuss. He disagrees strongly with Diabloss and I highly suspect he's going to try something stupid with those who are allied with him. But that is up to him. Diabloss says we should be prepared and not jump to conclusions and I agree. His plan is a good one and in keeping with how things have been with us since forever. We defend with strength but we don't go looking for fights."

Leida nodded in agreement.

"However," continued Stervia, "if war breaks out then we will go on the offensive. We are fully within our right to protect our Forest and we will recruit as many others as we can to fight alongside us."

"Are the other Gryphies allied with us?" asked Leida.

"The ones from the high mountains are. The Sky Gryphies would probably help if we needed it. As for the Deamons, they would only help if it affected them. So if war broke out and got to the Dark Plains, they would attack back. If it didn't affect them though, they wouldn't bother." Stervia explained.

"They seem selfish and unfriendly to me. How on earth did Diabloss's father end up with a Deamon mate?" Leida asked as they glided through the air together.

"They are unfriendly. As for selfish, well they keep to themselves is all. His father was injured in a fight with a rogue Sky Gryphie. His mother found him and couldn't leave him. Usually a Deamon won't help a pureblood unless the pureblood is in their territory. Then, they help them so that they will leave. Well, she sat with him over the moon cycle with some healing herbs until the sunrise came and he was strong enough to return to the Forest. They formed a bond though, something just clicked with them and he came back to see her. After that, they spent much time together and she took him as her mate. However, the other Deamons banished her since he could not and would not be allowed to live on the Dark Plains. So they came back to the Forest and had Diabloss. They lived on the outskirts of the Forest though, which is why you never knew his parents. They both died younger than they should have, taken by a disease, which is why Diabloss never speaks of them. After that, he began to train for the squadron and became the leader when the previous leader died..."

"And then he met me" finished Leida.

Stervia nodded.

"You know an awful lot about all this" said Leida.

"Yeah, well, I get out. Well, actually I listen a lot. I pay attention to the world around me and learn things. In my line of work I fly a lot, I go places and find new things, learn more. Always be observant, Leida." Stervia smiled and flew higher. The air was mild but a small breeze had picked up. It was breezier around the high mountains.

Leida nodded and followed her. It was so interesting learning all these things. She was surprised she knew so little. Then again, all her life she had kept to herself. When she was a kitten, she was often singled out and left by herself. After a while, she got used to it and made an effort to try and be alone as much as possible. She found that if she only had herself to hang out with, she could do what she wanted and when she wanted without having to come to an agreement with anyone else. She liked this a lot. She still occasionally wondered why the strongest Gryphie in the Forest had chosen the shyest, quietest Gryphie in the Forest. He was her strength though, he made up for where she had been weak and unconfident. In return, she was the caring, gentle side to his strong, powerful, tough side. So they complimented each other. She had hated the jealousy though. A lot of females had found Diabloss desirable of course, including Mettalika. Leida was thankful Mettalika had never harmed her to get at Diabloss.

She and Stervia flew at a cruising speed until the sun had reached its peak and there were the mountains nearing them now. They seemed so close in the distance but when she actually flew to them, they were further away than they looked. Much further. In fact, Leida's wings were starting to ache but she said nothing. She had learnt from her training with Otuss not to complain about things. It was a sign of weakness and also no one likes a whiner.

"Nearly there now, you'll like it in the high mountains I think. The Gryphies are hard workers but friendly. Some are short tempered though but I'm sure they'll be ok." Stervia told her as they flew.

Leida listened and took it all in. They had nearly reached the high mountains now and Stervia planned that they should land on one of the Steel Mountains. Leida saw Gryphies flying around in the air. Some recognised Stervia and called out a greeting. She called back and explained why they were there.

Soon, she and Leida had landed and Leida looked around with interest. The mountains were harsh and jagged and likewise, their inhabitants had sharp claws for climbing and their wings were a slightly different shape. They used their wings to help them climb and they had developed to be more flexible than regular Gryphie wings. They gathered rocks and mined the metal and steel from the mountains. It looked to be a prosperous place and pleasant enough. The Gryphies were large and bulky and many wore metal helmets to protect their heads and armour on their legs and tails. They also utilised their tails to help them work. They were covered in flexible metal like Mettalika's steel tail armour. The steel shone silver but the regular metal was dull and seemed to wear more easily.

Stervia found a friend, Kangrass and introduced him to Leida.

"She wants to learn more" explained Stervia.

Kangrass nodded. "Sure thing, I can show her around the mines and tell her how we make the armour and tools." He smiled at Leida and she felt at ease. She hoped he didn't have a temper, however, because he was massive and bulky. He was about Diabloss's size.

"I have some errands to run so I'll see you back here when the sun is down there" said Stervia, pointing to the sky. Leida nodded and walked with Kangrass.

"So, you've never visited before then?" he asked. Leida shook her head.

"No, I've only ever seen the high mountains in the distance. I've wondered what it was like to come here. My mate's cousin lives here. Iseera?"

"Oh yeah, I know her. She doesn't work in the mines though. She's a Sky hybrid and not strong enough for this heavy work but she's a nice enough soul" replied Kangrass.

"A Sky hybrid?" asked Leida.

"Yeah, her mother's a Sky Gryphie. Her father wanted to get into the Sky Elite but they won't let him. He's too big and heavy and would slow them down. Plus he can't pass their initiation anyway."

"Initiation?" Leida looked puzzled.

"Yeah it's a super hard task he has to complete and he can't do it. It's pretty much impossible to do, which is why of course, they asked him to do it. They don't like "outsiders" in their flying elite so they say that anyone who wants to join has to pass the test. No one has yet though and I doubt they ever will." Kangrass and Leida reached the entrance to the first mine.

Leida thought Gryphies weren't as friendly as she had always known. It seemed each gathering liked to keep within its subspecies and she found this weird and a bit sad too.

"So, here is the first mine. I'll take you inside but you gotta wear this helmet" Kangrass handed her a helmet which she put on, although it was a little too big for her and kept falling over her eyes. She tried to use her ears to keep it on right.

"Follow me and stay close" said Kangrass and headed in. This was a big mine. The entrance reached way up but the cavern got lower towards the tunnel at the back of it. Glowbugs lit up the walls, which dripped with syrup to keep them there. It seemed as though a large colony had set up home in this place of plentiful food, since they flew around everywhere Leida looked. It was pretty and somehow haunting at the same time. They walked through a low tunnel and came out in a vast cavern inside the mountain. Kangrass flew onto a platform and Leida followed. They didn't need a means to walk anywhere, since they had wings and although a few platforms had been made here and there, most of the cavern was how it was naturally. Everywhere Leida looked, there were Gryphies working and mining the steel. Kangrass began to speak.

"Well, here we are; this is one of the larger steel mines in the mountains. You can see everyone hard at work mining the steel. We use our wings to get anywhere we need to. The only problems we have are in small tunnels that we can't get through, so we have to dig them out. See, over there" he pointed to a Gryphie who was busy digging with steel gloves that ended in sharp steel claws on his hands. Leida gazed, fascinated.

"I've heard steel and metal both used, what is the difference though?" she asked.

(Author's Note: Although the names "steel" and "metal" are used, they aren't like our steel and metal, these are materials unique to Shernaron. I use human names for them so they can be differentiated more easily.)

"Steel is stronger and doesn't wear. It's used for attack armour. Metal is softer and can rust in time; it also wears faster and is heavier. It's good for defence armour. Also, steel is a brighter material, having a nice shine to it if kept well. "Kangrass explained, happy that Leida showed interest.

"So, Mettalika would have had steel?"

"Yeah, we kitted her out with steel. We'd never made anything like that before. Usually the steel is used as a tail or hand glove to help us when we work. We'd never fused it to flesh like that but Mystik was sure it would work. It did, with a lot of luck and careful preparation. Even the helmet was fused, she was so badly damaged." Kangrass's expression clouded. It had not been a pleasant operation.

"Well, it didn't help her for all that" said Leida.

"No, now she's gone all strange and nasty. We've sworn never to fuse it to flesh again; we think the chemicals in it might make the wearer hostile." Kangrass didn't know Mettalika was dead.

"That's probably a good idea" replied Leida. "She was killed, didn't you hear?"

"No, when?" Kangrass looked at her now.

"A couple of sun cycles ago by the Lizariaouses." Leida replied.

Kangrass's eyes grew wide. "Wow, well, it's probably for the best. I wonder why we never found out earlier. Mind you, I've been sleeping in the mines these last few moon cycles. We thought there was a leak so I stayed in here and didn't go out except to get a meal. There wasn't a leak in the end so my efforts were pretty worthless but never mind."

They carried on walking through the mine. A few Gryphies greeted Leida but most of them were too busy to pay attention. There were a lot of tunnels. Some were being widened, which seemed to take a long time. Gryphies weren't as strong as Lizariaouses and digging took more effort and power. Even though these mountain Gryphies were bulkier, they still didn't have the stamina required to work as fast.

"These tunnels go all round this mountain. There are entrances in a lot of different places though, should there be a cave in, there are enough places we can escape if we need to."

"Has there ever been a cave in?" asked Leida.

"Well, there was one once. It was seasons ago; I had just started working in this mountain. I didn't cause the cave in though, nor did I get caught in it. They were digging a tunnel out to the west of the mountain and I heard that it had collapsed on the diggers and some of the older, more experienced workers went and rescued them. I've never been involved in an accident yet, thank grik." Kangrass told her.

327

"Were they ok?" Leida asked.

"Yeah, they were ok. One had a broken leg I think but for the most part they were fine, just shaken up and scared. They all still work here so it didn't do too much damage. However I've known Gryphies get into accidents and develop a fear of the tunnels. They never work in the mines again. The metal mines are much like this steel one. Each mountain has a mine in except for the smallest mountain and they've been working for seasons to try and see whether one could be made in it. Many of them are natural but some are dug by us. For example, this is a natural one. Come with me and I'll show you how different one we dug ourselves is." Kangrass lead the way down a small tunnel. He had to duck when he walked down it but Leida managed to walk and only needed to lower her head a little as she did so. She kept her wings close to her. The walls were jagged and nasty looking and she didn't want to catch herself on them. She wondered if anyone else had so she asked.

"Yeah, there's been plenty of injuries down here. Every sun cycle someone manages to mess up and hurt themselves in some way. I have a few times. It's dangerous work in here but we enjoy it. What's life without the excitement, eh?" he laughed and they came out of another entrance. Kangrass pointed to another mountain. "That metal mountain over there; that has a Gryphie dug mine."

They flew over to the ledge he pointed to and Leida looked in, her helmet falling over her eyes as she did so. She pushed it back and saw that this mine was pokey and cramped looking.

"In you go" said Kangrass and Leida walked in ahead of him. The tunnel opened a little and branched off to many others, like a catacomb in the mountain.

There were plenty of glowbugs here too, so it was well lit up.

It has been made wide enough and high enough that a large Gryphie could walk through with ease but it seemed cramped because it didn't open into a cavern like the previous mine had done and there wasn't much room to turn around but it was fine if you were just walking along.

"See how this was dug? Gryphies are still working on it further in. We can't fit as many workers in here, which is why there are so many tunnels. Some of the walls are pretty thin because we tunnel close to existing tunnels to get the most out of the mountain. We use the mountains and resources well and above all, we waste nothing. When we have enough metal and steel to last us a while, mining stops and then continues when we start to run low. Obviously, when the tools and armour are used a lot, they wear out. The steel takes much longer to wear down so we have used more metal than steel. When the metal runs out, then we will just have the steel, which will keep us for hundreds of seasons."

"What do you do when you aren't mining?" asked Leida as they stopped in a connection area where several tunnels opened into and there was more room to move.

Kangrass sat down and motioned for Leida to do the same, for a rest. He didn't need one but he figured she might. He was right and she sat down gratefully.

"Well, when we're not working, we relax, we work out and train a little, strengthen our stamina but we also rest a lot, in equal measure because working is hard and we need to take a break so we don't damage our bodies from over working them. So we rest and train a little. I'll show you where the armour is made after this. When we start walking again, I want you to find our way out. As you can see, the walls are marked so we know where we are. They are marked with levels and tunnel numbers. Follow these and use common sense and see if you can work out the way to the east entrance. That's not the one we came in; it's in a different direction. Think you can do that? You've been training with Stervia so your sense of direction and sign following should be good."

Leida nodded. "I'll do my best. I'm pretty good at tracking and navigating."

"Ah but there's nothing to track. You can't take our scent because it will lead you back the way we came and I don't want you to do that. Also, you can't follow anyone else's scent because there are so many of us working in here; it's all mixed in together. So you have to read the signs."

They both sat back as a worker passed them, heading into the tunnel to their right. He nodded to them as he passed and flicked his tail in a brief greeting. Leida and Kangrass reciprocated.

"Are you ready?" asked Kangrass. Leida nodded firmly so he told her to lead the way, which she did.

Each tunnel had a sign at the entrance and exit to it. If a tunnel entrance was halfway through it, those also had signs. Kangrass told her the level didn't matter, so long as they left at the east entrance. There were several of these of course, on each level. Of course, levels and tunnel numbers aren't very useful when you're looking for a direction to travel in. Leida felt the air with her nose, to see how close they were to an entrance. If she felt a breeze, it would mean they were nearby. The nearer they got, the more signs had the direction as well as the tunnel number and level. This was to give an early idea to a worker, which entrance he was going to leave by, so if he wanted a west entrance instead, he could turn around and head in the opposite direction. Leida found a tunnel leading up and saw it was to the north entrance at the top of the mountain and this is how she found the extra sign that appeared in the case of tunnels that are near an entrance. She looked around more, Kangrass patiently following. From the north sign, she headed left and soon came across a sign saying that if she kept on in that direction, she would come out in the east. So she headed in that direction and soon they were outside again.

"Well done! Most of the Gryphies I've set that task to when I was training them get completely put off by the fact that most of the tunnels have tunnel and level numbers and it never occurs to them that if they head near an entrance, they will get a sign that also says the direction they are headed. Stervia taught you well." Kangrass smiled and took to the sky, Leida following.

"Well I'm glad I got it right. I haven't been training with Stervia for long. My mate seems to think I should be in his squadron."

"Your mate has a squadron?" asked Kangrass.

"Yeah, my mate is Diabloss" Leida told him.

"Wow, really? Hmm, I never knew he took a mate. I'm impressed though. I think you'd make a good addition to his squadron."

Leida just smiled and said nothing. She never knew what reply to give to compliments, besides the usual "thanks".

"Now I know how Iseera is his cousin. When you told me that your mate's cousin was her, it never occurred to me that he was Diabloss, even though I know he and Iseera are related."

They flew down and landed at the foot of one of the mountains. This was the first time Leida had set foot on the ground since she got there. Here, there was a cluster of little caves, each one a workshop for Gryphies making things out of steel and metal, using their fire to soften, sculpt and create things. It was a hot and noisy place. They were all hard at work and didn't notice Kangrass and Leida approach so they were free to walk around and have a look. No one minded so long as they stayed out of the way. Leida nearly tripped one of the workers with her tail at one point and he snapped and snarled at her, telling her to be careful or she would get hurt and also to keep out of the way since he was busy and didn't need to be interrupted. Leida was very careful after that. Her helmet had fallen over her eyes again, which was why she had stumbled into his way in the first place. Kangrass took it off her and put it to one side. She wouldn't need it now they were out of the mountains anyway, although she was half afraid someone would throw a tantrum and chuck something at her. She was safe though. She watched a Gryphie making a tail fixture with a large steel tail spade on it. It seemed like this was either to enhance or make up for a Gryphie's current tail spade.

"Interesting, isn't it?" said Kangrass.

Leida nodded, she had learnt a lot. Although the metal and steel mines were similar, a wide variety of objects could be made from both and both materials had different uses. Leida found she much preferred the natural mine to the slightly cramped Gryphie dug one.

"Can I see Iseera? I think Diabloss hoped I'd see her, he probably wants to catch up with what's been going on here." Leida said.

Kangrass nodded. "Well sure, but nothing much happens here except mining. You're the ones with all the action these sun cycles."

"Trust me, I'd rather we weren't" replied Leida.

Kangrass agreed that the action wasn't of the good kind and they headed away from the workshops to go find Iseera. Kangrass told Leida she would find her at the top of the mountains although she may have to fly around a bit. Iseera spent most of her time around the top, making sure all the entrances were secure. Sometimes there could be a cave in at one of the entrances and no one would know about it if it was one that wasn't used much.

Leida thanked him for showing her around and took off to find Iseera. The mountains were rightly named, they certainly were high! Leida didn't realise just how high until she tried to reach the top from the ground. They were vast! She wondered where the Gryphies slept at moon cycle. She saw a few living places around the foot of the mountains so she assumed they must return there after a hard sun cycle of work in the mines. Then of course there was Kangrass telling her that he spent the moon cycle in a mine, so maybe others did that too for whatever reason. It was all so different from the Forest and she loved it. She had discovered she loved to explore and travel.

Climbing higher in the sky, further up the mountain, she finally reached the top and had a look round for Iseera. There were Gryphies on top of the mountains too; some flying around carrying mined metal and some just sat having a rest, enjoying the view. It was a spectacular view too. Leida flew up and landed on a high ledge to rest and look around. She saw the Forest in the distance to the west and to the east she saw a great long expanse of rather unfriendly looking, barren land. The Dark Plains. They were dark too; the sky was a dark blood red mixed with deep blue and black and way off in the distance there was a flash of lightning. Between the high mountains and the dark plains were more Outlands, barren and dry, that no one could live on, not even a resourceful Gryphie. Some had tried to live in the Outlands of course but realised that there was no food to catch and no shelter. Quite often there were high winds and it was best not to stay around for more than a moon cycle in passing. The stretch of the Outlands was far wider between the high mountains and the Dark Plains than it was between the Forest and Dyarkroeen. The high mountains, Forest and all in between was Shernaron. Dyarkroeen was the territory of course of the Lizariaouses, the other side of the Outlands. They probably had their own sections too that they lived in but Leida wasn't aware of them, except some smaller mountains they had made their homes at the foot of. It was debatable as to whether or not the Dark Plains was a part of Shernaron or a place all of its own. Most Gryphies counted it as part of Shernaron.

Leida's gaze drifted away from the Dark Plains and to the tops of the mountains, seeking out Iseera. She found her, or what she thought was her, looking around in some small trees. Leida flew over to see. Yes, it was Iseera.

"Iseera!" she called and landed nearby. The other Gryphie looked round and recognised Leida, trotting up to greet her.

"Leida! What brings you here?" she asked.

"Stervia brought me. She thought it would be a good endurance exercise since it's a long flight." Leida replied, stretching out a wing and yawning a little. "The flight back will be just as long."

Iseera smiled. "Well, since you're here, maybe you can help me. I'm looking for berries in the trees. I'm collecting them for the kittens. They want to paint and berries are good for painting, since they are round and juicy. The kittens are making a mountain side mural about what life is like here. It's not that big of course and the rain will soon wash it away, but it's fun and they enjoy it."

Leida took a look at the position of the sun to make sure she had time before going to meet Stervia. She did, so she agreed to help.

"I heard about Mettalika" said Iseera as they picked berries. Leida was in one tree and Iseera was in another, clinging on and picking the berries. They dropped them to the ground to be picked up afterwards and put in the large pouches Iseera had brought. It was hard to hold a pouch while also holding onto a tree and trying to pick berries when your wings kept getting in the way as well. The Gryphies were really too big for the small trees.

"Yes, I hope that things will settle down now she's gone. It seems to be somehow more peaceful and nearer to how it was before without her" replied Leida.

"I can imagine it must be worrying having to think constantly about what might happen over that. For once, I know it's cruel to think this, but the Lizariaouses did a good thing." Iseera grabbed a bunch of high berries in her hand and nearly fell out of the tree.

"I'd be inclined to agree, although Diabloss told me that Zephirak is taking all the credit for something that his soldiers did." Leida ate a berry as she worked.

"Well, you know him. He couldn't have brought her down without help anyway, any of those guys must be aware of that. He's not saying he did it singlehandedly is he? Cos that's too farfetched for even those morons to believe" Iseera was amused at the thought of it.

"No, I think they think he had his soldiers there to help but that he did all the work. I reckon he just watched as they brought her down, he mocked her and told his lackeys to kill her while he watched" said Leida, the thought making her shudder a little.

"Na, he would've made the killing blow. Lizariaouses like to repay in full. Mettalika killed his mate so he killed her and so the dept was repaid. He wouldn't have wanted to just watch it." Iseera told her.

Leida pondered this and it made more sense than her theory. She had never been that good with theories anyway. She climbed down and put the fallen berries in the pouches as Iseera picked some more from the other tree.

"Hmm, I think you're right. Oh well, what's done is past now. However it happened, she's not coming back and we must try and return things to how they were. It's just too bad Sinxo had to die in the process. I wish we could have stopped it before that happened." Leida sat for a while, missing Sinxo again. She had been such a bright, positive Gryphie.

"Yeah" replied Iseera, picking the last of her berries and jumping to the ground to pick up the fallen ones. "It is a shame. But still, she didn't die in vain I guess…or something. I'm bad at this."

"Bad at what?" asked Leida.

"Sympathies. I never know what to say. Sinxo was cool though."

Leida decided to change the subject as Iseera was running out of things to say about the whole thing.

"Have you ever been to the Dark Plains?" she asked her.

"The Dark Plains? My aunt was a Deamon Gryphie. She told me a lot about it. Diabloss's Mum, you know? Well of course she was only my aunt through mating; she wasn't my blood aunt, obviously. But I was lucky since my mother is a Sky Gryphie and my aunt was a Deamon, I've learnt a lot about us all through them. I've never been there, no. I wanted to go and I asked my aunt a lot but she said no. She visited the mountains a lot with Diabloss, she was often returning to visit her family on the Dark Plains. I also visited the Forest a lot, especially after my aunt died and I made a lot of friends there like Mystik for example. Diabloss needed me then and I lived in the Forest for a while before returning here when his squadron duties kept him busy. The Dark Plains are completely different to here or the Forest or even the sky. Things there aren't tough but they are treated strictly, even from small kittens. They rarely speak or play like us; they seem to be half way between us and Lizariaouses. Whereas Lizariaouses are warlike, they are not so much but they are strict. And we are peaceful; well they aren't peaceful either. They keep to themselves like we do but if something upsets them; they will go out of their way to take vengeance. They bear a horrible grudge which is why those who have gone up against them have never lived to be heard from again. Basically, stay away from them as best you can. They are not to be messed with and my aunt told me they are not to be disturbed either. I've never known anyone dare go to the Dark Plains." Iseera closed the pouches and hung both round her neck. Leida followed her as they took them to the kittens.

"They don't hunt us though, do they? I mean, would they kill us if we strayed over there?" asked Leida as they flew.

"No they wouldn't kill us, just tell us to leave. If we did, no harm would come to us. If we didn't, then they would challenge us and we would back down but if we still didn't, then they would kill us. They aren't bloodthirsty but they are dangerous. I don't know how they live over there though. I've gone across the Outlands and as near as I can without being seen or warned away and I can see no places where they could make their homes. I think there are some kinds of mountains there like here or Dyarkroeen. Each territory has its own mountain range. But it's always so dark over there, I can't see that far. It makes me wonder and I've often wanted to visit but it just wouldn't be allowed. I don't think I could even sneak in and it would be a risk not worth taking." Iseera and Leida landed near a class of waiting kittens and passed the pouches to their teacher who took them gratefully and thanked her and Leida.

Leida had a load more questions now but felt she had asked enough. She wanted to go to the Dark Plains and have a look herself without being seen but she knew that wouldn't be possible so she dropped the subject. It was nearly time to meet Stervia now anyway; the sun had dropped to the right point in the sky.

"Well thanks for the information, Iseera. Is there a message you would like taken back to Diabloss?" asked Leida.

"Just send him my thoughts, I'm thinking of him and all you guys in the Forest. I hope things continue as they are and you've heard the last of Zephirak and his stupidity." Iseera smiled and they said their farewells.

When Leida reached Stervia, she had been waiting there some time.

"Where were you? I told you to be here on time, it will be dark before we reach home otherwise!" Stervia scolded her.

Leida apologised and explained that Iseera had been telling her about the Dark Plains.

"Yeah, well stay away from there. You don't want to end up dead or something. They don't take kindly to trespassers." Stervia told her.

"So I've heard" replied Leida. "But I had an interesting time seeing the mines and workshops."

"Glad it was a good experience. We'll come back here again sometime or you can visit them. This gathering doesn't mind visitors. Now, let's get back to the Forest!" Stervia spread her wings and leaped into the sky, closely followed by Leida.

They took off back to the Forest. This time they flew mostly in silence. Leida was a little tired from all the flying and she knew her wings would ache in the morning. Stervia had things on her mind and was thinking also about getting back to her tree for a rest.

The sun had nearly set when they reached home. Stervia flew off to her tree and Leida returned to hers. She was hungry but she thought she would rest before going to catch a meal. She was happy to find she didn't need to hunt; Diabloss had already caught something for her and was sat at the foot of the tree with it. It was a small bear hog. Bear hogs only come out as the sun sets and so aren't often caught unless a Gryphie goes hunting at that time. They resemble pig sized bears. They are really plump and make a filling meal, even the small ones.

Leida tucked in thankfully after greeting Diabloss. He had already eaten his.

"So, did you learn anything new?" He knew what the answer would be though.

"Yes, lots!" she said in between mouthfuls. "I learnt about the mines, how they make things out of steel and metal and Iseera sends her good wishes also. She told me a bit about the Dark Plains but not much, sadly. It's a shame I can't go there and see for myself what it's like."

"No, no one can go there, it's far too dangerous. Besides, they leave us alone, we leave them alone and that is how we get along. Deamons don't bother us."

339

Diabloss yawned. "Well, I've been busy scouting, training and making sure my squadron is in shape. No word about Zephirak. I saw a lot of hunting packs though this sun cycle. They seemed to be everywhere. I didn't like that but they only caught meal creatures. They keep food in the backs of their caves, it's cool in there and the meat keeps for a while. They seem to be restocking. I've no doubt there were celebrations a few sun cycles ago when they got Mettalika and they've gone through all their food reserves."

"They couldn't have been keeping much anyway, not in this warm weather" said Leida.

"No, it's only in the colder weather that they keep a lot of stock. I'm not entirely sure how it works. Still, I didn't see them catch any of us so for that I am happy. We'll see how it goes."

As this conversation was taking place, Jadariol was hobbling about with Lunara.

"Hey, what's that she's eating?" he asked her, referring to Leida's bear hog.

"It's a bear hog. We don't catch them often. Hey, look at this!" Lunara had found a round, shiny pebble. It looked like it came from the coast to the south of the Forest. Lunara was fascinated by the sheen on it but Jadariol wasn't that impressed. He wrinkled his red scaly snout and sniffed it.

"It's just a pebble" he said.

Lunara's face lit up suddenly. "Have you ever been to the cliffs?"

"No why?"

"Then tomorrow I'll get my Mum to take us! I'll see if Hiryasis and some of the others want to come along too. It's fun and we can find loads more pebbles like this." She skipped about excitedly and Jadariol couldn't help but smile at her antics. He wasn't quite sure about the whole fascination with the pebbles though. It was just a small rock to him.

Lunara went to ask Shen and Jadariol headed back to Mystik's tree, slowly. He was able to stand for longer now but it was still difficult for him. His legs still hurt. He also hadn't told anyone but his dreams had been haunted by Mettalika attacking him. Quite a few moon cycles he had had the same dream, of the attack all over again and he'd woken up in a cold sweat, realised where he was and gone back to sleep again. Those images would stay with him the rest of his life and he was secretly afraid her ghost would come back and haunt him, although he didn't tell anyone since that would be a sign of weakness, even around those who wouldn't take it as that. When he reached Mystik's tree, he settled down on his bed and rested. Mystik was out getting her meal or something he thought. So he had the place to himself. As he'd gotten better, he became more aware and interested in his surroundings. He knew now where a lot of herbs were kept and how close Mystik was to running out of the ones she needed for his dressings. This was all strange to him since he had never been hurt badly enough to require things like this before. His own species would approach it in a different way; they didn't use herbs or anything much. Sometimes they would wrap a damaged leg, give the wounded rest and hope that it healed ok. So a lot of Lizariaouses had scarred limbs and limbs that had not healed correctly. In fact some even lost them if they didn't heal right and then got in the way. The limb would be amputated. If the wounded didn't bleed to death or get an infection and die, they might live. Jadariol was happy to note that his leg was looking like it had always looked. He could flex his toes with almost no pain now on the broken leg and the fractured one was even better. He sighed and went to sleep.

Lunara was pleading with Shen at that moment.

"I don't know. Both your father and I are very busy." Lunara gave her pleading eyes and murred softly to persuade her.

"But," she continued, "I suppose I can take you just for the beginning of the sun cycle. Your father can take over for me until we return."

"Yippee!" yelled Lunara and flitted about in glee. Shen shook her head and smiled. She was growing used to Jadariol now. Lunara was rarely away from him and he was also getting on well with her other friends as well. Shen was almost accepting him as just another member of the gathering and she kept having to remind herself that he wasn't and that soon he would be returning to Dyarkroeen. It was hard though, he was so much like a kitten in many ways. Also the sight of him was to take pity on, since he still had trouble walking. He was bigger than Lunara though and as big as the male kittens. She wasn't sure of his age.

Lunara had run off to tell him and her other friends that it was on for the next sun cycle. She bounded into the tree to tell Jadariol first and found him sleeping.

"Jaddy! Jaddy? Hmm..." she wandered up to him and peered at him. He was sleeping peacefully and she wasn't sure disturbing him would be good, since he needed his rest so she decided to give Mystik the message when she returned.

Lunara left the sleeping Lizariaous and bumped straight into Mystik as she left the tree.

"Mystik! Could you tell Jadariol that we're going to the coast tomorrow?" asked Lunara sweetly.

Mystik nodded. "Of course, dear" she replied. "Who are you going with?"

"Mum's taking us. I'm gunna ask Hiryasis, Len, Kammy, Hevia and Zephyr too."

"Well, I am sure it will be fun and educational and I will tell Jadariol about it." Mystik smiled and headed into her tree while Lunara ran off to ask her other friends if they wanted to accompany them.

Jadariol stirred when Mystik entered.

"Ah, you are awake now. Lunara says Shen is taking you to the coast the next sun cycle. You haven't been to the coast, have you?"

"No" was the one word reply. Jadariol wasn't sure what the coast entailed, exactly.

"It will be fun" smiled Mystik.

Jadariol smiled, yawned and went back to sleep.

Chapter 29
Surprise Date

In Dyarkroeen, Mordred was keeping up his promise to find Zephirak a new mate. He thought it was a good idea of Schaarl's but it had to be done with care. He had found a suitable female in the last few sun cycles and told her about it. She was very interested in him, she had been for a long while now but of course had never acted on it since, like most of the others, she feared him a bit and of course, there was the subject of his previous mate and how much he missed her. This female was called Zetarzo. She was deep green with a few yellow scales here and there, the mix of the dark and light colours made her look truly stunning and flashy. She had a curious black streak down her muzzle and deep fiery orange eyes. She was large but slim and Mordred felt she would compliment Zephirak perfectly. Now he had to get them together. The sun was setting in the sky but it would be light for a while longer and Zephirak was outside his cavern having an evening meal. Mordred was wearing the spiked cuff on his leg from Mettalika and the setting sun made the steel look orange as it reflected on it.

"Ok, Zetarzo, just walk up to him and make conversation. Try to sit close to him, you know what body language to use to show you're interested in him, be natural, be yourself, don't mention Salvariss and make sure to flatter him. You like him, right? Then show how much you like him, tell him what you like best about him, compliment him on being brave enough to take down Mettalika. You got all that?"

Zetarzo nodded. "Yes, I think I have."

"Don't think; you must be confident. You get one shot at this and one shot only; you mess it up and not only won't you get to be with him, he will also get in a horrible mood again. We have to keep him happy, remember?" Mordred told her. He wanted it to be completely clear and planned well.

Zetarzo nodded again. "I have it."

"Then go do it!" said Mordred and pushed her forward with a paw. "I'll be over here watching. I won't intervene though; that's not my place. If it all goes wrong, just walk off."

"Ok" replied Zetarzo and headed over to Zephirak. No females had shown their interest to him since the scenario with his mate so she was honestly not sure if he would give her a chance or instantly dismiss her advances and tell her to leave. She swallowed and walked up to him. It didn't help that she had feelings for him either. That made her even more nervous about messing up.

"Lord Zephirak" she said, approaching him slowly and respectfully.

His red eyes flicked up to her and he nodded. "Yes?"

She sat beside him. "I heard you speak of how you defeated Mettalika. Such bravery is rarely seen among us. We hunt and fight every sun cycle but to singlehandedly take down such a powerful creature as her and come out without so much of a scratch; well your story will go down as legend among Lizariaouses. Your memory will live on forever in that."

"And do you think I will die anytime soon then?" he asked, looking her straight in the eye. Zetarzo swallowed. He was being challenging.

"No, I meant that you will never die. Your story will make you immortal in all Lizariaous eyes! No Lizariaous has ever done what you did, Sir." She lowered her head in submission so he could cuff her if he felt she was being insolent. He didn't, though.

345

"Ah yes, I see what you mean. You are very observant..." he looked at her questioningly, not knowing her name. He only really knew the names of his closest soldiers.

"Zetarzo, Sir" she said.

"Zetarzo, hmm, yes, well you are very observant."

"Thank you, Sir; it is an honour to hear such a compliment from you. I have looked up to you all my life and admired you and all you stand for." She gazed at him now, her body language suggesting she might be interested in getting to know him better.

"You want to be in my army? Are you a good fighter?" Whether he knew she was interested in him as a mate and tried to ignore it or whether he merely thought she was interested in joining his army, she wasn't sure.

"I am here to serve you" she replied. "Do with me as you wish."

"Hmm, well it depends how good a fighter you are, how dedicated you are to your work and how hard you train. Do you have any experience in the army or any other fighting tasks?"

"Yes Sir. I am in one of the lower ranking scout and hunting packs. I have knowledge with fighting and seeking." She moved a little closer to him, still submissively in case he saw and took offence. If she kept her profile low, he would have nothing to complain about.

"Well then go to Karnos and sign up with the soldiers. He'll put you through your paces and see what you can do to see if you are suitable." Zephirak's claws dug into the ground as he scraped at it in boredom as he chewed his food.

Zetarzo felt she was losing this and thought about something to talk to him about.

"I will go first thing at sunrise" she said with confidence. "Mind if I sit with you for a while? My...family is busy with other things and I would be honoured if you allowed me to sit here a while."

Zephirak looked at her, then shrugged and carried on chewing. "Just don't annoy me" he said shortly.

"Oh no Sir, I'll be well behaved. So, what was it like in the swamp the other sun cycle? I heard a lot about it but with all the celebrations and things, I didn't really catch much of what was happening at the time."

"We had her surrounded and I killed her. Heheh, she screamed for mercy but I told her that she showed no mercy to my mate so why should I show her mercy when she needed it?" Zephirak's lips curled up into a small and cruel smile, showing his teeth. Zetarzo found this to be cute, well, as cute as a Lizariaous could be anyway. She listened with intense interest and Zephirak saw she hung on his every word so he continued.

"I told her what I thought of her, the scum she was and that she would die and never be remembered for anything good, that she was worthless and neither Lizariaous nor Gryphie cared what happened to her." Zephirak was making a lot of this up since his speech hadn't been that long for fear she would still escape and kill him. Whatever he said out loud, inside he had feared her and as is the case with a lot of creatures, if it's feared, it must either be escaped from or destroyed, depending on the tendency of the creature in question. Zephirak had been afraid of her. Even after her wings were destroyed and she was worn out and held down, even then he was afraid she might, by some miracle, escape and kill him. Maybe jump up, escaping the soldiers' grasp and lunge for his throat. Even now he had moonmares about her returning and wiping out the whole clan while he slept. She had affected him way more than he let on. But as far as the rest of the pack was concerned, Zephirak had never feared her and he had dispatched her like a true hero, freeing them all from her threat. In all their eyes, he was a hero. Even his soldiers saw him as heroic and it never occurred to them that his boasting was wrong. He was the leader and whatever he said went, even if he lied about it.

Zetarzo listened. Then she decided to try the flattery Mordred had mentioned Zephirak enjoyed.

"Oh wow, you're so brave to take her on singlehandedly like that. She couldn't escape because she was surrounded and you took her out like a forest deer."

"Yes, she tried to run once she knew she was up against me. That's why she never came into our territory after killing my mate. She feared coming up against me. She snuck in here while I was out on a hunt anyway when she killed her. Once she realised I was in the swamp and she was surrounded by my soldiers, she wanted to flee but I broke both her wings and all her legs." Zephirak was exaggerating now.

"Wow, how strong you are, Lord Zephirak" crooned Zetarzo.

"Yes, well, my anger helped. She needed to die, it was a requirement and I needed to avenge the death of my beloved Salvariss. So I did. I'm sure word has got back to the other Gryphies about her death. They will know not to mess with me either now. If any of them choose to avenge her that is."

"Was it hard to do? I imagine not for someone as strong as you." Zetarzo flicked her tail and gazed at him, a dreamy look on her face.

"No, it wasn't hard. She wasn't as strong as she looked. The armour she wore was just a front to scare us all off. She killed weaker Lizariaouses because she herself was weak. Then again I am the strongest in the whole of Dyarkroeen, which is why I am your leader."

"And you lead us so well Sir." Zetarzo growled softly.

Zephirak smiled; something he didn't do very often these sun cycles but now Mettalika was dead, something he was starting to do more frequently.

Zetarzo laid her needles flat and growled at him. He ignored her. She tried again and he ignored her again.

"I've always admired you...you're so handsome and brave"

"Thank you" replied Zephirak. "You have good taste."

"Oh, I do. I have very high standards, after all." Zetarzo was right beside him now.

"Do you now? Very high standards for what, exactly?" asked Zephirak, turning and smirking at her.

"Well, for males I'm interested in" she replied.

"Oh, I see where this is going, the flattery, the questions, the fact you didn't rush straight off to Karnos and sign up with my army like any normal female would have done. You're interested in me as a mate, aren't you?" He looked her straight in the eye.

Zetarzo nodded. "Well...yes, I've...I've always liked you."

Suddenly Zephirak snarled and lunged at her. She jumped up and back just in time. "HOW DARE YOU!! I am not ready to take another mate! Whatever the grik gave you that idea?? Do I show any signs of being interested in choosing a new mate? No! So go now, or I'll kill you where you cower before me!" He roared at her, all his needles thrust forward in her direction.

Zetarzo yelped in sheer fear and bolted. Zephirak threw back his head and roared powerfully, it echoed all around Dyarkroeen for miles around, letting anyone else who might be interested know that he was *not* looking for a new mate and anyone who tried it on would be severely damaged, if not killed for their insolence. He grabbed what was left of his meal and stalked into his cavern in a rage. How *dare* she!

Zetarzo had fled back to her own cave, the only place she knew she would be marginally safe and she sat down and whimpered. She had moved too fast because she thought he was relaxed with her. She felt so stupid.

Someone appeared at the entrance to her cave and she shrank back in the shadows, fearful it might be Zephirak. It wasn't though, it was Mordred. He had been keeping an eye on her from afar.

"Zetarzo? Are you ok?" He wandered in slowly.

"No, now he hates me." She came forward, revealing herself now she knew it wasn't a threat. Normally she would have defended her cave fiercely but she thought he'd been Zephirak and she would never go up against him or even try.

"I suppose it was my fault for suggesting it. I didn't know he wasn't ready. But you shouldn't have said you were looking to be his mate; that was a little fast. I thought you were going to give it a few sun cycles and see what happened."

"Well, he asked me! He asked if I was interested in him as a mate. I couldn't lie, he is our ruler and lying to him would result in punishment or worse. Plus if I had lied, my expression or body language or something would have given me away." Zetarzo sat down miserably. "And now I've lost my chance forever. I wish I'd never listened to you."

"I'm sorry" Mordred sighed. "Well when he is looking for a new mate, maybe you can try again? Maybe he'll have forgotten."

"I doubt that. He was so angry; I could feel it in the very depth of my being. I felt his rage and hurt. He's still sad about Salvariss. I don't blame him. She was pregnant with their first youngster too. I won't try again. He's way out of my league. Rondo's interested in me anyway; I think I might take him instead. He's a good strong Lizariaous and a good fighter, though his attitude can be a bit bone headed at times. I hope Lord Zephirak gets a good mate, one worthy of him. That certainly isn't me." Zetarzo didn't cry but she felt like it. Crying wasn't the Lizariaous way.

"Well, whatever you wish. I hope you find someone too though, you deserve happiness just as much as Zephirak does." Mordred left her cave and headed back to his. He was annoyed with Zephirak. Sure, Zeph was sad about losing his mate, anyone would be. But it was such a long time ago and he bore such a grudge still, even after Mettalika's death. This whole thing made Mordred worried. Zephirak's temper had not gotten better and what this entire scenario proved was that he was still extremely upset about all that had happened. Mordred doubted that he would let this go. If he didn't, it would eat away at him and destroy his sanity, what little of it he had left at any rate. He really wished someone would overthrow Zephirak and become the new leader of the pack. He suggested this to Schaarl when he got home.

"Why don't you do it?" she suggested.

"Me? I could never go up against him. He's bigger, heavier and stronger than me. Plus, he's already lost his temper with me once. This scar on my eye will always be a reminder of that." Mordred thought the idea was insane and dangerous.

"Maybe you wouldn't have to use strength. Maybe you could outsmart him? You don't have to kill him, just prove that you're the better Lizariaous."

"Yes, which is done by fighting and overpowering the opponent. I appreciate that you have faith in me but this is ridiculous. Besides, I could never lead us. No one would respect me like they do him" said Mordred, sitting down beside her at the entrance to their cave.

"You're already his favourite pack commander and his advisor. Surely there must be some way you could get in there?" Schaarl pressed on.

"Schaarl, no. I'm not doing that. There is no way it could work and it's just asking for trouble. You don't want to lose your mate, do you?"

Schaarl shook her head.

"Then get rid of these silly ideas." He nuzzled her to reassure her and she smiled.

"Very well. I still think you'd make a great leader though."

"I appreciate that, thanks" he said and settled down with her. At least someone had faith in him. He had only been trying to help Zephirak and the rest of them. He felt sorry for Zetarzo though, she must really have had her spirit and her sense of self confidence run down. He knew how scary Zephirak was when he was angry. He also assumed that Zephirak would react the same way if he himself suggested Zeph get a new mate. Mordred decided to keep quiet about this for a while and try to get back into his old pre-Mettalika routine. He figured this couldn't be too hard. These last few sun cycles, the whole clan had been taking it easy. Everyone seemed so much more relaxed and happy. Mordred didn't want this to end.

***

352

The next sun cycle dawned brightly over the Forest and Jadariol slowly woke up upon hearing Mystik doing her usual morning chores around the tree. He stretched, winced and sat up slowly. This sun cycle they were going to the coast, whatever that was. He'd heard about it before from various sources but he'd never seen it himself. He knew that sea vultures came from there and the hunters often returned with tales of lots of water.

He watched Mystik and then looked out of the entrance of the tree. Lots of Gryphies were going about their morning business out there, getting food, water, taking their kittens training and other morning activities. He saw Leida and Diabloss head into the Forest and some of the kittens running about. Len and Hiryasis were running after an older Gryphie who seemed annoyed by their presence. Jadariol grinned to himself and wandered outside to see what was going on. Zephyr ran past and greeted him briefly. Jadariol wanted someone to talk to but everyone was so busy with their own things that he was mostly ignored. This made him annoyed and he stuck his tail out and tripped up Kammy. She yelled at him.

"When are we going to the coast?" asked Jadariol.

"After breakfast, honestly, have you no patience?" she picked herself up and trotted off, nose in the air. Jadariol imitated her and stuck his tongue out at her as she left. He heard laughing. It was Hevia.

"She's so stuck up! She thinks she knows everything" said Hevia. Jadariol sniggered and then stared at Hevia. He couldn't work out if the little Gryphie was a boy or a girl. He raised on eye ridge and cocked his head to one side.

"What's up? Is my mane a mess or what?" asked Hevia.

353

"Err...are you a boy?" asked Jadariol. But Hevia just laughed and bounced off with a wave of the tail. Jadariol watched Hevia and still couldn't work it out.

"Jadariol! Come inside, please. I need to check your dressings before your big outing this sun cycle" Mystik called.

"Big outing? How far is this coast place?" asked Jadariol, worried now because he might get tired along the way and be left behind. He assumed the Gryphies were like the Lizariaouses and left behind anyone who couldn't keep up. Lizariaouses showed no pity, not even to their own youngsters or the injured.

"It's pretty far. You will be flying." Mystik said, taking a look at Jadariol's dressings and replenishing the herbs in them.

"Flying? I can't fly!" Jadariol sounded panicky now.

"No, you will be given a lift by Shen."

"What?" Jadariol was completely confused now.

"Lunara's mother, Shen. She will carry you. The flight is not that far and while you are heavy, it is not too much stress on her muscles to carry you there. You would never be able to walk it, nor would I advise it. Walking, you would slow everyone down and probably strain yourself, hindering your healing."

"She's gunna *carry* me? What if she drops me? I don't want to go now." Jadariol complained.

"You will be going. The salt air will do you good and help you. If this were Dyarkroeen, I would have given you a rough slap in the face for complaining." Mystik told him sternly.

"But it's not Dyarkroeen, you're not my parent and I don't have to listen" growled Jadariol obstinently. "I don't trust that a Gryphie wouldn't drop me. They're not that strong."

Mystik suddenly did something very unlike her and cuffed his ear, taking him by surprise. "Be quiet! You are complaining like a spoiled kitten. And why would she drop you? We have been working to heal you and killing you now would make all this work pointless. We would have left you for Mettalika if we had wanted that. Don't be so ungrateful! Now, hold still while I change these."

Jadariol sat silently in shock. He'd thought he could have appealed to Mystik's better nature and got some sympathy but the quick old Gryphie knew the tricks of the young and he was not going to wimp out of this one. He suddenly felt ashamed. What would his father think? His father would be angry that a prospective soldier would ever suggest anything like that. Wimping out of the trip was the wuss's way out and there was no way Jadariol was a wuss. He decided not to complain any more. Even if he did get nervous he knew he mustn't let it show. Being around these Gryphies, who always made their true feelings known had made him start to do the same and this was not allowed in his species. He held still.

Lunara bounded in a little later while Jadariol was eating his breakfast.

"Are you ready?" she asked happily, leaping about. "Len, Kammy, Hevia, Hiryasis and Zephyr are all outside and ready to go! My Mum will be along soon to take us. She's with my Dad right now, sorting things out that he can get on with while we're gone. My parents are very busy so it will only be a morning outing. We'll be back at mid sun but I can guarantee that you'll love the coast! There are so many awesome things there!"

Jadariol finished his meal and stood up carefully. "Like what?" he asked.

"Oh, beaches, caves, water, rock pools, sea creatures, sand, pebbles, hidden places that are great to explore…loads of stuff!"

"I don't know what any of those are except the water and the caves. What's "sand"?" asked Jadariol tentatively.

"It's like teeny little stones, really, really small ones and it's soft underfoot but sometimes rough. It's hard to describe but you'll see it. Oh hey, here's Mum! Come on!" Lunara rushed to Shen and the other kittens crowded around her. Jadariol hesitated. He knew that she was here to pick him up…literally. He waited for Mystik to say goodbye.

"Go on then" she said, "Go and have fun!"

Jadariol left without replying and walked up to Shen.

"Are you ready? I'll have to carry you, but it isn't far if we fly. Stand still so I can pick you up" Shen said, smiling. Jadariol did as he was told. The kittens were already headed up a nearby tree. Shen picked up Jadariol and tucked him under one arm, following them. He tried to relax but he knew his body was as stiff as wood. He was terrified.

"Are you ok?" asked Shen as she carried him up the tree after the kittens.

"Yes, I'm fine…I've just never been picked up before but I'm ok." Jadariol lied.

Shen reached the top, held Jadariol in both her arms and swooped her wings, pushing off of a high and thick branch with her feet, taking to the sky. The kittens were already flying around. They could have taken off down on the forest floor but Shen's wings were too big and she would have had difficulty trying to take off while also holding onto Jadariol so she needed a more open space higher up to get into the air.

Jadariol looked around as they flew; now his fear had been replaced by amazement. He had never seen the world from this view before and he liked what he saw. Everything was small down below and he could see the layout of the land better, it amazed him. He started to relax, forgetting his nervousness.

"How are you? Not feeling sick are you?" asked Shen.

"No, this is amazing!" yelled Jadariol.

"See? This is what we see every sun cycle! Isn't it great?" yelled Lunara, flying by with ease and closely followed by the weird Hevia.

"Yeah! Wow, I wish I could fly and see this every sun cycle. It sure beats living in a cave and only seeing the wastelands or the training grounds. How come your territory is so much prettier? I can see mine and yours and mine seems boring. Yours has all the trees and stuff and mine just has caves and a few mountains." Jadariol could see well now, since they were high up. They were flying over Shernaron but he could still see Dyarkroeen off in the distance. It did seem very boring in comparison. He could see why his leader hated the Gryphies so much; they could fly and had a larger and nicer territory.

"I don't know; that's just the way things are" replied Shen. Jadariol hardly heard her, his mind was off in his own thoughts. It was amazing. He'd never even dreamed of anything like this. The kittens wheeled and soared in the sky nearby. Jadariol envied them; they seemed to have it so good. He ignored them for a while though; everything else was so distracting and beautiful. He had grown up in a place where beauty was almost nonexistent and now to see so much of it all in one place really made him speechless. It was incredible beyond words.

After a while, he saw a wide and sparkling expanse of blue, stretching off into the distance. The ocean. He had no idea what it was though; it just looked like a much vaster version of the reservoir where the Lizariaouses got their water from. He wondered if this was the Gryphies' reservoir. They seemed to have everything else bigger and better; maybe their watering place was too.

"There it is! We're nearly there now, Jadariol!" Lunara laughed and flew on ahead, followed by Hiryasis. Zephyr was flying upside down.

"Hey Shen! I bet you can't do this while holding Jadariol!" he laughed.

"I bet I can. But I might drop Jadariol so I won't. I'll show you I can later, though." Shen grinned at him. She was a young mother and still knew how to play along with the kittens and join them in their tricks.

Jadariol went pale at the thought of being dropped and Zephyr saw and laughed. Jadariol shot him a nasty look but he'd flown off.

Hevia was teasing Kammy, who resolutely ignored Hevia. Jadariol still didn't know the kitten's gender and he thought he would ask Lunara about it later, seeing as Hevia was no help on the subject.

Shen landed on the cliff overlooking the sea; Leida's favourite lookout spot and put Jadariol down. He wandered to the edge of the cliff and looked out at the ocean.

"Wow...it's so big! How big is it?" he asked.

Shen stood beside him. "I'm not sure. None of us have crossed it so we don't know how long it goes on for. We only know that we can't see to the other side, if there is another side."

"You can't try to cross it, then?" asked Jadariol.

"We have no reason to" replied Shen.

Jadariol didn't reply. Now his mind was filled with thoughts of adventure, if the ocean was like an extra big puddle; that meant there must be another side to it. He wondered what was out there. He looked down the cliff and at the bottom the kittens were running about on the beach.

Lunara saw him and flew up.

"So? What do you think? I think it's great here! I wish we could visit more but Mum says that when I'm old enough, I can visit with my friends or by myself. We haven't been allowed out of the Forest lately so we haven't been here for a while."

"It's cool but how do I get down there" asked Jadariol pointing to the beach down below. "It looks more interesting down there."

"I'll take you" said Shen and picked him up. "Hold on tight!" she said as she dived off the cliff edge and down to the beach. Jadariol yelped in spite of himself and quickly pretended it was a cough.

Shen landed and put him down. The others ran up to him and Lunara landed nearby.

"Welcome to the beach!" she said with enthusiasm. "I'll show you around and then we can go play." Jadariol nodded and followed her while the others ran off. Hiryasis followed Lunara and Jadariol though.

"There are caves here, like where you come from but they aren't nice to live in because the water comes in and floods them" explained Lunara.

"Why does the water come in?" asked Jadariol.

"Because they're on the beach, silly!" replied Lunara with a laugh. "What we're standing on is sand. Err, what are you doing?"

Jadariol was thirsty and he was having a drink from a nearby pool. He spat out the water in disgust though.

"Ergh! What is this stuff?" he spat with a grimace.

"Its yukky tasting, you don't want to drink it; it's not fresh like the water from our spring." Lunara said, trying not to laugh. Hiryasis laughed though. Jadariol glared at him.

"Look!" Lunara pointed to an odd creature that was wandering along the beach. It had a shell like a turtle and was the same size but tentacles stuck out of it like an octopus. Jadariol went up to it and poked it and it wiggled at him in defiance.

"What is it?" he asked.

"It's a shell squid" replied Hiryasis. "They live in the water but sometimes come out and wander about on the beach. They like to stick their tentacles in the sand and look for sand leeches." Almost as if on cue, the shell squid plopped itself down in the wet sand and stuck all its tentacles down into the sand. It made clicking noises and remained motionless.

"What's it doing now?" asked Jadariol, "looking for sand leeches?"

"Yeah and it's making those sounds to attract them." Hiryasis explained.

Lunara giggled. "Hiry knows everything about beach creatures" she said.

"Don't call my Hiry or I'll call you Loony again" Hiryasis scowled.

"Loony Lunara heheh, that's funny!" laughed Jadariol.

"Hey! Don't you start too!" yelled Lunara.

"Oh come on, you call me Jaddy."

"She calls you *Jaddy*? Wow, that's worse than Hiry!" Hiryasis laughed and Jadariol pounced on him, forgetting his injuries. They started to wrestle about in the sand while Lunara fretted about Jadariol's legs. They didn't wrestle for long though, as the pain soon told Jadariol to stop and he did, sitting down and gritting his teeth.

"Oww, I forgot about these grikking legs" he groaned.

Lunara rushed to his side to see if he was ok and she told Hiryasis off for starting a fight.

"I didn't start it! Besides, we were playing, that was his decision to pounce on me like that, I can't help if his legs don't work right yet." Hiryasis countered.

Jadariol stood up. "Hey, I'm fine, let's continue exploring." He was once again hiding how he really felt. He'd landed on his front leg awkwardly when he pounced on Hiryasis and now it was really hurting. He thought the pain would go though and besides, he was so used to it, it didn't affect him in any large way any more. The others took his word for it and they carried on exploring the beach. Lunara showed Jadariol the secret path around the rocks that could only be reached when the tide was far enough out.

"You have to be careful not to stay too long on this little beach or when the tide comes in, you're stranded there. I got stuck here once before I could fly and I had to call to Mum for help. Then I was banned from going round here until I could fly. It's fine now but if you got stuck here, Jadariol, you would have to swim back. Do you know how to swim?" Lunara said as they headed around the path and to the smaller beach.

"I don't know if I know how to swim. I've never tried" replied Jadariol.

"When you're better, we'll come back and see" suggested Lunara.

"He's going back home when he's better, Lunara." Hiryasis pointed out.

"Well before he goes back then" said Lunara shortly and bounded onto the little beach. It was a nice beach;

361

the sun hit it just right. Lunara also didn't want to admit, but she didn't want Jadariol to be taken back home. He was one of her best friends now too and to see him go wouldn't be easy. She wanted to suggest to Mystik that he stay.

The three of them didn't spend that long on this beach for fear the water would come in and Jadariol would be stuck. So they explored quickly and left it. They were lucky, the tide was on its way out but they wanted to get back to the others so they could all play together. They returned to the first beach and found the other four. Len was sitting in a rock pool, Zephyr was stalking a shell squid and Hevia was laughing at Kammy while she yelled at Hevia to stop. She had sea plants (like seaweed) on her head and didn't realise it. Hevia had sneakily put them there.

Jadariol found this was a good time to ask about Hevia's gender.

"Hey Lunara, that one over there, Hevia. What gender is it? I can't tell and it really frustrates me" he said quietly.

Lunara giggled. "Hevia's a boy. I know it's hard to tell, I couldn't when we first met. I had to ask his Mum, I felt pretty embarrassed I couldn't tell what gender he was. He talks a bit like a girl and acts like one but his ears and tail are longer which boys have. So yeah, he's a boy. A weird boy!"

Jadariol nodded in understanding.

"But, when I asked him, he wouldn't tell me" he said.

"He never does. I think he acts like a girl because he likes others to be confused. I think it's silly, he's been doing it too long now."

"I think it's silly too" replied Jadariol. Hiryasis was teasing Kammy about the sea plants on her head and she found out Hevia put them there. She ran after him trying to breathe fire at him and failing badly at it.

"When do you guys learn to breathe fire?" asked Jadariol, sitting on a rock. Lunara sat beside him.

"It comes naturally but we are taught how to control it and use it like our parents do. We have special classes for it like we do with flight. I've passed my flight class. We also have fighting classes too now. Those are fun but way harder than the others. Flying and breathing fire is natural for us but fighting isn't except in self defence. We're taught by a big Gryphie called Strassor. He's cool. He's got two grown up kittens called Odax and Otuss. Otuss is scary, he reminds me of a Lizariaous. He's got teeth and a scar and only one eye. They don't train us though. Strassor is better. We have classes at the beginning of each sun cycle. Not all of them, just most of them. I'd ask if you could come but it might be dangerous and I don't think they'd let me bring you." Lunara told him.

"Dangerous? You think I'm scared of that? A bit of fighting and fire? Ha!" Jadariol chided.

"No, I think you might get hurt cos of your legs. I know you're not scared of fights. It's better not to get you in trouble." Lunara cared about Jadariol highly and she didn't want to risk him in any way. She felt that half the reason he was getting better was because she had been looking after him for Mystik. She was partially right. Although he was recovering fine by himself, the care she had given him had helped a lot whether he wanted to admit it or not.

Jadariol brushed off her kind comments, not really understanding why someone would be so stupid as to not allow him to join in or at least watch. "So, can you breathe fire?" he asked.

"Yeah, but not very well yet" she replied.

"Can I see?" he asked, interested now.

Lunara looked unsure. "Well, I was told not to use my fire outside training time until I got the hang of it." She paused, thinking about it but knew she couldn't resist. "Oh, ok then!" She hopped off the rock and walked a little way away, telling him not to follow her. She stood, facing away from him, with her face aimed towards the sea and wagged her tail, looking out, composing herself. For a young Gryphie, although breathing fire comes naturally, unless something causes them to do it in attack or defence, they need to psyche themselves up to it. She breathed in, felt the air inside her, filling up her lungs and the organs that produced the fire and churned it up inside her. Then she opened her mouth and blew out a few small flames. Because she was only small, the fire chambers inside her were only small so her fire wasn't impressive. It was of course, blue though. Jadariol was fairly impressed. He'd seen Gryphies blow out fire before but never Lunara and he found it neat how she could do it.

"Hey, nice job!" he said. "Can you do more?"

Lunara shook her head, walking back to him. "No, I can't. I'm only a beginner. Older Gryphies can do more or those who've practised more. Hiry can breathe fire better than me. Hevia is rubbish at it though. Kammy's ok. She wants to become a Fire Master. I dunno if she's better than me though, I haven't seen her breathe fire lately, she's not in my practise group."

"What's a Fire Master?" asked Jadariol, lying down on his warm rock in the sun.

"Fire Masters are awesome! It takes a lot of skill to become one though. They can make the flames into shapes. The best ones can make the flame shapes dance and tell a story and sometimes when several Fire Masters come together, they can make all their flames work together to make stories and things. It's really great to see. They do it at story telling sometimes. Tranzoss is a Fire Master. She's in Diabloss's Gryphie squadron. She doesn't perform much though. I don't know why, I think she's good at it. But she's busy a lot so that's probably why."

"So they just play with the fire? That's all? That's pretty stupid because they should be working with it to defend and hunt, not play with it. We don't play with our needles. They are tools for battle, not things to be used in games." Jadariol snorted.

"It's called Art. That's when we use things to make stuff that's beautiful, creative or interesting" explained Lunara. Jadariol didn't look impressed.

"Well it's ok if you have time to play games and be silly with it." He shrugged. Lunara found this close minded and annoying. Lizariaouses just aggravated her at times like this.

"Well ok then, show me what you can do with your needles" she challenged.

"I can do what anyone else can with theirs; shoot them at enemies and prey." Jadariol wasn't being that helpful.

"No, I mean shoot some off. I want to see. I did my fire for you; you do your needles for me!" Lunara plonked herself down and watched him with anticipation.

Jadariol sighed and stood up. "It's not a game you know. We take our needles seriously." Lunara sniggered at this; it sounded a silly, funny thing to say, taking your needles seriously.

Jadariol glared at her and she stopped sniggering, looking solemn and serious now, sitting to attention. She had to admit, seeing a Lizariaous shoot off needles up close and not aimed at her would be interesting to see.

Jadariol was stood on his rock. When she stopped sniggering, he stood up straight and told her to give him something to aim for. She pointed to a shell squid not too far away that was looking for leeches in the sand. Jadariol aimed for it. All the needles on his back lowered and pointed forward, he lowered his head and glared at the shell squid, snarling and narrowing his eyes; targeting in on it. Then he shot a single needle at it, the needle hit it and bounced off the shell, onto the ground beside the shell squid. Lunara watched, completely fascinated.

Jadariol straightened and his needles returned to their regular position, sticking straight up along his spine. One was missing though; the one he had shot.

"Oooh shoot another!" said Lunara, wibbling with glee.

"No, that would be wasted. This one was wasted as it is. This is why we have deadly accuracy. We can't afford to miss because the needles take a sun cycle to grow back again. We also only use needles when we absolutely have to. For everything else, we use our teeth, claws, tails and weight. You can breathe fire all the time but we can't shoot needles all the time. Most of us carry about 10 to 12 of them. Zephirak has 11. I'll grow more as I get older. I have 7 right now. They come out of our spines and when the vertebrae get bigger as we get older, we can get more needles." He sat back down again and yawned; the hot sun was making him tired.

"But, why don't they grow back faster? If you guys are in a big battle and run out of needles, then you only have teeth and claws." Lunara sat beside him now.

"I don't know. But in large battles, we use them sparingly." Jadariol rattled his. "We rattle them to warn enemies we're gunna shoot them. Hopefully then the enemy will run away so we don't have to use them."

"So you don't like using them?" asked Lunara.

"We like using them, we just can't use too many."

Lunara nodded, understanding and hopped off the rock, going over to the needle in the sand and picking it up. She was careful not to touch the sharp, poisoned tip of it. She had found needles before but never touched them since her mother had warned her not to in case she got poisoned. She waved it about in the air.

"Hey! You could use them for weapons after you've shot them you know. Like, carry them around. Like this!" She stood up on her hind legs. Gryphies can walk on all fours or two legs; they are quadrabipedal. She proceeded to thrash the needle around like someone would with a sword.

"Yeah, one problem? We can't stay on our back legs very long, we're too heavy" said Jadariol. Lunara sat down, putting the needle down beside her. Hmm, it had been a silly suggestion anyway. Seeing a Lizariaous using its needles like a sword was a funny image. They were much more threatening when they shot them at you.

"Does the poison kill anything?" she asked.

"It kills slow or fast, depending how many needles we've shot into the enemy. The more we use, the faster it kills. But with only one, the enemy is greatly weakened. If it isn't treated, the enemy will be slowly poisoned to death." Jadariol grinned evilly. Even though he was her friend, he was still a Lizariaous and still had their tendencies.

Just then, Shen called them. It was time to leave.

Lunara and Jadariol ran up the beach and joined the others. Jadariol slowed down after a while though. His legs were feeling much better but he still couldn't keep a lot of excursion on them for long.

"Did you have fun everyone?" asked Shen.

The kittens and Jadariol all nodded. "Then let's go back to the Forest and have something to eat!" Shen picked up Jadariol and took to the sky, the kittens all following. They took off towards the sea so they had a good runway and then flew higher, turned around and flew over the cliffs. Flying from the beach vertically to the cliffs could be done but it was just easier to fly out in a semi circle and then fly up and over.

Jadariol had enjoyed his time at the beach. He still wished he could fly though. Lunara, Kammy, Len, Zephyr, Hiryasis and Hevia flew about, playing in the sky. Jadariol wanted to play too. It really seemed like Gryphies got the best of everything; larger territory, water nearby, more places to live, constant fire, flight abilities. He started to wish he was one. Only a little, though, he liked being a Lizariaous. He still thought Gryphies were weak. The sun was high in the sky now, which was why it was so hot; it was mid sun cycle. The journey back didn't seem to take as long and they were soon back in the Forest and eating their meal. Shen's mate had caught a forest deer and some sea vultures for them.

"So, did you enjoy seeing the beach?" asked Lunara.

Jadariol nodded with his mouth full. It had been fun and until that sun cycle, he hadn't even realised such a place existed. He thought he'd go back one sun cycle.

Later, Lunara walked Jadariol back to Mystik's tree and he went in, flopped onto his bed and fell asleep almost instantly. Mystik was there too, she was having her mid sun cycle meal at the entrance to the tree in the sun.

Lunara passed her on the way out and then stopped.

368

"Mystik?" The old Gryphie looked at her, smiling kindly. Lunara continued. "Does Jadariol have to go back? I mean, surely his father will think he's died and won't notice if he lives here now. I don't want him to go back, he's my friend."

"There are several reasons why he must go back my dear. Firstly, he is a peace offering. If they see how well we have looked after him, they will surely see that all we want is peace and mutual understanding. Secondly, it isn't fair to leave his father thinking he has been killed. His father probably willingly accepted that but think how happy he will be when he is united with his kid. Thirdly if the Lizariaouses found out we had one of them living here, they would either think we had taken him and were keeping him against his will to bargain with when the time came or they would think he was siding with us and kill him. So you see; he needs to go back when he is better. He can't stay with us. And he is well on the road to being better."

Lunara looked as though she might cry but she mumbled "Ok" and accepted it. She wandered out and off to her tree.

Mystik watched her go. It was a shame to break them apart but hopefully they would see each other a lot more if the plan worked.

Chapter 30
Rebellion

Over in the training grounds, Otuss had been gathering like-minded Gryphies over the last lunar or so. All these Gryphies were of the same opinion; Diabloss was wrong to try and stay out of trouble, action needed to be taken and they were the ones who were going to take it. It was planned that moon cycle to go into Dyarkroeen under cover of darkness and take out Zephirak quietly while he slept. They didn't want anyone knowing, hearing, stopping them. Otuss had kept quiet about it. Very quiet. Everyone thought his words about recruiting and taking out soldiers to kill Zephirak was just a passing comment. How wrong they were.

This sun cycle was the last one they had before their plan was put into action. Otuss had trained those who wanted to fight but didn't have the experience and the others trained themselves. They were ready. He had a gathering of twenty four of them, including himself.

Right now they were sat under his tree at the far side of the Forest where he, Strassor and Odax lived. The others were out training. Otuss had taken the second half of this sun cycle off.

"You all know what to do, yes?" he asked them. They all nodded. They were soldiers and a few residents of the Forest. One was Conosza, the Gryphie whose voice it was hard to understand because of his heavy accent. He had been very angry when the Lizariaouses threatened his home and he'd had to leave so he wanted to get them back. He hated how they walked around like they owned everything and also how they killed the Gryphies. He didn't agree with Diabloss because he felt that if they'd gone on the offensive back when this all started, it wouldn't have gone this far. Also,

Otuss and all his gathering were of the mutual opinion that even though Mettalika was dead, the Lizariaouses would want more and would eventually break their silence, those who had a taste for Gryphie unable to hold back any longer. They didn't trust Zephirak any further than they could throw him if given the chance and they were determined to put things right but in their own way and without help.

"This moon cycle we'll sneak out, kill him and then return. Should we bring back the body and hide it though, I can't decide. If we sneak it out, they might think he left during the moon cycle for some reason or other. If we leave it there, they will see he's been killed and so they might want to take revenge. I know that they'd blame us even if we hadn't done it. Because they're stupid like that. So we'll take it with us. Everyone agree?"

The others all nodded. They'd agreed with everything he'd said so far, mostly because if they disagreed, he'd hurt them and also because they trusted he knew what he was doing and this was the best way they could get rid of Zephirak. The way they saw it, Zephirak had taken out a group and killed Mettalika so there was no reason why a similar plan wouldn't work. Under cover of darkness of course, they didn't need to be worried about rushing into Dyarkroeen and being killed for trespassing since hopefully, everyone would be asleep.

"Ok, you guys know what to do, right? Kando, you, Rezzin and I will do the killing. When we reach the edge of their territory, I want five of you to fly in and check the place out. Check if there are any guards, check Zephirak's cave…it has a skylight in the top I heard so carefully land up there and see if you can hear anything like snoring or breathing in his cave to make sure he's there. I dunno if he walks about at moon cycle or anything so we still need to be sure before we go in. I'm not risking us unless Zephirak is actually there. Of course, in the highly unlikely but very lucky event that he's not there and has in fact gone to get a drink or is taking a walk away from the main residential area, we're laughing because we can all attack at once! I doubt that will happen though. When Kando, Rezzin and I are in his cave, all the rest of you, keep watch out of sight. See if you can immobilise any Lizariaous who finds that we're there. Keep them quiet or kill them or something. It's best to just make as little noise as possible. Are we all clear on what must be done?"

The group around him nodded. This was a very risky plan and there was more a chance it wouldn't work than that it would but Otuss still wanted to try. He was confident enough with it at least and they all trusted his judgement since he had always been a fighter and was Strassor's son. They believed that if anyone could take Zephirak out, Otuss could. And they were right; Otuss did have the potential to. He was large and heavy, a good match for any Lizariaous. Plus he had killed them before. Or he said he had. In truth he had, but only two.

"We'll meet back here at sun down. Those who don't arrive on time won't be waited for so if you change your mind about coming, then is the time to do it. We will assume you don't wish to come if you don't turn up. We'll fly to Dyarkroeen but we'll start out walking. We'll walk to the edge of the Forest. We can't get there too fast because I want to be sure the Lizariaouses are all asleep. Now, go and I'll see you all later."

The gathering dispersed and Otuss climbed up his tree. He would need rest for the long moon cycle ahead, so he took a nap.

Otuss woke up a few hours later. The sun was low in the sky now and he flew off and caught himself a meal. He was eating it when the first of his gathering arrived. This one was a female. She was the only female who had chosen to team up with him and she was a real fighter. He liked this about her. In fact, he liked her. But relationships were never easy for him; a Gryphie who only knew fighting and violence so he had never pursued it further.

"You're the first to arrive, well done" he said. He had nearly finished his meal.

"Yes Sir!" she saluted. "I came on time, Sir, just as you ordered. I even missed out on my meal."

"Why?" asked Otuss, his mouth full.

"I live the other side of the Forest and I took a nap before I came. I woke up late and came right over. I didn't want to be left behind, Sir."

"Well you're the first one here so go catch yourself something quickly. We'll wait but don't take too long. Once the sun sets in the sky, we leave."

She nodded gratefully and bounded off into the Forest to catch a quick snack.

Soon, the others turned up. All twenty two of them arrived. The female came back, making twenty three and Otuss was twenty four so they were all there.

"Good work everyone, I'm happy to see you all turned up." Otuss smiled at them in his creepy, toothy, snarly way. A couple swallowed quietly and had second thoughts about coming with him on this crazy escapade. What if it didn't work and they all got killed? He had always reminded them of a Gryphie pretending to be a Lizariaous, or maybe and scarily, a Lizariaous in a Gryphie's skin. What if he had been disguised all along? Just waiting for this moment? The idea was utterly stupid and farfetched but the moon cycle gave room for these weird ideas and thoughts. In the half light, Otuss looked even scarier than usual.

"Are we ready?" asked Otuss, looking at the assembled gathering.

They all nodded, the female finishing her meal off quickly.

"Good, then let's go!" Otuss stood and the others followed. They headed through the Forest and out near the swamp. The Outlands stretched ahead of them, looking pale and eerie in the early moonlight. None of them gave themselves a chance to dwell on that because Otuss was already heading out. They followed, walking close as a group. And they walked in silence. They didn't want to be heard. Furmines often frequented the Outlands and since they could understand Gryphies and vice versa, you never knew who might be listening. If anyone asked, Otuss would say it was a training exercise. No one asked though, no one saw except the odd wasteland rat. About a quarter of the way there, they started flying high up so no one would see them reach Dyarkroeen. They reached the border of Dyarkroeen a while later. It was completely dark now but both Gryphies and Lizariaouses have some darkness vision, much like cats. They could see dull shapes instead of pitch blackness.

Otuss nodded to the group who was to fly overhead and check out the area. They did so and returned a while later, reporting that as far as they could see, all the Lizariaouses were in their caves asleep. They didn't see any wandering around at any rate. Also, when one listened at Zephirak's cavern, he heard Zephirak's heavy breathing and that proved that Zephirak was there and that the plan was worth going through with.

Otuss grinned. This was perfect. Now, so long as none woke up and decided to leave their caves while the Gryphie gathering were there, they could kill Zephirak and take the body away quietly.

They headed in.

Otuss was the lead Gryphie, followed by Kando and Rezzin. The others flanked them, keeping watch at all times. Everything was quiet. Glowbugs flew around a little, here and there some small insect made some loud sound but it was peaceful. It was hard to believe this was the territory of some of the most dangerous creatures alive.

They reached Zephirak's cavern. Most of them hid themselves on top of caves, one in the tree that grew around the back of Zephirak's cavern and a few others sat on the cavern itself, the female one, whose name was Sarna, she sat on top of the cavern and kept watch discretely at the skylight.

Otuss and the other two headed in. The cavern smelled damp, bloody, it smelled of death and cruelty. None of them liked the smell. It threatened their every sense. They wandered further in, silently, padding, keeping their wings close to them. They saw the moon light shining down through the skylight and a large, flat rock beneath. This was where Leida had been captured and held all those lunars ago. Otuss didn't know this and wouldn't really have cared if he did. Right now the only thing on his mind was the form of the creature sleeping on the large flat rock. Zephirak. Sarna stared excitedly down. She could just about make out the form of the sleeping Zephirak and hear his breathing. When the Gryphie had checked the cavern before, he hadn't looked, he had listened. If he had looked, he would have seen Zephirak for himself.

Otuss, Rezzin and Kando crept closer and poised themselves over Zephirak. Otuss looked at the other two, giving them signals with his ears and expressions.

He was telling them to hold Zephirak down and he'd kill him quickly. They nodded, understanding and readied themselves. Sarna watched on. Otuss looked up at her, telling her to spread her wings so it kept out the light. In the dark, Zephirak would be confused and less likely to hit them should he wake before Otuss killed him. Otuss gave a small twitch of his wing and Sarna opened hers, blocking out the moonlight. After a few moments given so the three Gryphies inside could let their eyes adjust to the darkness, Otuss gave the signal; a small snarl, and Kando and Rezzin pounced on Zephirak, holding him down. He immediately woke up, Otuss had lunged for his throat but foolish Kando hadn't pinned Zephirak's tail down. He had his back legs and Rezzin had his front ones. Otuss had one hand on his head and the other on his shoulder and Zephirak was on his side. Zephirak roared, panicked completely. His tail thrashed out and caught Kando, slashing his thigh with its tail spade. Kando squealed and instinctively leaped back out of the way, freeing Zephirak's hind legs, which now kicked about. Otuss was desperately trying to get his jaws round the Lizariaous's neck while Rezzin effectively stood on him, pinning him down with his body and trying to stop the back legs thrashing. His own tail was pinning down Zephirak's tail while Kando tried to check his wound out. It had gone deep, down to the bone.

Otuss blew fire in Zephirak's face to try and get him to stop moving but it only panicked him more and he started shooting needles everywhere. One narrowly missed Rezzin but hit Kando in the chest. Kando screamed in pain as he felt the burning sensation of the poison spreading into his body. He knew he'd been hit and now he too panicked. He pulled himself further into the cavern, trying to get out the way. Because of all the commotion, Sarna had moved her wing so she could see in and now Zephirak saw his attackers were Gryphies, which enraged him. Now his movements were stronger because they were done in anger and this soon turned into a blind rage. He threw Rezzin off him and Otuss leaped back at this. Rezzin had landed towards the cavern entrance and he ran down the cavern and out as fast as he could, leaving Otuss to deal with Zephirak on his own. Zephirak roared and lunged at Otuss but got nowhere. Sarna had dived through the skylight, landing beside Zephirak and shoving him violently away, getting him in the side and winding him. Zephirak was momentarily stunned, which gave Otuss and Sarna the chance to escape. When they exited the cavern, they flew, calling the others, telling that the plan had failed. Rezzin was halfway back to Shernaron; he had never flown so fast in his whole life.

Zephirak had recovered and rushed to the entrance of his cavern. He saw the vague shape of several Gryphies flying away and snarled, throwing back his head and roaring with sheer rage into the moonlit sky. How dare they come into his territory, into his cavern and try to kill him! He heard a noise behind him as Kando coughed, the poison getting into his system. Zephirak turned and went in to deal with him.

The others had made it to the Outlands and were well on their way home. Otuss was flying so fast, his wings ached. The others noticed that Kando wasn't there and they knew it had gone badly. None of them said a word.

Sarna wondered if Kando had made it out alive but she highly doubted it.

They made it back to the Forest and flew out to the cliffs. They could have headed back to Otuss's tree but there they risked waking others because they all wanted to talk about this.

They landed near the lookout point and composed themselves, catching their breath, their wings drooping at their sides. Most of them flopped down on the ground panting. And most of them hadn't flown that fast either before or in a very long time.

Finally, when he was able to speak, because that was what the others were waiting for, Otuss said what he had to say.

"Well, you probably guessed that didn't go well. Kando was hit and he crawled to the back of the cave. I don't think he made it out alive. As for you, Rezzin, what the grik were you thinking running away like that? I needed your grikking help! And you ran off like a scared kitten. You are pathetic."

"Well I may be pathetic but you're a fool for ever wanting to go up against the leader of the Lizariaouses. I don't know why I joined you. It was the stupidest plan ever and we all went along with it simply because you were *so sure* that it would work. Pah! I'm not listening to you again, Otuss. Diabloss might be wrong in some of his decisions but at least he isn't reckless." Rezzin snapped, growling at Otuss.

Otuss snarled twice as much and dug his claws into the ground angrily. "No one invited you, Rezzin. It was your choice and you wanted to be one of the Gryphies I took to kill Zephirak. You knew there would be risks, I knew too and most of all, all three of us knew our lives would be in danger. And yet you still agreed to be a part of it. So don't grikking blame me! If you didn't think you were up to the job then you shouldn't have gone with us. You could have been a lookout. But no, somehow you wanted to prove yourself. At least you're not dead like Kando!"

"Kando was my *brother*!" growled Rezzin.

"And *you* were the first to run away. You could have helped him; didn't you see he'd been hit? Don't you DARE put the guilt trip on me, Rezzin. You're grabbing at grass blades now. You feel guilty and you want to blame it on me."

"You never helped him either" snapped back Rezzin.

"Did you think I had the time to help him? As soon as Sarna hit Zephirak, I got out of there. I knew if I wasted any more time, he'd recover and kill the both of us. So we fled. What were we supposed to do eh?" Otuss thrashed his tail. He was angry at himself for failing but for a member of his gathering to suddenly get on his case like this? Well that angered him even more. "If you had any grikking sense whatsoever, you would have carried Kando out that hole in the top of Zephirak's cave while he was trying to fight me."

"That wouldn't have worked and you know it. The place wasn't big enough to open our wings properly, let alone try to fly upwards and out of the hole in the roof." Rezzin laid his ears back in annoyance.

"Well then, the only choice was to get out of there. If we had gotten Kando back here, he would either be dead by now or weakened to an extent where he was as good as dead. So stop grikking trying to blame that on me. We failed, so it was a stupid plan, we learnt from it."

"Yes but we gained nothing and lost a life. That's what griks me off so damn badly." Rezzin wasn't ready to let it go that easily.

"Shut the grik up and go home, Rezzin. It was a failed plan; you don't think I feel as bad about this as you do? Stop guilt tripping me" Otuss turned his back on Rezzin and swished his tail.

"Arguing about it won't help" said Sarna. "Let's all go home and go to sleep."

But Rezzin didn't listen. He went for Otuss, landing on his back and digging all his claws in, growling and flaming him.

Otuss threw him off and retaliated, taking out Rezzin's legs with his tail and knocking him off the cliff. Rezzin caught himself and flew back up.

"Go HOME!" yelled Otuss, flaming Rezzin right in the face. Rezzin yelped and fell back. "Or I'll kill you right here and now. I am in no mood to grik about with you."

Rezzin swooped his wings down, rose into the sky and flew off across the Forest. He and Otuss never spoke to one another again after that, which was probably for the best.

Otuss turned to the others. "You guys go home too" he said and turned away, heading towards the lookout point. Any other Gryphie would have apologised for dragging them into a stupid plan like that but Otuss was not one to apologise. The others flew off, all except Sarna. She followed Otuss.

He sat at the lookout point, looking out to sea. She sat beside him. They were silent for a long time before he spoke.

"It's late" he said.

"I know" she replied.

"Well then shouldn't you be going home now?" he asked. Sarna looked at him. She didn't want to go home; she wanted to be there for him.

"I just wanted you to know that you have my respect. It takes a lot of courage to not only go into Dyarkroeen but also to go into Zephirak's cave and ambush him. Even though it didn't work out, you were very brave for following through with it."

"Brave? I see, I suppose you want me to say you were brave too, for winding Zephirak and saving me.

Well thanks. You can go now." Otuss carried on looking out to sea.

"I just wanted to make sure you were ok." Sarna said, looking up at him.

"I will be. I'm leaving the Forest" he replied.

"Leaving? But why?" she asked.

Otuss looked at her. "Could you show your face in the Forest again after doing something like this? Rezzin hates me. Well I don't really care about him but word will get round of my stupid plan and how I failed. Diabloss will have more reason to think I'm foolish and as for my father, well, he'll be so disappointed in me. I've never really fitted in, all my life I felt like I was a bit outcast. So I'm going away to be a solitary and find myself and find somewhere I belong. Away from here and away from those who know me. I'll never forget the mistake I made if I continue to live here. Someone is bound to mention it every so often or remind me every now and then even if it's a passing comment or a joke. So I'm leaving. I had hoped no one would see me go, I wanted to leave in private but I can't seem to get rid of you."

"Well…if you're leaving, can I come along too?" asked Sarna.

"Why would you want to? After what I've done. I feel guilty being around any of you guys, let alone the ones who came with me on this dumb escapade." Otuss was opening up a little. He felt he had nothing to lose; no reputation to protect now that he was leaving.

"Because…I like you. I've admired you for a long time and this hasn't tainted that. And I feel you need someone to be with you. Hey if it doesn't work out, I'll leave you in peace. But you don't want to become like Mettalika." Sarna moved closer to him carefully.

Otuss looked at her. "I wouldn't. Solitary madness is a rare thing. I don't have time for mates though. I live to fight and train."

"Who said anything about mates? I was only suggesting that we flew together. Or are you interested in me as a mate?" Sarna smiled inwardly.

"Well, to be honest, I have been for a while but...I just; I'm just not...I've never had a mate before." He sighed. He was unsure of what having a mate entailed. He hoped it was nothing soppy or mushy.

"You? Never had a mate?" Sarna laughed. "I find that hard to believe. Hey, we don't have to be. We can take it a step at a time and see where it goes. I know this plan failed but we all make mistakes. Can I fly with you? We can travel and fight together."

"Ok. If that's what you want." Otuss replied. He felt awkward but in a strange way he was happy that she had suggested going with him.

"I do" she replied and leaned against him, nuzzling him. Otuss smiled.

"Well then, let's get out of here. No one knows we've gone." He spread his wings and took off. Sarna followed and they flew off into the moonlight together to start a new life away from Otuss's guilt and the Gryphies they knew.

***

The next sun cycle dawned bright and early for the Forest. Strassor awoke and headed down from his tree. Odax was soon up too and after their meal, they met at the training grounds as they did every sunrise.

"Now where be Otuss" asked Strassor. "It ain't like him ter be late."

"I haven't seen him this sunrise" replied Odax, stretching out his wings and doing his sunrise workout.

Strassor called for him. Nothing happened.

"Hmm well that be odd. Well I'm sure he'll be 'round soon. Go check his tree, see if he's not ill or somethin'. Yeh know what he's like." It was widely known that if Otuss was sick, he'd stay in his tree and not come to training sessions. So if his students wondered where he was, it was likely he was ill and never told anyone he wouldn't turn up.

Odax flew off and returned.

"No, he's not there" he told Strassor.

"Hmm, that there's very odd. Ah well, we'll look fer him later. Right now we be havin' work ter do." Strassor was in the middle of training some young Gryphies by that time. Their training was going well. Most of the gathering from the Forest knew how to defend themselves now. However, with Otuss gone, they couldn't train as many as they would have liked. They had to send all his groups home this sun cycle.

At mid sun, Odax called for Diabloss.

"Diabloss, we can't find Otuss, can you get out a search team and look for him please?" he asked.

Diabloss nodded and soon he, Tranzoss, Stervia and Kayto were out looking for him.

Odax and Strassor were going to leave it but lately Otuss had been so quiet and secretive, they were worried he was ill and he hadn't told anyone. They thought he'd gotten really sick and gone off to die somewhere. When he was sick, Strassor always had to go find the cure for him from Mystik because he would never admit weakness and go off himself.

Kayto had been asking passers-by if they had seen Otuss anywhere. No one had until he came across Rezzin.

"Hey you! Have you seen Otuss, you know the fighter Gryphie...trains at the training grounds?" he asked.

"Oh that idiot? No, thank grik. And I don't want to see him either, not after last moon cycle." Rezzin spat.

"What happened?" asked Kayto.

"He took a bunch of us to Dyarkroeen because he thought he could kill Zephirak under cover of darkness. He got my brother killed and I nearly got killed as well. He was trying to prove himself or something, prove he was better than Diabloss, I dunno. I think he was trying to fix this war thing. I believe too that the Lizariaouses are playing quiet and are gunna attack again and I was foolish enough to get dragged into Otuss's stupid plan. I wish I hadn't. As for my brother, Kando, I wish he hadn't too but it's too late for that now isn't it?"

"What? Tell me in details please. I'm confused" said Kayto.

"He took twenty three of us to Dyarkroeen last moon cycle. Otuss, Kando and I went into Zephirak's cave to kill him while he slept but it all went wrong and he woke up. He shot Kando and I managed to escape. Sarna flew in and saved Otuss from what I heard. Then we all flew back here and he told us to leave. It was at the cliffs. We left him and Sarna there. I haven't seen either of them this sun cycle. I dunno what they've done...I don't want to even think to be honest."

"So that was what he was planning. We suspected he'd been planning something, we just weren't sure what it was." Kayto looked thoughtful. He now wondered where Sarna and Otuss were. Had anyone seen Sarna this sun cycle? He searched a little more, for both of them this time but no one had seen either of them.

The team met back with Diabloss again.

"Well? Any luck guys?" asked Diabloss.

Kayto explained what Rezzin had told him.

"The idiot!" growled Diabloss. "I bet he and Sarna went to try again or something and right what went wrong!" He growled again in frustration and went to tell Strassor.

Strassor was shocked. "I knew he were quiet but I never thought he'd be planning somethin' like that there. Then again he were completely against yer plans of bein' more passive."

"I know and I should have seen it coming so I could have sent someone to keep an eye on him. He could have gone back and tried to do it again or he could have run away." Diabloss pondered.

"I've no doubt he's feelin' guilty now and fears I'll be angry with him. As fer Sarna, I dunno why she'd be with him. They didn't know each other that well really or talk much" replied Strassor.

"So what would you like us to do?" asked Diabloss. "We can go out and search for them beyond the Forest?"

"No, leave 'em. When he be ready, he'll come back. Just leave him to himself. If yeh go out lookin' fer him, he'll be actin' all aggressive like and he certainly won't come back 'ere. He's like that. He'll be ok. It'll put a fair strain on the training procedures though without him."

"Tranzoss can take his place for a while" said Diabloss. "I'll send her along later. She's a great teacher and she's taught training exercises both basic and advanced before."

"Thank you" replied Strassor. "I'm sorry 'bout all this. I dunno what went wrong when I were raising him."

"There'll always be one like that" replied Diabloss. Strassor nodded.

Soon, Tranzoss had taken Otuss's place in the training grounds.

Later that sun cycle, Diabloss told Leida what had happened. She worried a bit.

"You don't think he's gone back do you? Back to finish what he started and took Sarna with him too? And what about Zephirak? I bet he's really angry now and this might even cause a full on war to start out. For Gryphies to actually go and ambush him in his own home while he slept. He's probably now thinking that we want to start a war. It could happen all over again, he could start hunting us again!"

"Don't think I haven't thought about that. And they have still been hunting us but to a lesser extent now Mettalika's gone. I've seen packs out around the edge of Shernaron. There aren't as many though. As for Otuss, if he's that stupid as to go back there after what happened and try the whole thing again then he should expect to get killed. Personally I think he took Sarna and ran away. He ran from his guilt. It will catch up to him. Then again, maybe he did go on a suicide mission to Dyarkroeen. Quite frankly I've had enough of him and his stupid thick headedness. Whatever he gets, he deserves. In this time of unpredictability, I don't have time to think about him." Diabloss had never really liked Otuss. He hadn't liked how he'd treated Leida and he certainly hadn't liked how he rebelled against authority. He'd merely put up with him because he knew he would train Leida well.

Leida was thoughtful. "Maybe Zephirak got him. We seem to be being picked off one by one, first Sinxo, Mettalika we know about and now Otuss and Sarna. I honestly don't like where this is heading. We need to find out more, we need some kind of proof or we need to talk to Zephirak and find his views on it, try to reason with him or I dunno, attack if he doesn't?"

"It's a tough situation for all of us" replied Diabloss. "I'm at a loss for what to do. I don't know if they plan to attack and we can't assume that's the case. We've worked so hard for peace." He shook his head. "I'm going to call my squadron and have a meeting with them. I think we'll all go to Dyarkroeen together and see if Zephirak will listen this time. But this will be the last time. We should also apologise for Otuss's behaviour."

"And you think that will make him forgive us? Apologies? What Otuss did is unforgivable. He's ruined any chance we had for peace with them. If his plan had worked we would either have seen this whole thing end or they would have launched a full on attack on us for killing their leader. He should have known the risk was too big for if the plan failed."

They sat there in silence. All the Gryphies wanted peace but it didn't look as though they would get it.

"I need to think. I'll see you later. You're going to spend time with Lunara this sun cycle yes?" Diabloss paused before he took to the sky.

"Yes, she's been wanting to show me all the things she's learnt while training. I promised her I'd spend some time with her" replied Leida.

Diabloss nodded and smiled, then took to the sky and headed for his squadrons' base.

Leida headed for the clearing where she and Lunara lived.

Lunara was out with Jadariol and Hiryasis. They were playing Which One. Hevia and the others weren't there.

"Hey guys" said Leida cheerfully, coming over and looking to see what they were doing. Jadariol had a stone under his back foot and the others couldn't guess which one it was. He found this all very amusing seeing them struggle to guess and laughed his head off as they kept getting it wrong.

"You're changing it when we aren't looking! That's cheating!" said Hiryasis.

"I am not! You're just a rubbish guesser" replied Jadariol with a grin.

"But I've guessed all your feet, you must be changing it" growled Hiry.

In truth, Jadariol had been sneaking the stone under his tail by laying his tail close to his foot and then moving it away with the stone underneath. Then he'd place his tail near another foot and move the stone there instead, making it seem as though the others had gotten it wrong and that he wasn't cheating at all.

Leida saw what he was doing and smirked.

"Hey Jadariol, don't move your tail when you play; keep it in one place" she told him.

"Why?" he asked.

"Because that's the rules. Didn't Lunara and Hiry tell you?" She quickly glanced at the others, signalling for them not to say anything. It wasn't a rule to do this of course. Jadariol looked a bit worried now.

Soon, Hiryasis guessed right. After that it was easier for them. Whoever got it right got the stone and it was their turn. Each time Jadariol tried now, one of the other two would guess right. He wasn't happy about this and frowned at Leida. She simply smiled and told him that was the rules and that if he wanted to play properly, he had to abide by them.

They played until the sun was high in the sky and then it was time for something to eat. Leida caught a forest deer and brought it back for them all to share. It was her treat because lately she hadn't spent as much time with Lunara and her friends as she used to.

After their meal, Lunara showed Leida some of the moves she now knew from her training. Leida was genuinely impressed; Strassor had taught them well. Hiryasis showed some too and Lunara tried to get Jadariol to shoot some needles but he wouldn't because he thought it would be a waste. Lunara was saddened at this because she really wanted Leida to see.

"I've seen more times than I care to remember" said Leida. "So Jadariol can save his needles."

Jadariol looked relieved at this. He'd always been taught that wasting needles was very bad and been reprimanded harshly when he shot them at friends in play. None of the Lizariaous kids were allowed to use them to play with. Lizariaouses of course are immune to their own poison but getting a needle stuck in you still isn't fun.

Lunara thought he was a bit of a party pooper but Leida explained that Jadariol's needles are important and not infinite like Gryphie fire. Lunara still didn't really grasp that idea. She said that if she was a Lizariaous, she would use her needles all the time.

Jadariol thought she was crazy.

That afternoon, they played in the Forest and then went for a flight. Jadariol was left behind because Mystik wanted to check his wounds and see how they were healing.

Lunara flew around in circles. "Hey! I know! One of us has to do some moves in the air and the others have to copy them." She flew upside down. "Copy that!" she said with a grin.

Leida did it easily but Hiryasis had problems; he couldn't control himself as easily when he was flying on his back.

"Haven't you been training?" asked Lunara.

"Well I never got the hang of that" replied Hiryasis. He had been training but he struggled with a lot of it more than he cared to admit.

"I'll teach you then" said Lunara, "Leida you got it so you choose what we do next!"

Leida flapped her wings and moved her legs as though she was walking in the air. Then she rose up on her back legs and walked upright while flying. "I bet you can't do that!" she said with a smirk.

Neither of them could; they could only walk on all fours while flying. So Leida gave them an easier one by doing loop the loops and they could both do that. Hiryasis had a turn next since he hadn't before.

"Ok, check this out, I learned this recently while I was learning to defend myself." He spun around in circles breathing blue fire. Stopping he said, "If you're surrounded by enemies then that's what you have to do. Flame them all at once and drive them away. Of course it's harder to do when you're stood on the ground. I learnt to spin on one back leg and breathe fire at them. They're all taller than me so I'll still get them in the face!" He chuckled proud of his trick.

Leida could do this but Lunara hadn't learnt how to so she made a mental note to ask Strassor how to do that at her next lesson.

They spent the afternoon until the sun lowered in the sky playing and flying around. Leida had fun, it was great to be able to forget your worries for a little while and just be a kitten again. The others enjoyed it too. Even though they were kittens themselves, they still had more responsibility than Leida had when she was their age. When Leida was growing up, there wasn't so much trouble in Dyarkroeen.

As the sun began to set, they all headed home. Jadariol was waiting for them but Lunara and Hiry ran off home to have their meals. Jadariol had had his.

He walked up to Leida as she was about to go. She wanted to get back to her tree and wait for Diabloss to see what he was going to do about the situation with the Lizariaouses.

"Leida, Lunara and I waited for Moon Wraiths this one time and we actually saw one! But it wasn't what we expected. Can I show you and you tell me a bit more about it?" he asked.

"Well sure, when do you want to show me?" asked Leida.

"This moon cycle, over there at the edge of the trees. We saw it a little way in and I'm sure it'll be in there somewhere still. In fact there might be more of them but I don't want to go alone and Lunara didn't want to come this moon cycle so I can show you one and we can see if we can spot any others." He'd taken a liking to Leida because she had played with them and not many of the adults bothered to do that.

"Ok, so long as Mystik doesn't mind you wandering around after it's time to sleep. I'll meet you here this moon cycle as soon as the sun has disappeared."

"Ok! Cos they only come out after dark anyway so it'll have to be when the sun is gone." Jadariol smiled happily and Leida smiled back, heading back to her tree.

Diabloss was already there when she returned. She greeted him with a nuzzle and he had a few sea vultures and a bear hog for them to eat.

"Have a good time with the kittens?" he asked as they tucked in to their meal.

Leida nodded. "Yes I did. It makes me miss being a kitten. They're still so carefree and happy even in this time of uncertainty."

"That's because they don't know what war is and they haven't known battles or hard times. They are safe here in the Forest and I want to ensure that they will be safe for generations to come which is why this moon cycle my squadron and I are going to the Dark Plains to see if the Deamons can help."

Leida looked shocked. "The Deamons? Why? We've never asked for their help. They will kill all of you if you trespass on their plains."

"I am half Deamon, that's already a bargaining point. Plus if the war develops into something bigger and the Forest is brought down, do you honestly think that Zephirak will stop there? After what Otuss did, the war is pretty much declared. I bet he's thinking what a bunch of ungrateful grikheads we are. They took down Mettalika who was a pain to all of us and then we retaliate by launching an attack while he sleeps."

"Well he probably thinks we're mad at him for killing her" replied Leida.

"Exactly, so he probably thinks we're all the same and if he doesn't get us first, we'll do something much worse some other moon cycle or turn the tables and start hunting Lizariaouses. My mind is made up. If I can get the Deamons to help by scaring the Lizariaouses a bit, then we can keep the peace. All they have to do is threaten them a bit. Everyone is terrified of the Deamons, heck, even I am and my mother was one. So if they think that attacking us will get the Deamons involved then I'm all for it. I will be careful." He added the last sentence when he saw how worried Leida looked.

"Can't you go in the next sun cycle?" she asked.

"No, they seem to be more placid at moon cycle in the darkness, where they feel most at home so I will go in a while. My squad will be with me so you have nothing to worry about, we'll be fine. And we'll only go to the edge of the plains and call them. We won't go in and that way they can't get hostile with us since we won't be in their territory." Diabloss explained.

Leida still looked worried but she nodded. She wasn't going to change her mate's mind.

"Don't worry, we'll be back by sunrise" he told her and finished his meal. He stretched his mighty wings with some difficulty due to the fact their tree was in the way and he climbed up it.

Leida watched him go and sighed. She hoped he and the others were doing the right thing by getting the Deamons involved.

She heard him call the others and their response and then he was gone. She heard the beat of their wings as they flew off. She left the rest of her sea vulture. She wasn't hungry and it was time to meet Jadariol anyway.

At the edge of the Forest, Jadariol waited for her. Every so often he looked around; half afraid something would leap out and eat him. He still thought of his encounter with Mettalika. He willed her to hurry up. He hadn't been out on his own really after dark and the Forest seemed more ominous. He scanned around. Nothing much stirred apart from the faint chatting of the guards at the entrance path to the clearing.

Leida found him sat waiting. He saw her vaguely before she reached him and he smiled and stood up when she arrived.

"Ok, let's see these Moon Wraiths then!" she said.

"Ok, I'll show you where we saw it!" said Jadariol excitedly and squeezed his way into the undergrowth. Leida followed, holding her wings close to herself so they didn't catch on anything.

It was darker where the moon didn't shine through and they used their senses to find their way. Then Jadariol stopped.

"Ok, this was where we saw it" he told her and sat down. "It had a strange glow and it wandered right past us. It didn't really notice us though. It was kinda feathery and a bit smaller than a Gryphie."

Leida sat beside him and they waited. They waited a long while and Jadariol started to get fidgety.

"Maybe there are more a bit deeper in" he suggested and stood up.

"Hmm, but we don't want to go too far in. The Forest isn't safe at moon cycle" replied Leida. Jadariol nodded and they wandered a little further in. They had reached the little waterfall now and the spring.

"We never came this far" said Jadariol. "Maybe we should go back or shall we sit and wait?"

"I think we should go back. We've been out here a good time and seen nothing really."

"Yeah I guess you're right. I really wanted to show you…" he trailed off as he heard something. They both heard something and Leida stopped in her tracks listening.

"Ooh, maybe it's one of them?" Jadariol suggested excitedly.

Leida listened and sniffed. Then she laid her ears back. "Jadariol, run!" she said, flashing him a fearful look and suddenly she was bowled to one side by a large, dark form.

Jadariol shrieked and skittered about, trying to find a place to hide in his terror. Leida got to her feet and used her senses to find where her attackers were. She had no idea what it was that had attacked her at first but then she could smell it. Lizariaouses! She wasn't sure how many but they seemed all around her. Danger in the darkness! Like her dreams! She heard low growls and something that sounded like a chuckle. She heard Jadariol's whimpers too. She wanted to get to him and save him but she figured they were after her, not him. Then again they might kill him because he was with her but right now she just wanted to escape. Lizariaouses are much more at home in covered places whereas Gryphies, if they can't spread their wings, are pretty much grounded and helpless.

It lunged at her again and she smacked out with a wing. She feared using her fire in case she set the whole Forest alight. So she used her claws and wings instead. A needle flew at her and she deftly hit it aside. One tried to jump on her back. It seemed like it was a hunting pack of three although she couldn't be sure. Many things flew through her mind, one of them being why were these guys here in the middle of the moon cycle. Maybe they were planning to get revenge after dark, using Otuss's plan against the whole gathering. She was more determined to escape and warn everyone because of this.

One Lizariaous lunged at her neck, getting a grip and pulling her down. She tried to raise herself on her back legs and throw him off but another had a grip on one of her back legs. She smacked the one on her neck away with her tail and her head flew round and grabbed, getting her leg assailant's ear and pulling. He kept his vice grip on her leg and she pulled harder on his ear. Both of them growled viciously. Another jumped on her back and she managed to slash him away with her wing. There were three of them it seemed. As soon as she threw one off, another attacked. She was starting to get worn out. She would have to do some serious damage to them because throwing them off and trying to escape wasn't working. She needed to slow them down and knock them back so she had a chance to run. She knew she couldn't kill them, there were too many and to waste time trying to kill them would only use more energy. She yanked her head upward and tore off the ear she had hold of. The Lizariaous cried out in pain and eased off her leg; she pulled it away from his jaws and kicked him in the face. He fell back and she tried to move away. Another had jumped on her though, his claws digging into her fur and raking her flesh painfully. She snapped and snarled at him, swiping with her tail. He swiped back with his own tail as the third Lizariaous went for her back legs again. She tried to kick with them but this threw her off balance and gave the one pushing down on her side an advantage. Leida cursed her legs, they were failing her again. They always seemed to be the first thing that was hurt. She wished sorely that she had the armour for them that the mountain Gryphies were making. She had no idea where Jadariol was. She only hoped he'd escaped. Right now her own safety and only her own safety was on her mind. They had her pretty much pinned. The one she had torn the ear off previously was back on his feet again.

With one huge forceful heave, she threw off the Lizariaous who was clawing at her side. He tore off clumps of her fur as he fell back and a small chunk of flesh too but nothing too serious.

Leida was in a deadly rage now and without thinking, she lunged on him, her claws digging into his belly and tearing it to shreds. He screamed in pain but Leida wasn't listening. Nor was she paying attention to another Lizariaous behind her who was holding a large boulder. He smashed it over her head, knocking her out cold.

Chapter 31
Recaptured

"He'll be ok. She really tore into him though. He lost an ear too. If all the Gryphies have become as good a fighter as her then we'll have a really tough battle on our hands Sir. Rondo is fine. Croter made it ok too and I never participated. I just wanted to make sure they took her down. If she had done more damage, I would have stepped in."

"You did a good job, Karnos. We have her captured; that is all that matters. Now the plan can go ahead as it was supposed to in the first place. There will be no rescue, no hope of doing anything but obey my orders."

Leida heard this conversation faintly as she came round. It was the next sun cycle. She had been out cold all moon cycle. She didn't even know how high the sun was in the sky. She couldn't see anything but darkness and vague forms. Her wings were bound like they had been the last time. Her legs were bound this time too. And there was no skylight either. She sighed. Crying was no longer an option. She had been caught and she knew that Zephirak would no doubt plan to get Diabloss with her as he had the last time. She wondered where Jadariol was, if he had remained hidden or gone back to warn the rest of the gathering. She hoped it was the latter. They needed to know. Then her stomach churned and she felt sick. What if they had been all around, not just the three that had attacked her? What if at the same time, they were attacking the rest of the Forest too? The others…what had become of them. With this on her mind, she tried to stand or move but could do neither. This time she was completely immobilized.

She heard footsteps. Claws kicking up the few bits of gravel in this part of the cave she was in.

"So, we meet again Leida." She knew that voice, that horrible hateful tone, those red eyes glowing with malice in the dark. She merely glanced in Zephirak's direction.

"You put up quite a fight this time. You shouldn't have bothered. We would have caught you anyway. We were waiting you know." Zephirak walked towards her. She noticed someone beside him, a smaller Lizariaous. So, he had a new mate now did he? She simply sighed.

"I have to say, I ever intended to put my plan into motion this soon but after those grikheads so rudely decided to kill me while I slept, I felt well, the sooner the better really." He gritted his teeth with annoyance on certain words such as "kill". It was clear he was fighting to maintain his temper. He was angry that she had damaged a soldier so badly. How dare they get stronger and fight back with such a will!

Leida glanced up at him again.

Zephirak continued. "You had a betrayer in your midst and you didn't even know." He grinned in the darkness and another voice spoke up.

"I think the plan went very well, Uncle Zephirak." Leida's eyes flew open with shock and she gasped. Her stomach turned inside out and upside down when she heard the voice. It was Jadariol. It couldn't be! He had been working for Zephirak this whole time? But he was just a kid!

"Jadariol? *You* were betraying us this whole time?" she looked at him in horror.

Jadariol grinned. "Yep" he said. "Pretty neat huh? And you guys never suspected a thing! I did it so well!"

"But…but, Mettalika attacked you, you weren't faking those wounds."

"He was bait" Zephirak said, "His father agreed to let him be bait for Mettalika. We waited for a Gryphie to be passing near her and sent Jadariol off to be attacked.

398

We knew the Gryphie in its foolishness would try and save him. If he died, he would have died with honour, helping me with my plan. But he survived and you stupid creatures took pity on him and took him in. After his wounds healed enough for him to walk, he would head to the edge of the Forest and meet with his father on arranged moon cycles where he would tell us all he'd learnt about you. He listened in on all your meetings, he found your weaknesses. It had been agreed that if the plan got this far, he would be friends with you by now and able to lure you into the Forest where a pack would be stationed to ambush you. I had planned to leave it a little longer but it seems this war won't hold off any more. We haven't entirely finished our plans for attack but no matter. We know *when* to attack now at least, we were just waiting for that time. A sun cycle when the rains are here. We know when you are weak." Zephirak stopped on that nasty point and grinned.

"Bait? You used a youngster as bait? And he *willingly* did it?" Leida was beside herself with horror and shock.

"Oh yes, you see Jadariol is the next in line to be leader. I selected him very carefully. If he passed this test and allowed himself to be thrown to Mettalika, I would confirm his leadership. He is a Lizariaous after my own mind. Devious, cunning and strong willed. I will now train him up fully to follow in my footsteps." Zephirak placed a paw on Jadariol's head and the young Lizariaous beamed happily.

"But what about his father? Surely he wouldn't agree to having his own kid thrown to the jaws of death" Leida snapped.

"He had no choice. I had chosen Jadariol. If Karnos had refused or not let me take the youngster, I would have had him demoted or killed. And he did not want to die before the eyes of his own kid. As it happens, Karnos was honoured I would choose Jadariol and was all for the plan."

Leida's view of Lizariaouses had fallen the lowest it had ever done. At least she used to think that the youngsters were just misinformed and were still innocent in some way. Now they seemed as corrupt as the adults. She wished she had never let her guard down and trusted Jadariol. He was after all a Lizariaous and they were all the same. The voices she had heard at moon cycle had been Jadariol consorting with his father at the edge of the Forest. Leida would never, ever trust any of them again. Of course, it was too late now and she was caught. Diabloss would come running to rescue her and he would get caught too. With the pair of them held prisoner, Zephirak would wreak his bloody vengeance on as many gatherings as he could, maybe even wiping them all out.

"I had the idea when Jadariol told me a young Gryphie had wandered into our territory." Zephirak said.

Leida remembered when Lunara had wandered into Dyarkroeen, nearly been killed on the way back and Leida had saved her.

"That was quite a while ago now. We killed Mettalika since then. I assume your friends wanted vengeance for that the other moon cycle." Zephirak snarled, walking right up to Leida who quivered a little.

"I can smell your FEAR" snarled Zephirak, his face inches from hers and a grotesque snarl on his face.

Leida bravely snarled back. "They didn't want vengeance. They suspected you still had plans to destroy us and they wanted to stop it before you started a war. We thought it would stop at Mettalika but some of us knew it wouldn't and they were right."

"Oh don't worry, a lot of my soldiers did too. But I never intended for that. Still, they don't know that though. After the attack on me, they're all ready to go again now. So they'll never know this was what I intended all along. Oh and if you happen to escape and tell them, why would they believe you? It was after all, your kind who attacked us in apparent cold blood when we had ended it with Mettalika." He laughed loudly. "It's all so amusing. And you're all going to be under my rule. Anyone who disagrees or disobeys will be killed immediately. There is no room for mistakes any more." He tilted his head and something flashed.

Leida looked up, just noticing it now.

"Oh, you see my new battle armour. Yes, it was a gift from Mettalika!" He erupted into amused laughter again. The shining spike of the helmet he wore flashed as his head moved in the dull light. "I have a matching tail piece too." He swung his tail round and the blades on the end flashed. "She did have some use in the end. This armour will protect me when I kill all of you!"

"Kill us? I thought you just wanted to have us under your rule" said Leida.

"Kill, rule, whichever. It's all the same to me really. I don't care. If I want to rule you I shall and if I want to kill you I shall. If I let my soldiers hunt you for sport we shall. Or breed you and use you as workers so we can all have a break we shall. It doesn't matter to me. When I killed Mettalika, I knew from that moment on that I would succeed. I'd just taken out the most powerful Gryphie in the Forest! She had power greater than even Diabloss. She was first. He will be next. We'll get him here and attack once we have him captive. Without his Deamon power and strength to protect you, you will all bow before me or die."

Leida was enraged now. How dare he speak of her species like that! She struggled and snarled, desperate to get her claws and teeth around his neck. Her legs were bound together though and her wings bound folded against her back. She couldn't get them free no matter how she tried and it hurt to do so. Zephirak just watched with mild amusement. Jadariol stood beside him, his expression that of a child tormenting some poor insect. Leida called out distress calls and then she suddenly snapped her gaze on Zephirak and breathed fire at him. But with her wings bound and the bindings going tightly around her stomach this time, it was harder to breathe in enough to ignite her fire chamber. The flames came out in a large blast to begin with but soon waned and she lay panting.

"Now now if you do that we'll have to muzzle you. You don't want that now do you?" Zephirak placed a paw under her chin and raised her head to look at him in the eye. His claws dug unpleasantly into her throat.

She snarled and snapped in response but couldn't hurt him. She had so much rage and hatred in her and it frustrated her that she couldn't release it on him. This made her even madder. She also feared for Diabloss's life.

Zephirak removed his paw, shoving her head downwards as he did so and turned away from her.

"Come Jadariol. Let's put this war into motion!" Jadariol followed not even looking back at Leida. Leida watched them go. She was nothing to them. The little Lizariaous who had befriended Lunara, the one she had played with and thought was such a good friend to Lunara, was nothing but a betrayer. A hateful minion of Zephirak.

In desperation, Leida pulled herself a little way forward. And more. Maybe she could crawl away from there, it was her only hope. Then she found she could crawl no more, something stopped her. She looked back at her tail. It had a thick metal ring round it and was chained and shackled to the rocky wall of the cave. Her tail spade prevented her pulling her tail out of it too. She would have to chew off her own tail if she wanted to escape and that idea didn't enthral her so she lay back down, defeated. Plus even then she would only be able to crawl of course and they would soon find her from the trail of blood her tail left. She didn't blame herself though. She had fought well this time and that had annoyed Zephirak. Plus she had seriously injured one of them; maybe it would make the soldier a little more fearful and respectful of her kind. She could always hope.

Zephirak was with Mordred.

"Mordred, you will travel to Shernaron and return with Diabloss. You will go alone. Tell him we have Leida and if he doesn't go with you, she will be killed. Also if you do not return within the time limit, we will assume you are dead, kill her anyway and launch a full on attack on their territory. If he comes with you, we will let her go on the proviso that he takes her place. We will then hold him hostage instead and still launch an all out attack on Shernaron. Is this clear?"

"Yes Sir! One question if I may, Sir..." Mordred saluted before he looked puzzled.

"Yes what?" asked Zephirak.

"He won't give himself up if he knows we are going to launch a war on them."

"You idiot! We won't tell them that. He will be exchanged for her. He will think we'll kill him or hold him prisoner. I will tell them it's in return for those attacking me. It's not like you to be so thick headed, Mordred, grikking pay attention to the plan. We *need* Diabloss because he is the strongest of them. He is a half-breed and without him they won't have as much power. He can keep his fire burning longer and is immune to our poison. If we kill all the rest of them, it's likely he will still be standing. Plus without him, it will break the others' spirits somewhat and they'll surrender more easily. Do you understand?" Zephirak snarled threateningly at him.

"Yes, I go and tell Diabloss we have Leida and if he gives himself up she will be freed. If he fails to obey, she will be killed. And if he gives himself up, we will end it there. Right?" Mordred had been horrified when he learned that Zephirak still planned to carry out the war. He had been even more horrified to learn that he had to be the messenger. He was still Zephirak's favourite commander and advisor though.

"Hmm no. He won't trust us that way" Zephirak looked thoughtful for a while. "I know! A while ago he tried to talk sense into me. I'll say that. We'll kill Leida unless he comes back to talk. When he gets here, we'll have her ready and prepared to kill her in one blow if he tries anything. He won't have time to react or she will be dead. We'll bind him and throw him in the back of the cave. We'll leave guards outside. He'll be chained up like she is so he won't escape anyway but it's better to be on the safe side."

"That sounds like a better plan, Sir." Mordred hated it. "Shall I go now?"

"Yes, run. You have until mid sun. If you have not returned by then, Leida will die and we will launch the war regardless of Diabloss."

Mordred nodded and bounded off.

Zephirak chuckled and went to get something to eat.

Croter and Rondo were stationed outside his cavern.

"Ahh, I remember when me and Zarkiz used to do this" sighed Croter with nostalgia in his eyes. "We guarded her before but her mate came and saved her. It won't happen this time though" he chuckled.

Rondo glanced at him. "Do you think we'll really be able to bring all these guys down? I mean, do you think Zephirak will one sun cycle rule over everyone?"

"I don't see why not. He's a great leader after all. Why? You don't think he can do it?" Croter gave him a shifty look.

"Na, he can do it, I know that. But I just can't imagine him ruling over everything. We'll have to kill a lot of them before they'll let us be the dominant species."

"Ah shuttup, Zephirak knows what he's doing." Croter didn't really have the mental capacity to argue about it.

So they sat guarding in silence.

Mordred had reached the Outlands by now. He was galloping at a good pace and not tiring. Thoughts ran through his head like water. He foolishly thought Mettalika's death was the end of all this stupidity. He wanted to tell Diabloss the truth when he met him but he knew that if he did and Diabloss went in to Dyarkroeen fire blazing, Leida would die as soon as Zephirak saw. There was no way but to obey orders. Zephirak had fooled those Lizariaouses who wanted peace just as much as Jadariol had fooled the Gryphies. And Mordred had heard all about that too. He had no choice but to do as he was told and so he bounded across the wastelands and on to Shernaron.

Diabloss had returned from the Dark Plains. It had been fruitless though. The Deamon who greeted them told them that since the war would be nowhere near the Dark Plains for a very long while, it did not concern the

Deamons. Diabloss and his soldiers had flown back downhearted. All they had to hope now was that Zephirak didn't declare war. On the way back though, Diabloss and his squad had paid the high mountains a visit and told them to build up a good stock of armour. They would be ready for this. They were all trained. At the slightest notion of Zephirak attacking, they would fight back relentlessly and prove that they would never be taken down.

Diabloss was puzzled that Leida was not in the tree when he returned. He called for her but no answer.

Very soon, after not being able to find her anywhere, he got his squad to help him. They were all tired from the long moon cycle flight and would much rather have slept than flown around, Diabloss included.

He searched and called all morning and the sun was just reaching its peak when he saw Mordred. Mordred had just arrived and he was searching out Diabloss on the outskirts of the Forest. He didn't want to go in because he might get attacked.

He called out Diabloss's name and wandered around. Diabloss flew down, landing squarely in front of him.

"What do you want Lizariaous?" he said gruffly.

"Diabloss, Zephirak has your mate hostage and..." but Mordred didn't have time to finish because Diabloss was upon him. He shoved him to the ground, snapped off one of his needles and aimed it at the unfortunate Lizariaous's eye.

"What did you say?" he demanded.

"He's got Leida and he wants to talk. If you kill me, he'll kill her and if you don't go he'll kill her." Mordred choked out.

Diabloss let him up and flew into the sky.

"Hey! We have to go back together!" called Mordred but Diabloss was gone. If his kind were threatened, he would defend them with fierce savagery but if his mate was threatened, nothing else mattered, nor did he care. He didn't even remember that Mordred was the Lizariaous who had shown kindness to Leida. Zephirak was right; his love for her was a weakness.

Diabloss saw red. Zephirak had caught her once, how did he have her again? It didn't really matter. All that mattered to Diabloss was getting her back, getting her free. His powerful wings were far stronger than regular Gryphies' and with the extra determination and speed; he made it to Dyarkroeen fast. However, Zephirak had anticipated this and was ready with Leida.

Diabloss saw and he also saw the situation his mate was in. If he made a wrong move, she would be killed by Karnos. He landed carefully and stayed a fair distance away.

"Zephirak, I've come. Let her go." He almost pleaded.

"Not so fast. I want a trade. We'll release her but we want you instead." Zephirak spoke with a level tone.

Diabloss stepped back and growled. "I was told you wanted to talk. Now let her go."

"I do want to talk. But we need to bind you first. Don't move or try to stop my soldiers. If you do, Karnos will kill your precious mate before your eyes." Zephirak's snarling smile was spiteful and malevolent.

Diabloss had no choice but to allow himself to be roughly bound. Wings, legs and a soldier prepared a muzzle for him too, though that wasn't placed on just yet. Diabloss was bound as Leida had been. The bindings dug into him, they wanted to make sure he couldn't slip out or break out in any way. Leida just watched sadly. She had been ordered not to move or attempt anything or she would die then. In truth that had been an idle threat because of course they wouldn't kill her if they still needed her. At that moment though, she put nothing past them. She didn't trust them not to keep their word so she did exactly as she was told. She now realised how deadly and evil they were under the control of Zephirak.

"Now we can talk" said Zephirak, pacing back and forth before Diabloss. Diabloss snarled. "So, you thought you'd take me hostage and then gain control of us? That was foolish. I may be half Deamon but I'm not the only good fighter in Shernaron."

"Yes but you have the highest amount of stamina. Your fire is more powerful and you are twice as strong as the others. Now we can go ahead and conquer the Forest and everything beyond it. Anything to make the job a little easier you know? My soldiers are ready, my troops are assembled and I will have gained control of the Forest by this moon cycle. It's only a matter of time then. I plan to use Gryphies to fight Gryphies and bring down the mountains as well. If they don't fight for me, they will die."

"Then they'll all die. No one would fight for you, none of us anyway. You are bitter and corrupt. It was wishful thinking to assume that you would stop at Mettalika." Diabloss growled angrily.

"You stupid creatures already foiled my previous plan. We were going to attack when the rains came and you would be weaker but we have to attack now in case you send in more Gryphies to *kill us in our sleep*" Zephirak spat out the last words with malice and lunged at Diabloss as he did so. Diabloss didn't even flinch. He wasn't afraid, he was just filled with anger and loathing for the vile creature before him.

"We planned to let the dust settle a little, let you think we'd stopped. And then attack. Still, we are prepared and you will all fall before me under my command. I will rule over Shernaron and Dyarkroeen!" he laughed.

"Then the least I could do is warn them you're coming!" Leida spoke up.

"No, because I'm not letting you go..." Zephirak trailed off as he saw Leida had escaped her bindings, her wings flew out, smacking the guards either side of her as she rose into the sky. She had sneakily loosened her bindings with the sharp edges of her tail spade while Zephirak had been busy with Diabloss. No one had noticed and it was a sudden idea she had had. She was more resourceful than she used to be.

"Shoot her down!" yelled Zephirak and Leida was showered with a barrage of needles. She hit most of them away and flew higher, blowing flames back down at them. She had enough time to see Diabloss's expression of hope and relief before she turned and headed back for Shernaron.

"Fly Leida!! Warn everyone!" he called after her.

"Shut up!" snapped Zephirak and cuffed Diabloss across the face. Diabloss snarled and snapped at the air as Zephirak moved away.

"We attack now!" yelled Zephirak. "Get those soldiers moving to the Forest!"

Karnos and Croter nodded and called to the troops. There was a rumbling and the soldiers who had been assembled near the training grounds galloped towards them. There were hundreds, thousands of them from all over Dyarkroeen. Every single one was under Zephirak's command and control and they were sub commanded by Croter and Karnos. Jadariol was among them and Diabloss looked at him with horror as he sneered cruelly at the captive Gryphie.

"Take them out! Take down the Forest and kill anyone who opposes you! Make it clear if they surrender they won't get hurt and kill those who don't agree to that. GO!! KILL!! CONQUER!! Bring down the Gryphies of the Forest!! We begin now!! Have no mercy!! GO!!" Zephirak roared and the troops galloped in formation towards the Outlands.

Diabloss struggled and strained but he couldn't escape. A soldier had bound his tail now too, so he couldn't do what Leida had done.

His angry face snapped towards Zephirak. "You'll never take us down, we fly high and keep the fire burning and we will drive you back here with your tails between your legs and your needles obliterated" he growled through clenched teeth.

"Oh I don't think so. They are all trained for this. They will defeat and conquer whatever comes their way. You are nothing Diabloss, nothing" he seethed out the last word. "Take him to the cavern, shackle him down and place guards outside" he commanded the soldiers who had Diabloss. They dragged him away to Zephirak's cavern.

Diabloss felt helpless, he mentally kicked himself for not taking back up. Then again if he had, Zephirak would have killed Leida. He tried to flame the soldiers and he was muzzled. He was also weakened and tired after the moon cycle flight to the Dark Plains so he didn't have as much strength as he would have normally. He had no choice but to allow himself to be made prisoner. He stared up at the sky before they dragged him into the darkness and only hoped that Leida would make it back to the Forest and the message would go out to all the others that they would soon be invaded.

Leida was well on her way to the Forest. Her wing muscles burned from flying so fast and hard. She called out as she went. "Lizariaouses are coming! Warn everyone, prepare everyone! Get ready to fight! Call the Gryphies from the mountains, tell them to bring armour! War is coming!!" She called this over and over, nearby Gryphies went to spread the word. She was soon joined by Kayto and Tranzoss.

"War? They declared war?" asked Kayto as they flew together.

"Yes! They're coming to invade the Forest and take us down. They'll kill us all if we don't surrender. We have to protect the Forest, get those soldiers out there to slow them down in the Outlands. We don't want to give them the chance to reach the Forest. Tell the squadron!" Leida hurriedly explained.

"But where's Diabloss?" asked Tranzoss.

"They have him captive. He's out of this for now, we have to take charge and do this ourselves. Don't fly around talking, get to it! I don't know how much time we have. Get everyone who can fight! Quickly!" Leida was surprised at her own leadership.

The others nodded and flew off. Stervia was just up ahead.

"They've declared war?" she asked.

"YES!! Weren't you listening? We need to stop them before they get here! I'm going to warn Mystik. We have to protect the kittens and keep them out of harm's way. Round up the fastest flyers to go to the mountains and help bring back armour! I never thought they would attack this fast. We aren't properly prepared." Leida was worrying. Stervia flew off. It was a long way to the high mountains. She headed for the Forest and landed on top of Mystik's tree. All around her, she could hear siren calls, warning cries and general panic.

411

She leaped down the tree in great bounds.

"Mystik! You have to help make sure the kittens are safe. The Lizariaouses have declared war and are coming to take down the Forest!"

Mystik had heard beforehand about the invasion.

"Yes, I already know. I was told by him" she motioned to Mordred who came out from the back of the tree.

Leida immediately growled. "Get out of the Forest! You are not welcome here Lizariaous!"

"No, he's with us." Mystik tried to explain.

"I don't believe him and you shouldn't either. We thought Jadariol was just a helpless kid but he took me into the Forest and got me ambushed by their soldiers. None of them can be trusted!" Leida opened her wings threateningly at Mordred and growled. "Get out."

"You don't remember me do you" replied Mordred, not making any attempt to move.

"No and I don't care about you either. Go back to your master." Leida snapped.

"That time when Zephirak had you prisoner the first time. I came to see you, I told you my views and that I disapproved of how Zephirak treated you. I got this scar on my eye because he caught me talking to you, remember? I had no choice but to obey; he would have killed you if I hadn't. Please believe me Leida, I only want peace." Mordred tried to explain but Leida didn't trust him at all.

"I don't believe you. I hate all your kind. You have never proved yourselves to be anything but evil, controlling, vicious creatures who want to rule over everything in every territory. Now get out of the Forest! You're trying to take over from the inside with your hateful lies."

Mystik spoke up. "He can be trusted…"

Leida snapped at her. "And what do you know? You saved Mettalika and started this whole thing. You said we should look after Jadariol and then he got me ambushed and used me to bribe my mate. This is all your fault! Maybe you should go with him? You aren't as wise as you make out. You're just a crazy old Gryphie who for some reason everyone put their faith in simply because you're a healer. Well, anyone can heal, Mystik, you aren't so wise or great as you make yourself seem."

Mystik was taken aback. Was this the same sweet, shy Leida she had watched grow and learn, train and mature? But she was right. Mystik had been foolish. Her tail and wings dropped.

"You are right. I am not wise. I am just a foolish old dreamer who thought that things would work out through bargaining and had hope that we could stop this without a fight. For that, I will go and fight with you. I am not strong enough to hold up for long but I want to repair the damage I have done or at least try to."

"You can't fix it. It's beyond broken, Mystik. You're just a cog in the wheel. But Mettalika started this by killing Zephirak's mate and you were the reason Mettalika lived. We've lost Sinxo, Otuss and Sarna because of that. Your guilt is good enough punishment. Stay where you can be of use, looking after the kittens and any mothers who stay behind." Leida bounded out of the tree and didn't wait for a reply. Mordred followed.

"Leave the Forest! Are you deaf? Didn't you hear? We don't want or need your kind or your help here. I don't trust any of you. I remember you but I don't trust you so you can stop hoping I will." Leida snarled at Mordred. She had no time for this.

"Fine, I will fight alongside you. You don't need to trust me but if I get killed by one of my own kind, defending you and fighting for what I believe is right,

413

maybe you will see then. I am one of the few of us left who still want peace and don't agree with our leader." Mordred galloped off into the Forest.

Leida watched him go briefly before Tranzoss alighted beside her.

"Sir, I've sent off our best fighters to drive them back at the Outlands" she told Leida.

Leida stared at her for a moment. Sir? She was referring to Leida as their commander. Leida had never expected this.

"Err, good. Don't use all our best fighters at once though; we need some to fall back on should some be killed."

"I haven't, don't worry. But I've called Gryphies from all over. They are coming down from the high mountains and beyond the Forest. The Sky Gryphies haven't been persuaded just yet but if we're losing too badly, they will I've no doubt come to our aid too. There are as many Gryphies out there as I've seen Lizariaouses in the distance. We won't let them get past us. Are the kittens secure?"

"Yes, all the young ones are at the centre of the Forest and protected by guards. If you see a grey Lizariaous with a scarred eye running about, keep an eye on him. He says he wants to fight with us but I don't believe him. Still, I do remember he was the only one who showed me any kindness back when I was kidnapped so let him be for now. Kill him if he causes any trouble though."

"Yes Sir!" replied Tranzoss.

Leida nodded. "Let's go. We need to make sure the ones who aren't out facing the battle are kitted up with armour. Then we can call them back and send out the armoured Gryphies while they put on their own armour."

414

"We don't have nearly enough armour for all of them, you do realise that. We only have a handful. The squadron is already in armour. They came back from the Dark Plains and stopped off at the high mountains to tell them to crank up the armour making. I have no armour just because I believe that I can fight well without it. I'm a good fighter, fast and strong. It's my opinion that only the weaker ones would need armour and so it should be reserved for them instead of used on everyone. Just leave it to ones who need it. Speaking of which, you still need some for your legs. I remember they were your weakness a while back, do they still cause you trouble?" asked Tranzoss.

"Yes, I'll have to get some armour for them when they bring it back. I really hope we can keep them away from the Forest. If they get past us, I don't know what we'll do." Leida was worried and now she had time to stop and dwell on it; that made it worse.

"We'll kill them all if we have to! Or until they see sense and back off. Come on, let's go get you that armour and join the others on the front line. Those grikheads will have reached the halfway point by now." Tranzoss climbed a nearby tree, followed by Leida and they took off to go find a Gryphie bringing back some armour to the Forest.

They didn't need to search long, Kanzo had gotten back with some armour and he let Leida have some leg protectors. She landed in a tree and put them on. They were nicely made, in shining steel with patterns on them. She put one on each back leg.

"You'd better put them on your front legs too" said Tranzoss. "Better to be safe than sorry, after all."

Leida nodded and soon her legs were nicely armoured. The armour plating covered the whole leg with a joint where the knees and elbows were.

"Let's go!" said Leida and they headed for the Outlands.

"Plan?" asked Tranzoss as they flew.

"We warn them to stay away first. If they don't listen, we attack. We'll give them the chance to back down. I've no doubt they'll tell us to surrender or die or something so we'll tell them our side of it. They won't listen anyway but if they start to fight us, I want them to make the first move." Leida told her. "After all, we're stopping them from passing. We will form a barrier of defence. If we rush out there fire blazing, it won't be organised enough and some of them will slip by us. We must act as one unit and keep them away like that."

Tranzoss nodded, thinking this was a good idea and they flew on.

Back at the Forest clearing, Shen was having trouble keeping Lunara in the tree. Lunara wanted to go check out what was going on with Leida and the others. She also wanted to know where Jadariol had gone and was worried.

"Stay in the tree! All kittens must stay in their homes and are forbidden to leave them." Shen told her, pushing her back into the safety of the hollow part of the tree where Lunara slept.

"But I want to know where Jadariol is. He's gone and I haven't seen him all sun cycle" she persisted.

"I don't know where he is but he can take care of himself, he's a big boy" said Shen, worrying for Lunara's safety. "You must stay inside. Once this is over, you can go look for him but not until then."

Lunara was obstinate but she shut up and stayed where she was. Until her mother's back was turned that is. Then she was off down the tree and over to Mystik's tree. Mystik would know where he was.

416

Mystik was sat at the back of the tree staring at her medicines in their little compartments in the walls of the tree. Her ears and wings were down and she looked a shadow of her former self. Leida's words echoed in her mind. It *was* all her fault. All of this and she couldn't put it right. It was too late now.

She heard Lunara rush up beside her. "Mystik! I haven't seen Jadariol all day and I'm worried. He is ok isn't he? Where is he?" She bounded about in agitation.

"He has gone back to Dyarkroeen and I was wrong to let us take him in. He should have been given back when Sinxo found him. Maybe he shouldn't have been rescued at all." Mystik replied, not even looking at her.

"What do you mean? Of course he should've been rescued. If we hadn't have helped him, he'd be dead." Lunara sat and looked up at Mystik.

The old Gryphie looked down at her; the old face was tired and tear stained.

"No my dear, I was wrong. Jadariol took Leida into the Forest where some other Lizariaouses ambushed her. He was working for Zephirak all along."

"What? No! Not Jadariol! It's not true! He's one of my best friends and I know he'd never do a thing like that!" cried Lunara.

"Then you didn't really know him. He had all of us tricked. Go back to your tree dear and hope that they don't invade this far. Remember your training." Mystik turned away.

Lunara shook her head, backing away. Then she turned and ran. She didn't run back to her tree though; she ran into the Forest. She needed to know this was true; she needed to see for herself. She needed to see Jadariol working for Zephirak before she would believe it.

417

She had no real idea where she was running, except she assumed she needed to get to the edge of the Forest. She saw Mordred and hid from him. Whether she simply didn't want to believe Jadariol would do such a thing or that she genuinely didn't believe it remained unclear but she needed to find the truth for herself.

After a while she realised she wasn't alone. She was being followed. Lunara stopped in her tracks and spun round coming face to face with Hiryasis.

"What are you doing here? You should be safe at home" she told him.

"I could say the same for you" he replied. "I heard what happened and although I don't like Jadariol, I didn't want you going alone."

"Thanks Hiry!" Lunara was glad of the company. "You don't think he'd betray us do you?" she asked.

"Well...yeah I do. But that's not the point. If you get there and he tries to kill you, you need your friends. I asked the others to come too but they wouldn't. So...you need your friend. Me. I was your best friend way before he came along and he's not here now, he ran off but I won't run off." Hiryasis told her kindly.

Lunara smiled. "Ok then, let's go find the truth!"

Zephirak had joined his army on the wastelands of the Outlands. He told Karnos and Croter to halt the army before it reached the Forest and see if they could bargain with the Gryphies. They wanted to make it clear that they would keep their lives if they surrendered. Zephirak had decided now that he wanted as many of the Gryphies alive as possible because he realised for one, ruling over the dead has no benefits and for another, he needed to gather fighters who could fly in order to take down the Sky Gryphies and the Gryphies from the high mountains. He didn't really have any idea how he would do this but right now he was in his element and that didn't really matter.

On the other side, the Gryphie army was waiting. It was headed by Strassor and Odax and they hovered menacingly in the sky, keeping watch over the barren Outlands. They saw the Lizariaouses approach from a long way off.

"What do we do if they won't leave?" asked Odax.

"We give 'em all we got! We be backin' down fer no one, yeh hear?" growled Strassor. "They won't be takin' this territory, not while I be alive. They might have Diabloss but I can fight as well as he can." Word had got round very fast that the Lizariaouses had Diabloss. Kayto wanted to send out a rescue party to fetch him but Strassor told him that everyone was needed to protect the Forest, this was what was most important and Diabloss would say the same. One Gryphie or the whole territory. The latter held far more importance. Kayto had reluctantly agreed and fallen under the command of Leida, along with the rest of the squadron. As Tranzoss had noticed before, Leida was now wiser and more thoughtful and that made her stronger. Although in this situation, keeping a level head was becoming increasingly hard for her.

Leida and Tranzoss arrived on the scene and the approaching Lizariaous army grew closer.

Leida scanned across, her eyes viewing as far as she could see. "Wow, how many are there? He must have brought the whole population of Dyarkroeen" she said.

Tranzoss looked grim. "We can hope that's what he's done. Once these guys are taken down, he won't have any backup and we can drive the rest of them back if they try anything. We do have backup though and we will rotate our army. The mountain Gryphies are arriving.

A lot of them are tired from their fast flight and they're resting until we need them. As we fight, more will arrive and be able to rest. The Sky Gryphies will arrive later if it gets so bad that they need to."

"I suggest tryin' ter take down that there Zephirak" said Strassor. "With 'im gone; I doubt they'll be as bold."

"Good idea. If we can get to him that is, they're protecting him very well, he's right in the middle of that fray." Leida said, watching the approaching army. Zephirak was in the middle and he was making his way through them as they galloped, ready to tell the Gryphies to back down or die defending their territory. He was wearing Mettalika's steel helmet and tail armour. As the army got nearer, the full scale of it was apparent. Leida worried a little now. Strassor flew up beside her.

"Don't worry m'dear, yer a great fighter and we're here beside yeh. They don't stand a chance, no matter how many there are of 'em." Leida nodded but wished with all her heart that Diabloss was there.

The vast army slowed to a halt and Zephirak stepped forward, the blade on the helmet glinting in the sun.

"Gryphies!" he roared, "We have come to request your surrender. Accept me as your leader and we will live in peace once again! Those who refuse will die and we will invade your forest and take it by force if you do not agree. I am Zephirak, lord of all I command. If you do not back down and accept me as your new ruler, I will allow my army to do as it wishes. What is your answer?"

Leida flew up in the sky high above them before Strassor could speak.

"We do not accept. Go back to Dyarkroeen and never bother us again. We are sick of living in your shadow, living in fear that you will hunt and kill our kind.

You killed Mettalika; the battle was over when she died. You will not pass and you will not invade our home. Don't sacrifice your soldiers for nothing."

"You can't expect me to just go back. My armies are ready and waiting. They have lived for this sun cycle and besides, it was you who started it back up again by sending in Gryphies to kill me. Surrender or die." Zephirak roared.

"You were going to do it anyway. You are a liar and a filthy, corrupt, power hungry creature. Our answer is no. We will never surrender to you and your kind and we will drive you out long before you reach the Forest." Behind her, the Gryphie army roared and fired out blasts of blue flames.

And from behind the front row of Gryphie soldiers stationed on the ground came Mordred.

"I say no too, Zephirak" he growled.

"Mordred?" Zephirak was briefly taken aback.

"Yes, I am fighting for them. I wanted peace, I thought you would give up on this stupid plan after we got Mettalika but you never intended to stop there, did you? I would rather fight alongside the enemy than fight for you." He lowered his head and growled.

"You filthy betrayer!" roared Zephirak.

"Then I am no better than that youngster you sent in to betray the Gryphies. Since it was your idea to get him to betray them, that makes me no better than you. I find that likeness insulting and I am fighting against you."

Zephirak snarled with rage. His favourite commander, his advisor, the one that he himself had put trust in had betrayed him. It came back to him now, when he had Leida kidnapped and Mordred had seemingly turned a blind eye to her escape, aided her in that way and he mentally kicked himself for forgiving the grey Lizariaous.

"Then you will die with them Mordred" he roared. His tail thrashed and his needles rattled. The army rattled their needles in response, creating a deafening sound that echoed over the Outlands.

"ATTACK!" roared Zephirak and the army charged forward as one.

"Go!! Take them down!" roared Leida and the Gryphies took to the sky, speeding at the Lizariaous army. The rest charged towards them on the ground. The Lizariaouses kicked up dust as they ran, their muscles rippling in the sun as they charged full on. The Gryphies' fur shone as their wings moved with a flash of speed, claws extended, teeth bared, awaiting the inevitable clash of contact with the enemy.

Chapter 32
War!

Time seemed to slow down; it was as though the impact was being dragged out between the two species as they charged for one another. Rage burned in the eyes of the Lizariaouses and fire blazed in the eyes of the Gryphies. Leida, Strassor, Odax and the squadron headed the Gryphie army and Mordred ran with the Gryphies on the ground. They didn't pay much attention to him. He was one Lizariaous and if he tried anything, there were so many around him they could easily kill him if he did. He wouldn't have though, he was determined that if he did die, it wouldn't be fighting for his corrupt leader. Zephirak had lost his mind long ago, he was only concerned with one thing and that was becoming ruler over all.

The armies made contact in a vicious hard clash of teeth and claws. Needles were fired into the sky, shooting down the Gryphies whose wings they hit. The front line Lizariaouses were blinded by Gryphie fire as the Gryphies flamed them upon their approach. Those saving their needles charged with their heads down so they weren't blinded and they barraged right through the front line Gryphies who were concentrating more on fire than fighting. Lizariaouses on the outermost ranks of the army tried to get past into the Forest without being spotted but the outermost trees had sentries posted in them to watch out for such things and they didn't make it that far. As the Lizariaous army hit the Gryphies, the Lizariaouses at the back of the throng charged out and round, the more that came, the better the chance they could overpower the Gryphies with their sheer numbers.

While the front ones fought, others made their way around to get past while the others were distracted and met their fate at the hands of the sentries. Leida used her legs to hit away needles now they had the armour to protect them. Her wings and legs were great shields and defensive weapons. Because both Gryphies and Lizariaouses were more or less evenly matched, this made the battles longer unless they were caught off guard or with a particularly accurate shot.

The needles gave the Lizariaouses a great advantage because it meant that the Gryphies couldn't land on their backs from out of the sky. Likewise, the needles, although they were excellent weapons, they could only be shot so high and a lot of the Gryphies flew up higher and went to take down the furthest lines in the army nearer the back.

Mordred found it easy to kill the enemy soldiers. He was immune to the poison and the biting and clawing didn't bother him. He was also an expert fighter and knew all their tricks from commanding his own armies.

Zephirak was the most vicious fighter; he killed left and right, charging in with unrivalled anger and hatred for the enemy. He knew that they wouldn't back down but it angered him even more that they didn't.

The other side of the Forest, more and more Gryphies arrived bearing armour from the mountains. They rested and waited to be called to battle. Nothing this huge had ever been witnessed in either territory, the war that had been culminating all these seasons was finally here, let go with power and anger, for all the years they had lived in mere tolerance, now, like a wildfire it spread through each and every member of the two species. The Gryphies, angry at always trying to maintain peace, tired of it, now got to let it out and release what had been pent up all this time. The Lizariaouses, always having felt their existence with the Gryphies was competition for dominant species finally got to release their might upon them. One side fighting to conquer, one side fighting for freedom.

Fire engulfed the battle; needles flew like rain, roars, anger, savagery and brute strength. The glint of steel armour, Zephirak's helmet blade gouging and gutting any opponents unlucky enough to come up against him, claws and fur flying. Two species, one land bound and furless, the other masters of the sky and fire. One once peaceful and the other always savage. Two opposites from each other.

Mordred fought with the Gryphies in total harmony, he even double teamed with a couple of them. He was proving himself and soon others realised he was really fighting for them. He'd been sick of Zephirak's corruption for so long now; it was good to get back. One thing left to do for him, even if he died doing it. He was fighting, working his way through the army, heading for Zephirak. He would kill Zephirak, it was clear to him now. He wanted to put a stop to it. It wasn't to prove himself; it was because he was utterly sick and tired of living under such a corrupt leader. If he died doing it then so be it, at least he would have tried. He wanted to kill him to ensure the future for both sides would be better.

Strassor and Odax fought as a unit together, they had trained for this often before. They knew this would happen sooner or later and had been prepared in their own minds. One would flame the opponent's face while the other lunged in for the kill while the opponent was confused and bewildered trying to escape the flames. They did this over and over with every single opponent they battled. The flamer would swap with the attacker every so often to recharge resources and stamina.

Tranzoss fought alone, she was picking off the furthest soldiers at the back of the throng. Because she fought alone however, she would attack one Lizariaous and a bunch of others would come to its aid so it was hard to fend them all off at once. However, she was a Fire Master. She used her fire to create multiple images of Gryphies, surrounding the soldiers, confusing them so she could pick them off one by one. Some soldiers would be alarmed, others fascinated and it only took for them to be distracted for a few seconds before they realised they were staring straight into the jaws of death.

Kayto and Stervia picked off the outer soldiers, the ones who were trying to make their way to the Forest. As well as the sentries in the trees, they kept the soldiers from getting too far. Sometimes the fight would move forward, sometimes the Gryphies would force it backwards again. Lizariaouses who had been foolish and used up all their needles now had to rely on physical teeth and claws contact. They were vulnerable like this however because it meant a Gryphie could get closer to them, close enough to kill them.

Some soldiers had taken to aiming their needles for more vulnerable Gryphie body areas such as eyes. They had to be really good shots though in order to hit such a small place on a moving target. Those who had target trained managed to hit the eyes every so often or the throat. The Gryphie would either claw at its eyes in confusion and pain or fall crashing to the ground where it would be trampled by the rest of the throng.

It was harder for airborne Gryphies to hit Lizariaouses because of the needles but engulfing them with flames blinded and confused them.

And then there were the front line soldiers, Gryphies and Lizariaouses going full on at each other on the ground, biting and slashing and destroying. Some Gryphies charged in with no fear, they would die with honour defending Shernaron. Likewise with the Lizariaouses. Of course, some of the latter thought they were invincible. Some who had a high tolerance to the fire thought they couldn't be burned and ended up as charred corpses. And some were just so tied up and lost in the moment that they carried on slashing and biting even after they'd been partly disembowelled by the opponent. These ones were left to snarl and gargle angrily as they died. The Gryphies fought with practicality. Once an opponent had been disabled enough that they would not be able to get up and continue fighting, they would move to the next soldier. Some they managed to hit with instant fatality but the more difficult fighters were merely disabled. The longer they took fighting and killing, the higher the chance that members of the Lizariaous army could get past them to the Forest.

Somewhere in the massive throng were the younger Lizariaous soldiers such as Jadariol. They fought together side by side; they were fully aware that their smaller size made them vulnerable and worked together. They killed a fair amount of enemies. Some foolish Gryphies wouldn't fight kids. The kids however would tear them apart. They had no remorse; it was how they had been raised. They all looked up to Zephirak because they were young and easily mislead. They were too young really to develop their own ideas through looking practically at both sides of the argument. They followed Zephirak without question because he was their leader and they were dedicated to him.

They also fought near to Zephirak; most had the hope that if Zephirak got into trouble that they could be there and save or help him. Jadariol saw him as an uncle figure even though they weren't related. Zephirak had taken him under his teachings, which honoured Jadariol and he wanted to prove what a brave fighter he could be. So far none of the younger soldiers had been harmed; the Gryphie soldiers were concentrating on the larger, more powerful adult Lizariaouses. The kids weren't considered to be a threat. It was because of this that very slowly they were edging away from Zephirak and making their way to the Forest.

A sentry saw them and flamed at them in warning and they stayed where they were. Since the betrayal of Jadariol, most of the Gryphies knew that even youngsters were dangerous. Another technique they were using was to get under Gryphies who were in the middle of fighting and slash their stomachs open. The smallest of the young Lizariaous soldiers did this. Now Gryphies were starting to catch on and make sure they kept flapping their wings or moving so much that any kid who tried this couldn't get beneath them. Jadariol was commanding them to do most of this stuff and more as he observed the battle. Zephirak had told him he could command the others because he did so well at betraying the Gryphies and carrying out the plan.

Suddenly a gathering of new Gryphies appeared, most of them armour clad and the current fighters fell back. They had their first soldier rotation, allowing the fighters to fall back to the Forest and rest. The new fighters stormed in roaring and flaming, taking out a bunch of enemy soldiers with fresh energy.

Zephirak roared out his anger at this and fought twice as hard. His rage was what kept his stamina up. It was renewed tenfold when he realised the Gryphies were rotating their troops.

Somewhere at the edge of the Forest, Lunara and Hiryasis peered out and watched the battle. So far they hadn't seen Jadariol and then they spotted him and a few others when they tried to get closer to the Forest. A Gryphie flew down in front of them, growling at them and telling them to get back. Jadariol snarled at it, giving the others a chance to jump on it. There were about four other Lizariaous kids and they clambered and pounced on the Gryphie, causing it to cry out as they dug their claws in, forcing it down. Jadariol paced back and forth in front of it. Lunara and Hiryasis couldn't hear what he was saying. He was mocking it as he knew Zephirak would. The others held it down laughing. The Gryphie flapped its wings, trying to get away. A Lizariaous sat on each wing, one on its back and one holding its tail down. Suddenly Jadariol lunged forward and snapped his jaws down on its neck, biting down hard and breaking it.

Lunara and Hiryasis stared in horror. This was the little Lizariaous they had hung around with and called a friend. This was the kid Lunara had cared for, looked after, helped and watched over, played Which One? with. Her own mother had carried him to the beach. Lunara just stared, she couldn't stop staring. She wanted the event that had occurred before her to be a dream or for the Gryphie to get up, laugh about it and Jadariol tell it he was only joking and that he was really on their side and that he had pretended to kill it as a ruse, to trick the other soldiers.

The Gryphie didn't get up.

Hiryasis snorted. "I knew it! I knew all along he was bad. I tried to tell you but noo, you wanted to give it a chance and so I relented against my better thoughts and accepted him. I even thought he was cool at one point. I can't believe it took you to actually *see* him in action betraying us before you'd believe me."

Lunara said nothing. She felt numb. It was as though Jadariol had killed her and not someone else. He *had* killed her, he had killed their friendship and trust, everything she had ever shared with him had meant nothing because all along he had just been pretending, their friendship had been a lie all along.

"You happy now Lunara? Now you've seen your "best friend" kill one of us? From now on, only Gryphies can be friends. Lizariaouses know nothing about friendship. I hope you can see I was right all along." Hiryasis snapped at her.

Lunara shook her head and a tear rolled down her cheek. "I…I didn't want to believe. Maybe I did suspect him at one point, I can't remember. He was grumpy a lot of the time but after we spent so much time together, I saw him change, I swear he did."

"That was a lie too. He pretended to change once he realised that we were stupid enough to accept him. And to think you wanted him to stay. Let's go back home Lunara. I don't want to be here any more. I don't want to see them kill us. We're too young to put up a good fight" said Hiryasis turning to go.

Lunara was about to speak when suddenly a small gathering of Gryphies trampled past heading for battle. The two kittens got caught up in it. They couldn't head back into the Forest and had no choice but to go forward into the Outlands. So they ran with the gathering, hoping to turn around once they got out there and head back unseen. It was hard for smaller Gryphies to keep up though and soon the soldiers had left them behind. They turned to head back, bumping right into a snarling Lizariaous soldier.

"Oh look! I didn't know they had free food running around here. I need a little sustenance to keep on running" he grinned hideously and snapped his jaws down at the pair of hapless Gryphies. Lunara and Hiryasis screamed and ran for it, parting and running off either side of the soldier. He spun round and chased after them laughing.

"I can taste you already! Taste your fear!" he laughed cruelly and gained on them.

"Fly Hiry!!" yelled Lunara and they took to the sky. The soldier fired needles at them but they were faster and smaller targets to hit than adult Gryphies, managing to escape while the soldier cursed them below.

They decided to stay in the sky and watch what was going on. They saw Leida, Strassor and Odax fighting, Tranzoss in the distance with her fire and Stervia. Kayto was nowhere to be seen but he was there on the ground. A Gryphie called out to them.

"You aren't supposed to be here, kittens, go back to the Forest and home to your trees" she was hovering a little way away; it was Keela, a mountain Gryphie who was kitted out in full armour. She was the leader of their squadron. Iseera flew past them, fire blazing and Keela called out a command to her, momentarily distracted. Hiry and Lunara flew away.

"We're going back home" said Hiryasis.

"Ok" replied Lunara and they headed for the Forest. Suddenly, a needle flew past them and then another and another. It was the soldier, he'd found them again. Hiryasis swore loudly and they flew higher. However, Lunara flew straight into a passing needle as they hurried to get back to safety. It didn't hit her, not the tip anyway; it was flying past her as she headed for the Forest and she flew into it. Momentarily stunned, she stopped flapping her wings and fell to the ground.

Groggily she got up. The soldier was standing over her. Hiry flew about in the sky, then lunged at the soldier, flaming him. He merely swung out his tail and hit Hiry aside. Hiry fell to the ground a little way away as the soldier turned his attention on Lunara.

"Mmm, I can nearly taste you now" he chuckled. Lunara was trying to get to her feet. She saw Hiryasis

431

on the ground a little way away and wanted to get to him.

The soldier's jaws lunged down at her and she crouched in fear. She would not be fast enough to get away.

Over where Hiryasis watched in fear, he saw Jadariol also watching. Jadariol saw Lunara crouching, shaking and crying and stared at her, not moving.

"Hey you! Go grikking save her you lousy good for nothing betrayer! If the time you spent with Lunara means anything to you, you'll go in and help her!" Hiryasis called to Jadariol.

Jadariol turned to him, smirked at him and turned away. Hiryasis roared in anger at him, calling him every insult under the sun. How could he turn away at such a time? Even if he killed Gryphies, surely there was a shred of honour in him and that he would save his friend. Hiryasis was too weak to get over to her.

Lunara took it into her mind to dodge at the last moment and the soldier missed. She kept on dodging but she was getting worn out.

"Oho you can't keep that up forever little one! I'll get you!" The soldier found this game amusing. Lunara managed to get to her feet and try to run but the soldier didn't like this and pounced on her, holding her down.

"Enough fun, time to eat now" he said. Lunara quivered in terror as she stared into his bloodthirsty eyes and saw up close the real meaning of fear. Suddenly he screamed out and let go of her. She got up, looking around, thinking she'd see Hiryasis attacking the soldier. It wasn't Hiry though, it was Jadariol that had hold of the soldier's tail and was biting down on it.

"That Gryphie is MINE! Go find another!" he yelled at him. "If you don't, I'll tell Uncle Zephirak and he'll kill you because you wouldn't let me have my kill!"

The soldier grumbled and backed down. He knew better than to answer back to anyone who Zephirak smiled upon. With a snarl, he ran off.

Lunara was unsure of Jadariol. She stayed where she was, quite terrified after she'd seen him kill that Gryphie in front of her.

Jadariol sneered, walking up to her. "I hate all of your kind" he said. "Except one. You. I like you. I don't want you to die. You were the only friend I had when I was in that stinking forest of yours. Everyone else saw me as something to be distrustful of. You were gullible enough to believe me. I like when plans go well and how you reacted was just how I wanted all of you to react. If the rest of your kind were like you and wanted to be friends, we wouldn't have to kill you."

"But Jadariol, doesn't our friendship mean anything? Is the only reason you like me because I believed that you couldn't be as evil as everyone thought you were? You really only like me because of that?"

"What is friendship? It's weak. Like love. My master knows true strength lies in force and conquering. Holding down the weak and getting them to do our bidding. I found something I'd never experienced with you and for that I'm thankful because I know what friendship is like now and just how weak and pathetic it is." He laughed nastily.

"But we had so much fun…didn't you enjoy it?" asked Lunara sitting up and dusting herself off.

Jadariol shrugged. "What's fun? You think playing games is fun, I think killing is fun. You think flying is fun but I think using my needles is for work and war. We don't agree on anything that is fun and because we're so different, we can never live together in harmony unless you back down and allow us to rule you. Then we will be kinder. Those who please my master will have good lives and be able to do as they wish. Those who anger him will die."

"If you really didn't care, you wouldn't have saved me. If you really thought I was weak then you would've watched him kill me and laughed about it" said Lunara.

"I don't care! But I don't kill you guys for no reason. My master wants those who don't need to be killed alive so they can fight for us when the time comes to take over the rest of Shernaron. We started with the Forest because you were closest and easiest. We only ever killed you for food until Mettalika came along. Then we killed you for pleasure because we wanted to get back at you for her killing us, like she did my mother. See, we're fair; we've gone back to only killing you for food now and those of you who oppose us. We don't kill you without reason. All your other little friends will survive." Jadariol explained.

"That still doesn't make it right! We all deserve to live in peace and co-operate with each other. You only don't kill kittens because we're too young and weak to be a real threat" growled Lunara.

"Well yeah, there is that too. I mean if you were adults, we'd kill you cos you'd be fighting and trying to stop us. Get this straight Lunara, we will trample, tear, slash and destroy those who go against us." Jadariol pulled himself up to his full height and glowered.

"Yeah but you still saved me which means you cared about what happened to me" said Lunara.

"Think what you want" Jadariol replied shortly and ran off. Lunara watched him go. She was still convinced that he cared about her in some small way, even if it wasn't completely clear or apparent. He'd seemed like he wanted to do as Zephirak said but also wanted to be her friend somehow. She watched him run back to where a group of other kids were fighting another

Gryphie. She saw the Gryphie kill one of the young Lizariaouses and Jadariol flew at it in anger, biting and tearing. It seemed whatever he said; he was there for his friends.

Hiryasis limped up to Lunara. "Well I never thought he'd save you. Let's go back home."

Lunara shook her head. "No, I want to leave with Jadariol. I want to convince him to join us."

"WHAT?? That's crazy! He might have saved you but he's right back fighting us again. He wouldn't have saved me you know. The only way he's gunna stop fighting us is if he sees Zephirak isn't so great and there's no way in Shernaron you're gunna convince him of that. He worships the ground his leader walks on. Look how savagely he fights! There is no good in him, Lunara." Hiryasis started to head for the Forest. "Come on!"

But Lunara was running the other way. "Lunara!" called Hiry but she didn't listen. He sighed and headed for home. If she wanted to go in there fire blazing like a soldier, he'd let her but he wouldn't compromise himself trying to convince her not to. Once Lunara got an idea into her head, she went with it with determination. He sat at the Forest's edge, hidden under a bush. Somehow he couldn't get himself to return to his tree. He knew their mothers would be worrying about them and if he returned home without her, how upset Shen would be.

Lunara was scared with all the fighting going on around her but she was determined that after sharing so much of her time with the Lizariaous and getting close to him that she didn't want to lose what they had built together. She was convinced he cared.

Meanwhile, the other side of the throng, Leida was fighting with speed and strength. Those Lizariaouses who had seen her be captured and held in Dyarkroeen either time were surprised by how she fought. All the training she'd had paid off. She dodged, hit, defended, even smacked needles back at her attackers. One needle even flew straight at a Lizariaous's eye, blinding her. None of them could hit her with their needles now she had the armour. It often bounced off her legs and she was thankful a million times over for wearing it. Her legs would have been taken out and she would have been badly poisoned and fallen long before now. She felt unstoppable and wanting the war to be over so she could free Diabloss made her fight even harder. She fought for Shernaron but most of all she fought for her beloved Diabloss. She knew if he was watching, he would be proud. The soldiers cursed her and growled in anger as they got frustrated over not being able to hit her.

A little way away Strassor saw how she fought and smiled. Otuss may be gone but he'd trained her well and it was showing in her battle prowess. She was fighting a whole group of them at once and dodging every needle shot at her with speed and skill. Like any female member of Diabloss's squadron, she relied on her lightweight speed to get away. She flew higher if it got too much. The Lizariaouses below her were getting badly burnt and had to fall back, allowing another group to attack her.

Zephirak was having problems of his own. There was a group of Gryphies above him, flaming him and as he fought, soldiers were protecting him, getting burned and shooting their needles at the attackers. These were the soldiers who used their needles up the fastest. If they hung around too much covering Zephirak, they

436

would get burnt to a crisp so they had to use their needles to try and get rid of the threat. Early on it had been easier. The Gryphies were easily taken out or driven back but now with the soldier rotations they were using, the Gryphies were wearing armour and could easily stop the needles and carry on flaming. The Lizariaouses stood against them until they died doing so. They were completely loyal to Zephirak and to die protecting him was a great honour. The Gryphies thought they were foolish dying while protecting such an awful leader. Still, it was up to them and if they died that was less Lizariaouses to worry about.

Zephirak himself had probably killed the most Gryphies. He was a raging ball of adrenalin and nothing was going to stop him. There was a reason he was the undisputed leader; he was the strongest and no one had been able to overthrow him. For the moment at least, it seemed as though the only way they would get a new leader was if he died or he passed leadership down to a favourite soldier. Neither was likely, chances were that he would go on to rule until he was either sick or old and weak and could be overthrown that way. And by that time, the whole of Dyarkroeen would be so brainwashed by him that they would never dare try it.

The Gryphies continued to attack him, the Lizariaouses to defend him.

Stervia was in trouble. She had been hit by a needle in her thigh and was having trouble keeping in the air. She'd managed to pull the needle out with one hand but the poison was already coursing through her veins and she wouldn't be able to stay in the air much longer. Kayto saw and came to her aide.

"There is a healer at the edge of the Forest, go there and see if they have any herbs that might help" he told her.

"I…I don't know if I can make it. My muscles are freezing up" she was sinking in the sky. Kayto managed to carry her to the Forest's edge and set her down there with the healer before he continued to fight. There was a huge gathering of Gryphies all around.

"Nearly all the soldiers from the High Mountains are here now" the healer told her. "The Sky Gryphies are now on alert. I'm not sure how the battle is going, the Gryphie who was returning every so often to tell us has been killed and no one else has given us an update."

Stervia shivered, the poison taking effect. Her temperature was normal but she felt freezing cold. Her muscles had all frozen up and her veins burned. "I think you may be too late, it got…got in my…leg too…deep" She lay on her side and panted. Now she felt boiling hot.

The healer sat beside her and stroked her head. "The darkness will come soon" he said "but then the light of Forever and you will fly high always my friend." He spoke of the death and how Gryphies believed it worked when they died. Dark of leaving the world and then the light of what they called "Forever", the afterlife and the endless bright sky that they would fly forever free in.

Stervia's breathing became slower and she looked up at him, her vision dying. She paused in her breathing, took one final deep breath, let it out and rested forever more. The healer shook his head sadly and moved her body out of the way. He was dreading the collecting of the bodies after this mighty battle. He wondered what they would do with them all. Have a funeral pyre he supposed. Gryphies didn't bury their dead; they burned them in a large grassy area near the edge of the Forest towards the east. The pyre from this battle would be the biggest ever though. He figured it may even need to be split into more than one burning.

Back in the heat of the battle, Iseera was fighting well. In reality though, she wanted to go and rescue her cousin. She missed Diabloss and knew that they would have a clear upper hand if he was there to help them. She couldn't go alone though, she needed help. She'd heard Kayto mention that it was more important to keep battling and not waste soldiers going to rescue Diabloss. He would be heavily guarded and it would be a fight they wouldn't need. Once the battle was won, then they could go rescue him. Iseera wondered though, what if the battle wasn't won because Diabloss wasn't helping. She had an idea that they could rescue him and use him as a secret weapon. He'd be rested fully from his trip to the High Mountains and so be full of fresh energy. Iseera still couldn't go on her own though and she couldn't see anyone who could come with her. Plus Keela wouldn't be happy about her leaving. She carried on fighting, thinking about it.

Lunara was watching Jadariol. Well, keeping an eye on his position at least. She couldn't bear to watch him and his friends taking down Gryphies but she dare not interfere or she might lose the chance to get him on their side. Mordred she saw fighting for the Gryphies. Mordred was fighting with anger and might; she had lost count of the Lizariaouses he'd killed. Right now he was surrounded by about seven of them and they all jumped on him at the same time. He threw them off one by one, usually with fatal injuries caused by a well aimed smack by his tail or slash by his claws. Being a commander and soldier, he knew all the places to hit in order to disable an opponent. Lunara watched him with interest.

Jadariol and the others had just taken out another opponent and Jadariol saw her.

"What are you doing here? Go back to the Forest you idiot!" he yelled.

"Why? Because you're worried I might get hurt? Why don't you join us? That guy has." Lunara pointed at Mordred who was battling fiercely. "You don't need to listen to Zephirak any more. Please Jadariol, if our friendship means anything at all, please stop fighting against us."

Jadariol said nothing but turned and ran off into the fray. In reality his mind was confused. He wanted to work hard for his master, the one he looked up to and admired but he wanted to remain friends with Lunara. Right now though, his loyalties lay with his own kind. Lunara sadly watched him go and flew into the sky. She remained hovering, hoping she would see him change his mind. He didn't though.

Meanwhile Iseera was still dwelling on her plan. She saw Leida zoom past and flamed a Lizariaous in the face who was aiming his needles at her. She looked around and saw Lunara.

"What are you doing here, kitten? Go back home! It's too dangerous." A few needles flew past to remind them both of this.

"I was trying to get my friend to change his mind and join us." Lunara replied.

"A Lizariaous? Not going to happen, kitto. Go home." Iseera swerved a needle and zoomed down at the attacker.

Lunara growled in anger. Just because she was young, they thought she shouldn't be there. The young Lizariaouses fought alongside the adults, why couldn't she help defend the land she loved? Everyone counted as far as she was concerned. However, she knew she was small and weaker than an adult. She watched the battle a moment, then she knew what to do. She might

440

not stand much of a chance in battle but she knew who would and what she must do to help out. She turned and headed for Dyarkroeen. Hiryasis had been keeping an eye on her and saw her leave. He followed her a little way off, wondering why she was flying away, into enemy territory.

Down below, another rotation took place as the current Gryphie soldiers flew off to rest and new ones flew in to fight.

Leida met up with Strassor and Kayto.

"There have been many fatalities; the numbers of Lizariaouses don't seem to be going down very fast. This is our second rotation and still there are many of them. What's worse is a few nearly made it into the Forest" said Kayto.

"We have to keep going, we'll carry on, maybe rotate a little faster or something" replied Leida.

"Ay, they won't be getting' us so easily" growled Strassor.

Kayto shook his head. "It's those damn needles. Even our fastest movers are at risk, because of the sheer numbers of the needles. We can only hope they'll run out. They seem to be doing a little rotation of their own. Already I see the Lizariaouses who lost their needles at the beginning of this battle are sitting out in order to grow them back. It's not a very fast process and growing back the entire length of a needle usually takes a sun cycle to do but they've nearly all grown back long enough lengths of them to fire effectively now and they'll be coming back into battle soon."

"Well then there be only one thing ter do. We'll attack 'em while they be restin' and can't hit us. We can pounce on their backs and kill 'em that way" said Strassor.

"Yes, you and Odax take out the ones who are resting. They can't take out our resting soldiers because they're in the Forest and safe while they rest. The Lizariaouses have nowhere to go to rest other than a way away and sit out." Leida said, pondering.

Strassor nodded and flew off to get Odax so they could put their plan in motion.

"Stervia has died" Kayto said shortly.

Leida's face clouded. "I knew we'd lose friends in this, we may even lose our own lives but it's all we can do. Keep the fire blazing, Kayto!"

Kayto saluted and they both flew back into battle.

Iseera had gotten caught up in the fray now and her thoughts were far from getting Diabloss back. She knew that no one would go with her. She figured she should wait. Her commander wouldn't be too happy about her flying off anyway.

Luckily she needn't have worried; Lunara and Hiryasis were well on their way to Dyarkroeen.

Mordred was still trying to make his way to Zephirak. He charged through soldiers but got thrown back by two large ones. One was Croter. Mordred and Croter sized each other up, growling and snarling.

"So, you turned against us then, how foolish. Because now you will die." Croter lunged for Mordred and Mordred jumped to one side.

"You know, you were never that fast. Carrying too much weight, Croter. You should've stayed a guard, a nice simple job where you didn't need to move around too much!" Mordred laughed and dodged again.

Croter roared in rage. "Why you little grikhead! I'm bigger and stronger than you and I'll bring you down!"

"You might be bigger and stronger but you're not faster. There's a reason I was a commander. I can think on my feet, I'm fit and I have the speed needed to battle

442

effectively!" Mordred dodged him and lunged at him, gripping one of Croter's needles in a clawed paw and tearing it out. Croter roared in annoyance more so than pain and spun around at Mordred as he took out another needle. "You won't need these where you're going!" Mordred snarled and his tail swung round to hit Croter in the face, his sharp black tail spade tearing across the Lizariaous's eyes and blinding him. He was easy to take out then and Mordred wasted no time in doing so before galloping on to the next challenger. He had hardly a scratch on him. He'd fought better fighters than these and now he knew if anyone had the skill and power needed to take out Zephirak, it was him.

Lunara had nearly made it to Dyarkroeen but she was pretty tired. Although her flying had gotten better and stronger, she still didn't have the stamina and soon landed to walk. Hiryasis followed, not letting her know he was there just yet. Lunara wondered how she would save Diabloss. She wasn't even sure where he was but she presumed and rightly too, that wherever he was, there would be guards there. As she neared the outskirts of Dyarkroeen, she started to feel just a little apprehensive. It had felt like such a good idea at the time but now the slow realisation was dawning on her that she probably had no chance against Lizariaous guards. The sun had past its highest peak in the sky. Lunara knew that they needed Diabloss and she was determined to face all the odds and do her best as she had been taught in battle training. So she carried on.

Things weren't looking too good in Shernaron. A few sniper Lizariaouses had found if they were careful and had good aim, they could shoot down the sentries at the Forest's edge and were slowly picking them off one by one. Others flew down to stop them but more and more

443

soldiers were appearing to help shoot them down. Since the sentries were for the most part, unmoving, they made easy targets and soon there were only a few left. A few of the Lizariaous soldiers headed into the Forest where they were greeted with angry guards and forced back out again. Further down, more tried to get in and more of the huge throng were making their way to the Forest now that most of the Gryphie sentries had been taken out.

All the resting Gryphie soldiers were brought out to help defend now and the Lizariaouses were slowly manoeuvred out again.

"They're getting in! Quick! Defend the Forest!" called Leida. More Gryphies flew in to attack. Using their fire around the Forest was risky but luckily the Lizariaouses weren't so good at aiming their needles either, since there was so much foliage everywhere and they didn't have a clear shot. Teeth and claws were used and fur and scales flew.

Kayto and the squadron flew in roaring in anger and telling the enemy to get out. The enemy of course didn't listen.

Elsewhere, Zephirak saw their progress and grinned to himself. It was working. They would have the Forest under control by moon cycle! He fought with even more ferocity at this thought and made his way to the Forest, still flanked and covered by soldiers.

Strassor saw him moving closer and flew in. He was nearly as big as Diabloss and could pack a fair punch. He knew it was now or never to stop Zephirak. He wouldn't be such an easy target to hit or fight under cover of the trees. He landed before Zephirak and roared.

"Yeh'll hafta get past me first! Bring it on Zephirak!" he roared. Zephirak lunged at him without pausing and they fought savagely. Sadly, Zephirak was still surrounded by those soldiers and they worked with him as a unit. Strassor needed help. Odax was just finishing off the rest of the resting soldiers and was too far away to hear his father call in the noise of the battle. Strassor had to fall back; he had no other choice unless he wanted to die. Already he had deep gashes on his side and legs from Zephirak's helmet and tail armour. He needed to get that helmet off Zephirak somehow. He hovered above, trying to get close enough to grab the blade in his hands and pull the helmet off. However, the soldiers immediately fired needles at him whenever he tried. When they ran out of needles, more just came in and shot them. Strassor fell back again. It was no use! He needed a whole group of Gryphies but they were all busy defending themselves and the Forest and all the spare soldiers had been brought out so there was no one who could help. Strassor roared in anger and defiance.

In Dyarkroeen, Lunara had found the cave where Diabloss was being kept. It was Zephirak's cavern again. She flew around without being noticed by Rondo or the other guards. And there were a *lot* of other guards. Lunara found the hole in the roof of the cavern and flew down, peering inside. Diabloss was being kept further back. Lunara flew through the hole and landed inside the cavern, looking around and keeping close to the wall. She found Diabloss but there was a guard stationed nearby. Somehow she needed to free Diabloss. She crept quietly along the floor near the wall, keeping well in. Nearing Diabloss, she made a soft murring kitten sound. He looked around and saw her and she headed closer.

The guard looked around at the sound and Diabloss mimicked it as best he could to make it look like he'd made it. The guard snorted at him.

Lunara crept behind Diabloss and worked to chew through his bindings. It was hard but she managed to free his tail. Suddenly she felt something beside her and saw the face of Hiry smiling at her. He'd flown in to help. She looked grateful and they worked on the bindings together, freeing Diabloss's wings. Diabloss helped by using his tail to work on the bindings on his legs. He was still shackled and muzzled though. He removed the muzzle once his hands were free. The shackles wouldn't be so easy to remove though.

They looked at each other. Lunara and Hiryasis tried to get the shackles loose but they found it very hard. There was no key, they had to be pulled apart and the kittens didn't have the strength. Diabloss used his hands to pull apart the shackles on his legs. They made a chinking sound and the guard looked round again. Diabloss bowed his head so the guard wouldn't notice he wasn't muzzled. The guard growled and turned away again. Now the shackles on his wrists wouldn't be so easy. He managed to get his tail spade under one of them and used that and his hand to pull it apart. Chinking again. The guard looked round and Diabloss bowed his head, doing his best to make it look like he was still bound and shackled. The guard growled and walked over to him. He'd noticed the lack of muzzle.

He placed a clawed hand under Diabloss's chin and forced his head up to look at him.

"Where's your muzzle?" he demanded but suddenly Lunara and Hiryasis were upon him, grabbing hold of his sides and digging in their claws. He let go of Diabloss and roared, spinning around. Diabloss freed his other hand in the commotion and flamed the guard. The kittens jumped off but all three heard the other guards piling into the cavern to see what the fuss was about. How would they get out? The kittens could make it out of the hole in the roof but Diabloss was too big to open his wings inside the cavern and fly out of course so he'd have to get out the conventional way.

Lunara called Hiry and they rushed towards the oncoming Lizariaouses before Diabloss could stop them. They managed to run straight through the guards, between their legs while yelling rude things to them to get them to give chase, which of course they all did. Diabloss saw this and headed out a little way behind them so they wouldn't notice him and come back in again.

He reached the entrance of the cavern but saw with horror that the kittens were in trouble. They were surrounded by guards, having been ambushed by the ones who were outside. Rondo was questioning them.

"What are you doing here? Are you spies? Answer or we'll kill you!" He aimed all his needles at them threateningly. Lunara and Hiryasis shivered in fear, cuddled together. Rondo was intimidating when angered. He had a lot of battle scars and they could see he had made many kills. He was also an older soldier.

"Hey! Maybe you should start caring more that I've escaped than bothering with those harmless kittens!" roared Diabloss from on top of Zephirak's cavern. He spread his wings, blocking out the sun and causing his mighty shadow to fall on the ground and cover the guards in shade. They all roared and rushed for him. However, one of them still had hold of Lunara and Hiryasis. Diabloss thought they would release them when they saw he'd escaped. He hated being wrong. He roared and flamed the guards but he aimed for the one with the kittens. The guard held onto them tighter. Then the kittens started struggling and flaming him too, burning his legs so he had to let them go.

"Damn Gryphies!" he yelled, leaping back and shaking his legs in irritation and pain. The other guards all lunged at the kittens, who ran in terror while Diabloss tried to protect them with his fire so they could take to the sky.

Seeing that Diabloss was trying to protect the kittens, some of the guards aimed their needles for them instead. Diabloss flew in front of them, using his body as a shield.

"Leave them! It's me you want!" he roared.

"Oh no, we want the young ones. They'll make a good snack" laughed an unpleasant female Lizariaous.

Lunara and Hiryasis took to the sky and headed away from Dyarkroeen with relief. Diabloss joined them.

"Who sent you? And why would they send kittens to do a soldier's work?" asked Diabloss.

"We came ourselves. We wanted you to be free so you could fight with us. Things aren't looking very good. The Lizariaouses are getting closer to the Forest and they don't seem to be stopping" replied Lunara.

"You came yourselves? Just like that?" Diabloss was shocked that they would risk their lives like that.

"Yeah, we aren't very good at fighting because we're too..." Lunara cringed and sighed at the word, "weak" she said. "So we thought we'd come rescue you instead because we really wanted to help. Although I didn't know Hiryasis was following me but I'm glad he did!" Lunara smiled warmly at Hiryasis and he blushed, trying to hide it.

"Well," he said, "I wanted to make sure you were safe. You couldn't take on all those guards by yourself. Plus it's what a *true* friend would do."

Lunara nodded. She knew he was her true friend anyway and she also knew that remark was a poke at Jadariol.

"Have there been many casualties?" asked Diabloss.

"I don't know...I never saw anyone I knew die. There's a Lizariaous fighting with us though, a grey one with a scratched eye. I don't know why he's fighting with us" Lunara told him.

"Hmm, he sounds like the one who told me Zephirak had Leida. I think he's one of Zephirak's closest and highest ranking soldiers. Why would he be fighting for us? That makes no sense unless he wanted us to trust him so he could turn on us like that little red youngster did. I don't trust them and neither does Leida. I wonder why she'd let him fight for us. They're too sneaky." Diabloss pondered this as they flew. The kittens were getting tired again so he let them ride on his back.

"You should see Leida! She's totally taking control! The others all call her Sir" said Lunara.

Diabloss smiled. His mate had matured.

"And you should see her fight!" put in Hiryasis. "She's amazing and really fast too."

"I'd expect nothing less of her" said Diabloss proudly. "In these seasons she's learned and grown so much. She escaped the guards here earlier when they had both of us held prisoner. It was very resourceful; she used her tail to cut her bindings and flew off to warn everyone. If she hadn't, the Lizariaouses would have taken us by surprise and would already have the Forest under their control by now."

"I don't like all this fighting. I've never seen anyone killed in front of me before and it's scary" said Hiryasis.

"Don't worry, we'll soon be back and I'll put a stop to all of it" growled Diabloss and flew faster. He dreaded the state their territory would be in when they got back.

He didn't worry for nothing either, back in Shernaron, the Lizariaouses had broken into the Forest fully now. The Gryphies couldn't hold them back and now that it was difficult to use fire against them in case they burned down the trees, they had to try and get ahead of them in order to push them back. The forest guards were already ahead of them and did their best to kill and disable as many as they could but once a few made it through, the others behind them found it a lot easier. Zephirak had reached the Forest too now. The rest of the army carried on fighting outside, keeping Gryphies busy so they couldn't help the others rid the Forest of the Lizariaouses.

"Yes!! We've made it! Strike them down! Kill all who oppose you! Take their Forest, break through to the centre! This place will soon be MINE!!" Zephirak erupted into cruel laughter and charged ahead, his bladed helmet striking attacking Gryphies away.

Strassor, Leida, Odax and the rest of Diabloss's squadron entered the Forest ahead of the Lizariaouses and lay in wait. Up ahead they saw the flash of wings and needles as the other Gryphies fought to push the Lizariaouses back.

"It's not working!" yelled Leida. "They're too strong, too determined and too many!"

"We mustn't stop, we mustn't let them reach the centre, that be where the kittens are and they could easily threaten to kill 'em if we don't surrender. We can't be lettin' that happen!" Strassor growled, watching up ahead carefully. "We must fight harder than we've done before. All the soldiers from here and them there mountains are fighting now. We need the Sky Gryphies to help. Their stupid poisoned needles have killed off too many of us."

450

That was the problem, the poisoned needles. Leida wished more than ever that Diabloss was there to fight with them. He was immune to their poison; it would have no effect on him. She wasn't personally sure if he was entirely immune or not but it was still a strength and they really needed that right now. That was the main reason Zephirak wanted to keep him away. With his strength, stamina and resistance, he was a truly powerful fighter.

They saw the Lizariaouses get closer and roaring in rage, they charged in to fight.

Mordred was also in the Forest trying to drive the Lizariaouses back. He'd followed Zephirak. Still he couldn't get close enough for a strike but under cover of the Forest, Zephirak's guards couldn't keep so close to him, nor did they need to because the Gryphies weren't flying overhead flaming them. The Gryphies could climb the trees and drop down on the soldiers to take them out but none of them wanted to be skewered on the needles.

Now Mordred could get closer to his target. Soldiers still flanked Zephirak and they continued to fight as a unit. Mordred just had to wait for his moment and rush in there.

The first soldiers who had broken through and so were the furthest in had nearly reached the centre. Again, more guards defended and attacked them.

In the trees, calls of terror and distress went out as mothers heard the fray getting closer. Kittens shivered in the hollows of their trees and Mystik stood agitated at the entrance of her big old tree. It would end here, they would take down the Forest and no one could stop them. She felt sick. None of this would have happened if it wasn't for her thinking that saving a life was the right thing to do or trusting an enemy in the hopes it would make everything better was the wise thing to do. She

451

threw back her head and let out a sorrowful roar as the enemy closed in.

Suddenly another roar joined hers, a mighty, powerful roar. Her ears pricked up. Could it be? It was! Diabloss had reached the Forest and he was letting everyone know. She climbed to the top of her tree just in time to see the deep green half breed dive into the trees followed by angry roars which turned into screams of horror and terror and sounds of struggling.

Diabloss flew straight at a pack of attacking soldiers and took them all down in a fit of rage at being held captive while his kind needed him. Now was the time to make up on all the action he'd missed. The enemy, completely taken by surprise, was stunned at first. Diabloss took down a lot of them with ease. Others lunged at him in defence of their dead and he took those down too.

"GET OUT OF MY FOREST!!" he roared, his tail smacking a couple of soldiers flying while his wings swept up and hit a couple of others aside with ease. He lunged his head down and broke the neck of a soldier who was headed right for him. Diabloss didn't need his fire; he worked on sheer strength alone here.

Zephirak had heard his roar and paused, listening. No, how had he escaped? Now Zephirak knew he had to get to the centre of the Forest as fast as possible and put his plan into motion. Strassor had been right. Threatening the young in the Forest was exactly what Zephirak planned to do. He roared for his soldiers to follow. Now they wasted no time fighting and tried to make it through by barging past opponents.

Kayto and Strassor appeared before him, growling.

"Go back, Zephirak! Get out of here or we'll kill you." They spoke as one.

"Never! I've got this far, you think I'd really want to waste this hard work? I think not." Zephirak flicked his head slightly and the soldiers with him lunged at Strassor and Kayto, keeping them busy while Zephirak charged past them.

Elsewhere in the Forest, Lunara and Hiryasis had returned to their trees at Diabloss's orders. He told them they had helped enough and done well, there was nothing else to do so they must return home so their mothers knew they were safe. Needless to say both mothers were overjoyed that their kittens weren't dead. Shen told Lunara off strictly until Lunara told her what she and Hiry had done. Shen was still angry but she was also proud of her baby for being so brave.

Jadariol had parted from the other young Lizariaouses and searched for Zephirak. He ran through the Forest keeping a low profile. This was fairly easy but his deep red skin looked out of place in the Forest and he'd already had one confrontation from a Gryphie who he'd managed to shoot in the belly. He had most of his needles left. He had been wise in using his friends to bring down the Gryphies and then just breaking their necks, thus saving his needles. He saw Zephirak up ahead as he charged past Strassor, Kayto and the Lizariaouses they fought.

"Uncle Zephirak!" yelled Jadariol running up to him.

"Ah Jadariol! I hope you have taken down many of those pathetic creatures" growled Zephirak as they ran.

"Yes Master! My friends and I worked as a unit like you told us to"

"Good, good. I'm heading for the centre of the Forest. That is where a lot of young Gryphies being kept safe. They will die unless the Forest is passed over to me. Other soldiers are following me as they can. We're nearly there boy! Soon this place will be mine! We must get there before Diabloss catches up" Zephirak ran faster at this comment.

"Diabloss? How did he get free?" asked Jadariol.

"I have no grikking idea but it doesn't matter. He won't be able to stop me; he's too busy fighting my army." Zephirak chuckled.

"Will you actually kill any of the youngsters?" asked Jadariol.

"Only if they don't co-operate with me. I'll kill a few to prove my point. Once they see I'm deadly serious, they will co-operate, oh yes!" Zephirak smirked cruelly.

Jadariol felt a bit worried. He hoped Lunara was still in the Outlands. "But only if they won't obey us right?" he asked.

"Yes, I won't kill any unless they won't come quietly. Why do you ask? You don't need to care about it. They may be young like you but they are nothing but worthless scum who don't know the true meaning of battle and fear."

"Yes Master." Jadariol replied shortly. He trusted Zephirak to keep his word and only hoped that the Gryphies would listen.

Diabloss had taken out a large chunk of the invading army. Leida had heard his roar when he arrived and couldn't believe her ears. She headed for the source of the roar as fast as she could and soon found him, joining to fight alongside him.

He looked pleased to see her. "I hear you've been doing a great job with your battle moves" he said.

"See for yourself" she replied and hit a few needles aside with her legs, swerving a charging Lizariaous, tripping him with her tail and cuffing him across the face with a back foot as he fell. He got up and headed for her again, leaping towards her. As he leaped into the air, she spun round, her tail sweeping out and the blade on the end slicing into his belly. He fell, bloody and sprawling.

Diabloss watched, speechless and immensely impressed.

"Wow, nice job!" he said.

She merely nodded and stood tall.

"Zephirak is heading for the centre of the Forest, we have to cut him off" she told him.

"Then let's go!" growled Diabloss and they headed to the centre of the Forest together. Soldiers tried to stop them along the way but they took them down. Leida was happy now her mate was there beside her. Finally she got to battle alongside him; the greatest fighter in Shernaron. Now she knew she was a fighter worthy of calling herself his mate and this made her proud of herself. There was no more self consciousness or under confidence. She knew she had what it took now to be a leader and a fighter.

Diabloss called to a couple of other Gryphies to follow them as they headed for the centre of the Forest. They would need backup because chances were that Zephirak would also have backup. There was no way he'd attempt to take over by himself.

Strassor, Odax and Kayto wanted to go as well but they were too busy keeping other soldiers away so kept up their fighting against them.

Mystik knew Zephirak was closing in even before he arrived. She felt fearful and the terrified cries all around her didn't help ease her nerves. She remained sat at the entrance of her tree, looking out into the clearing and at the parting in the trees she assumed Zephirak would come through.

A Lizariaous appeared at the very place she was watching. But it wasn't Zephirak, it was Mordred. A guard went for him until he realised who it was. Mordred stationed himself near the parting in the trees.

"Make sure all your youngsters are safe and hidden" he told the Gryphies watching from the trees. "I will take Zephirak down as soon as he enters here." He positioned himself and watched for his leader. He felt relieved he had reached the centre of the Forest first.

"And what are you watching for, traitor?" A voice behind him spoke and he spun round. There was Zephirak and Jadariol. They had entered through the trees the other side. Two more Lizariaouses leaped out either side of them and snarled at Mordred.

Behind Mordred, Leida and Diabloss arrived. They halted when they saw Zephirak.

"Get out of our Forest" Diabloss rumbled angrily. "You have one more chance to turn and leave now. I suggest you use it and go before we kill you and your little sidekick there."

Jadariol snarled and snapped at Diabloss in defiance.

"You know I'm not going to leave. Nothing will stop me now, Diabloss. Gryphies! Surrender or I'll kill your kittens. For each time you refuse, a kitten will die. I wonder, how many will lose their lives until you decide to be wise and give in to me." He flicked his head slightly and one of the soldiers with him started to scale a tree to get a kitten. Mordred shot needles at him to try and knock him down but the other soldier lunged at Mordred and fought him viciously.

"You leave them out of this! They are nothing to do with it" growled Diabloss.

"Oh but they are. Each of those kittens is a future soldier in my army. They are born to be raised to fight. I will have a Gryphie army to take over the rest of Shernaron. Those who do not side with me will die. Of course if too many of you decide on that path, your species may well be wiped into extinction so I would think very carefully about what you decide." Zephirak grinned cruelly.

The mother of the kitten in the tree was attacking the Lizariaous soldier, who shot needles at her. She managed to knock him out of the tree but he simply climbed up again. Leida rushed to help, grabbing the Lizariaous's tail in her teeth and pulling him down again so he turned on her instead.

"Leave them alone" snarled Mordred. His face was bloody and the hapless soldier he had been fighting lay at his feet dead. "I'm tired of all these seasons of you trying to start a war with them. We killed Mettalika; we stopped the senseless deaths of our kind so let's stop the senseless deaths of theirs. You are no better than she was. So she killed your mate, you've paid the Gryphies back one hundredfold for that. I don't want to raise a family under your control and that was why I sided with them. I and a lot of others are tired of your killing. You are corrupt and insane. It's all gone to your head and I won't take any more. I will kill you here and now and I will put a stop to this. You were given enough chances and it seems that the only way this will stop is with your death. I was your favourite commander but I will also be your destroyer."

"You really think you can take me on? I am stronger, faster, bigger and more powerful than you can ever imagine. You have no chance. Don't throw your life away you pathetic fool." Zephirak took a few steps forward and Mordred reciprocated, rattling his needles and snarling.

"You might be able to take him on but I doubt you would stand a chance against *me*" Diabloss growled, stepping up beside Mordred.

"Or me." Leida roared; having killed the soldier she had been fighting. Zephirak and Jadariol faced Leida, Diabloss and Mordred. Behind Zephirak, a couple more soldiers arrived and waited for commands.

Zephirak wasn't stupid though and he knew he wouldn't stand a good chance against Diabloss. He flicked his tail and another soldier scaled a tree.

"As I said, all you have to do is come willingly. My soldiers outnumber yours and they will kill you on mass, I have no need to even lift a claw to defeat you. As for you, Mordred you will be the first to die. You want to kill me? Then I will fight you to the death. Your death that is!" Zephirak laughed spitefully.

There was a sudden shriek from in the trees and the soldier came back down, holding a kitten in his jaws. The kitten struggled and called out for help but the soldier kept a good grip on her and offered her to Zephirak who grabbed her by the scruff in his claws.

Jadariol glanced round and suddenly stared in horror. Zephirak had Lunara!

"OK, enough talk. Surrender or I'll kill this kitten. It's up to you. Do you wish to allow her mother to see her die before her eyes?" Zephirak held Lunara out, aiming a needle at her belly.

Mordred went to lunge forward but Zephirak gave him a look. "You try anything and she dies. You only have one chance to save her. Diabloss, surrender. Oh, and pretending to surrender and then attacking me won't work either, I will keep hold of her until the rest of my army arrives and I can ensure you will all obey."

Leida was overcome with rage but she remained where she was, growling angrily, unable to do anything since if she tried it, Lunara would die.

Diabloss snarled at him with sheer hatred. "There is no way you can control us. We will simply wait for the right time and reclaim our leadership over Shernaron."

"Then more kittens will die. Decision time Diabloss. Surrender; yes or no." Zephirak moved his needle to point blank range. It would kill Lunara instantly.

"NO!" With a sudden cry, Jadariol flew at Zephirak, charging into the side of him and knocking him off balance. He dropped Lunara who ran off and hid.

Zephirak found his balance and spun to face Jadariol.

"WHAT? What did you just do?" His red eyes were flaming with rage now.

"I don't want you to hurt Lunara. I don't care about the others but...but not her."

Before Jadariol could react, Zephirak had his claws around the smaller Lizariaous's throat. "How DARE you, after I took you under my command, you have the total utter cheek to do this? You have become soft from hanging around with them so long. I'll kill you instead." His grip tightened.

Jadariol was terrified now. He had acted out of reflex and not considered the consequences. More soldiers arrived as well as a couple of Gryphie guards who tried to fight them and force them back into the trees.

Mordred charged at Zephirak, fighting off soldiers who tried to defend him. Leida and Diabloss joined in the fight now.

In his fear, Jadariol shot out needles, trying to hit Zephirak. One lodged in his neck and Zephirak pulled it out angrily.

"This will be the last thing you see, traitorous little kid!" Zephirak's voice had lowered to a rumbling growl of sheer anger, his face contorted into a hideous malicious snarl. Jadariol was really terrified now and he whimpered and moaned in fear.

Suddenly, Mordred slammed into Zephirak and attacked him full on. Jadariol was released and forgotten as the grey and brown Lizariaouses slashed and sparred.

Diabloss and Leida had driven off the rest of the attacking soldiers who now rushed to the aid of their leader.

Leida stepped forward but Diabloss held her back.

"No, it's their battle, not ours. Let Mordred fight him with the honour of a warrior. He needs to do this; it's why he's here."

"But what if he dies and we could've helped?" Leida questioned.

"Then he dies fighting for what he knows is right and he will have a proud death. In that case, I will take Zephirak down but for now we must wait."

They stood at the ready nearby.

Mordred fended off the attacking soldiers with his tail as he fought Zephirak.

"Let me kill him!" Zephirak called to his soldiers and they reluctantly fell back. Jadariol had found Lunara and they sat together hidden under some large bushes as the fight went on.

Zephirak had been right; he was bigger and more powerful than the lean and swift Mordred. In a true fight between two Lizariaouses, the bigger and stronger one always wins. Mordred kept going, fuelled by his honour and wanting this war to stop. He would never surrender or give in to such a corrupt and hateful leader.

Chapter 33
Final Showdown

Zephirak was enjoying the battle, he was even laughing at Mordred's fighting skills. He allowed Mordred to fly at him and knocked him back every time. Mordred knew that if he wanted to win, he must think strategically. The main problem was Zephirak's size and weight. When he hit, he hit with power.

"You'll never defeat me, Mordred. There's a reason I'm the leader of the Lizariaouses and those who come up against me die at my claws."

"Don't bet on it!" growled back Mordred and lunged at Zephirak again. He narrowly missed being hit by the blade on Zephirak's helmet. Zephirak swung his steel tail round and caught Mordred's leg in the tail spade at the end. The steel tail spade closed around Mordred's leg and started to cut into it. Mordred struggled and whipped his tail round to try and throw Zephirak off balance but Zephirak wasn't falling for that again and he stayed clear, dodging each time and closing the tail spade around Mordred's leg more. Mordred had seen his opponents lose their legs to this tactic and he didn't want to be the next victim. Mordred grabbed the spade in his claws and tried to pull it apart to release his leg but he couldn't budge it. He didn't call for help though, this was *his* battle and only by fighting alone would he prove to himself his evil master could be defeated. Zephirak pulled his tail upwards, taking Mordred's leg with it and dragging him along the ground.

"Seems Mettalika was useful after all" he chuckled and watched his hapless opponent struggle in the dirt.

Mordred managed to get close to Zephirak's front leg and clamped his jaws around it, biting down hard and causing Zephirak to scream out in pain.

Unfortunately, it also made him close the tail spade on Mordred's leg completely and cut into it. Mordred's pained cries mixed with Zephirak's but Mordred didn't give up, he whipped his tail around and slashed the spade down Zephirak's side deeply. Zephirak snarled and lowered his head down to Mordred, trying to reach his neck so he could break it.

Mordred moved around as best he could. With a roar and in one powerful motion, Zephirak pulled Mordred by his leg, making him let go and throwing him into the air with his steel tail. Mordred crashed into a tree and fell beneath it. It was Mystik's tree and she ran inside in fear. Zephirak's leg was torn through to the bone where Mordred's jaws had been pulled off it and he panted and limped a little, holding his leg up and snarling at Mordred.

"Is that the best you have? Grabbing me by the leg and hoping that would disable me? Ha!" Zephirak gazed hatefully as Mordred got to his feet.

It's what you did thought Mordred.

Being thrown by his leg hasn't done any good and he also held that back leg up a little. Blood splashed to the ground from the deep wound caused by the tail spade.

"I will kill you!" roared Mordred and charged at Zephirak. Zephirak stood his ground, the blade on his helmet lowered. Mordred swerved just in time and flew at him from the side; Zephirak dodged and turned the blade on him again. Mordred rushed at him again, jumping over his head while the blade of the helmet was still lowered and as he did so, grabbing it with his claws and pulling the helmet off Zephirak's head. Mordred threw it to one side and Leida grabbed it swiftly so Zephirak couldn't get it back again.

Zephirak roared in rage at having his main weapon removed and charged at Mordred, who dodged him. Now Mordred just had to stay away from that tail. The tail spade could easily slice through Mordred's legs if Zephirak wanted it to happen. Mordred wondered why Zephirak hadn't done that before but he was thankful he hadn't. He supposed Zephirak wanted a good fight that lasted so he could show the onlookers why he was a superior fighter. He concentrated on rushing at Zephirak and trying to lay a little damage on him each time. Now he was working out how to get rid of that tail armour in the same way. It wouldn't just pull off like the helmet. Suddenly he felt a searing pain go through his tail and he spun round to see what had caused it. His tail was no longer there. Zephirak had sliced it off with his tail spade. Zephirak laughed cruelly at him.

"That was what you wanted to do to me, wasn't it? Ha ha you fool! Now you have no tail you freak!"

Mordred gritted his teeth and snarled in pain and anger.

Over by the trees, Leida hid her eyes when she saw Mordred's tail sliced off. Diabloss tried to roar in warning but it all happened so fast, there was no way to warn Mordred in time.

Lunara had buried her face in Jadariol's chest and was shaking in fear, not wanting to see any more. Jadariol solemnly watched, now seeing the true colours of his "master". He growled low in his throat and wished with all his heart he was bigger and could help.

The other soldiers from both species watched. The fight was still going on in the Forest; there were roars and crashes all around them. The others still fighting had no idea their leader was now fighting to the death. No more had broken through because when they tried to, they saw Zephirak fighting and the other soldiers sat merely watching and wisely stayed out of the way.

Without his own tail spade to lay damage into Zephirak, Mordred was running out of options. It was really hard to get near enough to damage Zephirak with his claws and now he had to be more careful of that tail armour than ever.

"Face it, you're losing!" Zephirak smirked.

"I might be, but that doesn't mean I'll give up!" snarled back Mordred and charged at him again. In agitation, he shot a needle at Zephirak, aiming for his face but he missed. Zephirak just laughed.

"Like that would stop me! You're more of a fool than I thought."

Mordred seethed at him and suddenly had an idea. He broke off a needle and held it in his jaws, standing his ground facing Zephirak.

"And what are you going to do with that? Poke me to death??" Zephirak laughed his head off, his sharp sickle like teeth glinting. It had gotten quite dark now as moon cycle was fast drawing in. Zephirak and his soldiers had this planned though since if the Gryphies wouldn't give up during the sun cycle; in the darkness they would easily be confused.

Mordred watched Zephirak carefully. He made no move to get near him, he just watched him at distance. He was building up his stamina and power, secretly resting until he felt the time was right. Also, the longer he remained there not doing anything, the more Zephirak's mind was working out the possible things Mordred *might* do. And the more he thought, the more the ideas became implausible. This was what Mordred wanted; he wanted Zephirak to slowly become confused.

"Well? Come on and fight me then! Or are you scared now you have no tail and look like a freak!" Zephirak laughed. But his body language told Mordred he was starting to feel nervous. Still, Mordred stood and stared him down, not blinking, just staring at him in a strange way while he held the needle in his mouth. Zephirak didn't make any attempt to make the first move since he had no idea what Mordred had planned and it would be too risky. For once, he was becoming unsure and a little nervous.

Mordred smirked and remained still where he was.

"Come ON!! Or I'll come over there and kill you myself." Zephirak snarled.

Mordred still watched him unmoving and silent.

Zephirak put one foot forward towards him and suddenly Mordred shot out at him, charging towards Zephirak full speed and holding his needle like a lance. Zephirak hadn't been expecting this. From Mordred's body language it looked like he might start circling and sizing him up. How wrong he was.

Zephirak managed to dodge at the last moment but Mordred came again and again, running around him in circles, judging his time and distance carefully. His injured leg burned with pain but he knew it was now or never.

Suddenly he saw an opening and went for it. Zephirak had raised himself up a bit, trying to get a move in to hit Mordred aside with his front legs. Exposing a bit of his chest for just a moment gave Mordred the chance he needed. Mordred charged around, targeting Zephirak's chest as fast as he could and plunging the needle deep into it, running it through and piercing Zephirak's heart. He plunged it in as deep as he could before Zephirak tried to hit him aside. Mordred leaped back and watched as Zephirak fell.

Zephirak's eyes stared at him with contempt and hatred, nothing Mordred had ever seen in his life had more malice and loathing in it than Zephirak's final expression as he died.

Mordred stood, panting, still staring at Zephirak. He was half afraid the cruel leader of Dyarkroeen would get back up again.

All around, the watching soldiers looked on in silence, unable to believe what had just taken place before their eyes. Leida and Diabloss, Jadariol, even Lunara looked up when the silence fell. Zephirak lay in a heap a little way away from Mordred with the needle sticking out of his chest at an uncomfortable angle.

"Zephirak is dead!" roared Mordred. "The corrupt ruler has fallen. Now I, Mordred will rule over Dyarkroeen!"

The soldiers just stood and watched, it was hard for it to sink in to them since most of them thought that Zephirak was practically immortal and certainly unbeatable.

Diabloss and Leida's roars joined Mordred's as they let the Forest and all around know that the Gryphies had won. All around, Gryphies and Lizariaouses stopped fighting, Gryphies' roars joining with Diabloss, Leida and Mordred.

It was finally over! No more would Zephirak rule over the Lizariaouses and cause the Gryphies to cower in fear.

Karnos rushed into the clearing and saw Zephirak; his face went blank with shock and horror.

Mordred lowered his head and stared him down, challenging him. Karnos stepped back; he was not one to argue. Anyone who could defeat Zephirak must be a worthy opponent and a powerful leader.

Jadariol left his hiding place and went to his father. Karnos was happy to see him.

No one said much. They weren't sure what to say, it was a relief for all of them now, aside from those who truly believed in Zephirak but many of them had died in battle. The remaining ones stayed out of the way, angry and snarling that the one they had looked up to and revered had been killed.

Shen leaped down from her tree and went to fetch Lunara who ran to her mother in relief.

Diabloss let Mordred have his moment of glory before he spoke.

"Well done, Mordred. I hope that you will take the rest of the army and go back to Dyarkroeen to live in peace with us now. There will be no more killing of my kind, am I right in assuming this?" He looked Mordred straight in the eyes.

Mordred was still breathing heavily. "Yes, we won't kill your kind again. Anyone who is found killing a Gryphie will be put to death. I don't want this starting up again, ever. This has caused both our kinds nothing but pain and misery. I would not be a good leader if I allowed it to start up again. If anyone here still thinks Zephirak was right and are still loyal to him, they are not welcome back in Dyarkroeen. I will not have traitors in our midst." He stared pointedly at Jadariol with his scarred eye and cocked his head to one side. Jadariol looked right back and hung his head. He knew after seeing how Zephirak truly was, that he had lead the young Lizariaous on all this time and Jadariol felt foolish and stupid for trusting and believing in Zephirak.

Karnos put a paw on Jadariol's shoulder. "There will be no more betrayal, Sir. You have our promise on that and our word." He saluted Mordred.

Mordred smiled. "Good" he replied. "I expect you all to follow that example. Now, let's get rid of Zephirak once and for all. Karnos, carry him."

Karnos removed the needle from Zephirak's body and slung it over his shoulder. He groaned a bit under the dead weight but tried not to show it.

"Diabloss, Leida, bring your closest soldiers and see what we do to those who die in disgrace." Mordred said and headed into the trees with Karnos and Jadariol. Diabloss called Kayto and the squadron as well as Strassor and Odax. Iseera and Keela came as well. Lunara wanted to go so Leida took her; Shen was too fearful to leave.

They headed out of the Forest and towards the cliffs where Leida had mocked the Lizariaous pack seasons ago. The moon shone over the sea and the moon cycle was clear, the stars were bright in the sky above.

Mordred and Karnos stood at the edge of the cliff, the others gathering around them.

"Zephirak is no more, let his body become waterlogged and rot beneath the sea for all eternity for what he has done" Mordred called into the dark sky.

Then he and Karnos took Zephirak by the legs and threw him out far into the ocean where his heavy body, also weighed down with the steel tail armour, sank beneath the water.

Mordred, Karnos and Jadariol threw back their heads and roared as one in victory. Soon the Gryphies' roars mixed in harmony with their own. They carried on like this for a long while, letting it all out and defying Zephirak's spirit, should it be watching over them and driving it away forever.

Leida rested her head on Diabloss's shoulder and Lunara sat on her back, watching out to sea. Jadariol now stood strong and tall, his betrayal was forgiven with the death of his leader and as long as he never did it again, it would be forgotten.

Strassor stood with Odax, Iseera with Keela and the squadron together on a higher cliff outcrop. It was a moment they all made the most of, all lost in their own thoughts of victory and relief. The killing, fear and death was over now and the war had been worth it because at the end they had destroyed the corruption that blighted both their species.

A while later they headed back to the Forest.

"I will take my soldiers back to Dyarkroeen now. I need to tell the mothers, kids and the soldiers who stayed behind about our victory. Luckily those who followed Zephirak all came along so I won't be breaking the news to anyone back home who would disapprove or get angry about it. I don't need any more arguments or fights over this. I will meet with you next sun cycle at mid sun and we can discuss what will happen now. I want my kind to make it up to you for the seasons of pointless killing." Mordred told Diabloss.

"You don't have to; living in peace and not taking the lives of my kind is good enough for me, Mordred. But yes, I will meet with you. I will bring Leida too" replied Diabloss. Leida smiled.

"Yeah, I couldn't believe how well you fought out there" said Mordred. Leida smiled more.

They were nearing the Forest again.

"I'll call my soldiers with Karnos and Jadariol's help and we will go back home." Mordred limped off, calling out along with Jadariol and Karnos.

"I will take my soldiers home also" said Keela and she and Iseera flew off to gather them. It was over for them now; they would go back to the High Mountains and hear about what was going to happen next whenever anyone next visited them unless it was urgent.

Diabloss smiled at Leida and they headed back to their tree while Kayto and the rest of the squadron went to make sure everyone else went home. They would have a big clean up job the following sun cycle and they were all tired from battle.

The healer had gone to Mystik to get more herbs and medicines and now she busied herself helping the queue of injured soldiers that was slowly forming outside her tree.

Mystik would now have to live with the fact her rescuing Mettalika had caused so much death and torment and that was her punishment. She was thankful that they had won though and that the Forest was finally safe, as was the rest of Shernaron. If Zephirak had succeeded, she didn't know what she would do. Still, there was no point thinking and worrying about that because he hadn't won, they had and they would forever stand tall with the knowledge that no one would ever force them into submission or prey on them again. Shernaron would forever be the Gryphies' home.

Diabloss and Leida climbed up their tree. Leida had a few cuts and bruises but nothing serious. Diabloss had hardly any wounds at all. He had hit them so fast and so hard that they barely had time to see him, let alone react against him. Leida settled in the hollow of the huge tree and Diabloss squeezed in beside her, wrapping a wing round her lovingly. She cuddled against his green fur and sighed. It was good to finally lie down and relax.

"I can't believe it's all over. After all these seasons, all this training and practise, it's finally over. No more worrying about Mettalika and Zephirak. Oh Diabloss, I almost forgot how it felt to have things back to normal again." She rested her head on him and sighed.

"Me too. It's a great relief. I dunno what my squad will do now though, there's no Zephirak to look out for, no Lizariaouses to spy on, no Mettalika. It feels weird, like there's something missing now. But in a good way. The meeting with Mordred will be interesting; I'd like to know what he has planned and how he intends to run things over there." Diabloss looked thoughtful.

"Well however he runs it, it will be better than how Zephirak ran it" said Leida. Diabloss nodded in agreement. Leida still had her leg armour on and she sat up to remove it since it was uncomfortable to lie on.

"Did that prove useful?" asked Diabloss.

"Yes, I found that I could use my legs to block needles with it. I'm glad we had quite a bit of armour in the end."

"I think they had a supply of it in the mountains anyway because we were always so close to war that they needed to be constantly prepared. All the same, I'm glad I warned them to make a bit more. I had no idea when I got back that you would be kidnapped again. It scared me more than death itself that something awful could have happened to you." Diabloss nuzzled her and Leida murred.

"Well I was fine and I'm glad I was. And I'm glad I managed to escape or Zephirak would have the Forest under his control by now."

"Yes. I'm only glad they didn't attack when it was raining. I guess we have Otuss to thank for that. We were all heroes out there. You for escaping and taking charge, Lunara and Hiryasis for freeing me and Mordred for killing Zephirak despite the loss of his tail and his dignity. He should have kept that tail armour of Mettalika's." Diabloss said.

"No" replied Leida, "that armour was tainted with greed and corruption. Mordred would rather have no tail than wear the armour that caused him to lose his tail. He would never wear or associate himself with anything Zephirak owned. You could see that from how he was."

"You are a very good judge of character" said Diabloss admiringly.

"And yet even I was fooled by Jadariol" she replied.

"But he saved Lunara in the end. So he did have a heart in there somewhere. However, I wonder if he would have done the same thing if it had been a different kitten in peril." Diabloss thought about this.

Leida shrugged. "Who knows. What matters is he saved her and even he was a hero in some way. We all worked together over this, helped each other and overcame Zephirak's evil. That's what really matters and counts."

"You're right" said Diabloss and rested his head down. "Well, we'd better go to sleep; we can talk about this in the next sun cycle. Right now I'm tired and I need sleep." He yawned to prove the point and they both fell asleep peacefully.

The next sun cycle dawned and Diabloss's squadron took out teams of Gryphies to clear up the carnage of the war. They gathered the bodies of their own kind and took them to the burning grounds to make the funeral pyre of all those brave soldiers who had died fighting to defend Shernaron. At the same time, Mordred sent out troops to gather the bodies of their soldiers too. He wasn't sure what to do with them all; Lizariaouses usually left their dead where they were but they couldn't leave them littered over the Outlands and they wanted to honour them even though Mordred was angry that most of these soldiers died fighting in the name of

Zephirak. Instead he got packs of diggers to work on a pit at the far side of Dyarkroeen and bury them there in a mass grave. He had been tempted to throw them all in the sea in disgrace but he wanted to respect their families and keep everyone happy so burying was the option.

The previous moon cycle when he arrived home with what was left of the army, Schaarl had been shocked at his lack of tail. It would now always serve as a constant reminder of the last battle with Zephirak. He had the scar on his eye to make him an example of one who Zephirak had been angry at and now he'd lost his tail and instead he was an example of a fine soldier who was strong enough to overthrow and destroy the evil leader of their kind. Schaarl said she would always love him despite how he looked and he was reassured by that fact. Now they could work to rebuild Dyarkroeen in a more peaceful way. They were natural killers but at least now they would only kill prey animals and not Gryphies. So far not even those left who had stood with Zephirak had argued with him and he doubted there would be an uprising since they were too few and they were far outnumbered by those who supported Mordred.

Mordred told Schaarl everything that happened. She was happy that it was over and that they could soon start a family without fear of a war breaking out.

Of course, during the battle most of the Lizariaouses left in Dyarkroeen were the mothers and kids. Some soldiers stayed behind to guard Diabloss which of course failed and this early dawn, Rondo and his pack had gone out with other soldiers to fetch the bodies while the diggers worked on the pit they were to be buried in.

Over in Shernaron, Diabloss and Leida helped carry bodies to the burning grounds. It was an unpleasant task and Diabloss told Leida she didn't have to help if she didn't want to. She wanted to though, now she was a soldier and with that responsibility came things that weren't very pleasant.

Lunara helped Mystik and she and some other kittens including Hiryasis, Len and Zephyr went to find more healing herbs and plants to replenish stocks in Mystik's tree. Now there was no fear of Lizariaouses or Mettalika, they could go out as they wished. Lunara was training to be Mystik's new assistant in Sinxo's footsteps. It made her feel grown up and mature and she had quite a bit of knowledge from looking after Jadariol.

Jadariol was with his father helping gather the dead. When they had left the previous moon cycle, he hadn't really said goodbye to Lunara and he planned to visit her later to see how she was doing. Mordred was now setting in new laws. Lizariaouses were able to do as they wished and those who wanted to be friends with Gryphies had no one to stop them now. Jadariol and anyone else would be able to come and go between territories as the Gryphies could as well. Mordred sat in his cave thinking up these new laws. Maybe they could even share battle tactics and give each other tips or advice on aspects of living or catching prey and share knowledge. He'd already thought about these things before once he knew that it would be he who put a stop to the war by destroying Zephirak.

The only one who hated that Zephirak had died was the female who had admired him so much; Zetarzo. Even though Zephirak had rejected her, a small part of her hoped he would take her to be his mate one day maybe when he'd felt better and gotten over the death of Salvariss. Zetarzo spent the whole sun cycle in her cave in misery. She hadn't gone with them to fight since she had to help guard Diabloss; a task she had offered to do. She now mentally kicked herself for not going to help. And now she found it was Mordred who had killed Zephirak, she hated him for it. However she couldn't do anything and she didn't try. She decided to drop out of the army and go back to scouting and hunting. She wasn't fighting for Mordred. She didn't think she would ever take a mate though unless Rondo showed interest.

Schaarl came back from a hunt with a fat cave cat and shared it with Mordred who was still thinking about the ideas he had for laws they should follow now. Many Lizariaouses, particularly young ones had come to him and asked what they were supposed to do now. They also wanted to know about how the battle went and Mordred said he would call a meeting for all the Lizariaouses once the bodies had been buried. Clearing up the Outlands was the most important thing to do now and get the bodies buried before they went bad in the sun. It would take all sun cycle to do it even with the amount of Lizariaouses who were working on it. Mordred told those who came to him to let others know the meeting would be the following sun cycle since he knew most of the soldiers wouldn't have finished by that moon cycle. He felt surprisingly organised, like he was meant to lead them.

Schaarl also saw him in a new light. She had chosen him for a mate because he had been a good fighter and a high ranker but now to her he was like a hero who had saved them from something they would surely regret later. After all, they could rule over the Gryphies but there would still be Gryphies who turned against them, maybe even form a rebellion army or some kind of freedom fighting gathering and work to bring down Zephirak. Or they could have got the Deamons involved. Chances were then that all the Lizariaouses would have

475

been wiped out. Deamons didn't care who they killed once they were angry and they wouldn't just have killed Zephirak.

Over in Shernaron, Diabloss was thinking the same thing as he helped to clear the bodies. He was flying to the burning grounds carrying two soldiers. He and the other larger Gryphies could carry two at a time easily. Diabloss could even carry three if he wished but he thought he'd take it easy and do just two. Leida could only carry one at a time. Tranzoss could carry two and he saw her fly overhead now.

Diabloss was thankful that it hadn't gotten to the Deamons. He knew that the Forest gathering would have surrendered at the threats Zephirak was giving to the kittens. There was no way he could have allowed any innocent youngster to die. Zephirak had known that too; the Gryphies' sympathy and gentle side was their weakness when Lizariaouses would easily put up their own kids for sacrifice as they had done with Jadariol. It disgusted Diabloss.

Since they could fly, they moved the bodies fairly fast. Already there were over a hundred piled at the burning grounds. Diabloss hoped they could burn them all in one go as it would be faster. He hated seeing so many dead, he had never seen carnage on this scale in his entire life and it upset him, as it did the others who saw it.

They made sure to keep all the kittens well away from the Outlands until the mess was cleared up. Even after that, Diabloss wanted to wait for the rains to come and wash the blood away. He didn't want their young minds tainted or disturbed by what they would see if they went there. Of course, some of them wanted to go see and their mothers had to keep a good eye on them. Lunara made sure to keep her friends away from the edge of the Forest where the Outlands were, Mystik had warned her not to let any of them see. Most of them didn't want to anyway. The sounds they heard of the battle had scared them enough.

Busying themselves with the cleanup operation made the time seem to go faster for Diabloss and Leida and soon it was mid sun and when they should meet Mordred. Mordred had never specified a place to meet so they flew to Dyarkroeen, keeping an eye out for him along the way. They found him travelling towards Shernaron and flew down to see him.

"Sorry, I only realised just now I never said where we should meet. I was tired last night. In fact I'm still tired today." Mordred apologised.

"It's ok, we'll go back to Dyarkroeen and talk there" Diabloss told him and they walked back together.

Mordred was still in his old cave. Zephirak's cavern he decided would be used for other things. Not many wanted to live there, the place smelled of death and fear. So Mordred took them to his cave where they sat outside to talk in the sun. Schaarl joined them too, to listen.

"How is the cleanup going?" asked Diabloss.

"It's going well. I think we'll have most of them by the end of the sun cycle. We're digging a pit for them to go in and we will bury them and mark the place with a large rock that the diggers are engraving a dedication into. It will take some time but we're just gathering the bodies and placing them in piles near the pit so we can bury them once the pit is big enough." Mordred told them.

"We've gotten a lot of ours back to the burning grounds. We have a ceremony where we burn the fallen in a funeral pyre" said Leida.

"I assume you have great plans for your kind now?" asked Diabloss. He wanted to know what Mordred had planned, to see if and how it would affect the Gryphies.

"Yes, I am making up some laws for us. No killing your kind. We are allowed to come and go as we wish so long as that is ok with you. Those Gryphies living near us who we drove out may come back to their homes if they wish. If you need help with anything, my soldiers would be happy to help. We need to make up for the damage Zephirak did" said Mordred solemnly.

"No, that was his doing; you shouldn't have to pay for something he did. He lead you all around and you have nothing to make up for. I won't have you putting yourselves out for something a corrupt leader did. It is all over. We will go back to how things were. How things should be. Mordred, I hope now both our species can live in harmony as it was meant to be and that this mistake will never be made again because you know next time the Deamons *will* be involved and I don't want to think of the consequences of that happening. I can have your honest word it will never happen again? I am eternally grateful that you fought alongside us but I must have your word that no one will try to become a new Zephirak; that no one will try to take his place and that if one tries and overthrows you, that they won't be allowed to build things up into a war like what has just taken place. I want peace for us all, now and forever."

"Yes" replied Mordred, "You have my word, Diabloss. It will never ever happen again. Not under my rule or anyone else who comes after me. From now on, Gryphies and Lizariaouses will live in harmony, not simply tolerance of each other, but in a mutual friendship. Those who have developed taste for Gryphies might try something but I've tried to find all those and keep an eye on them. Even though they may not necessarily have been supporting Zephirak, they may get cravings for Gryphie but they will be watched. Those are the only ones I have any concerns about. However, they are very few so you have nothing to worry about. If they won't co-operate then they will be killed and they are aware of that." Even with Mordred's new rule, the Lizariaouses would never drop their harsh ways towards each other.

"Good, see that you do keep an eye on them. And thank you" Diabloss put out a hand and Mordred took it in his paw to shake on peace and harmony now. He did the same with Leida too and Leida bowed her head. So, some Lizariaouses were good after all. She should have listened to her senses more and trusted Mordred but after Jadariol's betrayal, it couldn't really be expected that she would have done.

"What about your armies? I mean, we have soldiers but they have other jobs too and families." Diabloss asked.

"There will be a new law put in. If the kids of soldiers wish to become something other than a fighter, they may do. We don't need huge armies, we have enough soldiers. So the profession of the parents will no longer affect the profession of the kids. Also I want to see if I can get water closer to home. We have to wander a long way to get our water at the beginning of each sun cycle; I want to create a reservoir closer to home. With the help of the diggers, I think we could do that. We have never been as well off as you in our territory, I want to utilise our skills and research what you have to see if we can bring some of it here as well. Of course we're more at home in caves and mountains and don't need forests or plants very much but it would be nice if we had a few more useful things here. I want to start with the water source though. Do you think you could help if we need it?" asked Mordred.

"Yes, the Gryphies of the High Mountains can lend a hand with that. You would need to build a large hole in the ground and somehow channel the water from your reservoir to it so there would always be a fresh supply. We can help you with that and we would be happy to." Diabloss replied, smiling.

"Thank you. I think if we can help each other out, we will soon build a partnership and it will heal the damage my kind has done to your kind." Mordred smiled too, as did Schaarl.

"I will call a meeting of the Gryphies and tell them everything you have said. Also some of them still don't know the full extent of what happened in the battle." Diabloss said.

"Yes, I need to call a meeting too. I will be calling it after the bodies have been collected, in the next sun cycle" replied Mordred.

Diabloss nodded and stood, Leida followed.

"We will come and visit you again in a few sun cycles to see how you are doing" said Diabloss.

"No, we will visit you. My leg will feel better then and I want to come and see the Gryphies to show them we are friends now" said Mordred firmly.

"Very well" replied Diabloss. "Until then, farewell and good luck!"

They swept up their wings and took to the sky, flying off towards the Outlands to continue taking away the dead.

Mordred smiled after them and turned to Schaarl, who nuzzled him.

"I think this is the start of a great partnership between our species" he said to her proudly.

Chapter 34
New Beginnings

The next sun cycle, the Gryphies had gathered all their fallen and the pyre was set alight by the squadron. Blue flames swept up and swallowed the bodies as roars of respect were called into the sky. Way above, the Gryphies from the Forest and High Mountains put on a spectacular airborne display of honour for all those that had fallen.

Diabloss, Leida, Strassor, Odax, Lunara, Hiryasis and many more were there to see them off into the next world. Tranzoss put on amazing displays of fire shapes, her fire forming into figures of Gryphies defeating Lizariaouses and then roaring in victory. The flames of the funeral pyre rose high, past the highest trees and took up most of the burning grounds.

Over in Dyarkroeen, Mordred's soldiers were throwing the bodies in the pit and preparing to cover it over with soil. Due to their very nature, this was about as dignified as the Lizariaouses got. They slung bodies in instead of placing them in carefully because it took less time. Mordred wasn't happy with any of those who had died though since they had been fighting in the name of Zephirak so it was lucky enough that he was doing this at all. After the pit had been covered, the gathered Lizariaouses roared into the sky, sending their own soldiers off to the next world in a similar way to the Gryphies. Some workers moved the great stone to the centre of the grave and placed it there to show all who came across it that this was the final resting place of all those who died needlessly in Zephirak's corrupt war of greed.

Both species called their meetings after this.

In the Forest, the Gryphies met as usual. Kittens, parents, soldiers, the squadron, trainers and scouters all gathered around to hear the full story of how the war had begun and how it had ended. Anyone who wasn't at the meeting had perished in the battle. The whole of the Forest without exception was gathered around and it made it rather cramped.

"I will not keep you here long" began Diabloss and told them all how the war had begun, of his kidnapping, Leida's escape and all that commenced after it, culminating in the fight between Zephirak and Mordred, his number one commander. He told of how they had thrown Zephirak's body into the sea and how now they all intended to build a new partnership between the territories. The assembled Gryphies thought this was a brilliant idea; however most of them still didn't really trust the Lizariaouses. The trust would have to be built up over a long period of time and the Lizariaouses would have to earn it.

"Mordred wants to give his kind more of what we have so they can live more easily. That was one of the reasons Zephirak tried to control us. We have more resources and our water source is closer to us than theirs is to them. They wish to build one connected to their reservoir and I said we would help. I have Mordred's word that they will never attack or hunt us again and we will live in harmony instead of mere tolerance. I hope everyone here agrees that this is a good idea." He paused and the gathering nodded, talking quietly to each other. They all found this a great relief. Now they wouldn't have to live in fear and they could be happy and carefree again; the way Gryphies are meant to be.

In Dyarkroeen, a similar meeting took place.

"Now we have cleared away those who have fallen, we can start anew. The Gryphies will share what they know of certain things with us and we will form a partnership with them where we can work together and help each other. There will be no more hunting of Gryphies. I have said this before but if anyone is caught taking a pack to hunt them or even trying to alone, I will have you killed. It is not tolerable and it is certainly not forgivable. Those who have a taste for them; get rid of it or you will be punished. This applies to everyone. If you find a Gryphie in trouble, you are to help them. We need to really work to gain their trust and friendship after what we did. From now on, kids won't be forced to follow in the footsteps of their parents regarding on what they want to do with their lives. So if you are born to soldier or worker parents, you do not have to become that yourself. For example, a worker born Lizariaous may become a soldier if he wishes. It is freedom of choice." Mordred paused to glare at a father who looked very disapproving of this new law.

"We want all our kind to be happy with that they do. If they are happy doing it, they will put all their efforts into it. I expect you all to obey these laws and if you really have a big problem with any of them, to come to me about it and we can talk it over. However, watch out because if anyone crosses me, you know what happened to Zephirak." Mordred stood tall, watching over them all and he saw they looked at him with respect.

"Are there any questions?" he asked.

Rondo spoke up. "Sir, what do the soldiers do? We can go out in hunting packs I guess but we have no one to fight and nothing to work for."

"I'm sure in the future we will have other battles and we will need you for that, however right now I want us all to work on making it easier to live here. We need a closer supply of water and the Gryphies are going to help us build something to bring water in from the reservoir so we won't have the walk each morning to bring it back. Also, we have two main factions of working; soldiers and diggers. I want to make the other factions larger, like the scouters, hunters and those who train them. There is so much of our territory that is wasteland; we need more caves so we can spread out more. I have other plans too but those are probably good to start with. In time, we'll be able to do much more than we did when Zephirak was ruling. He only wanted us to work and fight. We could set up an arena for soldiers who miss battle and they could have sparring matches while others watch."

"We do that when we're training though, Sir." A soldier spoke up.

"Well this would be for leisure. We love to fight, so why not do it to ease our stress? It would be harmless enough and we'd be getting exercise at the same time." Mordred explained.

The gathered soldiers and other Lizariaouses talked amongst themselves and nodded in approval. Maybe Mordred would be a better leader than Zephirak. It certainly seemed that way right now.

Schaarl stood beside Mordred and smiled at him admiringly.

"Now, let's get started everyone. Rondo, choose some other high ranking soldiers to help you command and start planning how we're going to make the new reservoir and where we're gunna put it. It needs to be somewhere central without being in our main living area since it would get in the way there. However it needs to be easily reached by those who live in outlying areas." Mordred said.

Rondo nodded and went off with some others to start on this. The rest of the assembled Lizariaouses headed off to get on with their sun cycle, leaving Mordred and Schaarl stood alone outside Zephirak's cave. They headed back to Mordred's cave.

"Rondo will report back to me when he has a few ideas" said Mordred. "I think this will work out just fine."

Jadariol had followed them.

"Sir, can I go and see Lunara? I still haven't apologised for betraying her and my foolishness" he said quietly.

"Yeah go and have a talk with her. It needs to be done. Now Zephirak is gone you can do as you wish and follow who you wish." Mordred told him.

Jadariol smiled and nodded, then headed off for Shernaron.

Lunara was hanging around with Hiryasis when Jadariol arrived. They had been talking about the battle since they were the only two kittens who had had firsthand knowledge of it. A lot of the others had wanted to know what happened and they had told them at the meeting. They didn't exaggerate though even though Hiry was tempted to say he killed a Lizariaous.

Hiryasis's view of Jadariol was still tainted and he snarled a bit when he saw him approach. There were no longer guards at the entrance to the Forest clearing.

Lunara of course didn't snarl; she trotted up to him happily.

"How are things going over there, Jadariol?" she asked.

"Fine, we had a meeting and Mordred will soon have everything sorted. Hey, err, can we talk in private? I have some things to tell you." Jadariol lowered his voice for the last sentence and Hiryasis, put out by this, immediately got up and left without another word. He was still very untrusting of Jadariol after what he did to the Gryphies.

Lunara watched after him, about to say something but let it go. He'd forgive Jadariol in time. It would take a lot of time though.

"Can we go somewhere else then?" asked Jadariol. Lunara nodded and they walked through the Forest to the little spring with its waterfall where they could talk in private. Lunara sat down on a rock near the water's edge and Jadariol sat nearby. Both gazed into the water for a while before Jadariol finally spoke. It was hard for him because he felt so guilty at even thinking that Zephirak was anything good. It had occurred to him even back then that some of the other Lizariaouses didn't like their leader and seemed to have good reasoning behind it. Also, that a lot of them lived in fear of him as well.

"I suppose I grew up thinking Zephirak was really cool" he said finally. "I never saw much fault with him, he was strong, no one messed with him and he had a scary temper if they did. He took a liking to me which made me even happier and prouder too. Then I wanted to be like him when I grew up and he told me that I would be the next in line as the leader if I completed this task and that was to put myself up as bait for Mettalika. If the plan failed and a Gryphie didn't spot me, I would have been killed but I was prepared to take that risk. I would have done anything for Zephirak. I was foolish and I regret it every sun cycle. After all, Mettalika killed my mother. I never lied about that. So I was taken to the swamp and we waited around for the scouter Gryphie we often saw at that time of sun cycle. And she appeared. I guess I secretly hoped that she wouldn't. After all, it wouldn't have been my fault if she hadn't appeared and maybe I could have done some other task instead. But she did and they made me walk across Mettalika's path. I was terrified, I knew I would be. To see her up close for the first time was awful. And she attacked me. I wanted so bad to escape but before I knew it she'd hurt me so bad I couldn't run. Then the scouter appeared and saved me and I was taken to the Forest where I was healed and met you. Over the time we spent together I never really thought about disobeying Zephirak. I'd sneak out at moon cycle when I could walk better and meet with a soldier who snuck to the edge of the Forest to give him the report on how things were going and any dirt I could find on you guys to give us an advantage in the war. Usually it was my Dad I talked to. That was why I never missed him; because he'd visit me most moon cycles when I was feeling better. He told me I was doing a good job and that he was proud of me and so was Zephirak and that I'd definitely get the promotion to Zephirak's trainee. When I was well enough that I could walk without much trouble, I told Leida I wanted to show her a Moon Wraith and took her into the Forest where she was ambushed and taken back to Dyarkroeen. And so my task was complete. That was why I was used; I had to ultimately have her kidnapped so Zephirak could get her back again and have an advantage over Diabloss. Zephirak had always planned to take you guys down. Attacking Mettalika and killing her was just a side quest for him. I knew all this but of course told no one. I'd never known kindness like yours before I met you. Lizariaouses aren't like that. We get injured and we're left in our caves to get over it. We're given herbs or whatever but no one actually sits in and looks after us. We heal fast naturally or we would mostly be wiped out since if we can't fight or work, we have no use. Mordred says he'll give us other things to do aside from fighting and working and I'm going to make sure those who are injured are cared for as well as you cared for me. I'm not going to become another Zephirak. I was naïve and stupid. Now I will defy him by being the exact opposite." Jadariol told her, still mostly gazing into the water. His guilt wouldn't let him look her in the eyes when he told her his story.

"I thought it was cool to make friends with you. At first it was mostly curiosity which grew to friendship when I saw you would make a good friend and that you liked me. I enjoyed looking after you. My other friends were wary but you know what? Even though you betrayed us and you were lead around by Zephirak, I don't regret making friends with you. Even in the war when I saw you kill my kind and I should have hated you, I didn't because I knew that you were being mislead into these things. I'm glad you didn't let Zephirak make you completely evil." Lunara said with a smile, looking at him.

"Yeah, well, when I saw him holding you going to kill you I didn't want that to happen and I could finally see him for what he was. Corrupt and twisted. Who would kill a kid anyway? Plus I didn't care what happened to anyone else but I wanted you to be safe. I didn't want you to be hurt like I had been and it taken ages to heal from it cos I doubted you had anyone to look after you like I had." Lunara actually had her mother who would have cared for her but at this point in time she kept her mouth shut from telling him since she didn't want to ruin his moment and appreciated his kind words. Also, since he had no mother, it wouldn't have been very kind to say that.

"I would have killed him myself had I been bigger. Once I saw him do that, my heart was filled with hatred for him. I'd never look up to him again. I'm glad Mordred killed him and we can live more relaxed now. To be honest I'm used to living a relaxed life. I'm going to work to become a healer like Mystik." Jadariol sat up straight and looked at her proudly as he announced this and she smiled with joy.

"I'm going to be a healer too! We can share techniques and things! This is great" she laughed. Jadariol smiled and felt happy for the first time in a long time.

They sat together for a while, chatting or just enjoying the other's company. It was the beginning of an era for both species. Though they didn't realise it, Jadariol and Lunara's friendship was what had started the idea that maybe the two species could live in peace despite their differences and that they had more in common than they realised. The two of them had learned much about the other in their time together and this had brought them closer. Even though Jadariol had wanted to obey Zephirak, his friendship with Lunara burned strong inside him like Gryphie fire and won out in the end.

Diabloss and Leida were heading back to their tree. After the meeting, they had gone to catch a meal and now they were full and ready for a rest in their tree. Mystik was outside her own tree resting in the sun. She felt very tired these sun cycles even though she had not battled. She watched the two young mates climb up their tree and smiled. Leida had matured and Diabloss was still the most powerful Gryphie in the Forest. Maybe something good had come of all this. Maybe if Mettalika had never been saved, they would still be living in friction with the Lizariaouses and the war could well have broken out anyway. Mystik had never looked at it like that. But Zephirak was dead and gone and now they were all working to live in peace instead of mere tolerance. Mystik felt better for this thought. What is is what must be after all. That is what fate is. And she supposed maybe that was the reason she had insisted that Mettalika was saved. Sometimes things had to get worse before they finally turned out for the better. However, many had been killed in the war and there was no excuse for that. They had lost more of their own kind than the Lizariaouses had theirs. The Outlands remained stained with red for many lunars to come, as a symbol of something that must never happen again.

Leida settled down next to Diabloss and rested her head on him.

"I'm glad it's over. I know I gained more skills and experience but battle is still scary and when I was thrust into being a leader, I was terrified" said Leida.

"Well there's no need to worry now. Soon everything will be organised in Dyarkroeen and we can look to the future." Diabloss nuzzled her. Both of them felt like a weight had been taken off their shoulders.

"Yes! And now our future generations have nothing to fear either. I have a feeling things will be good from now on." Leida smiled and looked to the sky where Gryphies flew, happy and free.

Leida never had any more moonmares about the danger in the darkness, nor did she run when scared. Now she had seen the heat of battle and nothing ever compared to that again.

Soon she was Diabloss's second in command as well as his mate. Mystik trained Lunara up to be a healer and helped Jadariol too. Mordred was pleased that they would finally have a proper healer of their own.

The Lizariaouses got their new water source by channelling the reservoir with the help of the Gryphies and the Gryphies from the High Mountains who helped them dig more cave homes in the mountainous terrain further into Dyarkroeen. In return, the Lizariaouses gave the Gryphies some of their needles. Mystik developed a much better anti-venom with them so that they would have a proper cure in the unlikely event that friction between the two species started out again. The Gryphies also used the needles to help themselves in other ways too.

Seasons later, Leida and Diabloss had a son, Ellendrii. He was headstrong and determined like his father but could sense things like his mother. And there is a story about him too and his great quest.

Needless to say, war never broke out again. However, Leida never forgot those moonmares she had, warning her of the danger in the darkness.

END